HARRY's B

By

George Donald

Also by George Donald

Billy's Run
Charlie's Promise
A Question of Balance
Natural Justice
Logan
A Ripple of Murder
A Forgotten Murder
The Seed of Fear
The Knicker-knocker
The Cornishman
A Presumption of Murder
A Straight Forward Theft
The Medal
A Decent Wee Man
Charlie's Dilemma
The Second Agenda
Though the Brightest Fell
The ADAT
A Loan With Patsy
A Thread of Murder

CHAPTER ONE

She patiently waited till the young carer with a smile tapped in the code to unlock the security door, then opened it to permit Mary to pass through.
Turning, she was about to thank the carer who pre-empted her by saying, "It wasn't too bad a visit today, was it Missus Harris?"
"No," she returned a tight smile, "he was a wee bit more responsive, hen, and thanks again to you and everybody for what you're doing for him."
"Ach," the carer waved away the gratitude. "Michael's one of our favourites. He's a sweetheart, so he is," she replied before closing over the door.
Neither woman alluded to the fact that almost two years into his disease, Michael had wasted away from being a relatively fit and healthy twelve stone man to now weighing just over six stones and that his food and liquid intake was regular simply because he was incapable of now feeding himself; it was the staff's care and devotion to routine that kept him alive.
Mary sighed and turning, glanced up at the black clouds threatening to unleash their deluge upon the city of Glasgow below.
Readying her folding umbrella, she stepped out from the foyer and made her way to the exit of the care home that led out onto Brand Street. A short hurried walk took her to the corner of Cessnock Street then a couple of minutes later she was stood on the platform of the Underground.
The short ride to St George's Cross passed quickly during which time lost in her thoughts, she reflected on the visit to her husband.

Of course, the young nurse was being kind; there was no visible change in Michael's condition and it pained her no end that he no longer recognised her.

The onset of his dementia after the stroke had been rapid and God forgive her, she sometimes wondered if it might have been kinder to let him succumb to the stroke rather than waste away to become the shell of the man he had been.

"Are you okay, Missus?"

Startled, she stared at the young man, a student she guessed from his spiky, brightly coloured green hair and by the way he was dressed, holes in the knees of his jeans, his brightly polished black boots laced with bright red laces and who sat opposite with a phone in his hand and concern etched upon his face.

That's when she realised the tears were slowly trickling down her cheeks.

"Oh," she reached into her hand bag and withdrew a packet of tissues, withdrawing one and taking a deep breath, wiped at her face. As the young man continued to stare, she replied, "Sorry, son. Wee bit of bad news today," she explained rather than go into the real cause of her grief.

The living loss of her husband of thirty-eight years.

"Oh, so sorry," he mumbled and blushing, returned to staring at his phone.

The train began to slow as it prepared to stop. Rising from her seat, she swayed along the carriage of the slowing train to the door and then when it had come to a shuddering halt, up the stairs to the exit to find the rain had indeed begun, but thankfully not too heavily. Raising her brolly above her head, she quickly made her way to the bus stop in St George's Road where she joined the queue of eight or nine men and women, mostly commuters making their way home after working in the city centre.

Two teenage girls, shop assistants she thought, who were stood half way along the queue in front of Mary, giggled and loudly discussed their forthcoming weekend in what her Michael used to call 'industrial language' that was enough to make the fifty-seven-year old Mary blush.

The First Bus arrived with a hiss of air brakes as it jerked to a halt.

Waiting her turn, at last Mary stepped onto the platform and with a smile, presented her travel card at the dour driver who without a glance, waved her onto the bus.

As she stepped along the aisle, the bus took off and losing her balance, she almost fell into the lap of a middle-aged man who with a loud 'huff,' roughly pushed Mary back upright.

"Sorry," she gasped and making her way to an empty seat towards the back of the bus was conscious of the embarrassed stares of her fellow passengers.

Settling herself down into the seat, she placed her handbag on her lap and glanced along the aisle at her fellow travellers.

The slight fall of rain and the heater on the bus going full pelt had combined to cause condensation to form in small rivulets that now trickled down the inside of the windows.

The journey took no more than ten minutes and soon the bus was on Balmore Road, approaching the junction with Stonend Street. As it stopped at a red traffic light, several passengers including Mary arose from their seats to make their way to the door.

Passing through the junction, the bus pulled up sharply at the stop adjacent to the Lidl's Store.

Getting off, Mary turned and said, "Thank you," to the driver who moodily staring through his windscreen, ignored her.

Stepping off the platform into the drizzling rain, she hurriedly walked through the store's car park and spent five minutes shopping.

At the checkout, the cheery young woman greeted Mary, recognising her as a regular and said, "That the bloody rain on again, hen?"

"Aye," Mary returned a smile, "but we live in the west of Scotland, so I suppose we shouldn't be surprised, eh?"

"No, you're bang on, hen," replied the woman as she run Mary's purchases through the bar code till. "I suppose the predictable thing about our weather is it's *unpredictable*," the woman grinned.

Settling her bill, Mary loaded her shopping into a small nylon bag and with a cheery wave, made her way out of the store.

The short walk through the car park and across the busy junction took but a few moments and then she was turning into her close on Balmore Road.

Walking along the entrance path, she glanced into the small garden at the front of her ground floor flat and frowning, shook her head and tut-tutted.

A discarded beer can lay in the overgrown grass.
She didn't know whether to be more annoyed at the individual who had carelessly disposed of the can or the fact that the grass once carefully tended by her husband Michael, was so unkempt.
Opening the green painted metal gate that permitted her access into the garden, Mary fetched a paper hankie from her pack in her bag and using it to lift the can, carried it into the close and straight through to the rear door where she deposited it in the bin in the back court.
She glanced up at the skies and her eyes narrowed as she muttered to herself, "Looks like more rain," before wearily turning back into the close and into her flat.

Rain was the last thing on Kieran McMenamin's mind.
Stood nervously in front of the shaven headed Peter McGroarty in the smaller man's end-terraced council house in Ronaldsay Street in the Milton district of Glasgow, McMenamin was trying to explain why he was late with his payment when the unexpected backhanded slap came from nowhere to rattle his teeth.
As his head bounced round almost from his shoulders, he felt the blood seep from his gums and instinctively raised his hands to his face to avoid any further blows, but McGroarty had turned away to lift the half smoked joint from the ashtray on the table by the couch.
As he did so, Sharon Gale, his dyed blonde, live-in girlfriend who lay sprawled across the couch wearing a baby-doll nightie, shrieked with laughter and said, "Look at him, Peter, look! He's shitting himself, so he is," she pointed with a shaking hand at McMenamin while continuing to hysterically giggle.
Gale would have been pretty, perhaps even more than pretty, but the sunken eyes, too pale skin and needle marks on both inner arms were a turn-off for most men.
But not McGroarty who kept the twenty-two-year old woman eager and happy with her daily fix of heroin, though was beginning to wonder if she was worth the bother.
His legs shaking, McMenamin swallowed with difficulty and hands raised, stuttered, "Pete, you know me, man. I don't let you down. I'll get the dough. For fucks sake, you know I'll get it!"
McGroarty took a deep inhale of the cannabis cigarette before carefully returning it to the ashtray, then quicker than McMenamin

could anticipate, the former lightweight boxer turned back and shot across the few feet that separated them before taking McMenamin by the throat.

Slamming the twenty-three-year-old McMenamin against the wall, he hissed, "I'm sick of hearing your excuses, bawbag! But for the fact I'd need to wipe it up, I'd have your blood dripping right here onto my carpet, ya spineless wee shite!"

He glared at the frightened McMenamin, then said, "Now, here's what you're going to do, Kieran. You're going to find me my hundred and eighty quid by midday tomorrow morning or I'm coming for you, understand?"

"Aye," the terrified McMenamin, his throat constricted by McGroarty's powerful grip, managed to gasp.

Releasing him as suddenly as he had grabbed him, McGroarty stood back and grinning, playfully slapped McMenamin on the cheek before telling him, "Now get your arse out of here."

Turning towards the scantily clad Gale, he added with a lecherous grin, "I've a wee bit of business to attend to, haven't I doll?"

She was fortunate to find a parking bay outside the office and switching off the engine, glanced upwards at the cloudy sky.

The rain had for the moment thankfully stopped, but she was grateful that tonight there would be no soaking, for tonight's nightshift would be spent indoors.

Her attention was briefly taken by the staff of the B&M store on the corner directly across the road removing the stock from the pavement at the door and hurrying it inside.

Glancing at the dashboard clock, she saw she still had time before her seven o'clock shift commenced and lifting her mobile phone from her handbag, she scrolled down the index and pressed the button.

He answered almost immediately and smiling, she said, "Thought you'd be making your way home, by now."

"No," Ian replied. "Still got a bit of cleaning to do and then there's the blinking books as well."

"Getting near that time again," she grinned.

"Yes, and we really should be thinking about getting ourselves somebody to do the books, even if it's part time, Daisy. Not that it's beyond me, but it's so time consuming and to be honest, after a day's shift here in the café, doing the accounts is the last thing I need."

"Can the takings afford us hiring someone?"

"Well," she heard him exhale, "we're doing okay, staff wise I mean. The profit margin is a little better than we anticipated and now that summer's rolling in, we should be seeing a lot more passing trade. After all, you know as well as I do that Byres Road during the summer months can be *really* busy with tourists."

"Yes, well, maybe we should give it some thought. Look," she glanced towards the entrance to the office, "it's Tuesday today and I'm off this Thursday and Friday. I'm due to start in a couple of minutes, but here's an idea. Why don't you and I make time on say," her eyes narrowed as she thought, then continued, "Thursday evening. We'll book a table somewhere and discuss it further."

"Sounds like a plan," he cheerfully replied, then added, "Be careful. You know I worry about you."

"I told you, I'm indoors tonight and tomorrow evening too, so don't worry. Love you," she smiled at the phone.

"Love you too," he responded before ending the call.

With a sigh, she returned the phone to her handbag and checking the windows were closed, got out of the car and locked it.

Entering the building, the civilian bar officer smiled when she saw her and said, "Evening Sergeant. You're a bit early."

"I'm always early, Jeannie," she replied with a grin and waited to be buzzed through the security door.

It was as she was taking off her anorak that she heard her name called and turning, saw the Chief Inspector who called out, "Evening, Sergeant Cooper. My office, if you please."

With a puzzled glance at the young bar officer, Daisy followed him through the building and up the stairs to the upper floor where inviting her to take a seat, Dougie Kane slumped down with a sigh into the chair at his desk.

"Surprised to see you here at this time of the evening, sir," Daisy smiled.

"Aye, well I'm surprised myself," replied the portly Kane, who jokingly continued, "Particularly as I don't get paid overtime anymore. Right, the reason I need to speak with you is you're due your first annual appraisal since your promotion from Stewart Street."

Daisy frowned and asked, "Will that be a problem?"

"Problem?" Kane frowned then shaking his head, added, "No, not at all, Daisy. The year you have served here at Saracen office as a patrol sergeant as well as acting as our sub-Divisional collator dealing with all incoming intelligence reports has proven to me and the Divisional Commander that you are an asset to this Division. No," he shook his head again, "your appraisal will indicate that you are an exemplary officer."

"However?" her inner sense suspected that there must be a reason for this chat.

"Ah, however, there is the question that you might have some…how can I explain this? Some paid employment outside your calling as a police officer?"

Daisy smiled. "You mean my fiancé's business? Daisy's Café in Byres Road?"

"Exactly."

"Look, sir," shaking her head, she opened her hands wide, "I've already explained to the Personnel Department at Dalmarnock office that my fiancé, Ian McLeod is the sole owner of the café. Yes," she nodded, "I *do* have a financial interest in the place, but I do *not* take any part in the day to day running of the business. My financial interest is much the same as if I was say, buying shares or perhaps even investing with a bank. At the most, Ian and I will discuss the hire of a member of staff or even the décor and occasionally when he permits it," she mischievously smiled, "the menu. As for my involvement with the café, it's all been cleared and approved by the Personnel Department."

Kane raised his hands and slapping a hand down onto the buff coloured folder in front of him, replied, "I'm sorry, Daisy, but there's nothing in your file that explains what you've just told me. Hands up," he sighed, "it sounds like another balls-up on our part. Well," he widely grinned, "now that you've explained that, how about we set a date for your appraisal and be done with it?"

Trudging in the fading light towards his home in Crowhill Street, Kieran McMenamin was angry.

No, not just angry, but absolutely raging.

Raging at his treatment by Peter McGroarty and even more so in front of that skinny, wasted, junkie skank, Sharon.

As he walked, he pulled the hood of his navy blue NIKE sweater up over his head and imagined how he would revenge himself on McGroarty.

In his mind, he would kick the shit out of the former boxer then make him watch while he shagged the arse off his girlfriend before battering her too.

Aye, he worked at loosening his aching jaw and turning his head, spat a globule of blood-stained phlegm against the side of a parked car, grinning as he hurried on.

His hands thrust into the pockets of the sweater, his main concern for the moment was how he would find the money to pay off his weekly bill.

He thought again of how he had been scammed; of that bastard Lennie Robertson who yesterday, when visiting McMenamin's bedroom to purchase a joint, had stolen the grass and the poke of money from the stash under the floorboards when McMenamin had been having a shit, then fucked off before he had even got out of the toilet.

Bastard!

He'd get his, McMenamin vowed, thinking of how he would enjoy battering the junkie smackhead!

But the money, he wondered. How the hell was he to find a hundred and eighty quid before midday tomorrow?

He stopped and realising he was in Berneray Street, glanced at the houses on either side of the road.

It wasn't the first time he had screwed houses for an earner, but in an area with a high incidence of unemployment and most of the residents on welfare, even McMenamin realised he was unlikely to find that kind of money lying about in these homes.

With a sigh, he continued walking and smiling, it came to him. Wednesday was usually busy with the old folk out spending their pensions.

He'd go down early and hang about Saracen Cross and watch who drew their money from the cash machine at the bank.

It wouldn't be difficult to follow a couple of the old gits and after seeing them at the ATM, he could be certain they were carrying cash.

Sorted, he grinned and head down, hurried homewards.

CHAPTER TWO

Wednesday morning opened with bright sunshine, but stepping out of Saracen police office, all Daisy Cooper could think about was getting home to bed.
What she had hoped for during her nightshift was a quiet period to reflect on her upcoming appraisal, but the two noisy drunks arrested by the patrol officers for a breach of the peace and who through the night hammered constantly on their metal cell doors, put paid to that.
Driving home, her thoughts turned to her fiancé Ian and unconsciously she smiled, thinking how fortunate she was that during the recent terrorist attack in Glasgow, Ian had been there to save her.
Now, she now could not imagine her life without him.
Yes, she decided, she was lucky to have him and even more so that he didn't try to impose his will upon her, that though he worried for Daisy when she was at work, he supported her decision to continue her career in the police.
She sometime wondered if she had not been so involved during the terrorist attack, if the media had not made such a fuss about her courage when confronted by the armed Jihadists, her promotion might not have been so rapid. No matter that she had been so terrified she had almost wet herself when facing the Jihadist, the one called Abdul-hameed Muhammad who Ian killed before he shot Daisy.
She shook her head, angry with herself for doubting her own ability.
"That's what got you promoted, my girl," she muttered as she drove, "not the bloody newspapers."
Glancing into the rear view mirror, she saw she was pale and wondered if it was because she was tired after a restless nightshift or perhaps still suffering the effect of that dreadful day when so many innocent people had been murdered by the four gunmen.
In fairness to the police and in the aftermath of the attack, they offered counselling to Daisy and she was warned that there might come a time she would suffer from PTSD, Post-Traumatic Stress Disorder.
No, not me, she had tried to laugh it off, but lately and usually in the privacy of the bathroom, more and more found herself close to tears.

It was the most stupid things that would set her off. A soppy movie, an article in the newspaper or even watching some kids playing in the street.
So far she had coped, but recently on a number of occasions caught Ian staring suspiciously at her, as though he knew there was something not quite right.
She exhaled and shook her head.
No matter, it just isn't worth getting myself worked up about, she decided.
Turning the key, she started the engine and taking a deep breath, readied herself for the drive home to the ground floor flat she shared with Ian.
It was when she was driving that something else, something she had not considered, occurred to her.

Mary Harris had no need for an alarm clock, for every morning she awoke just before seven and was in the kitchen by five minutes past. Just over a year previously, her usual routine would have had her out of bed and straight into the kitchen, the kettle on the boil and Michael's breakfast on the table by quarter past. His pieces would have been prepared the night before and in the fridge, his flask topped up with boiling water and ready for his departure to catch the five past eight bus that would have taken him to his work as a janitor in the office building in the city centre's Hope Street.
For over twenty years, five days a week other than their annual two week break to Margate and the Christmas public holiday closures, that was their unchanging routine.
Then came the stroke that changed everything.
She lay in bed, her eyes closed as for the thousandth time she remembered the phone call to attend immediately at the Western Infirmary, then sitting in the ambulance holding his hand as its blue lights and siren hurried Michael across the River Clyde to the Southern General Hospital.
No, it isn't not the Southern anymore, she recalled.
It's the big modern hospital in Govan, whatever it is called these days.
The haste in which the ambulance men, both kind beyond words, who carried Michael from the ambulance, the nursing staff who hurried Michael and her through the long corridors and the young

staff nurse who politely, but firmly refused her entry to the curtained off cubicle, then took her by the elbow and seating her in the waiting room brought her a cup of hot, sweet tea.

She waited for what seemed an interminable time until the young doctor, even younger than her own children, arrived and sitting beside her gently confirmed, "Missus Harris, your husband has had a stroke."

The devastating news almost broke her as the doctor continued, "This occurs when there is a poor blood flow to the brain, Missus Harris," and went on to explain that there were two main types of stroke and that he suspected her Michael had what they called a haemorrhagic stroke, that for some unknown reason there had been a bleed in his brain.

"Has he fallen recently?" the doctor had asked. "Been struck on the head?"

Dazed with the shock of what was happening, she had said no, no, no, that Michael was a fit man for his sixty-two years.

Did he smoke, was there a history of high blood pressure and a dozen other questions that both bewildered and confused her.

"No," she had told the doctor. "He didn't smoke, walked a lot and I'm fussy what food I give him. It's like I said, he wasn't much of a drinker either and kept himself fit."

The following day the doctor organised what they told her was an MRI scan of Michael's brain and then broke the news that yes, it was as she feared. There was a bleed directly onto Michael's brain. Someone, she didn't know who, organised a taxi to take her home and then there was the phone calls.

Their son, young Michael had travelled overnight from his home in Dorset to be with her while their daughter Jennifer suggested she travel back to Scotland from her home in New Zealand, but Mary inwardly knew that Jenny fervently hoped her mother would say no. And Mary did say no, for she was aware that with two young children of her own and eight months pregnant with her third, Jenny was in no fit state to make the long journey home. Besides, with her husband having just set up his own construction business, he needed her there with him, if only to care for their sons while he worked the long hours at the business.

Slowly, she opened her eyes and turning back the quilt, swung her legs out of bed and her feet to the floor.

Standing, Mary reached for her dressing gown and slipping it on made her way into the kitchen.

For a full week Michael had lain unconscious, then after two weeks semi-conscious in the hospital came the dreadful news that the stroke had brought on dementia.

It was obvious she had neither the skill nor the experience to care for her husband at home and so for two months Mary visited a number of council residential homes in the Glasgow area in the hope that one would be found that would care for Michael.

At last, when she was both physically and mentally exhausted, Michael was finally accepted into the Ibrox home where Mary believed he would be and was well cared for.

Not that Michael knew any different, she sighed, for the man who excelled at the 'Glasgow News' crossword, fished with his angling pals on the second Sunday of every month at the Glenburn Reservoir and never missed a Partick Thistle home game, was now a shell of the man he had been.

A sob threatened to erupt from her as she took a deep breath, but she forced herself to be calm and slowly exhaled.

Fetching the loaf from the breadbin, she made her usual breakfast of toast and tea and sat at the table in the neat and tidy, narrow kitchen. She glanced at the wall clock.

Wednesday morning was one of the four days she volunteered at the cancer charity shop at Saracen Cross, though the recent lack of volunteers and old Jean McGraw, crippled with arthritis and finally standing down after almost ten years of service, meant that Mary was now there almost six days a week.

Not that she minded, for the company of her fellow volunteers and the craic with the customers kept her going and her mind off her own troubles.

Finishing her tea, she washed then dried the plate and the mug and returned them to the cupboard.

With a glance at the bright day outside she returned to her bedroom to get dressed.

Kieran McMenamin's father Brian knocked on his sons bedroom door and called out, "Hey, ya useless sod. Get your lazy arse out of your bed. You've to sign on at the Social this morning."

Brian turned around when his daughter Patricia, older than the twenty-year-three old Kieran by three years, passed him by in the hallway on her way to the bathroom and said, "Morning, Da. Can you lend me twenty quid for my bus fares and some lunch till I get my wages this Friday?"

"For heaven's sake," her father responded. "Do you think I'm made of money? That'll be fifty quid in total that you'll owe me, hen."

Turning her head, she smiled humourlessly at her father, knowing he wouldn't refuse her and closed the bathroom door behind her.

"And don't be too long in there, young lady," he yelled after her. "I've my work to go to in half an hour and I need a shite before I go!"

Lying in his bed, Kieran McMenamin idly listened to the exchange between them and sighed.

If Tricia didn't have money and likely his Da only had enough to see himself through the rest of the week before pay day, then it would be useless asking either of them for a bung. Besides, neither would have one hundred and eighty quid to give him anyway.

No, he sighed again, he'd need to go with his idea from last night. Find a couple of pensioners and take the cash from them.

Daisy Cooper turned the car into Kingsheath Avenue and slowing, came to a halt outside the house.

It was a relief to be home and she looked forward to getting to bed, but not before having a cuppa with Ian before he left to open the café for business at nine that morning.

Locking the car, she nodded to her next door neighbour then unlocking the door, called out, "That's me home."

Tossing her keys onto the small table behind the front door, Daisy slipped off her navy blue anorak and still stood in the hallway, rolled her head to ease the ache in her neck.

"Want me to do that for you?" said Ian from behind her as he placed both hands on her shoulders and gently massaged them.

"Mmmm," she smiled, her tiredness replaced with a longing for him. "Do you *really* need to go to work today, Mister MacLeod?"

He grinned and softly whispered in her ear, "Why, what do you have in mind?"

She turned into his encircling arms and staring up at the tall man, lightly stroked at the scarring on the left side of his neck and ear and replied, "Come to bed and find out."
It had taken the former soldier a long time to permit anyone, even Daisy, to touch his battle-wounds, but now accepted she was not repelled by his disfigurement.
He pretended to frown and making a theatrical glance at his watch, said, "Oh, I suppose I could give you half an hour, Sergeant Cooper."
"I'd rather you give me something else," she coyly grinned as she pulled him towards their bedroom.

Peter McGroarty awoke and drowsily reached a hand to the other side of the bed, but it was empty.
Suddenly awake, he snarled "Bitch!" and leaping from the bed strode quickly to the toilet, but the door was locked.
"Sharon!" he hammered on the door with his fist. "Open this fucking door or I'm putting it in!"
"Wait, I'm peeing," she replied and a few seconds later, heard her fumble with the door lock.
Pushing it open, the door swung against the blonde haired, naked Gale who stumbling back against the wall, said, "What the fuck, Peter!"
He grabbed her by the wrists and turning both arms outwards, inspected them for a fresh needle mark.
"I wasn't doing anything," she whined. "Honest. I told you. I'll wait till you give me the stuff."
He threw down her arms in disgust and hurried through to the second bedroom where he upended a single bed with tubular legs. From the bottom of one of the legs he removed twelve inches of the leg and emptied out more than a dozen small clear packets of heroin onto the wooden floor, counting them as he did so.
Turning, he saw Sharon standing in the doorway, one arm held protectively about her breasts and the other at her crotch as she fearfully watched him.
"See, I told you," she stuttered. "I didn't touch any of them."
Unable to admit he had made a mistake, his teeth bared, McGroarty scowled, "Well, make sure you don't or believe me, hen, I'll punch you so many times you'll think there's two of me."

So afraid of him, she couldn't speak and could only stare wide-eyed while nodding in understanding.

The tall and lanky form of Cornelius Doyle, known throughout the Saracen and Maryhill area as Popeye, lifted his lunchbox from the rear seat of his car before pushing through the doors of Saracen police office.
Nodding a cheery greeting to the young female civilian bar officer, he made his way through the building and upstairs to the Community Police office where after signing on in the duty roster, deposited his lunch into the fridge, but not before shaking his head at the state of it.
With a sigh, he took off his anorak and emptying the fridge of its contents, fetched a basin of hot water from the toilets and began to clean the food debris adhering to the inside.
About five minutes later, as satisfied as he could be the interior was now clean, he emptied the basin in the toilets and returned to the room to find Sergeant Anne Cassidy, a fair haired young woman with a pinched face who might have been described as pretty but for the permanent scowl affixed to her face. Seated behind her desk, her head was down as she pored over a file.
"Morning, Sergeant," Doyle courteously acknowledged her.
Cassidy didn't immediately respond, but without removing her gaze from the file almost grudgingly replied, "Good morning, Constable Doyle.
Knowing that was the most conversation he would get from the young woman, Doyle turned his attention to restoring the food items into the fridge.
"Morning Sarge, morning Popeye," called a chirpy voice and turning, he saw the grinning Fariq Mansoor, the twenty-six-year old probationary cop who was for the next month seconded to Community Policing. A strikingly handsome young man with a neatly trimmed beard, Mansoor was just two inches short of Popeye's six feet and eighteen months into his police career.
"Good morning, Constable Mansoor," replied Cassidy who nodding towards Popeye, icily added, "You'll be working today with Constable Doyle, so I expect as it's now just after nine o'clock, you'll both be ready to commence your beat duties."
"Sarge," Mansoor acknowledged with a nod.

Slipping on his utility belt and lifting his cap from his locker, Doyle turned to the young officer and with a smile said, "Ready?"
"Ready."
On their way to the uniform bar to collect their Airwave radios, Mansoor said, "She's not the most pleasant of women, is she?"
Doyle shrugged and replied, "She's still finding her feet, son. Remember, she's only been promoted within the last year and she's still finding her way as a supervisor. Give her time and I'm sure she'll settle down."
"You're too nice a guy and it's true what they say about you, Popeye. You've not got a bad word to say about anybody, have you?" laughed Mansoor. "Besides, what service has she got, four, five years? Surely the wise thing would be to get you onside, not what I've heard."
Handing Mansoor a radio from the recharging rack, Doyle stared keenly at him and asked, "What have you heard, then?"
"Well," he slowly drawled as he fitted the radio to his stab-proof vest, "the word is that she's been giving you a hard time, that she's asked the Chief Inspector to replace you and that she wants you out of Community Policing."
"Don't believe everything you hear," Doyle smiled at him.
"So, it's not true then? You're seeing out your time in the CP?"
"What time I have left," he shrugged, "yes, I believe so."
They continued towards the front entrance door of the station during which time Doyle reflected on what Mansoor had heard.
Anne Cassidy was one of a number of university graduates who upon joining the police were fast-tracked through the ranks by a system that assumed these individuals, by reason of their academic backgrounds, were suitable candidates for promotion to positions of supervision with the belief they would eventually reach senior management rank. While in the main the officers selected for this route proved to be ideal candidates, capable of learning and assimilating the job in a very short time and proving worthy of the trust placed in them by the selection procedure, a few such as Cassidy were incapable of accepting advice from their more experienced colleagues and subordinates and hid behind bluster and rank to conceal their inadequacies.
Not that it bothered Doyle so much, having decided within days of her appointment as his supervisor that for the short time he had

remaining in the job, arguing with or even trying to helpfully advise a young lassie like Cassidy just wasn't worth the bother.

Pushing open the entrance door to permit Doyle to pass through, Mansoor broke into his thoughts when he asked, "How long *do* you have left to serve, Popeye?"

"Counting today," he mused, "a little over six weeks, but with my two weeks' annual leave to take, I reckon I'll be gone in four weeks."

Reaching for his radio, he added, "Hang on and I'll sign us on with the Maryhill control room." That done, he continued, "If I've read the calendar correctly, four weeks and two days to be precise," and smiled.

"Wow, so that will be your thirty years in?"

"Aye, thirty years of toiling the beat here and at Maryhill."

"You must know most of the people round here then."

"A good number of them, yes."

"What do you intend doing when you retire? Put your feet up, I bet."

Turning from Barloch Street into Closeburn Street, Doyle indicated with his hand and said, "I've a return call to make at one of the flats here," and led the way into a close.

"So, what's the first thing you going to do when you retire?" persisted Mansoor.

"Sleep late in the morning," Doyle grinned and reaching the first floor, knocked on a door.

Kiernan McMenamin heard the front door close and with his father already left for work, knew that Dona was now also gone from the house.

Quickly, he jumped from his bed and pulled on black coloured jogging trousers, a Celtic football top and fetched his navy blue hooded top from his wardrobe.

Slipping on his training shoes, he inspected himself in the wardrobe mirror and grinned. With the hood pulled up and covering most of his face, he'd be hard to identify.

With a last look around his room, he headed for the door and then began to quickly make his way towards Saracen Cross.

CHAPTER THREE

Pulling on her coat, Mary Harris glanced through the bedroom window and was pleased to see that at least for now the rain had now given way to a bright and sunny morning.

Fetching her handbag from the kitchen, she ensured the charity shop keys were inside before locking the front door behind her.

"Away to the shop, Missus Harris?" asked her young upstairs neighbour, Elaine Findlay, who at twenty-six was trying to raise two toddlers alone after her wayward partner decided family life was not for him. Struggling to carry a heavy shopping bag and a two-year old on her hip while the four year-old raced up the stairs ahead of her, the younger woman seemed to Mary to be exhausted.

"Here, let me help you with that one," Mary plucked the two-year old from her and carrying the girl in her arms, followed the grateful Findlay up the stairs to the first floor flat directly above Mary's own home.

"Sorry about any noise during the night. The wee one was up crying again last night with a temperature," Findlay laid down the shopping bag as she searched in her shoulder bag for her door keys. "That's why I'm out so early doing my shopping, I just couldn't get any sleep and…"

"I never heard a thing," Mary graciously lied and continued, "I can see that you're exhausted."

"Any news about your husband, Missus Harris?"

"No, hen, nothing new and I've told you before," she gently rebuked Findlay. "Call me Mary," but was pleased that the younger woman had thought to ask.

Carrying the child through the door, she continued, "Look, it's me that's doing the opening at the shop which means I'll finish my shift about two. Why don't you let me take the wee ones for a couple of hours, let you get some rest? If you stick Megan in her pram and the wee pram step thing that goes on the back for Ross, I'll take them for a walk to Ruchill Park. How about that? Besides, I'll be needing the fresh air myself."

Close to tears at her neighbour's kindness, Findlay bit at her lower lip and nodded, unable to speak.

Feeling a little better about herself, but hoping that she hadn't taken too much on, Mary returned down the stairs to make her way to the charity shop.

He reached the Cross and stood in Copeland Road, leaned against the wall of the Saracen Bar, for the tenement building provided dark shadow from the bright sun.
The Cross was busy with shoppers, but nobody paid particular attention to a young man hanging around for the area was already populated with the unemployed and unemployable.
Tensely, he watched as an elderly, stooped man wearing a long, grey trench coat and a tartan bunnet crossed the street at the pedestrian lights and walked to the ATM machine located in the wall of the Royal Bank of Scotland. His eyes narrowed and he briefly considered following him as a potential target for mugging, but then that idea was dropped when the man was approached by a young woman pushing a buggy who accompanied him along the street in the opposite direction from where Kieran McMenamin stood. Disappointed, he unconsciously pulled his hood down and took a deep breath.
Across the road, Mary Harris took advantage of a break in the traffic to hurry across the road at the junction, then stopped outside the RBS on the corner to again check she had the charity shop keys. With a sigh of relief, she glanced across the road and her eyes narrowed.
What caused her to be suspicious, she couldn't say, but the sight of the young man stood watching her caused her to shiver and turning her head away hurriedly walked the forty yards to the shop doorway. Yet some inner sense made her look back to where the young man stood, but either he was gone or was now standing out of sight around the corner in the shadow of the building.
With a sigh of relief, she inserted the key and opening the door, startled when a voice said, "Morning, Mary."
"Oh, it's yourself, Alice," she greeted the elderly shop volunteer. "I got a wee bit of a fright there, hen."
"Oh?"
"It's just that…oh, nothing," she smiled at her own foolishness and dismissing the thought, switched on the shops lights.

Chief Inspector Dougie Kane had just taken off his jacket when his door knocked.
"Come in," he growled, thinking I've hardly got my arse onto my chair and already I'm busy.

The door opened to reveal Anne Cassidy, her face grimly set.
"Sergeant Cassidy," he forced a smile. "What can I do for you this lovely, sunny morning?"
"It's about Constable Doyle, sir," she began while he thought, it always bloody is.
"What about Constable Doyle?"
"If I may?" she nodded to the chair in front of his desk.
"Please," he returned her nod, already anxious for the coffee he had promised himself when he arrived at the office.
"As you may have read in my memo dated almost a week ago, sir, since I took over the job of Community Policing I have been extremely unhappy with Constable Doyle's performance. His arrests, of which there are very, *very* few," she stressed, "are so minor and trivial it's hardly worth reporting them to the Procurator Fiscal."
"You do realise that Popeye…I mean, Constable Doyle, has just over a month of reckonable service before he retires?"
"That may be so, but I intend running an efficient and effectual department, sir, and I do *not* and I will *not* tolerate slackers. No, sir, I will not."
"And you believe Constable Doyle to be such a slacker, Sergeant?"
"Yes, sir, I most certainly do."
"Hmmm," he elbows on his massive chest, clasped his fingers together, his hands in front of his bulbous nose as he leaned back in his chair."
"Those two medal ribbons that Doyle wears on his stab proof vest, Sergeant. Do you recognise them?"
"Well, yes sir," she frowned at the unexpected question. "The Long Service and Good Conduct Medal, anyway."
"And the other ribbon, the one with the little vertical red stripes. Do you recognise *that* ribbon?"
Her brow furrowed and she stared suspiciously at Kane as she replied, "No, sir. I thought it was something to do with his long service."
"No, indeed it is not," he softly replied. "That ribbon, Sergeant Cassidy, is the Queens Police Medal for Gallantry. Now, as Constable Doyle is one of your officers, I had presumed that you perhaps had read his personnel file, that you knew the officers under your supervision?"

Her face paled at the oversight and tight-lipped, she slowly shook her head.

"Well, the slacker you refer to is no ordinary constable. In fact, Cornelius Doyle is to me and every officer who knows him well, a hero, Sergeant Cassidy."

His eyes narrowed as he stared at her and asked, "What service have you to date?"

"Eh, a little over five years, sir," she quietly replied.

"And remind me again. How old are you?"

She was now swallowing with difficulty, for this complaint about that lazy bastard Doyle was not going the way she expected.

"I'm just short of my twenty-sixth birthday, sir."

"Almost twenty-six, eh? My, I sometimes wish I was that young again," he smiled humourlessly at her.

Wordlessly, she stared at him and thought him to be just another patronising bastard who should have been retired years ago.

"Now let me see. Almost twenty-six? That means before you were born and then when when you were sitting on your mammy's knee, Sergeant Cassidy, Constable Doyle was patrolling the streets of Maryhill and Saracen and let me tell you, those streets were a *lot* different in those days. Murder and mayhem, as we used to say. And it was in one of those very streets that your Constable Doyle chased down an armed robber who was carrying a handgun and who twice, yes twice, shot at Doyle before he bravely tackled the bugger and bringing him to the ground, arrested him! And that, Sergeant Cassidy," his voice now rose, "is why Constable Doyle wears the QPM for gallantry and why I will *not* have you come in here and whine to me about him! Are we clear?"

She didn't have time to respond, for there was a knock at the door.

"Come in!" shouted Kane, who when the door opened got to his feet for there in the doorway stood Detective Superintendent Cathy Mulgrew.

Staring from him to Cassidy and back to Kane, Mulgrew's perfectly plucked eyebrows arched as she said, "Sorry to interrupt, Chief Inspector Kane, but I was hoping to have a word about one of your officers."

Of course, Kane not only recognised Mulgrew, but knew her well and keeping his face straight, replied, "One of my officers, Ma'am?"

"Are you sure I'm not interrupting, Dougie?"

"No, Ma'am, not at all," he turned to see Cassidy rising to her feet and added, "The sergeant was just leaving."

"Oh, right," Mulgrew smiling, stepped into the room and added, "It's about a Constable Doyle and if I'm correct, I'm told he's more commonly known as Popeye."

"Popeye Doyle, Ma'am," his heart sunk a little, but then Mulgrew added, "Yes, I'd like to pass on my thanks to him through you, if that's okay."

Relief swept through him as he inhaled and said, "Perhaps Sergeant Cassidy, who is Doyle's supervisor, might remain?"

"Of course," Mulgrew smiled at the younger woman and indicating she sit back down, took the seat next to Cassidy and turning to her, continued, "I called in for a visit with the DI at Maryhill and he was telling me that last week, as a result of information obtained by your man Doyle that he passed timeously to the CID, a team of housebreakers were arrested as they were breaking into a large house in Dunellen Road up in Milngavie. The lads had been after this team for some time and Doyle apparently provided time, date and locus for the arrest. I'll be notifying the Divisional Commander about his information, but thought as I was passing, Dougie," she turned to him, "I'd pop in and let you know how grateful I am. Besides that, I figured I might get a decent coffee, knowing you to be a bit of a Barista and fussy about your blends," she grinned at him.

His face a fixed smile, Kane turned to Cassidy and said, "I take it you're aware of the good work done by your officer, Sergeant?"

Her mouth set in a tight smile, Cassidy replied, "I'll be sure to mention it to him, sir," then getting to her feet, left the room.

"Am I sensing a bit of an attitude there, Dougie?" asked Mulgrew.

"Not so much attitude as inexperience, Cathy," he shook his head, "but that's the way the polis is going these days, promoting some of these young people to a level of incompetence."

"Aye, well you're starting to sound like one of those old farts we knew in our youth," she grinned at him, "so, how about that coffee?"

Outside the Kane's room, Anne Cassidy slowly made her way to the Community Police office, her berating at the Chief Inspector's hands still smarting and teeth gritted, inwardly vowed that before his month was up she would see Cornelius Doyle revealed for the waster she really believed him to be.

Thanking the elderly couple for the tea and cake, Doyle and his probationer Fariq Mansoor made their way downstairs to the close entrance and out into the bright sunlight.

"At least we don't need our jackets," commented Mansoor, his head turned to stare at the cloudy sky, before asking, "Tell me this, how did you come by the nickname Popeye?"

"You mean you don't know?" he pretended to be surprised.

"No," Mansoor slowly replied, but guessing he was about to be wound up.

"Well," he drawled, "I used to have this girlfriend called Olive and then there's my tremendously muscular arms with an anchor tattoo on…"

"Aye, very good, but what's the *real* story?"

Doyle grinned and turning to the younger man, said, "Back in the seventies and *long* before you were a twinkle in your old man's eye, there was a popular movie called 'The French Connection'. One of the characters was called Popeye Doyle and heh-ho, when I joined the polis and because of my surname, I was christened Popeye."

"That's it?"

"What, you were expecting something more glamourous or exciting?"

"Maybe," Mansoor grinned, then continued, "That old couple back there," he cast a thumb back towards the close. "You said it was a repeat call, but you didn't ask them anything about anything. I mean, why were we *really* there? I mean, they seem to be a nice couple, but was it just for the tea and the cake?"

Doyle didn't immediately respond, his eyes narrowing as though trying to decide how to explain the visit to Mister and Missus Taylor before he replied, "About two months ago, I had to deliver a death message to that couple. Their son was only forty-seven when he got hit by a bus down in Sauchiehall Street. Drunk as a skunk and didn't make the other pavement like he intended. Anyway, cut a long story short, like any parents they took his death very badly. I knew Willie Taylor. He was a bit of a lad, was Willie. Not a bad guy, just a bloody nuisance, always getting himself locked up for a breach of the peace or a bit of shoplifting now and again and usually for stealing alcohol. I've probably made more calls to that house in the last couple of years than any other address in this sub-Division and always to inform them of Willie's arrest and on each occasion they were always very civil to me."

He paused as though reflecting. "Since he died, I try to get there at least once a week, just to let them know that whether Willie is here or not, *I'll* not forget *them*."

Turning to Mansoor, he softly smiled and said, "Policing is not always about locking up bad guys, son."

What he didn't disclose was that as a mark of respect to the deceased and his parents, Cornelius Doyle was one of the few non-family members who attended William Taylor's funeral service.

"Right then," he broadly smiled. "How's about you and me taking a wee turn down to the Cross, eh?"

He had his target.

The elderly and obviously infirm woman using a walking stick had withdrawn money from the Royal Bank of Scotland ATM.

He had almost nervously laughed out loud, anxiously watching and seeing the impatience of the two young women behind her as it took the woman four or five minutes to obtain her cash. She had begun with trying to find her spectacles in her coat pockets, then searched for a full minute through her purse for her bank card and then so very slowly typed in her PIN number. From the number of times she tried, he guessed she made a couple of mistakes.

Shaking his head at her antics, he sniggered and thought she's begging to get mugged.

When the drawer opened to dispense her notes it had taken her almost a minute to place them into the red coloured purse that she slipped into the tartan covered, four wheeled shopping trolley. He watched her drag the trolley behind her when crossing the Saracen Street to McMenamin's side of the road.

From the distance, he had been unable to see just how much she had withdrawn, but no matter.

Whatever money she had would soon be his.

His hood now pulled up, he continued to watch as the woman, her head down, shuffled past him and with a quick look about to ensure the polis were nowhere near, gave the woman a head start of twenty yards before slowly following her into the dead end of Saracen Street that run off the Cross.

Twenty-five yards into Saracen Street, a man who stepped out of the Credit Union doorway stopped and greeted the elderly woman and almost in panic, McMenamin crouched down and pretended to tie his shoelace.

A middle-aged woman walking towards him gave McMenamin an indifferent glance as she passed him by, though warily stepped almost to the edge of the pavement before continuing on.

Fuck, he thought, I can't stay here like this and was about to turn away when the man disappeared back into the building and the elderly woman carried on slowly walking.

With a sigh of relief, he watched as the woman passed by the row of shops in the Victoria tenement building and was then abreast the two storey more modern tenement flats.

He quickened his pace and watched as she turned into the pathway of the third close and hurrying after her, worried there might be a security door that would deny him entry.

Fixated on the woman, he didn't concern himself about who might be watching.

As the distance between them narrowed, he could see there was no security door and he too turned into the pathway where in the dim light of the close he saw the woman dragging her trolley towards the stairs.

With a sudden sprint, he was behind then upon her and without difficulty, pulled the trolley from her grasp.

The woman screamed in panic, but McMenamin was too busy rummaging through the trolley for her purse and didn't see she had raised her walking stick that she brought crashing down onto his head.

The pathetic blow didn't so much hurt as annoy him and in his anger, he shouted, "Fuck off!" and pushed at her arm that wielded the stick, but his swipe only enraged her more and again she tried to strike him, all the while screaming in a pitifully squeaky voice.

Ignoring her assault upon him, he grabbed the purse from among the shopping then snarling lifted the trolley and threw it at the woman. The confined space meant that there was no real power behind his throw, but when the trolley struck her on the upper half of her body

the weight of the shopping in the trolley and the frail woman's age combined to knock her down backwards onto the concrete stairs.
He watched her fall like a sack of potatoes then with a sigh, her body relaxed and her eyes closed.
McMenamin, stared down at her and seeing the crimson blood seep from the back of her head onto the stairs, panicked.
"Missus?" he quietly said, his voice faltering, then more loudly, "Missus!"
He was about to reach over to shake her, but his heart was racing and his chest felt tight, then with the purse in his hand he raced through the close to the open door at the rear exit and ran.

It was a neighbour, the young man who lived opposite her flat on the same landing, who discovered the old lady lying unconscious on the stairs and with shaking hands phoned from his mobile for an ambulance. Seeing the shopping trolley lying at the foot of the stairs with the shopping scattered about, it was almost as an afterthought he then told the nine-nine-nine operator she had better send the polis too.

CHAPTER FOUR

As it happened, the nearest police resource to the incident were Popeye Doyle and his young probationer, Fariq Mansoor who arrived at the close before the ambulance responded.
"Have you moved her?" Doyle asked the young neighbour and placed two fingers on the unconscious woman's carotid artery to satisfy himself she was still alive. Before the younger man replied, Doyle sighed and muttered, "Aye, she's still with us."
"No, I didn't move her," the neighbour shook his head. "When I saw the blood at the back of her head that's seeped onto the stairs I thought it better just to leave her. All I did was cover her with my jacket," he pointed to the thin yellow coloured anorak covering the old lady.
"What's her name?" Doyle asked.
"Missus Henderson. She lives on the first floor opposite me. I don't know her first name and I'm almost positive she lives alone. I only moved in a couple of weeks ago. Me and my girlfriend, I mean."

Doyle's eyes narrowed as he stared closely at the old lady, at last recognising her.

It had been a long time since their paths had crossed and at that time Harriet Henderson had been living in a ground flat in Stoneyhurst Street, but of course that building had been demolished to make way for the new housing that was now there.

He lifted what looked like house keys from the overturned trolley, unconsciously noting that there was no apparent sign of a purse or wallet that might hold money. Turning to Mansoor, he handed him the keys and said, "Here Fariq, away up to the woman's flat and grab a blanket or something. We need to keep her warm.

"Roger," the younger man said and carefully stepping over the unconscious woman, hurried up the stairs.

"While you're there, son," he called after Mansoor, "see if there's a telephone book or something that might have a next of kin number in it, okay?"

"Roger," Mansoor repeated and gave him a thumbs up before disappearing.

Doyle turned to see two ambulance personnel entering the close.

"What kept you layabouts?" he chided them and grinned.

The older of the two, Roberta 'Bobby' Dawson, her blonde hair tied back in a French ponytail, returned Doyle's grin and replied, "Trust you to get here first, Popeye. What we got then?" she asked as she bent down and first dumping a green coloured First Aid holdall at her feet, then tenderly moved the fallen woman's hair from her face before ever so gently running her fingers round the old lady's neck to the back of her head.

Doyle nodded to the young neighbour and eyes narrowing, said, "This young guy...sorry, son. What's your name?"

"Eh, Mark, Mark Caldwell."

"Young Mark here found his neighbour, Missus Harriet Henderson, lying on the stair as you see her and covered her with his jacket. He didn't move her, Bobby..."

"No, I didn't think it was safe to do so," Caldwell interrupted, wondering how the officer knew the woman's first name while he did not.

"Aye, well you did the right thing," Bobby muttered as she nodded, but her concentration was fixed on the old lady.

Turning to her young male colleague, Ian Forsyth, she said, "Frosty, go and fetch the stretcher and a collar. Better bring the portable oxygen too. Popeye," she turned towards him, "can you give me and Frosty a hand to get her into the back of the ambulance?"

"No problem, hen, whatever you need."

"Popeye," he turned as his name was called from the top of the stairs. "Do you still need this?" and saw that Mansoor held a folded blanket in his hand.

"No, you're okay, son. The cavalry are here," he grinned up at the younger man, before asking, "Any luck on a next of kin?"

"Still looking," Mansoor replied then disappeared again.

Forsyth returned with the stretcher, oxygen and a blanket and after a few minutes, the ambulance crew had the old lady secured in the stretcher and the oxygen mask on her face.

"Here," Bobby handed the oxygen bottle and First Aid holdall to Doyle, "make yourself useful."

It took but a few moments for the crew to convey and secure the old lady in the rear of the ambulance, then turning to Doyle as Bobby closed the rear doors on the victim and her colleague, she told him, "I don't like the look of that head injury. That and her age," she sighed. "If you guys are looking for her later I'm requesting that I take her straight to the Neuro at the Queen Elizabeth over in Govan. Besides, if I take her to the Western, they'll only transfer her anyway."

She stared curiously at Doyle and asked, "Do *you* think she fell?"

His brow furrowed as he shook his head and said, "No, I couldn't see her purse or any money lying around and it's obvious she's been shopping, so she must have bought the groceries. If I'm correct, I think she was attacked."

"By the young guy in there?" her voice lowered, Bobby subtly nodded back into the close towards the neighbour who remained standing at the bottom of the stairs, his jacket in his hand.

"I can't say for certain, but my gut tells me no," he quietly replied.

"Right then, we'll be away and Popeye," she began to walk to the front of the ambulance but turned to give him a dazzling smile, "it's nice to see you again. Stay in touch, eh?"

Taken aback, he watched her climb into the cab and almost immediately Bobby switched on the blue lights and the ambulance raced off. A moment later as it reached a busy junction and though

out of sight, Doyle could hear the 'blues and two's being activated and smiled.
Every opportunity, Bobby, he thought and grinned.
Turning, he made his way back into the close, his hand reaching for his Airwave radio as he prepared to request that the CID attend at the locus of what he suspected was a street robbery gone wrong.

He had the sense not to run through the rear court, but hurriedly made his way to across the metal railing that separated the rear courts and into the rear close of Barloch Street where he stood still and glanced behind him.
To his relief, there was no sound or sight of any pursuit and his body still shaking, he briefly glanced into the purse.
His eyes widened at the sight of the wad of notes in one compartment and stuffing the purse into his hoody, composed himself before making his way through the close to the front.
He hesitated, but other than a passing lorry, the street was quiet and as boldly as he dared, pulled down his hood and stepped out into the path and began to make his way along the pavement in the direction of Closeburn Street.
Once in Closeburn Street, McMenamin turned into a close and making his way through to the rear, retrieved the purse from under his hoody and calmer now, counted the notes.
"Eighty quid," he murmured then searching the zipped pockets, in one of the pockets found a man's worn gold wedding ring, a black and white and headshot picture of a man in army uniform who seemed to be not much older than himself and who was smiling at the camera. The rest of the pockets contained a bank card, pensioners bus travel pass, a bingo card and old till receipts, a thin, but broken gold chain and a St Christopher medal, none of which interested him. He stared hard at the wedding band, but decided it was too old and worn to be pawned and discounted both it and the thin broken chain with the medal.
His eyes narrowed then stuffing the photograph into his pocket, decided to keep it and he grinned. If ever asked he would pretend for a laugh the photo was of a long dead uncle; a war hero.
Listening for any sound, he was satisfied that so far there was nobody looking for him and ensuring the back court was clear,

slipped over to a waste bin and threw the purse and the rest of the contents inside.

Pleased that he had the eighty pounds, he knew that nevertheless he was still one hundred quid short of McGroarty's bill and decide that needs must, that the risk was worth it. He would return to the Cross and watch again for another pensioner drawing money from the ATM.

Duster in hand, Mary Harris was leaning forward, cleaning the shelving and articles for sale that were displayed in the charity shop front window when glancing outside, her eyes narrowed for she was certain the same youth who had worried her earlier that morning was again hanging about the same corner outside the pub, across the busy road.

The sound of a siren slowly fading in the distance was nothing unusual in that part of the city, but Mary hardly heard it for her concentration was taken by the young man wearing the hood on his head who to her mind, was acting most peculiarly. To her surprise, the youth darted back into the shadows and a few seconds later on the road outside, a police van passed by the shop.

That's when Mary realised why the youth didn't want to be seen. For some reason, he was hiding from the polis.

No sooner had the police van turned the corner into Balmore Road and out of her sight and the youth was back, keeking out from behind the corner, his attention fixed on something on the other side of the road that was out of sight of Mary.

"Mary?" said Alice's voice from behind her, startling her.

She turned to see the volunteer holding two mugs of tea, one of which she handed to Mary.

"As it's quiet I thought I'd get us a wee cuppa," she cheerfully toasted her colleague.

Mary smiled and sipping at the scalding liquid, turned again to glance through the front window, but now there was no sign of the youth and again mentally dismissed her suspicion as foolishness.

The young detective who arrived outside the close in Saracen Street in response to Doyle's radio message, greeted the older officer with, "What we got?"

Quickly, Doyle apprised him of the circumstances in which the old lady, now identified by Doyle as Harriet Henderson, had been discovered lying injured by her neighbour whose statement he had noted.

"And you let the guy go?" the detective gruffly asked while with his phone camera, began taking photographs of the blood-stained stairs as well as the walking stick, trolley and the spilled shopping.

"Why would I detain him? There's nothing to indicate he's anything more than a witness."

"I'd like to have interviewed him myself," the detective moodily replied.

Doyle tolerantly smiled before replying, "I'll type out his statement and his contact numbers for you if you want to ask him to attend the office."

"Aye, maybe do that for me. Right, the woman, Missus Henderson. She lived here in the close?"

"That's why she was here," Doyle patiently nodded and added, "The first floor, door on the left. I've my lad up there the now trying to find a contact number of a next of kin. We've knocked on the neighbour's doors, but other than an old guy who lives in one of the top flats, nobody's home right now."

"Right then. You're satisfied it's a mugging?"

"No sign of any purse and she must have paid for her messages," Doyle nodded to the shopping that lay scattered about, then added, "Also, there's this."

He handed the detective an ATM print-out. "You'll see that about ten minutes or so before the call came in, Missus Henderson drew eighty pounds for the RBS at the Cross. There's no trace of it anywhere here," he waved a hand about him, "and I'd say there even if she used some of the money, there's not much much more than twenty quid's worth of shopping lying here."

"Any likelihood the witness, this guy Caldwell might have pocketed it before you got here?"

"Every chance, but I'd no right to ask him to turn out his pockets and like I said, my gut tells me he's an innocent in this."

The detective didn't immediately respond, but then asked, "And it was him who identified the victim?"

Doyle paused, briefly wondering if he should disclose what he knew then realised the truth would probably come out at some later time and replied, "Caldwell knows her as Missus Henderson. It was me who recognised her as Harriet Henderson. She's a widowed lady who used to live in Stoneyhurst Street, back when it was the older buildings, not the houses that are there the now."

The detective smiled and said, "Popeye Doyle. Widely known for his local knowledge. Let me guess, you used to pop into her house for your fly cuppa?"

Doyle stared at him and shook his head.

"No, Missus Henderson was never that pro-polis. Her nephew was Harry Henderson," and knew full well the younger man would neither recognise nor associate the name.

It was clear on his face the detective had no idea who Harry Henderson was for he grinned and asked, "Some old gangster, was he?"

"Something like that. Now, anything else I can assist you with? If not, I'll see the crime report is submitted when I get back to the office, but right now I'd like to assist my probationer and try to find a next of kin. According to Bobby Dawson, the ambulance woman, she says Missus Henderson's injury and her age might mean she could prove."

'Could prove.' The widely used police term that indicates a victim might succumb to a life-threatening injury.

The detective's face paled and nodding, he said, "She's away to the Neuro over in Govan?"

"That's what Bobby told me, aye."

"Okay, I'll head back to the office and inform my boss. I'll arrange a Scene of Crime visit here too and they can photograph and obtain a sample of the blood from the stairs. I know I've got photos on my phone, but if the woman croaks, then we'd better get this done properly, so if you and your neighbour hang fire here to protect the locus, I'll square it with your sergeant. Needless to say, if you find anything in the flat that's of use, get me on the radio and let me know."

"Will do," Doyle nodded and watched the detective hurry through the close to return to his car.

Inhaling and then slowly exhaling, Doyle began to collect the spilled shopping and replaced it into the trolley. That done, he was bending to pick up the walking stick when he became aware of a woman standing staring at him from the front of the close.

"Hello there," he smiled at her. "Do you live in the close, hen?"
The woman, in her late forties he judged and heavyset with a world weary expression, dark hair pinned back in a ponytail and wearing a knee length tweed coat, denims and training shoes and carrying a black leather handbag in her hand, took a few nervous steps forward and said, "That's old Harriet's trolley."
"Aye, it is and again, do you live in the close?"
"No," she shook her head. "No, I've come to visit Harriet. Missus Henderson, I mean. She lives up the stairs. Why do you have her shopping trolley? Has there been an accident? Is she okay?" the woman gasped, her free hand rising to her mouth.
"Who *are* you, hen?"
"I'm a…" she hesitated before continuing, "I'm a friend and well," she paused, "I also do a bit of cleaning for Harriet. My name's Agnes Fleming. Missus Fleming," she sniffed.
Doyle guessed Fleming's cleaning duties were cash in hand and a wee unofficial job on top of her benefits, hence her hesitation at admitting it.
"And are you a local woman, Missus Fleming," now standing upright, he stared down at the smaller and obviously nervous woman.
"Eh, no, I'm from Shettleston. Dalness Street. I'm only over here visiting, you know?"
With the shopping trolley in one hand and the walking stick clutched in the other, Doyle stood aside and said, "Perhaps you might like to come upstairs, Missus Fleming and I'll tell you what I know."

Kieran McMenamin couldn't believe his luck.
Ten minutes back at the Cross and the old stooped guy with the grey coat and tartan bunnet he'd seen earlier at the ATM had come slowly walking along Saracen Street on the opposite side of the road, but this time without the woman pushing the buggy. He watched the man turn the corner at the RBS bank and continued walking in Balmore Road. He was about to cross the road and step out after the man when a police van travelling on Saracen Street towards Balmore Road approached and almost in panic, he stepped back into the shadow of the building, but the two officers in the van paid no attention to him.

With a sigh of relief, he saw the old man was now thirty yards away and passing by a small park area where in an attempt to improve the area, the council had cleared the land and set up benches. As the man approached Sunnylaw Street, he neared a lane partially hidden by heavy foliage that run the length of the lane where McMenamin, his hood pulled up over his head, grabbed him and to any passer-by seemed to be helping the elderly man along the lane. However, firmly holding the protesting man, he steered him deeper into the lane and out of sight of the roadway before throwing the man face down to the ground.
"Don't say a fucking word or you're getting it!" he snarled and raising a fist at the startled and frightened man then reaching down, began to search through the prostrate man's pockets.
Whimpering and shaking, the old man began to weep at the humiliation as McMenamin pulled first at his coat, then at his trousers, sniggering as he did so.
From an inside pocket of the coat he retrieved a worn leather wallet and opening it, pulled from it four ten pound notes that he stuffed into his trouser pocket.
"Is that it, you old bastard!" he hissed, by now his blood up and the adrenaline flowing through his veins.
Bad-temperedly and savagely he kicked twice at the mans prone body.
A car horn being sounded on the nearby road caused his head to snap around and almost in panic, he threw the wallet down at the man and took one final kick at the man's legs with the warning, "If you get up within the next couple of minutes, I'll come and find you! Understand?"
He saw the man nod and then with a backward glance, run down the lane as fast as his legs would carry him.

CHAPTER FIVE

Daisy Cooper awoke earlier than she intended in the unforgiving heat of the bedroom with a blinding headache.
She had forgotten to leave a window open and as the sun rose the humidity in the room had increased through the morning.
Inwardly cursing at her forgetfulness, she got out of bed and yawning, made her way through to the kitchen where after gulping a

large glass of water, swallowed two Paracetamol and downed a second glass of water.

Needing to pee, she staggered through to the bathroom and once there, decided against returning to bed and instead drew a bath. While waiting for the bath to fill, she thought again of a recent conversation with her fiancé Ian where he asked her to consider selling the ground floor flat in the block of four and buying a house. "A three-bedroom semi, maybe," he had shrugged. "I just feel that it's time we moved to somewhere a bit nicer."

She had argued that with their commitment to the café, perhaps right now wasn't the right time to think about changing houses: still, she mused, the prospect of moving to their own place was very appealing. Somewhere they would both choose rather than continuing in the two-bedroom flat that was Daisy's before Ian moved in.

She turned off the taps and slipping off her robe, removed her nightie and panties before sliding into the bath, gasping as the hot water toasted her skin.

She lay back in the water, letting the steam and heat gently invigorate her tired body.

She had suggested to Ian that this being her last nightshift, they could book a table somewhere tomorrow evening and inwardly decided that would be an appropriate time to discuss moving house.

Eyes closed, her thoughts turned to her conversation the previous evening with the Chief Inspector, Dougie Kane, and her upcoming annual appraisal due to occur on the morning of the forthcoming Monday.

She had nothing to worry about, he had assured her, but still it niggled her.

Of course, she was ambitious and hoped that her promotion to sergeant might be the first step towards further advancement, but then a thought struck her.

Though the discussion had never really taken a serious turn, both she and Ian had tentatively discussed their future that included family.

She had turned thirty-five just a few months ago while Ian was approaching his forty-third birthday.

It didn't leave a lot of time on her biological clock and with a start, recalled her mother had begun the change at forty.

Was that why she had been feeling out of sorts recently, she wondered? That and the puking?

Her brow creased as she further wondered; was the menopause hereditary?

Warm as she was in the hot bath, a cold shiver passed through her and she mentally made a note to check the Internet, see what she could find out about it.

Course there might be another reason, but she had been taking precautions so that wasn't even a consideration.

With a sigh, she stepped from the bath and enveloping herself in a large bath towel, began to vigorously dry herself.

He had a hundred and twenty quid now, but was still sixty pounds short of the bill to McGroarty.

His mouth was dry at the thought of offering the money to the twisted bastard, guessing the former boxer would not be pleased. Not be pleased? Fuck, he shook his head, for like it or not, Kieran McMenamin knew he was on to a hiding for the shortfall, but to try and dodge McGroarty and not turn up at all would only be the worse for him.

Glancing at his phone, he saw it was now quarter to midday and so with his head down, began to make his way to McGroarty's house in Ronaldsay Street.

"How's about you put the kettle on, Missus Fleming," suggested Popeye Doyle as he followed the woman through the door, "and while you're doing that, I'll tell you what I know."

Turning to his younger neighbour, he said, "Fariq, you've got the sharp end, son. Get yourself done to the close and wait for the Scene of Crime to show."

"Aye, no bother," Mansoor grinned at him before adding, "and if you can pass me a mug of tea down…?"

"I'll see you get a cuppa," he smiled.

In the kitchen, Fleming took off her tweed coat and hung if over a chair before busying herself filling the kettle and emptying the teapot.

Sitting himself down into a wooden chair, Doyle removed his cap and glancing about him his eyes narrowed when he saw not just a neat and tidy kitchen, but what struck him was the newness of the fitted units that were top of the range and definitely not council installed.

"I'll just make sure my young colleague hasn't disturbed anything," he rose from the chair and making his way through the two bedroomed flat was surprised to see that the furniture in the lounge and bedrooms as well as the décor, was also top of the range. The bathroom at the end of the hallway was completely tiled with a modern, walk-in shower and fitted with some of the disability aids that were provided to senior citizens.

It was while he was in the lounge and staring at the array of photographs neatly lined up in the dresser that his eyes narrowed. Lifting one black and white framed photo of a much younger Harriet Henderson and a young man who smiling, had his arm about her shoulders, Doyle sighed in recognition.

His suspicions confirmed, he returned to the kitchen and was resuming his seat when Fleming asked, "Milk and sugar?"

"Just milk, please hen," and made a great show of removing his notebook from his utility belt.

"Now," he begun, "tell me about Missus Henderson?"

"Eh, what about her?" she nervously replied. "I mean, what is it you need to know?"

"Well," he drawled, smiling to try and ease her concern, "let's start with her age, next of kin, that sort of thing."

"Can you first tell me what happened though?" she handed him a mug.

Before he could reply, he heard the front door opening and a few seconds later, Mansoor gasped, "Have you switched off your radio, Popeye?"

"Aye, what is it?"

"There's been another mugging. An old man apparently, over in a lane off Balmore Road. The panda car's attending. Should we go too?"

"No," he shook his head. "We're already committed here and the control room will already be aware this is the second attack and likely will inform the CID. Get back down to the close and here," he handed him his mug of tea. "Take that with you. I'll get another cup."

"Right," Mansoor nodded and was gone.

"Another mugging, did he say?" she stared at Doyle.

"So it would seem. Now, where was I? Oh, right, Missus Henderson. Well, as you might have guessed from what my young colleague said, it seems as if she was mugged. I couldn't find a purse and I suppose she *did* carry one when she went out shopping?"

Her hand to her mouth, Fleming nodded before stuttering, "Aye, a leather purse. It was red. Is she badly hurt?"

"I can't say for certain, but she was unconscious when we got here and remained like that when the ambulance took her to the hospital in Govan. She's away to the Neurological Department, Missus Fleming. I don't know what her condition is at the minute, but when I've got your details, I'll be in a better position to inform you later what I hear."

The next few minutes were spent by Doyle noting the distraught woman's statement, learning that she had known Missus Henderson for almost five years and admitting that she had been hired by a man called Harry Cavanagh of Cavanagh Accountancy who had an address and phone number in the city centre, to clean twice a week for the old lady.

"Mister Cavanagh also told me that if anything happened to Missus Henderson, I was to get in touch with him right away," she added.

"Well, I've his number now, so why don't you leave that to me," smiled Doyle, but his voice told her that it wasn't so much a request as an instruction.

While she poured a second mug of tea, he very obviously glanced about him and said, "Nice place that Missus Henderson has here and I can guess there's been a lot of money spent on the flat. You told me you don't know anything about any family she might have living locally, that as far as you're aware, she's a widow with a nephew who lives abroad. Does she ever speak about her nephew?"

He stared at her as she handed him the mug and saw her face pale.

"Sometimes," she replied, her voice almost a whisper, then continued, "I was told by Mister Cavanagh that I'm not to discuss anything Missus Henderson tells me with anybody. I signed a paper that said that I couldn't talk about what Missus Henderson told me, something called a …" she closed her eyes as she tried to remember, but was then prompted by Doyle who gently asked, "A non-disclosure form?"

"Aye, that's it," she vigorously nodded.

"Okay," he slowly nodded. "Then I'll ask just one question that will be between you and me, Missus Fleming and look," he closed his notebook and returned it to his utility belt pouch. "See, I won't even write anything down."
He paused and hands clasped together on the table top, stared at her and asked, "This nephew that Missus Henderson has abroad. Is his name Harry? Harry Henderson?"
Her eyes widened and her throat tightened, for she could not speak and could only nod.
"Well, like I said, Missus Fleming," he continued to smile at her, "let's just keep that between us, eh?"

CHAPTER SIX

The uniformed officers who attended the call to the old man discovered by a passer-by staggering in an obvious distraught and dishevelled state in Balmore Road, learned of the witness being told by the old man he had been robbed of his wallet.
Sitting the victim in their panda car, the officers realised how upset he was and because of his great age, wisely conveyed the victim in their panda car to the casualty ward at the Royal Infirmary in High Street where after being examined and calmed, the old man provided them with a statement.
However, irate as he was at the loss of his money he was sufficiently of sound mind to inform the officers that the youth who robbed and assaulted him was white, spoke with a local accent and had worn a Celtic top under a dark coloured hooded sweater, "...or whatever they call they bloody things these days," he had added.
In due course the CID, already alerted to the life-threatening attack upon Miss Henderson and now informed by the Divisional control room of this latest mugging, arrived at the Casualty Ward.
Learning the old man was not seriously injured, the detectives took him home where over a cuppa they tried to elicit more details about his attacker.
"No," he had shaken his head, "I can only guess he was in his late teens or maybe early twenties."
"No, like I told your uniform pals," he shook his head, "I didn't see his face."

"No, if he passed me in the street, son, I wouldn't recognise him. No, not at all."

Disheartened, the detectives bade the old man cheerio and returned to their office to check CCTV footage of the area in the hope of identifying a youth matching the vague description provided by the victim.

Hesitating at the corner of Ronaldsay Street, Kieran McMenamin took a deep breath and patting the envelope with the money that he had in his back pocket, he began to walk purposely towards McGroarty's house, though approaching the gate to the path his legs faltered, stomach tensed and he thought he would throw up.

He raised a fist but hesitated, then taking yet another deep breath knocked upon the door.

It was McGroarty's live-in girlfriend, Sharon Gale who opened the door, smirking at McMenamin as she called out over her shoulder, "Aye, it is, Peter, you were right enough. It's him," then standing to one side to permit McMenamin to pass her by, blew a kiss at him and giggled.

His eyes narrowed and he formed the opinion that though it was just midday, Gale already seemed to be out of her face with the smack, confirmed when she slurred, "Okay *wee* man?"

He ignored her and walked through to the front room where defensively raising his hands, he said, "Peter, my man. You know me. I've never let you down before…"

McGroarty raised his own hand and interrupting, said, "I think I can hear a 'but' coming. Is that right, wee man?" then quickly walking towards McMenamin, grabbed at the front of his hooded top and bunching the material into his fist, snarled, "Are you going to tell me you've not got my fucking dough?"

Terrified, he could only stare helplessly at McGroarty whose face, mere inches from his own, contorted with hatred as he sprayed small balls of spittle onto McMenamin's face.

"I've…" he swallowed his fear, "I've got some of the money, Peter," he stuttered and tried to wrestle the envelope from the back pocket of his jeans.

McGroarty snatched the envelope with his free hand and pushing McMenamin backwards, opened the envelope and counting the money, said, "There's only a hundred and twenty here."

"I'll get the rest, I swear on my mother's life."
McGroarty, staring at the notes, turned curiously towards him and said, "These are all new notes. Where the *fuck* did you get this money? And by the way, you lying shit. I know your Ma's dead. So, I'll ask again, wee man. Where did you get this money?"
"I...I..." he wiped his hands nervously on his jeans. "I knocked over a couple of people who got the money from an ATM."
McGroarty pushed the notes under McMenamin's nose and said, "These are Royal Bank of Scotland notes. New ones. Are you talking about the ATM at the side of the RBS at the Cross?"
"Aye," he gulped. "The one at the Cross."
McGroarty's head lowered as he stared down at his own feet, then slowly shaking his head as it rose, without warning butted McMenamin to the face, bursting the younger man's nose and spraying them both with droplets of blood.
"You fucking *turd*!" he screamed at the fallen man. "You've brought me stolen money! Don't you know the ATM records the serial numbers of the notes it dispenses! If the filth come here and turn my pitch over, they'll find these fucking notes and they'll jail *me*!"
Staring up at the enraged McGroarty, he raised his hands to ward off the expected blows, but did not imagine that from behind him Sharon Gale would also participate and so did not expect the booted foot that crashed into the back of his head.
"Do him, Peter!" he heard her screaming. "Fucking do him proper!"
He was dazed from her blow, but to his surprise McGroarty turned on Gale and with a vicious slap, knocked her across the room to land spread-eagled on the couch.
"If anyone's doing anybody, it will be me that's doing it," he sneered at her.
Gale, her hand held to her reddening cheek, began to cry as McGroarty stared down at McMenamin.
Thrusting the bank notes at him, he bent over and his voice almost a whisper, said, "I don't care how you do it and I don't want to know, but get these fuckers changed for used notes and be back here by five, okay?"
With that, he threw the notes at McMenamin who turning onto his knees hastily gathered them up and almost run from the room.

Before opening the front door, he stuffed the notes into his pocket and then heard McGroarty shouting, "You ever interfere in what I'm doing again, ya bitch and I'll kill you!"
He slammed the door behind him to the sound of slaps on skin and Gale screaming.

When the Scene of Crime officer had finished examining the stairs in the close, Doyle and Fariq Mansoor helped her pack equipment and carry it to her van before waving her off. That done, Doyle sent Mansoor to Missus Henderson's flat for a bucket of water and watched the young cop swill the blood off the stairs.
Ensuring the old lady's flat was secured, Doyle said, "Right, my son, let's you and me get back to the office. We'll get our statements done and passed to the CID and there's a phone call I need to make."
"About the victim?"
"Aye, the woman who turned up, Missus Fleming. She gave me the contact number for the man who hired her as a home help. He must be working for her nephew, so he's likely the man to inform the nephew that she's been attacked and is in the hospital."
"I wonder how she's doing, poor wee woman," Mansoor shook his head. "Dirty bastard that has a go at somebody that age. Do you think it might be connected to the other mugging that was on the radio? The old man in Balmore Road?"
Doyle pursed his lips and shaking his head, said, "No idea, but when we get back to the office, we should know more if the CID have attended the call."
"That's where I want to be," Mansoor grinned. "The CID. Once my probations out and I get my exams passed, I'm applying."
"Don't you think you would be better served getting some street experience in first? Say a couple of years on the beat rather than trying right away for the CID?"
He shrugged and replied, "You've got me for a month, old yin. What can anybody teach me that you can't do in four weeks?" he grinned.
"Can teach you to be more respectful of your elders, that's what," Doyle huffily replied, but with a glint in his eye.
"You sound like my grandfather. He's always on about respecting my elders, so he is. Says when he was a youngster in his village in India before it was Pakistan, if he was cheeky or ill-mannered to an uncle or an auntie, he'd get a slap across the back of his head."

"Not much different to where I was brought up in Partick, then," Doyle grinned at him and added, "It's like I'm always saying. The world is a village. If you're brought up properly you can live anywhere because no matter *where* you're born and bred, the rules are all the same. Do as you're told, don't be cheeky or devious and just try to get on with your neighbours. Aye, I've not met him, but I think I like your granddad."

At the police office, Doyle sent Mansoor to fetch two mugs of tea while he went to the writing room to commence copying the statements of the neighbour, Mark Caldwell and the woman, Agnes Fleming. That done, he copied them at the printer and with his own statement and the corroborating statement of his young neighbour, made his way to the CID general office on the upper floor.
Opening the door, he saw the only occupant in the room, a woman in her forties, greying fair hair bundled untidily on her head and wearing a white blouse and pinstriped trouser suit, who leaned back against a desk reading a report.
"Oh, hello," he smiled. "I was looking for some of the guys."
"Anything I can help you with," she returned his smile.
"Sorry, you are…?"
"I'm the newly appointed DI, Myra McColl. I've just been promoted couple of days ago from Stewart Street. You are?"
"Ah, Constable Doyle, Ma'am. I was looking for someone to hand over a couple of statements regarding a mugging, down just off Saracen Cross."
"The guys are all out the now following up a couple of inquiries, Constable…sorry, what's your first name?" she asked as she strode towards him, her hand extended.
"Cornelius, but most call me Popeye," he shook her hand and grinned.
"Well, Popeye, seen as how you look long in the tooth, I'm Myra, but don't let anybody else hear you call me by my first name," she winked, "I'm trying to create a good impression here or at least for my first week anyway. Can I see your statements, please?"
Doyle handed the sheaf of papers and watched as she skimmed through them.

"I can see you'll have done this once or twice, eh?" she nodded as she complimented him oh his statement taking.

"Aye," he smiled, "once or twice through the years."

"So, I gather this is the old lady that's lying in the Queen Elizabeth neuro at the minute?"

"Aye, Harriet Henderson, aged eighty-six according to her pension book we found in her flat. Have you had any word back yet about how she is?"

The door opened behind him to admit young Mansoor who stared curiously at the DI.

"This is DI McColl," Doyle introduced him and winking at her, added, "Constable Mansoor, Ma'am. My probationer for the next month, but he wants to be a detective."

"Indeed," she smiled and shook the hand of the blushing cop who said, "I've left the tea downstairs, Popeye."

"I'll be down in a minute, Fariq."

When the door had closed, he turned to McColl who said, "Right, the old lady. Well, the young DC I sent over there to the hospital…" and raising her hand, grimaced when she added, "Please don't ask me to remember his name, I'm still trying to get my head round the names of all the guys in the Department. Anyway, he phoned in twenty minutes ago to say the victim is unconscious, but because of a swelling at the back of the head and her age, the medics are reluctant to probe any further. They're content to monitor her condition meantime in the hope the swelling subsides, but apparently as a matter of urgency are seeking as much information as they can about her medical history. They want to contact her GP and find out what if any kind of medication she might currently be prescribed in case it interferes with what they intend giving her."

"I've got her personal details from the pension book and as she lives in Saracen, likely she'll either be a patient of the health centre in Bardowie Street or the Possilpark Health and Care Centre in Saracen Street. Do you want me to go ahead and make that inquiry?"

She pulled a face and replied, "I'd be grateful if you would, Popeye. Like I said, I'm just arrived here and a wee bit out of my depth at the minute."

He paused for a second. The new DI, Myra McColl seemed a decent enough sort and it briefly occurred to him to tell her what he suspected, but then in the heartbeat that passed, made his decision.

"No bother," he smiled and with a nod, left to join his neighbour in the writing room and use the phone.

Kieran McMenamin was a lucky man; lucky because he still had all his teeth while wondering where the hell he would exchange the stolen money for used notes. That and McGroarty hadn't demanded he find the extra sixty quid, just get the new notes changed for old ones.
He thought about the discount store among the row of shops on Saracen Street near to the Possilpark Health Centre.
Ali Rahmani, the miserable bastard who owned the shop, wasn't beyond resetting the occasional items that McMenamin shoplifted and reselling them at a bargain price to cover the pittance Ali paid for them, while still making a profit.
But change the new notes for old ones? He shook his head, knowing that while Ali undoubtedly would agree, likely there would be a cost.
He briefly considered mugging another pensioner, but suspected that with two done within an hour, the cops would probably by now have flooded the area with plainclothes officers, all looking for him or somebody like him.
His eyes narrowed and he tore off his hoody and wrapped it about his waist, knotting the arms at the front. It wasn't a big change in his appearance, but might just be enough to throw off any suspicious copper.
He wore a white tee shirt under his Celtic top and glancing at the sky, decided he'd also remove the Celtic top too and slipping it off, bundled it under his arm.
There, he unconsciously grinned. Nothing like the guy that mugged the two old bastards.
He made his way to the shop and arriving there, with a quick glance about him ducked inside.
Ali, the almost obese man in his mid-fifties with the badly pock-marked face, glanced warily as McMenamin entered, but continued serving the elderly woman.
"I'm telling you," she whined at him, "I gave you a ten pound note, you bugger. You've given me change for a fiver."
"Okay, missus, let me check," Ali replied and opening the till, pretended surprise and said, "Oh, you're right enough. Sorry, my

mistake," he smiled broadly as he returned a five pound note to the woman who left the shop with a scowl on her face.

"Got caught out there, Ali," McMenamin cheerfully remarked.

Ali shrugged and said, "Aye, she noticed this time, but it's not really theft, it's just good business. If they check their change then what's the harm in saying I'm sorry and if they don't…" he shrugged again, but this time with a grin on his face.

"So, young Kieran, what can I do you for?" he quipped.

"Can you change new notes for me for used notes?"

Ali's eyes narrowed as he replied, "What's wrong with them? Are they duds, forgeries?"

"No, nothing like that," McMenamin hastily replied and shook his head.

"Then why do you want to change them?"

"Let's just say I shouldn't have them in the first place," he slyly grinned.

"But if they're dodgy, then why would I want them?"

"I'm telling you, Ali, they're not dodgy. I've a debt to pay and the guy I owe doesn't want new notes, that's all there is to it.

"How many notes are you talking about?"

"One hundred and twenty quid's worth."

"And what's in it for me?"

"What do you mean? Jesus, Ali, don't I do enough for you, bringing gear that you sell on for a good profit? How's about this time doing me a favour instead?"

"Not much of a favour if the polis is involved, is it?"

"I never said the cops are involved."

"Then why not just go to the bank?"

Caught out, McMenamin glared at Ali, then quietly said, "Okay, how much to change the notes for used ones?"

"Twenty quid."

"Fuck off, I'm going elsewhere," he replied and turned towards the door, but his bluff didn't work and Ali, with a grin on his face and his arms folded, simply stared at him.

His hand on the door handle, he stopped and turning said, "A tenner."

"Call it fifteen and we've a deal."

Muttering under his breath, McMenamin threw the notes onto the counter and watched as Ali first counted the new notes and

apparently satisfied, lifted a metal box from under the counter. Removing a rubber band from a roll of bank notes, he carefully peeled off one-hundred and five pound that he handed to the younger man.
"Nice doing business with you, Kiernan," he grinned.
"Fuck off," McMenamin replied with a dirty look and left the shop.

Mary Harris turned as the chime above the shop door activated.
"I thought I'd come in a wee bit earlier and let you away, hen," the young man who was her afternoon relief smiled at her. "After all, you're the one that's always doing wee favours for the rest of us, eh?"
Now, her coat on and waving cheerio to the young man and Alice, she briskly made her way home and looked forward to the afternoon walk in the Ruchill Park with young Megan and Ross.
As she turned into Balmore Road, her eyes narrowed at the sight of the police van parked beside the lane near to Sunnylaw Street. Crossing over to the north side of Balmore Road, Mary slowed as she drew parallel with the van, her natural curiosity getting the better of her. Down the lane she could see two uniformed officers with large poles, probing the bushes on either side of the lane and wondered what was going on.
None of my business, she sniffed and continued on her way.
She stopped in at her own house to use the toilet and freshen up before heading up stairs where the weary looking Elaine Findlay was so pleased and grateful to see her.
"I know I'm a wee bit early, but if you'd still like me to take the weans for a couple of hours?"
"A couple of hours? What," Findlay pretended surprise as she stared down at her children and added, "you mean you don't want to keep them forever? Now, if they give you any cheek," she pretended to scold her children, "bring them straight back Missus Harris and it'll be straight to bed without any television."
In my day, thought Mary, cheeky weans meant no dinner, but times have certainly changed as she smiled and waved away Findlay's assistance to help carry the buggy downstairs.
"I might be in my late fifties," she joked, "but I'm still as fit as a fiddle."

"You'll need to be to handle these wee devils," Findlay wryly grinned as she kissed the excited children cheerio.

"I'm really, really grateful, Missus Harris."

"*Please*, I've told you a dozen times, hen. Call me Mary. Now, when I get back I'll keep them for a couple of hours and will fish fingers and chips be okay for their dinner?"

"If you're sure and if it's not too much trouble?"

"It'll be no bother. You just make sure that you get a sleep now and I'll see you say, round about six?"

"Are you really sure?"

"Course I am," Mary scoffed. "Besides, it will take my mind off my own problems," and with that and the wee boy self-importantly carrying her handbag, Mary carefully bumped the buggy down the stairs.

Aware that as soon as his probation period of two years concluded the keen and enthusiastic Fariq Mansoor intended sitting the first of his police examinations, Popeye Doyle told the young cop that while he was making his phone calls in the writing room, Mansoor take a break and find somewhere quiet if he wanted to catch up on his studies.

"Thanks, old yin," Mansoor grinned and disappeared through the door.

Doyle's first call was to the Bardowie Street health centre where identifying himself to the receptionist to whom he was known, he hit the jackpot. Without fuss, the receptionist put him straight through to Missus Henderson's GP who upon learning of her assault and the requirement by her attending staff for information of any medication the old woman was prescribed, instead suggested that she herself phone the Neuro Ward 65 and speak directly with the attending staff.

"Thanks, doctor," Doyle concluded the call then fetching his notebook from his utility belt pouch, flipped to the page with the details provided to him by Missus Henderson's friend, Agnes Fleming.

Seated behind his large desk in his Wellington Street office, Harry Cavanagh waited patiently for his secretary Helen to return with the milk and his afternoon lunch of a roll and hot pie.

The door opened to admit the young woman with the pink coloured hair that erupted from her head like a burst pillow, black cropped top and a skirt that was so short it could hardly be described as such; however, the skirt showed off the most marvellous pair of legs that were perhaps the young woman's only redeeming feature for she could barely type and her disdain for her boss was at best insubordinate.

Why the fiftyish Cavanagh suffered the twentyish Helen to be in his employ was the cause of much speculation among his many disreputable clients, the most plausible reason being he was sleeping with the acerbic young woman.

However, what *was* generally agreed was though rough as the proverbial badger's arse Helen was the perfect defence against anyone, large or small, friendly or otherwise, who arrived at the office with the intention of meeting with Cavanagh, for if the rotund man did not wish to meet with that individual they most certainly did not get beyond Helen's desk.

That and though Cavanagh himself walked a fine line between honesty and criminality, Helen was completely trustworthy and one of a select few Cavanagh himself trusted.

"Have you any idea at all the amount of cholesterol in that greasy pie?" she slammed the paper bag down in front of him.

"Aye," he nodded and withdrew the pie, then to tease her took a large bite out of it before sliding the remaining into the roll, ignoring the trickle of grease running down his chin.

Staring in disgust, Helen was about to further lambast him again, but his desk phone rang and leaning across she lifted it from its cradle and softly replied, "Harry Cavanagh Accountancy, how might I direct your call?"

It never ceased to amaze him that she could switch from her caustic Glasgow slang to such a sexy, enticing voice.

He saw her eyebrows narrow and before pressing a silent button on the phone cradle, said, "Please hold, constable and I'll buzz to see if Mister Cavanagh is at his desk, thank you."

Turning to him, she said, "It's a polis guy. Says he wants to speak with you about a Missus Henderson. Would that be…?"

Cavanagh raised his hand to stop her then nodding in response to her unfinished question, heard her say, "Putting you through now," before handing him the phone.

He pressed the sound button and taking a breath, a pencil ready in his other hand, he said, "Good morning. Harry Cavanagh speaking, how might I assist you?" while waving Helen back through to her own office.

"Mister Cavanagh, I'm Constable Cornelius Doyle at Saracen office. I was given your number by a Missus Fleming regarding a lady she cleans for, Harriet Henderson."

"Ah, yes, Missus Henderson," he felt a tightening in his gut. "Has there been a problem? Is the lady well?"

"First, sir, can I ask what your association with the lady is?"

"I am contracted by her nephew to provide for her needs while he is employed overseas," he smoothly replied.

"And would that nephew be Harry Henderson?"

Cavanagh, eyes narrowed and licking at his lips, slowly asked, "Again, Constable Doyle, is the lady well?"

There was a slight pause while Doyle considered his response before replying, "I regret, Mister Cavanagh, that earlier today in her close, Missus Henderson was the subject of an assault and robbery. She is currently detained at the new Queen Elizabeth Hospital over in Govan. The neurological ward. I regret I don't know what ward she has been removed to, but my understanding is that she is unconscious."

Cavanagh closed his eyes before asking, "Do you have a suspect or anyone in custody for this assault?"

"Not at the minute. The inquiry is being dealt with by Saracen CID, though I'm not certain which officer is designated the inquiry."

There was a definite pause and Cavanagh's curiosity got the better of him and he asked, "Is there something else that you're not telling me and no disrespect intended, Constable Doyle, but why are you phoning me? Surely if this is a CID matter…"

Doyle interrupted and said, "Yes, you're quite right, it is the CID who will investigate the assault, but strictly off the record and between you and me, Missus Henderson's assault has all the hallmarks of a junkie looking for cash, nothing more. You understand that's just my personal opinion based on my own experience?"

"As you said, Constable Doyle, it's strictly off the record, but I'm still puzzled as to why it's you who is are phoning me rather than the detective in the inquiry?"

There was that pause again, thought Cavanagh and was about to speak when Doyle replied, "Because, Mister Cavanagh, unless I'm mistaken Missus Henderson's nephew is known to me from some time ago. Back then of course, he was better known as Headcase Henderson and that's why I'm phoning. If I'm correct, you might want to let him know his wee auntie has been mugged. As far as I am aware, nobody has yet connected Missus Henderson with her nephew, but the CID are not daft. I owe Harry a small debt and I'm simply giving him a heads up. Do we understand each other, Mister Cavanagh?"

"This small debt, Constable Doyle…"

"Not what you think, Mister Cavanagh, it's not…financial. Let's just say that early in my career I made a mistake that might have cost me my job, but Harry kept his mouth shut and for that I was and still am grateful. When you contact him, tell him Popeye said hello."

At that the line went dead leaving Cavanagh holding the phone to his ear and wondering what the fuck that was all about.

CHAPTER SEVEN

A little over four and a half thousand miles away from the indifferent Glasgow weather, he sat on the shaded balcony of the bungalow, showered and changed into a fresh tee shirt and shorts and relaxing after his strenuous workout at the homemade punch-bag in the room he had converted to a makeshift gym. True, his particular skills honed through the years of his criminal activities in Glasgow and the West of Scotland were no longer needed and for that he was thankful, but after a lifetime of disciplined physical exertion he didn't relish what muscle he had turning to fat. Besides, he inwardly grinned and blushed as he did, Donna was always telling him she liked her man to be in good shape.

His attention was attracted to the beautiful sea nymph who walked quickly from the water across the 50 metres of burning sand towards him and he unconsciously grimaced, for he knew that he was about to upset her, yet it had to be done.

Her collar length dark hair, wet from her swim, was plastered to her head and he watched while walking, she used her fingers to comb the hair back from her face.

The white one-piece swimming costume glistened as droplets of water fell from her. Her tanned physique was that of a woman fifteen years her junior and now almost as brown as Maria, their cook cum cleaning woman who he could hear in the kitchen singing tunelessly to the radio while she prepared their early morning breakfast. Standing, he lifted a beach towel and readied to wrap it about her, grinned widely as she stepped warily onto the already burning wooden steps that led up to the veranda.
"I still find it hard to believe that you're mine," he enveloped her in the towel and held her close.
"You'll get all wet," she smiled and turning towards him, nuzzled her face into his, then as if some finely tuned female intuition struck her, turned to stare into his face. Frowning, she asked, "What?"
He took a deep breath, deciding to get it over with sooner rather than later for knowing she would be dismayed, realised there would be no right time. Gently stroking her cheek with his fingers, he said, "I've had a phone call from Harry Cavanagh. About my auntie Harriet. She's been attacked. I need to go back."
She pushed a step away from him, her hands flat on his muscled chest, her eyes opening wide and flickering as though not understanding, then said, "You can't go back, Harry. They'll catch you. No," she vigorously shook her head, her hands waving in front of her, "I won't let you. I can't lose you."
"Donna, please," he firmly took her by the elbows, but not to hurt her. "She's the woman who raised me. She was almost like a mother to me, I don't have any choice."
"Is she…I mean…she's not…"
"No," he slowly shook his head, "at least I don't think so. Harry called to tell me that Harriet's suffered a head wound and is unconscious. A policeman phoned him to tell him she was found in her close and she's been taken to some new hospital over in Govan. She's in the neuro there, but the cop didn't know how badly hurt she is, only that she's unconscious. Harry's made some inquiry and been told she's stable though remains critical, but of course it's early afternoon there so that might change as we speak. However," he paused as though the very thought upset him, "because of her age, there is a likelihood she might not recover."

Tearful now, her lips trembling, she replied, "But if the police know that you're going back, that you're returning, they'll be waiting for you. It might not be true. It might be a trap."

He inhaled, then sighing, said, "The cop that phoned Harry told him he owed me a favour from years ago; a cop called Popeye Doyle. I remember him," he nodded with a tight smile before light-heartedly adding, "I mean, with a name like that I'm hardly going to forget him, am I?"

Pulling her towards him, he reached for her hands and held them tightly as he recounted, "Back when I was a stupid teenager, there was a gang fight in the Saracen area. A running battle with knives and swords and axes and God knows what. One of these parochial things that the young teenagers back then got caught up in, between the Saracen boys and a crew from Possilpark. We were *all* young and bloody stupid," he smiled as he reminisced. "Anyway, I got separated from my team and cornered by two of the Possil mob and just as they were about to set about me with an axe and a bloody great sword, this young cop turns up wielding his baton, but he's as mad as the two sods facing me," he grinned, "and just wanted to batter *anybody*. Anyhow, before the two lads got to me, this young polis is behind them and laying into them and by God, he fairly went his dinger, so he did," he slowly nodded at the memory. "Knocked them both down to the ground and then as if realising what he's done, stares at me. I'll not kid you, I thought he was a right nutter and by this time I've my hands up and I'm surrendering, but he's calmed down and so shocked at what he did he starts shaking. He didn't try to grab me or anything so I thought about running and even to this day I can't explain it, but instead I grab him and hustle him into a nearby tenement close out of sight of his mates and wait with him while he gets it together. Anyway, with all the bedlam that's going on outside the close, we stood there and shared a fag," he smiles, "and he tells me his name is Popeye. But just then two other polis come into the back of the close and *they* think he's arrested me. I was about to run out the front when I heard one say that they've called an ambulance because they found two guys outside who are unconscious and with what look like fractured skulls. I realised Popeye could be in serious bother and anyway, he's saved me for getting a right hiding, so I just went along with it and pretended that he had arrested me, I mean."

"Didn't you tell the other policemen what he'd done?"
"What," he smiled tolerantly, "after he's saved me from getting the…" he smiled, "battered? No, I whispered to him to say he'd caught me running away and to deny knowing anything about the two he'd battered. I think he was that shocked he just did like I suggested."
"What happened to you? I mean after you were arrested?"
"Like the rest who were caught, I went to court. Some were fined, but I got six weeks in a juvenile detention centre at Low Moss on the outskirts of Glasgow," he smiled again.
She sees he has a faraway look in his eyes as he quietly continues, "I saw him a few times over the years when I was in the Saracen area visiting my auntie Harriet, but we never spoke again. And now this," he sighs.
Turning to her, he slowly nods as he tells her, "I don't think it's a trap, Donna. I think Popeye's being honest when he told Harry Cavanagh that he's returning a favour."

While Mary Harris pushed the buggy along the concrete path with the squealing Megan happily clapping her hands at the antics of her boisterous brother Ross, the four-year-old run up the slight incline of the path in the direction of the flagpole located in the centre of Ruchill Park.
"Ross!" Mary called out, a little alarmed that the agile lad was ducking in and out of the thick foliage and out of her sight, "Please come back here. Ross? Ross!"
The curly haired boy, suddenly appeared and a little chastened at the sternness in her voice, began to slowly meander down towards her, his hands tightly clenched behind his back and a dark scowl on his face.
Mary fought her smile, knowing that if she didn't he would ignore her stern voice and she would have lost any control over his behaviour.
"Now," she began as he started to sullenly walk beside her, "when we get to the top, I'll find somewhere to sit and you and Megan can play together. I mean, you will help me to look after your wee sister, won't you? I'm an old lady," she fluttered her eyes at him, "and I need a young man like you to help me. Okay?"
His face brightened at the sudden responsibility and he eagerly

nodded and without prompting, placed a hand on the buggy to help Mary push it up the incline.

Pleased that she now had things under control, Mary and the children had continued just a little over ten yards when her eyes caught movement to her left and in the shadow of the bushes saw a dark haired youth with something wrapped about his waist making his way through the bushes up the hill in the direction of the flagpole. Though she thought he had not apparently seen Mary and the children, the youth's very actions made her suspicious and almost fearfully, she glanced about her, but there was no one in sight if she had to call out.

She hesitated, wondering if she should carry on, but then thought perhaps she was being too alarmist, that the youth was probably just out for a stroll.

Now a little over thirty yards in front, the youth stepped out from the bushes onto the path in front of her and with a glance at Mary and the children, continued making his way towards the flagpole.

Mary stopped dead, her instinct telling her that something was wrong for the brief glance from the youth in her direction was enough.

She had seen the face earlier that today when the youth had been hanging about the corner of Saracen Street and if she had been suspicious then, she was more than apprehensive now.

Stopping dead, she brightly smiled at the puzzled Ross and said, "I'm fair puffed out, so I am. Listen, why don't we not bother going to the flagpole, but instead see if we can find somewhere that sells ice-cream?"

The grin on his face was enough and turning the buggy, they set off back down the incline.

Returning to the CID office, Popeye Doyle knocked on the DI's door and informed Myra McColl that he had traced a contact who would inform Missus Henderson's next of kin of the attack upon the old lady.

"So, did you get any details of this next of kin?"

"Apparently it's a nephew who's working abroad," he shrugged. "The man I spoke with has been contracted to take care of Missus Henderson's bills and any needs she has."

Concentrating on a file before her, McColl glanced up and with a tight smile, said, "Thanks, Popeye."

He was about to turn away when she asked, "The man you spoke with. I'm giving the inquiry to DS Fraser, so what's his name if he phones so that I can let Fraser know?"

Doyle tensed, but he didn't hesitate and with a forced smile replied, "Cavanagh. Mister Cavanagh of Cavanagh Accountancy in the city centre somewhere."

However, he did not expect McColl to stare at him with surprise as she asked, "*Harry* Cavanagh?"

"Eh, yes, that's the name. Have you heard of him?"

She didn't immediately reply, but then slowly said, "My God, Harry Cavanagh. Now that's a name I haven't heard for a while. Take a seat, Popeye," and nodded to the chair opposite her desk before continuing, "Harry Cavanagh is the accountant to half if not most of the major players in the city and elsewhere. He's a wee fat guy who operates out of a tenement office in Wellington Street. You haven't heard his name mentioned before?"

"No," he truthfully told her with a shake of his head.

"Well, this is a turn up," she grimaced. "Let me explain. Harry Cavanagh *is* a legally qualified accountant, but with a portfolio of some of the major criminals known to Police Scotland. He's been on the go for years and to my knowledge, evaded prosecution by the Fraud Squad with whom he was and likely still is the number one target. He's the man who, dare I say it, finds the means to *legitimately* funnel the ill-gotten proceed of crime into off-shore accounts, property abroad and if memory serves me correctly the last crime bulletin I read about him reported he has recently begun to invest his clients' money into IT and the pharmaceutical industry and I'm *not* talking about illegal drugs; I mean some of the large Swiss based pharmacological conglomerates. He's a sharp and shrewd individual, but to look at him you'd think he was a successful businessman because he's a right dandy looking wee shite. Favours white shirts, bright red ties and red braces and looks like a character out of that Hollywood movie 'Wall Street.' However," she grinned, "I also have to admit that he's a real charmer. I visited his office once in connection with a money laundering operation I was investigating when I was a DS, just before I left the Fraud Squad and once I got past his secretary, who believe me is a *real* piece of work, the wee bugger charmed the knickers off me. Had me laughing so hard I almost forgot why I was there to see him. Anyway, I couldn't prove he had done anything illegal and a week after my report to the Procurator Fiscal was marked down as No Proceedings, Cavanagh sent me a huge bunch of flowers with a card that read, 'Better luck next time' and you know," she shook her head, "he signed it off with an invitation to dinner."

"And before you ask, no," she grinned as she raised a hand, "I did *not* accept."

She smiled as she shook her head at the memory then said, "When you spoke with him, did he happen to name the woman's nephew?"

Doyle realised that to lie would only provoke further suspicion and replied, "Actually, the woman who cleans for Missus Henderson already gave me the nephew's name. She told me it. He's called Harry Henderson."

"Harry Henderson," McColl drawled as she stared at him. "Do you know who *he* is?"

Doyle pursed his lips and slowly shook his head.

"Did Cavanagh mention anything about contacting the nephew?"

"Not directly. I suppose I just assumed he would pass the message on."

"Well, no matter," she decided not to press the issue and with a smile said, "Thanks, Popeye, I'll see that DS Fraser gets all that."

He had closed the door behind him, but could not know he was correct; she had seen through his lie when he told her he denied knowing who the nephew was.

Thoughtfully tapping her fingers on the desk, McColl wondered why Doyle had so blatantly lied about knowing Harry 'Headcase' Henderson.

Slowing as he furtively approached the area of the flagpole in Ruchill Park, Kieran McMenamin's eyes darted back and forth. If he was right, this is where that lying, thieving junkie bastard Lennie Robertson hung around when he was trying to score or sell smack and with the money he'd stolen from under McMenamin's floorboards and the sale of the weed, he'd have enough for him to buy and then sell smack for at least three, maybe four days.

He stopped dead, the sound of low voices coming from the grassy embankment in front of him, a distance of no more than fifteen or sixteen yards.

Creeping forward, he crouched down and slowly peering from behind a bush saw Robertson, easily identifiable from his usual outfit of an ex-army camouflage jacket, skinny red coloured jeans and worn navy blue baseball cap, standing with his back to McMenamin and in front of someone. His eyes narrowed when he saw it was a young girl who though her face was hidden by Robertson's body, he could see was wearing a long black coat and tight black coloured jeans with scuffed Doc Marten boots.

He held his breath and watched as Robertson's head swivelled back and forth, waved his hands in the air and heard him loudly say, "Aye, Maggie, right! You must think I'm a mug, that I'm going to give you tick again!"

Then he heard the girl mutter, "I'm not fucking joking, Lennie, I've got the cash and I'm telling you, for *two* bags this time."

He couldn't hear the Robertson's response, but saw him shake her head then the girl threw her arms up and heard her hiss, "I know, but that was the last time. I'm telling you. This time I've got the money, honest."

His eyes widened.

The bastard was selling dope and even if he no longer had the money he'd stole from McMenamin the drugs would be worth something.

He made his decision. With Robertson's back to him and obscuring the girl's view of him, he decided he'd lunge forward and catch the bastard before he could make off.

Steeling himself, he took a deep breath and sprinted from behind the bush, running as fast as he could towards the pair.

He'd covered the short distance in seconds and was reaching for Robertson when the girl saw him and screamed. Colliding with Robertson who was in the act of turning, they both fell to the grass and he was vaguely aware of the girl turning and running off.

"Bastard!" he screamed at the skinny Robertson and pounded at his head and face with his fists.

Totally surprised by the attack, Robertson raised his arms to defend himself and to protect his face while he screeched, "I'm sorry! I'm sorry!" but McMenamin was in no mood to accept an apology and now astride the fallen man, continued to rain angry blows down onto him, ignoring the blood that spurted from Robertson's nose and mouth and covered McMenamin's fists.

Panicking, Robertson's fear lent him strength and in desperation, almost wriggled free from McMenamin's weight. In his attempt to stop him, McMenamin clamped his hands about the slighter man's throat and teeth gritted, began to squeeze.

Gasping for air, the terrified man tried to prise McMenamin's fingers from his throat, but his drug addiction and weakened state conspired to deny him the energy he needed to save himself.

His face turning red as his lungs were denied air, Robertson's eyes widened and mouth open, the small veins within his bulging eyes began to enlarge then burst.

But there was no stopping McMenamin who astride the weaker man and with savage fury, ignored Robertson's panicky and gradually weakening attempts to claw McMenamin's hands away as he continued to compress the Robertson's throat until at last there was no movement from beneath him.

He did not intend to nor did he immediately realise that he was strangling Robertson to death. Yes, his intention was to hurt him and to make him pay for the theft of the money and drugs from under the floorboards in the bedroom that resulted in the indignities McMenamin's had later suffered at the hands of Peter McGroarty. But killing him? No, that had not been part of the plan.

Now, as he stared in horror at the lifeless man, he scrambled off him then getting to his feet, staggered a few feet away, unconsciously wiping his blood-stained hands on the hoodie wrapped about his waist and unable to take his eyes from the awfulness of what he had done.

He had committed murder and in terror was about to turn to run from that awful place when he stopped.

The drugs.

Fearfully glancing about him, he quickly searched the pockets of the camouflage jacket and found not just a half dozen small, cellophane bags that each contained a small quantity of the brown powder, but a wad of notes too. Stuffing the money into his pockets, he glanced about him again and hurried to the safety of the nearby bushes.

CHAPTER EIGHT

He had persuaded Donna to remain at the bungalow, deciding he would ask Maria's husband Rodrigo to borrow Father Rodriquez' old Pontiac car and drive him to Havana to catch the UK flight. He knew she would protest, but steeled himself against her tears and insisted. Now four hours later, here he was at the José Martí International Airport waving goodbye to Rodrigo and checking he had his passport. He had decided against packing a suitcase, preferring instead to carry a travel bag that he could stow in the overhead locker. Anything else he needed he would purchase locally in Glasgow.

In the busy terminal, he made his way to a phone booth and inserting the payment card, checked the number against his diary before dialling.

"Harry Cavanagh Accountancy, how might I direct your call," said the polite, sexy voice.

Conscious of the ongoing police interest in Cavanagh and suspecting the call might be monitored, he chose not to identify himself and instead replied with a smile playing on his lips, "Helen, it's your suntanned friend here. Is the man in?"

He heard the gasp and could almost hear at the pleasure in the young woman's voice when reverting to her native slang, she picked up immediately on his caution and said, "Hello, stranger. Are you bringing me something nice from where you are and is my pal coming with you?"

He hadn't thought of a gift for Helen, but mentally reminded himself to purchase something for both her and Cavanagh before responding, "Just me, hen. So, is he in?"

"Wait a minute, I'm putting you through," then grinned when he heard her screech, "Harry, it's him! Him!" he heard her repeat. "You know who!"

Seconds later, Cavanagh said, "Hello there. No news, I'm afraid. She's still sedated. Are you on your way?"

"Catching the flight in just under an hour. You got my e-mail?"

"Aye, I did. Accommodation is booked for you at the last place your lovely lady stayed before she took off for the sun. You know where I mean?"

"I do, yes," he recalled that before fleeing to Cuba, Donna had been booked into the Glasgow Hilton Hotel in William Street by the M8 motorway.

"I took the liberty of leaving a package at the desk for your arrival. It's under your own name, though I'm not sure coming as you are that was such a good idea."

"I'll be using my own passport anyway, Harry, because there's nowhere here that I would be able to obtain a bummer, so if they want to find me, they will. Because I'm using my own passport to re-enter the UK, I'll either be passed through immigration with no bother or if there *is* a Ports Watch for me I'll be detained. Besides, they'll need evidence to lift me, won't they?"

"I wish I had your confidence and don't forget, a lack of evidence in the past didn't stop them, son. Who's to say it will this time when you arrive in the Smoke? On that point, when *do* you get in?"

"Flight time is just under ten hours direct to Gatwick and then there's a connecting internal flight to Glasgow, so I expect I'll be with you in," he paused and turning, glanced at the large digital clock hanging on the far wall, "say early morning."

"Right then, you have my number. Soon as you're settled, give me a bell. Is the lovely lady accompanying you?"

"No," Harry shook his head. "I've asked her to stay here just in case…well, just in case things don't work out and I don't make it back. One further thing. How are my finances?"

"On that issue, you have nothing to worry about. You and the lovely lady are set for life. In the parcel at the hotel you'll find new credit cards for a temporary account I've set up locally and I've transferred sufficient funds to see you through your stay. Any further cash you need all you have to do is call me and I'll transfer more funds."

"Let's hope it doesn't work out like that. Right, I'll cut this short and we'll speak soon."

"Good luck, my son."

"Thanks, Harry."

He replaced the phone into the cradle and stared at it for a few seconds before bending to lift his flight bag and then turning, headed towards the Jet Airways desk to collect his ticket.

Watching the two children seated at her kitchen table tucking into their fish fingers and beans, Mary Harris smiled with pleasure. Her son young Michael, who lived in Dorset with his new wife, had still to present her with grandchildren though her daughter and her husband already had two sons with Jenny now eight months pregnant with their third child.

Her eyes narrowed when she thought of her daughter. Of course she had many photographs of the two boys scattered about the house, but had last seen the oldest when he was but three months old as a tearful Jenny and her husband boarded the flight at Glasgow Airport that started them on their new life. Now Thomas was seven years old and a big brother to Conor, who was almost four. She longed to meet the children, but the cost of travelling to New Zealand was far too expensive and besides, she could never leave her husband while he was in such poor health.

"Can I have more juice, please," Ross interrupted her thoughts and held up the plastic beaker. She almost laughed when little Megan, copying her adored big brother, also handed her half full beaker to Mary, ignoring the drips that trailed across her plate and the table to the floor.

The door knocked before she could fill the beakers and wagging a finger at the children that they were to remain seated, hurried to the door.

Her neighbour Elaine Findlay, looking far fresher than she did a few hours previously, said, "I hope they haven't been too much trouble Missus…I mean, Mary."

"Come away in, hen and no, they've been grand," Mary beamed at her before asking, "Have you time for a cuppa?"

"Eh, aye, if it's not too much trouble," she replied, then entering the kitchen was besieged by two excited children who screamed, "Mummy!" as throwing themselves from the chairs, they embraced her.

"Right you pair," Mary, hands on hips, pretended to be annoyed, "what did I say about getting off those chairs?" before turning to Findlay and quietly adding, "You'd think they'd not seen you for a year."

While the children disengaged themselves from their mother, Mary continued, "If I put on the cartoons and find some ice-cream in my freezer, will that keep you pair quiet while I make your mum some tea?"

They both eagerly nodded and so, a few minutes later and with the children seated quietly in the front room watching 'Masha and the

Bear,' Mary and her neighbour settled down at the kitchen table for a chat.

Comfortable with the younger woman, Mary admitted it had been some time since she had visitors in her home.

"I'm not saying I don't have friends. I mean, I get on very well with the women at the charity shop, for instance, but neither Michael nor I have any family left in Glasgow and with my two away living down south and abroad…" she sighed as if that was enough explanation.

"It's a son and daughter you have, isn't it?"

"Aye, young Michael and Jennifer; Jenny, she prefers, who's in New Zealand with her husband and my two grandsons and another on the way."

"You'll miss them," Findlay sipped at her tea.

"More than I can admit," Mary nodded.

"No chance you can visit?"

"Huh," she huffed. "Not on my benefits or Michael's work pension and anyway, I can't leave him with nobody to visit him. Besides that, the monthly payments for the nursing home take up most of Michael's pension anyway so I'm really only living on my own benefits."

"I know I sound rotten saying this, Mary, but from what you've told me, would your husband even know you were gone?"

She didn't immediately reply, but then reached across to gently lay her hand upon the younger woman's hand and said, "No, hen, *he* wouldn't know, but *I* would."

They sat in awkward silence for moment then Mary, her eyes narrowing, said, "I *think* I saw something funny today. Not funny, a bit strange."

"Strange?"

"Aye, when I was in the shop where I volunteer, I saw a young man across the road at the Cross who looked to me like he was hiding on the corner next to the pub. You know where I mean?"

Findlay nodded.

"Then when I was with the children in Ruchill Park going up the path to the flagpole, I saw the same young man, but this time he had taken off his top, one of those with the hoods attached."

"A hoody," Findlay smiled.

"Aye," she returned the smile, "but it looked to me like he was creeping through the bushes."

"Why was he doing that?"
"No idea," she sighed with a shake of her head, then sipped at her tea before adding, "but something inside me didn't like the look of him so I just turned about and came back down the hill. Weird, eh?"
"You know there was a mugging earlier today? Just along the road in the lane that runs off Balmore Road?"
"A mugging?"
"So it said on the five o'clock news on the radio and I remember looking out of the window when I was pulling the curtains closed before I went for a lie-down …"
"The police van," Mary's eyes opened wide. "That's why it was there?"
"You saw it too, then?" Findlay nodded.
"I did, yes. So, do you know who got mugged?"
"No," Finlay shook her head, but then her eyes widened when she added, "You don't think it might have been anything to do with the guy you saw standing at the Cross?"
"Let's not run away with ourselves, Elaine," Mary replied, but though she smiled there was a lingering suspicion in her mind.

He could not believe his luck.
Not only did he have the half dozen deals of smack, but the wad of notes was the one hundred and eighty-quid stolen from him and demanded by that bastard McGroarty. Once the debt was paid, the money left over would enable him to buy even more smack to add to the half dozen deals that he would cut with baking soda and sell on for a greater profit.
Would he purchase the smack from McGroarty, he wondered, then decided no, there were other dealers who were willing to sell the gear without the threat of handing him a kicking.
Approaching McGroarty's house in Ronaldsay Street, he walked a little more confidently and imagined himself throwing the money in the startled former boxer's face.
However, imagination was one thing and instead settled himself to deliver the cash and get out of there as quickly as he could. But there was one thing he needed to do and getting down onto one knee, rolled down his sock and hid the extra cash inside.

Returning to his feet, he fetched his mobile phone from his pocket and saw that he had a couple of minutes to spare before the deadline of five o'clock and decided to place a call to his sister.

When she answered, he glanced about him as though fearing being overheard and said, "Tricia? It's me. Listen, I'm out doing a bit of business…"

He angrily shook his head and hissed, "No, I'm not doing fucking drugs! Look, the reason I'm phoning is I'll be in a bit late tonight so stick my dinner in the oven and I'll get it when I get home."

He angrily ended the call when his sister told him that if he wasn't in for dinner, he'd better make another arrangement for she wasn't running a buffet.

Taking a deep breath, he turned into McGroarty's path and knocked on the front door.

It was Sharon Gale who answered his knock, her face sporting a fresh blackened eye and a visible bruise on her jaw.

"Is he in?" McMenamin asked.

She didn't reply, but nodded and head down, timidly stood to one side to permit him to enter before leading the way into the front room where McGroarty sat in an armchair in front of a huge plasma television, watching that afternoon's horse racing.

"Wee man," he drawled as he greeted McMenamin without taking his gaze from the screen. "Got my dough?"

Wordlessly, he approached McGroarty and from his green coloured, nylon wallet embossed with the logo of Celtic football club, handed him the folded notes.

"It's all there. Count it if you need to."

"I don't need to count it, my son. If you're short, you're dead."

McMenamin felt a chill run down his spine at the threat then was turning to leave when McGroarty asked, "Where did you get the outstanding money, Kieran?"

He hesitated, then replied, "I met somebody that owed me."

"Anybody I know?" he asked, but McGroarty's voice was too casual, too friendly and it took all of McMenamin's nerve to simply shake his head before replying, "Just a lassie that I sometimes deal to. A student I think she is," he added to support the lie.

McGroarty didn't respond, but simply nodded, his eyes fixed to the screen.

"Nice wallet. Did you nick it?"

"Eh, what? My wallet? No," he grinned nervously. "Bought it at the Barra's a couple of weeks ago."

McGroarty turned towards him and hand outstretched, said, "Show me it."

Inwardly relieved he had the good sense to stow his extra cash into his sock, he reached across and handed it to McGroarty who casually inspecting the wallet, opened it and peered into the pockets.

"What's this," he grinned and held up the black and white photograph of the soldier, before asking, "Who's this, then?"

"Eh, that's my dead uncle. Died in the Falklands war. He was a hero," McMenamin proudly replied.

McGroarty stared at him, then broke into a wide grin.

"You're full of shit, you are. Dead uncle, war hero," he slowly shook his head. "Your family have always been Irish republicans. I can't imagine a worse embarrassment than your lot having a British army soldier in the family and besides," he peered closely at the photograph. "Look at it. This photo is a lot older than one that was taken in the eighties. Who is he really?"

Deflated that he was so easily caught out, McMenamin, his face bright red, shrugged and said, "I don't really know. Just a photograph I found in a purse," but didn't say how he had come by the purse.

Throwing the photograph onto the cluttered sideboard and tossing the wallet at McMenamin, McGroarty sat back down again and said, "Away to fuck before I give you a slapping for lying to me. Go on, get out!" he roared.

Leaving the room, Gale followed him to the door where pointing to her face, she whispered, "He didn't mean it. It was my fault. I upset him."

"Like I fucking care," he sneered and a few steps along the path, grinned when he heard the door slam behind him.

The two middle-aged joggers wearing their newly purchased, brightly coloured designer tracksuits with headbands to hold back their fashionably cut hair and each carrying a bottle of water, were slowing plodding up the steep incline towards the flagpole in the park when the older by three years, her legs shaking and pulse racing, stopped and said, "Give me a minute, hen, this bloody hill is killing me, so it is."

Her equally unfit and red-faced friend, secretly pleased that she wasn't the one to call a halt to their first day of fitness training, could only gasp and nod her agreement.

Together, the women stood for a moment hands on hips to catch their breath before gamely resuming their meandering stagger towards the top of the hill.

It was when they crested the hill they saw what seemed to be a young man lying nearby on the grass and while their initial instinct was to ignore him, the younger of the two continued to stare.

"I think there's something wrong with him, Jean," she hesitantly pointed towards the figure who lay on his back, his arms and legs splayed at angles that made him look like an abandoned mannequin. The woman continued to stare, her breath returning but her nerves now tautly stretched.

"No, he's only sleeping," Jean attempted to assure her, glancing at the fading light that seemed to have suddenly arrived and dreading the thought that Liz might want to approach the man. "Come on, it'll be a lot easier running down the other side of the path," she tried to joke, but Jean continued to stare and ignoring Liz's pull at her arm, hesitantly stepped towards the man.

She did not need to reach down to touch him for his bulging eyes, his mouth slackly open with dried spit at the corners, the large wet stain at his groin where he had wet himself and a redness about his throat clearly indicated to her that he was dead.

"Oh my God, Jean," her hands went instinctively to her face, "I think we'd better phone for the polis!"

CHAPTER NINE

The two uniformed officers who responded to the jogger's frantic phone call agreed that the man discovered in the grass was certainly dead. Seating both women in the rear of their patrol car, the senior of the two officers used her Airwave radio to request immediate uniform and CID back-up and instructed her younger neighbour to secure the location as best he could with the blue and white tape from the boot of the car.

It was fortunate that there were few early evening walkers in the area while the occasional keep-fit enthusiast who happened by was waved away.

In a short time, further resources arrived to assist the first responders and very quickly, the crime scene was completely taped off with officers deployed to carefully search the nearby shrubbery for anything that might prove to be of evidential value.

The Scene of Crime officers set up a tent over the body of the deceased to both protect the locus and deny any passers-by the opportunity to gawp at the SOCO's, who in their white suits and following the casualty surgeon's pronouncement of life extinct, carried out their examination.

"Seems to me that he's been strangled, Miss McColl," the doctor sighed while he glanced impatiently at his watch and conscious his dinner would soon be on the table, waited for her approval to remove himself from the locus.

Detective Inspector Myra McColl, dressed in a one-piece white Forensic suit, thoughtfully nodded and tightly smiling, replied, "Yes, well, thanks for attending doc. Is there anything else that might be useful?"

"Needle marks on both arms and the legs and his general appearance, gaunt would be the best description, seems to suggest he is a regular drug abuser, but the post mortem will likely confirm that. I can't imagine that he would have just lay there as he was being strangled so your guys," he nodded towards the tent, "are bagging up both hands in the likelihood that there is some DNA trace evidence under the fingernails."

"Strangled? Any suggestion with what? I mean, something broad like a rope or belt or narrow like a wire?"

"The bruising on his throat is irregular rather than even and I'm only guessing here for again the PM will of course be more thorough, but I would venture an opinion it was the killer's hands for it appears to me to be finger-marks that caused the bruising."

They both turned as a Scene of Crime officer approached and handed McColl a clear, plastic bag that had been zipped closed.

"This was in an inside pocket of his jacket, Ma'am."

McColl held the bag up and peering at it, saw it contained a Job Centre attendance card.

"Leonard Robertson of Sheldaig Street," she murmured, than asked the SOCO, "that's up in the Milton, isn't it?"

"Aye, Ma'am, and if memory serves correctly, it runs off Castlebay Street."

"Well, this is a starter for ten," she grimly smiled and turning towards the casualty surgeon, said, "Thanks, doctor. I'll look forward to your report in due course," and with a nod, dismissed him to his home and evening meal.

She took a deep breath. As a recently appointed DI this was her first murder in the role of Senior Investigating Officer and conscious the detectives who stood nearby watched and waited for her instructions, McColl did not want to project anything other than confidence. Calling them to her, she cast an eye around the five detectives and said, "Right guys and gals, the PF Depute has been, the casualty surgeon pronounced life extinct, the SOCO people are on the ball so we're set to go. Right now," she held up the plastic bag containing the Job Centre attendance card and continued, "We have what seems to be an identification for the deceased, so this will be our first priority."

She turned to a tall, bearded and lanky man who dry-smoked a pipe and handing him the plastic bag, said, "DS Fraser, take this and DC…" she paused and smiling at a young female detective, said, "Sorry, hen. I'm still trying to get used to the names."

"Mhari Munroe, Ma'am," then as though in further explanation, pointed to her blonde hair, and added, "but this lot call me Marilyn."

McColl grinned and nodding, replied, "Well, Marilyn, you accompany DS Fraser to the address and," she turned again to Fraser, "before you go have a look at the victim to establish if the deceased is indeed Leonard Robertson and find out what you can about associates etcetera." She smiled and almost apologetically, added, "Sorry, Calum. I'm certain you don't need me to tell you what information we need."

"That's okay, Ma'am," he cheerfully shook his head. "If I forget anything, I've Marilyn here to keep me right."

Arranging for a second DC to accompany the body to the mortuary at the Queen Elizabeth Hospital in Govan, McColl concluded her briefing with, "The uniform have agreed to stand by the locus throughout the night to protect the scene. I'll be arranging for a Support Unit team to come out first thing to conduct an area search of the nearby shrubbery. In the meantime," she addressed the remaining DS and DC, "we'll get back to the office to set up an incident room and take statements from our two joggers."

The discovery of a body in Ruchill Park under what the police confirmed were suspicious circumstances was first reported that evening on local radio stations on the eight o'clock bulletins. However, what is generally known as the jungle drums began beating much earlier and the word soon spread among the local populace that a junkie had overdosed near the flagpole in Ruchill Park, but then the whisper grew that no, he had in fact been murdered.

Turning into Sheldaig Road, DS Calum Fraser pointed with the stem of his pipe to the house that was listed on the Job Centre attendance card he held in his other hand and said, "Over there, Marilyn." Munroe slowed then parked the CID car outside the former council semi-detached house.

Locking the car behind them, they saw a curtain twitch at a ground floor window, the lounge they supposed and upon approaching the door, it was opened by a middle-aged woman who anxiously greeted them with, "Is it my Lenny? Is he in the jail again?"

"Good evening, Madam," Fraser formally replied, then identifying both he and Munroe, asked, "Are you Missus Robertson?"

"Aye," she cast a glance behind them and face grimly set, said, "Please come in. There's too many nosey buggers about here that like to know my business."

Closing the door behind them and leading them into the neat and tidy lounge, she turned and wringing her hands, again asked, "I suppose you're here about my Lenny?"

With his hand, Fraser indicated the couch and said, "Can we please sit down?"

"Oh, aye, I'm sorry. Where are my manners?"

Once seated, Fraser gently asked, "Lenny I assume is your son Leonard, Missus Robertson. Do you have a recent photograph of your Leonard?"

"A photograph?" her eyes betrayed her curiosity before she stood and from a sideboard, fetched a paper wallet from which she withdrew a number of prints. Her hands visibly shaking, at last she selected one that she handed over saying, "This was taken about a year ago. Is that the sort of thing you mean?"

Peering at the photo of a young man who wore Highland dress and held a pint tumbler of lager in one hand while he grinned at the camera, Fraser was in no doubt the victim was indeed Leonard

Robertson and handing the photo to Munroe, took a breath before disclosing the awful news.

Knowing Ian was working late at the café, Daisy Cooper knew she wouldn't see him before she left for her last nightshift of the week and decided to leave a note to remind him to book a table for the following evening, adding, *'somewhere nice without background music so we can talk.'*
That done she collected her sandwiches and with a weary sigh, made her way to the front door.
She was leaving a little earlier than she needed to but had already made her mind up that just to be sure, just to be *absolutely* certain, she'd pop into Tesco on the way to work to buy what she needed.

Kieran McMenamin was on a high.
Lennie Robertson had spent twenty quid of the money he had stolen, but added to the one hundred and five pounds and now his debt to Peter McGroarty was settled, it still left McMenamin with eighty-five quid to score some smack that he would adulterate and sell on. As he trudged towards the dealers flat in the high rise in Wyndford Road, he thought again of doing Lennie Robertson. There was no doubt in his mind the skinny bastard had it coming to him, ripping him off like that. His eyes narrowed and his brow furrowed as he wondered who the young bird was that Lennie had been trying to score off. He had just glimpse of her before she run off and from what he saw, didn't think he knew her.
Yes, she was a witness to him attacking Lennie, but he was confident that she would never come forward for after all, she was unlikely to admit to the polis that she was scoring smack from the junkie bastard and risk herself getting the jail.
No, he was confident he was in the clear. There was no way the polis could identify him and grinned at his own cleverness.
Approaching the high rise flats he glanced up at the building and made his way to the front entrance. He stood for a few moments at the secure door entrance, his head low to avoid his face being recorded by the CCTV camera situated on the corner that covered the entrance area. The doors opened and was held by a woman with ebony coloured skin wearing brightly coloured clothes with a small toddler running after her.

Grunting with impatience and ignoring her fearful glance towards him, he held the door for the nervous woman to permit her to grab at the child before making his way across the foyer into the lift where he pressed the button for the ninth floor.

Seated comfortably in the worn armchair, one suited leg crossed over the other, Nigel Faraday idly picked at a loose thread on his shirt cuff while he stared at the bloodied Jackie Stone, a skinny man in his early forties, who was being forced to kneel in front of him. Sandy Craig, the large and threatening man who stood over Stone and held the terrified man's long, greasy hair in a tight grip, waited on his cue from Faraday.
"Now, Jackie, here's the thing," Faraday smiled while pulling a handful of tissues from a box on a side table that he reached across to hand to Stone. "First, though, wipe your nose before you spill your blood on my shoes."
He watched as Stone dabbed at his nose, the blood mingling with the tears of pain that run down his cheeks.
"A little bird has informed me, Jackie, that you have been a naughty lad. I'm told that the product my associates delivered last week has…how shall I put this," he pretended to ponder the question, "been adulterated far many times more than was agreed and so the customer base is quite correctly upset and hence my receiving numerous complaints. In short, my friend," he leaned menacingly towards the stricken Stone, "*you* are ripping me off."
He paused then sitting back, continued. "While I applaud your enterprise…"
"But Nigel…" Stone began, but was savagely jerked backwards by his tormentor behind him who slapping viciously at the side of his head, growled, "Mister Faraday to you, ya scummy wee shite!"
"Please, Sandy," Faraday raised his hands as though to calm the large man. "Let's hear what Jackie has to say."
Stone gasped with pain as Craig tightened his grip on Stone's hair before slowing permitting him to again lean forward.
"It's just that, well, you said that when I had the smack…"
"Product, Jackie, the product. I don't deal in smack, remember?"
Stone did remember, his mind suddenly casting him back to the first meeting with the snobby bastard and his lah-de-fucking-dah voice,

insisting they never used the word drugs or any similar connotation, but always referred to it as product.

"Anyway," he winced at the pain in his head, "when you said that you were happy for me to accept the product and put it out at a price that paid your bill, I didn't think you would mind if I spread it out a bit more than you wanted."

"With the product becoming much less potent and the profit margin for you rising, of course," he nodded in understanding to Stone.

"However, my dear boy, you did this without my authorisation and frankly, that rather *does* upset me. Do you not see how this would look to my rivals? One of my dealers going behind my back to adulterate the product without my permission? That and the customers taking their business elsewhere if our product is not up to scratch. You do see that, don't you, Jackie?"

"Yes, Mister Faraday," he winced at the pain in his head.

"Well, Jackie, we cannot have that, can we?"

He suddenly rose from the armchair and glancing over Stone's head to Craig, said, "I believe a suitable punishment…" but then stopped, for the doorbell rang.

His face tightened as he instructed, "See who it is," then staring down at Stone, added, "You fell and banged your face and we are here to assist you, Jackie. Do you understand?"

"Aye," Stone nodded, then remaining on his knees, his hair now free from Craig's grip, tilted his head back in an effort to stem the flow of blood from his nose.

Faraday waited anxiously for Craig to return from the front door and his eyes opened wide when he saw the large man was pushing a youth in front of him.

"Says he's come to speak with Jackie about some gear…I mean, product, boss," Craig growled and then pushed the youth into an armchair.

"What's your name, my young fellow?" Faraday, relieved it wasn't the police, tilted his head and stared curiously at the youth.

"Kieran McMenamin, sir," the youth respectfully replied, clearly frightened and cowering from Craig.

"And what do you expect to obtain here from Mister Stone?"

McMenamin stared in fright at the bloodied Stone who was still on his knees and his voice almost a whimper, replied, "A bit of gear, sir. I mean, some smack."

"Fortuitously, it seems this customer has saved you from my wrath, Jackie. I'll leave you now while you conduct your business, but am I assured you *will* heed my warning?"

"Aye, Mister Faraday," Stone gurgled through his blood and tears.

"Then, Sandy, our work here is done," he smiled at Craig.

The two men had been gone from the flat just a few minutes when McMenamin, still curled up in the armchair, whispered, "Who the *fuck* was that, Jackie?"

Stone, the red sodden tissues still held at his nose, struggled to his feet and wordlessly made his way to the bathroom where turning the taps on in the wash hand basin, he inserted the plug. Reaching for a soiled towel, he waited till the basin was filled before plunging his face into the lukewarm water.

"Jackie!" McMenamin stood in the doorway. "Who were they two guys?"

Raising his face from the blood-stained water, Stone shook his head as thought to clear it and pressed the towel against his face.

"It's better you don't know," he lifted the towel from his face and saw the bleeding had slowed to a trickle.

"Come on, who were they?" McMenamin persisted.

Stone pushed by the younger man and returned to the lounge where he flopped down into the armchair recently vacated by Faraday.

"*Jackie!*" McMenamin, who had followed him through to the lounge, persisted.

He gently dabbed at his nose, wincing at the pain and wondered if it was broken before replying, "The big guy. He's called Sandy Craig. A hard bastard who used to be one of the muscle for a team that run the drugs in this area. A family called McDonald, but they're all dead now. The flashy guy. He's my supplier, though I hardly ever see him. He usually works through third parties unless there's a problem and today," he hissed, "*I* was the fucking problem and that's why my nose got burst!"

McMenamin settled down into the opposite armchair and thought it best to keep his mouth shut as lightly touching his nose, Stone continued to rant.

"Faraday is a fucking, poncey bastard," he snarled, "who's running the smack in the Maryhill area. I don't know where he comes from, but for the last year he's been the main man for the deliveries around here."

"Faraday? I've not heard the name before," McMenamin's eyes narrowed, "but I did hear about a new guy that had set up business. Is that him, then? Faraday?"

"Oh, aye, that'll be him," Stone nodded. "Posh accent and fancy suits and that big thug Sandy Craig as his minder and top dog. He keeps another couple of bampots on the go that do the running around and smacking heads when he tells them, but he never usually gets involved himself."

"So why was he here today if he doesn't get involved?"

Stone sighed, then grimaced as a sudden pain caused his eyes to water. "I think my nose is broken," he whined, then turning to stare curiously at McMenamin, asked, "Why are you here again?"

Striding through the foyer at the bottom of the high rise flats, Craig followed Faraday across the car park to a gleaming white Range Rover Discovery where the bigger man got into the driving seat and asked, "Where to, boss?"

Seated in the rear seat, Faraday glanced at the dashboard clock and with a sigh, replied, "Drop me home, Sandy. I've had enough for one day."

He sat back as Craig started the engine and eyes closed, thought about the rapid progress he had made in such a short time.

The private schooling in Giffnock, the mediocre degree at Glasgow University and then the endlessly boring job in his father's accountancy job.

For what?

To face forty years of tedium?

No, eyes still closed, he smiled. It had been the luscious Lucy Barrowman in his second year at the Uni who quite unwittingly introduced him to the drug scene and the massive profits to be made. Lucy, bless her cold heart, who increasingly believed the drugs she scored from the local dealers would never control her life.

Well my dear, he thought of Lucy in her final weeks, the drugs didn't just control you, you stupid bitch, they took your life.

As was expected of someone with Lucy's pedigree, her death was covered up by her extremely affluent and high profile family who bought off not just her flatmate and fellow druggie who discovered her with the needle in her arm, but also the family doctor who diagnosing a previously unrecorded cardiac complaint, signed the cause of her death on the certificate as a heart attack. Thereafter it was simply a question of hiring the private ambulance that conveyed her body to the funeral home, who for the right price readied Lucy for the remarkably quick and private cremation.

Then of course there were the non-disclosure payments to those in the know who were aware of her addiction.

The experience piqued his curiosity about the drug scene and it was in the third year of the accountancy and finance degree that he made his decision to probe the world of drugs.

Through subtle and occasional amiable questioning of his fellow students he had recognised as users, he soon identified some of the minor dealers and from them, their distributors.

It was fortunate that his wealthy father permitted him such a large allowance for within a month, Faraday was arranging to buy and sell the commodity, during which time he began to recruit his own distributors.

He had decided heroin, that old favourite, was definitely where the real money was and invested a large part of his quick profits into smack or as he preferred to term it, the product.

Sooner than even he anticipated, he had come to the attention of some of the more notable Manchester and London based heroin suppliers and within six months, established his own network of not just distributors, but couriers too.

Conscious that the drug scene was heavily infiltrated by the police, he realised he would require some form of protection and of course, none of this administrative growth could be achieved without the muscle that he required to keep his organisation in line.

Sandy Craig has been his first choice as a minder, having seen the large man deal with a couple of rowdy drunks at the door of the Sauchiehall Street nightclub.

Brutally, he smiled at the memory.

And now here he was, twenty-seven years of age and already pulling in profits in excess of the high six figures in his first full year.

He opened his eyes as Craig turned the Discovery into the riverside car park by the plush apartment complex at Bulldale Street.

Switching off the engine, Craig turned in his seat and in a gravelly voice, asked, "Do you want me to leave the motor, boss? I can jump a taxi."

"No," he waved a hand as he opened the door with the other. "Take the Discovery home, Sandy. If I need you I'll give you a bell."

"Okay boss. What about that wee shite, Stone? Do you want me to go back and give him a leathering?"

"No, we'll leave it as it is. I believe our Jackie has had his warning and likely the word that I was not best pleased with his actions will quickly be circulated among his fellow dealers. Should he fail to heed the warning," he smiled, "then you may have your wicked way with him."

"Boss," Craig nodded and grinned in acknowledgement.

He didn't wait to watch Craig drive off, but quickly made his way to the newly purchased top floor flat that overlooked the River Clyde. Pushing open the security door, he glanced at a rusting and bashed looking Transit van that was parked in a bay outside the adjoining flats. The vehicle was so out of place among the Audi's, BMW's and four by fours it briefly occurred to him it might be a police surveillance vehicle.

No matter, he thought with a smile.

He was far too careful to be directly implicated in his drug business and with the confidence of a young man whose intellect was far above average, made his way to the front entrance of the flats.

CHAPTER TEN

Though he had travelled in the comfort of business class, he had not slept too well and bleary eyed, joined his fellow passengers as they grouped at the door.

Nodding his farewell to the young steward, Harry Henderson strode purposefully through the long restricted tunnel towards the Immigration desks with his travel bag in his hand.

Seated in his cubicle, the portly Immigration Officer looked up from his newspaper and saw the suntanned, slim man with gold, thin framed spectacles, wearing a white linen suit, open necked pale blue shirt and a Panama hat, approach his window with a smile. Handing the Immigration Officer his passport, Harry greeted him, with "Good morning. How are you today?" before removing his hat to reveal an almost bald head with just a wisp of closely cropped hair at the sides.

"Fine, sir," replied the Immigration Officer who first compared the passport photograph with the man stood before him, then passed the open passport across a scanner.

Unseen by Harry a red light flashed at the Immigration Officer's knee who continuing to stare at Harry and without expression, returned Harry's passport then pointed to the nearest wall and said, "Please step over to that door, sir. Someone will be with you in a minute or two."

Harry tightly smiled and inwardly thought, here we go then.

With no other option, he turned towards the door and assumed when the Immigration Officer passed the passport through the bar code reader, an alarm must have activated for the door was opened by two men in suits, one of whom beckoned Harry follow them through a narrow hallway to a small office.

Once seated in the office, the older of the two men first identified them as Metropolitan Police Port Coverage Unit officers, but not their names, then taking the passport and peering at it, politely asked, "Do you have any other luggage with you, Mister Henderson?"

"No, just the bag there," he nodded to the brown leather holdall.

While the younger detective searched the bag, the older officer said, "The use of your passport alerted us to a message that was sent some years ago by our colleagues in Strathclyde Police. Apparently they wish to interview you regarding an ongoing investigation."

Harry's demeanour didn't change, but the detective's comment 'interview you' made him think, so he asked, "Am I under arrest?"

"Eh, no, not exactly," replied the detective, his face reddening, "but we do have authority to detain you until such times we are satisfied that our Scottish colleagues are informed you have returned to the UK."

"But I'm *not* under arrest?"

"Technically, no…" the detective began, but stopped when Harry stood and with a confident smile, said, "I've nothing to hide so it is my intention to catch a connecting flight, officer and I can assure you I will make myself available to officers of Strathclyde Police when I arrive in Glasgow."

"That might be a bit difficult, Mister Henderson," shrugged the detective. "Strathclyde Police don't exist now, because our Scottish colleagues are now Police Scotland. However, if they still wish to interview you, I'm sure they'll be waiting for you to arrive. You see *we* will escort you to your Glasgow flight and also inform them of your arrival time," he grinned as though believing he had scored a point.

Harry glanced at his watch and with a disarming smile, replied, "Then as we have just over an hour before my flight departs, gentlemen, why don't I treat you to a coffee while we wait?"

Daisy Cooper arrived home to find that her fiancé Ian had already left for work, but smiled when she saw the note by the kettle.
Gone in early for the fish delivery. Missed you all through the night. Looking forward to us having a couple of days together. Booked the Indian in Ashton Lane, the same place we had our first date. Hope you get a sleep. Love you. xxx
Grinning, she switched on the kettle and was about to crumple the note, but stopped and read it again.
The nightshift had been far quieter than the previous night and with a yawn, prepared herself a coffee and a slice of toast.
As the kettle warmed then boiled, she thought again of her idea of discussing taking on someone to do the books. It would certainly relieve Ian of the pressure of trying to manage the accounts. But now, her brow furrowed, there was something else she needed to discuss with him. Something, she inwardly sighed, far more pressing and wasn't quite sure how he would take her news for the visit to Tesco had proved to be more startling than she anticipated.

Detective Superintendent Cathy Mulgrew was at her office desk in the Gartcosh Crime Campus when her secretary called through to inform her that she had a visitor.
"It's DI McBride, Ma'am."
"Tell him to come through," she replied, then smiled when he opened the door.
"Danny," she greeted him, "what brings you here all the way from across the corridor from Criminal Intelligence?"
"Morning, Ma'am," he sat in the chair opposite her. "Just over ten minutes ago, one of my guys took a call from the Met's Port Coverage Unit at Gatwick. It seems that a passenger arriving from Havana flagged up when his passport was passed through the scanner. Harry Henderson, aka Headcase Henderson, a convicted murderer. The Met PCU are escorting him to a connecting flight to

Glasgow Airport."

"The name sounds familiar, but remember, Danny. I spent a number of years working in the Special Branch and was kind of out of touch what was happening with the CID inquiries, so remind me," her eyes narrowed.

McBride, sleeves rolled up to his forearms and tie undone, sat comfortably back in his seat and said, "A number of years ago, the Maryhill area drug scene was controlled by an old guy called Wally McDonald. Him and his two sons, Mickey and Billy, a right pair of evil bastards, had the north of the city under lock and key. Wally had a younger wife, a blonde bimbo with big knockers called Donna," he smiled. "Pardon my description, but I do *not* exaggerate and I'll explain about Donna as I go on. Anyway, at that time Wally and his sons were in a turf war with a Southside drug dealer called Brian Murphy."

"Wait," she raised a hand and leaned forward. "I do know *that* name. Wasn't Murphy the guy who…"

"Yeah, he was responsible for the death of a mate of mine, DI Peter McKinley, who fell with him from the top of a block of high rise flats," McBride nodded, his face pale, for even after all these years it still pained him to think of it.

"Anyway," he exhaled and continued, "the word was that after Wally McDonald died, his sons were in line to continue the war against Murphy, but while their father was being cremated, they were driving out of the yard at their house in Maryhill when their vehicle was petrol bombed. Not just that but they were tooled up at the time; shotguns I think it was. No witnesses, though. When the polis arrived, Billy was burned alive, but Mickey," he shivered at the memory. "Mickey was also badly burned, but apparently got out of the vehicle.

Unfortunately, the McDonalds kept several large and ferocious dogs and, well," he grimaced, "the dogs finished Mickey off."

"Dear God, I *did* hear about that," she nodded. "And this man Henderson?"

"Headcase Henderson was suspected of being the petrol bomb thrower, but there was never any evidence to link him to the murders. However, the day the McDonald brothers were murdered, the grieving widow Donna left the country for Cuba and the word is, old Wally McDonalds large and illicitly gained fortune went with her. The fortune," he frowned, "was assessed to be in excess of six to eight million quid. To date, the inquiry on the McDonald brothers' murders remains open."

"Bloody hell! Six to eight million? And you said Henderson has just flown in from Cuba, so you're assuming…"

"We knew he had left the country a couple of months after the McDonald brothers were murdered, but not certain to where. However, the Intel Department of the former Strathclyde Police caused an all ports lookout to watch for him re-entering the UK."

"But you now think because he's arrived from Cuba…"

"That's where he's been all this time," he nodded. "With Wally's widow, Donna."

"And if you excuse the pun," she grimaced, "the million dollar question is, Danny, do we have evidence that might implicate Henderson in the outstanding murders?"

"Truthfully?" he shook his head. "No. All we have is gossip and speculation and Henderson's reputation as a former hitman who never left any evidence of his murders. However," he thoughtfully mused, "I am curious that after all these years, Harry's back and what worries me, is why?"

"Tell me more about Henderson?"

"He's a former lifer, went down after being arrested for murder, though he is suspected of carrying out far more killings than we ever learned about. Curiously, according to his file, a tout once reported that Henderson had his own code of honour. No women, no clergy and definitely no children. There *was* a rumour he had been fitted up by our colleagues of the former Serious Crime Squad for the murder he did time for, but he never appealed so perhaps it's just another one of these urban legends."

Mulgrew took a sharp breath and replied, "I hope so."

"Anyway, I've had a look at what we know of him, his antecedent history, but there's no family listed so his return does not seem to be social. I can only assume he's here for some criminal purpose."

"You said we were informed what, about ten or fifteen minutes ago? Does that mean he's not yet landed in Glasgow?"

"As far as I am informed, he's due to land in about an hour's time."

"Do you intend having him detained for interview regarding the McDonald brothers' murders?"

"That's why I'm here, Ma'am," he smiled mischievously at her. "As the Head of the north side of the city CID, you inherited the McDonalds' brothers' murders, so technically, *you* are the SIO."
"Thanks for that," she ungraciously scowled at him. "Right then, contact the Glasgow Airport Ports Coverage Unit and have them detain Henderson when he lands and you," she rose to her feet, "go and grab your coat, DI McBride, for as the bearer of this morning's bad news, you are coming with me to greet our Mister Henderson."

Kieran McMenamin was up early and had the television on and switched to the news channel before his sister Patricia awoke.
"What time did you get in last night?" she asked him as yawning, she flopped down onto the couch beside him, her dressing gown tightly wrapped about her. Tightly, for she neither liked nor trusted her younger sibling and in recent months had on several occasions caught him trying to sneak a look at her tits.
"Late," he surly replied, spooning the cereal into his mouth from the plate in his lap.
"Aye, very good," she shook her head. "Never been a morning person have you, wee bro," she slapped at his head.
"Fuck off!" he drew away and snapped at her.
"Language," his father, dressed for work, called out from the doorway then added, "Tricia, I've left a tenner on the dresser in the kitchen. Can you bring in the milk and bread and something for dinner, hen?"
"Aye, I'll get it when I finish, but I'm a late start today, Da, so I'll not be home till about six."
"That'll do fine hen. Cheerio for now," her father replied as he noisily closed the front door behind him.
Turning to her brother, she asked, "What are you doing today? Going to the Job Centre or what?"
"Maybe," he mumbled.
"Maybe? What the hell do you mean, maybe? Jesus, Kieran," she sat bolt upright and stared angrily at him. "You need to get out there and get yourself a job, son! It's me and our Da who's bringing in the money for the rent and the gas and the electricity and the food that you fucking take for granted! How about *you* trying to find a job and contributing something yourself, eh? Either that or *here's* a great idea," she sneered at him. "Go and find yourself somewhere else to

live!"

Pushing himself up from the couch, he slammed the plate down onto the low coffee table, spilling some of the milk over the side as the spoon clattered onto the floor and snarling at her, fished two twenty pound notes from his pocket that he threw at her.

"Here! Take my last forty quid, ya moaning faced bitch!"

She stared open-mouthed at the money and then, her lip curling, hissed, "Where did you get forty quid? Kieran! Answer me," she demanded as she arose from the couch.

He turned to walk off, but she grabbed at his arm as furiously, he pulled away from her and walking from the room, ignored her calling out again, "Tell me! Where did you get that money?"

Returning to his room, he knew it had been a mistake, giving her the two twenties. She wouldn't let it go and suspect that he had been dealing again. He was on his last warning from his father who after the local Drug Squad turned over the house two months previously, told him that any further visits from the police or dealings with them and he was out on his ear.

That and there was nothing on the BBC or Sky news about Lennie Robertson being found up in Ruchill Park.

It worried him that maybe he was a bit too confident, that he had gotten away with it. What worried him the most was the lassie who had run away, the lassie called Maggie somebody.

He had no worries that she would fire him in to the polis for he was confident she would not want implicated and her drug dealing coming to light.

But like it or not, she was a witness to him attacking Lennie and because of that, he shivered, he first had to find her then do something about her.

The subject of McMenamin's thoughts was at that time lying in a drug addled stupor on a filthy mattress that lay on the floor of her room in the first floor flat in which she squatted with two others. To call them friends or even acquaintances would be an overstatement, for the plain truth was that all three were associated simply because of their drug addictions.

Hovering between conscious and comatose, the twenty-year old Maggie Dalrymple, failed student and part-time prostitute, the latter occupation to earn the money to feed her addiction, had arrived in

Glasgow a year previously to commence her further education at the Strathclyde University. However, within a month of her arrival from Oban, the naïve Dalrymple fell prey to the social life that in turn degenerated into her use of drugs. With her new circle of friends, she first tried cannabis, then as the need for more powerful narcotics took a hold of her body, her addiction to heroin was complete.

Of course her parents, family and friends, worried at her lack of communication, arrived in Glasgow to search for her, but such was her reliance on the opiates that her spiral into the world of drug abuse occurred quickly and within weeks, she had lost all touch with her former life in Oban.

She took a deep breath and tightly closed her eyes.

There was something she had to remember, something she had seen. Tiredly, she turned in the mattress and laying her head to one side, burped then vomited a thick, yellow glutinous fluid. Shivering, she forced herself to push up from the prone position and using her sleeve, wiped at her mouth, nauseated at the smell of her own bile. She waited for a few minutes, trying to recollect what it was she had forgotten, then rolled onto her knees and with difficulty, pushed herself to her feet, her legs shaking and her body cold.

She wrapped her arms about her and then saw her long black coat lying abandoned near to the door. Stooping, she almost fell over, but managed to fetch the coat from the floor and slipped it on.

Opening the bedroom door, she listened, but could not hear any sound and in bare feet, wandered into the second bedroom and the lounge that her flatmate used as the third bedroom. Neither of the young men were in the flat and quickly, she searched both rooms, vainly searching for any sign of their drug stash.

Disappointed, she returned to her own room and sliding down the wall, stared at her bare, dirty feet, her mouth dry and a thousand invisible bugs crawling with their tiny clawed feet across her skin. If only she could remember what it was that itched at the back of her mind.

Truing the key in the padlock, Mary Harris again was the morning opener at the charity shop and pushing open the door, reached to switch on the interior lights.

She intended working just a half shift this morning and looked forward to visiting Michael at one o'clock in the nursing home, where the staff had willingly agreed she could serve him his lunch.
"Morning, Mary," her fellow volunteer Alice McLean greeted her from behind. "Right, first things first, I'll get the kettle on," Alice continued with a smile, taking off both her hat and coat while she made her way to the kitchen in the small room at the rear of the shop.
Mary, hanging her coat up in the storeroom, returned to the till where she unlocked it and ensured the small Tupperware box containing the float was still there. Not that she thought the shop had been broken into during the might but, she sighed and shook her head. Times were hard for folk and even charity shops experienced thieves and shoplifters these days.
"Did you hear about the murder, Mary?" Alice appeared at her back, two mugs of tea held in her hands.
"Murder? No, not the mugging round the corner in Balmore Road," Mary's eyes widened.
"No," Alice, the eyes and ears of the Saracen district, waved a dismissive hand. "That's another thing. There were *two* muggings. A wee man round the corner in Balmore Road and a woman in her close in Saracen Street. Did you not hear about her too? Place is becoming like a war zone," Alice shook her head.
Taken aback, Mary could only shake her head.
"Aye, bad business so it is. Makes you wonder if anybody's safe these days," she sighed.
"Anyway," Alice conspiratorially lowered her voice, "I heard there was a body found in Ruchill Park. Murdered. Up near the flagpole. You know where that is, don't you?"
She felt her knees shake, her chest tighten and a weakness overcome her as with her free hand, she reached out to steady herself on the counter.
"Mary. Mary? Mary! Are you okay, hen," Alice reached to solicitously help her sit down in a nearby wooden chair. "Mary, dear, you've gone as white as a sheet. Are you ill? Will I phone for an ambulance?"
She could hardly speak and was conscious of the mug slipping from her grasp that just in time was caught by Alice who laid it down onto the counter.

"What is it, hen? You're frightening me," she heard the older lady's voice breaking.
"A murder?" she heard herself whisper. "Up at the flagpole in the park?"
"Aye, that's what I heard. Is it somebody you know?"
She shook her head, but the memory of the young man skulking through the undergrowth flashed before her.
"Alice, dear," her voice was now a mere whisper, "can you phone the polis. I need to speak to Popeye; Popeye Doyle."

Harry Henderson stepped towards the domestic arrivals gate and saw them stood waiting for him, the tall, good looking woman with the copper red hair and the guy beside her in a crumpled navy blue business suit. They had CID written all over them and as he approached, he also noticed the two burly, fit looking guys in suits who stood discreetly a few paces behind them with their hands clasped in front.
"Mister Henderson?" the woman asked.
"What gave me away," he smiled then raising his free hand, added, "don't tell me, it's the white suit and the Panama hat."
She couldn't help herself and acknowledging his charm, returned his smile and replied, "My name is Detective Superintendent Cathy Mulgrew and this," she turned and nodded, "is Detective Inspector Danny McBride."
Harry nodded in greeting and before she could continue, said, "If I'm under arrest, so be it, I'll be coming quietly and there's no need for any fuss from your guys there," he nodded to the two detectives at the back. "But if I'm *not* being arrested, how about we find a coffee bar and we can speak there? My treat," he added with another smile.
Taken aback, Mulgrew stared for a few seconds then broke into a wide grin before responding, "Seems fair."
Turning, she dismissed the two detectives with a nod and then continued, "Follow me Mister Henderson. I know just the place."
A few moments later both she and McBride were seated opposite each other at a table, Harry's travel bag nestled at their feet, and watching as he ordered their coffee's at the bar. Returning, he shook his head and sighing, said, "Bloody prices they charge, they should be wearing masks. And they called *me* a criminal?"

Settling himself into a chair between them, he continued, "When the Met guys pulled me at Gatwick, they told me you're keen to interview me regarding an ongoing investigation, but nothing else. Now, I realise I'm not under arrest, but hopefully I'm only back in Glasgow for a short time so I'm not looking to cause you any trouble, Miss Mulgrew. So, go ahead and ask your questions and I'll do my best to assist you."

She glanced at McBride who taking his cue, said, "Mister Henderson…"

"Please, Harry."

"Fair enough. Harry, I won't labour your historical past. However, we have a number of outstanding murder inquiries that continue to be investigated, albeit I admit the investigations have been toned down through the passage of time, but the two murders I'm most interested in are the McDonald brothers, old Walters's sons Mickey and Billy. My information is that you were, during your history of criminality on a number of occasions engaged by Wally McDonald to deal with some of his rivals. Is that correct?"

He stared at McBride before replying, "I notice you didn't caution me, Mister McBride. Does that mean this is an informal chat or a police interrogation, I'm not quite sure."

"Would you prefer to be cautioned?"

"It doesn't really make any difference," he shrugged, then stopped speaking while the young waiter carefully laid three coffee's on the table.

When the waiter left, he continued. "My history is one of violence. I admit to having committed some horrible crimes, hurt people and as you are aware, served a life sentence for a murder. Now," he grimly smiled, "as far as I am concerned its history; water under the bridge if you like. Not that I wish to make anything of it at this time," he raised a hand, "but I didn't actually kill the man I served time for. No, that was fabricated evidence that got me sent down, but I didn't complain because the way I saw it, there was things I didn't get caught for so you could say," he extended his hands and smiled, "it was a bit of eachy-peachy."

"Are you saying you were fitted up, Harry?" Mulgrew leaned forward.

"What I'm saying, Miss Mulgrew, is I had a good run before the law caught up with me."

"I really don't quite know how to respond to that," her face flushed. "Let's forget what I told you, then. Now, I believe I'm correct in thinking you want to know if I killed the McDonald brothers, yes."
"That's correct, yes," nodded McBride.
"It strikes me that had you evidence to indicate that I was responsible, we wouldn't be having this chat, but when I landed in the UK I would have been handcuffed and transported to the nearest jail. It also strikes me that a verbal admission without corroborating evidence…" he smiled at Mulgrew and said, "Yes, I did a lot of reading when I was in the jail. To continue, a verbal admission without corroborating evidence is insufficient to convict. Unless since I've been away Scottish Law has drastically changed?"
"No, you're quite correct, Harry, the law hasn't changed that much."
"Then my reply to your question is," his voice tightened, "those pair of scummies deserved everything that happened to them. Their father, albeit Wally *was* a criminal, had his own code of conduct, but his sons had no such morals or scruples and were vile and dangerously out of control. All I will say is whoever did kill them saved some lives as well as you guys a power of work. Not for one instant do I regret their deaths and as you will also likely know, yes; I now live in Cuba with Wally's widow, Donna. We have a good life there and a quiet life, but for this trip home…"
"Why have you come back, Harry?" McBride interrupted.
Harry lifted his coffee and sipping at it, his brow knitted as he thought quickly before replying, "I received word from an associate that my only living relative, an elderly lady who lives in the city, has been admitted to a hospital. It just might be that this could be the last time I see her and so, here I am. In short, my visit is personal and nothing to do with my former life."
"And how long do you intend remaining?" Mulgrew asked.
"Miss Mulgrew, that really depends on my old auntie, but rest assured. As soon as I know she is recovering or…" he paused then exhaled through pursed lips, "the worst occurs, then I'm gone."
He smiled softly and added, "I should have asked. Do you fancy a cake with your coffee?"

They walked Harry to the taxi rank at the front of the terminal and hesitating as he glanced at the taxis, nodded to them before choosing the third taxi in the queue.

"Call me old fashioned," he smiled at them, "but I've never underestimated the Glasgow polis."
Returning to Mulgrew's car, McBride asked, "What do you think, Ma'am?"
"I think Mister Henderson…" she chuckled and corrected herself, "Harry…is one charming and suspicious individual. Did you get the taxi plate?"
"I did, but something tells me that when I check to find out where he was dropped, it won't be at his accommodation address."
"So, Danny, you ask what do I think?" she mused. "Well, like you I suspect he probably did murder the McDonald brothers and if you recall when you asked him, he didn't deny it, did he? However, can we prove it after this length of time? Unlikely and of course we can't arrest him purely on our suspicion alone."
"So, as the SIO for the murders, what's your next move," McBride opened the front passenger door of Mulgrew's Lexus and got in.
"I'll need time to consider that," she shook her head. "Right now, I've a number of other inquiries I'm overseeing, but what I'd like you to do, Danny, is make some discreet inquiry and try to check the veracity of his story about a sick auntie. We've nothing to hold him on, but if he *is* returned to Glasgow to commit some murder or other crime, I want us to be ready for him."
"Understood," McBride nodded. "I'll get right onto it when I return to Gartcosh."

Sitting on his veranda with a glass of freshly squeezed orange juice in his hand and staring out across the River Clyde, Nigel Faraday thought again about the Transit van he had seen parked outside the adjoining block and wondered if indeed it *was* the police.
But how would he go about finding out?
Certainly, he grinned, if the van returned he could always instruct Sandy to go along and bang on the side and try to provoke a reaction if there *were* officers inside, but that would show his hand, confirm their belief he was aware of their surveillance and make them even more suspicious of him.
No, he'd rather circumvent a direct approach and pondering the question, slowly smiled.
There *was* someone he hadn't spoken to for some time.
Someone who owed him a great favour.

Someone from his days at Uni who had come weeping and wailing to him and panic-stricken after discovering poor, stupid Lucy's body with the needle in her arm.

He smiled and reaching for his mobile phone, scrolled through the directory to find if he still had the number.

CHAPTER ELEVEN

Popeye Doyle was at the receiving end of another ball-busting tirade from Sergeant Anne Cassidy, but she was interrupted when her desk phone rung.

"Yes!" she irately snapped at the caller, then sighing, turned to Doyle to tell him, "That was the control room, Constable Doyle. They wished a message to be passed to you. Some lady at the charity shop in Saracen Cross wishes you to call there to see a Missus Harris. Right, on you go," she waved a hand. "You're dismissed."

He kept his cool and turning, picked up his cap from the desk and went into the corridor where Fariq Mansoor waited for him.

"What was *that* all about, Popeye?" the young cop hurried along the corridor with him.

"It seems that I've not been submitting enough of them motor traffic fines. You know, those bloody parking ticket things," he fumed then added, "No wonder the people round here don't trust us if we're out hunting for stupid wee things like broken lights to hit them with fines when all it takes is a quiet word to tell them to get the thing fixed. My God, son, I never thought I'd say it, but I'm actually looking forward to the day I'm out of here," he shook his head.

"Where are we going anyway?"

"Oh, sorry, Fariq, we're going to see Missus Harris down at the Cross. She's a volunteer with the charity shop there," he pushed open the front door to the office, smiling a nod at Jeannie Morris, the civilian bar officer. "Nice lady that lives with her…Oh," he stopped and slowly shook his head. "I'd forgotten. Her husband Michael, he's been admitted to a nursing home. Dementia, if I recall."

"Is there *anybody* in this sub-Division you don't know?" Mansoor grinned.

Continuing walking, Doyle shook his head and replied, "When you've walked the beat here for nigh on thirty years, son, it's harder *not* to know who the locals are."

Discreetly nodding to a couple walking arm in arm across the road, he quietly said, "That pair there. That's old Willie Johnson and his wife, Sadie. Seem like a happy couple, eh?"

"Aye, they do," Mansoor replied, his face expressing his curiosity at the comment.

"Well, would it surprise you to know he's doing a line with his downstairs widowed neighbour and spends his nights with her. His wife's okay with that because she says it gives her peace and quiet when he's out of the house."

"You're kidding!"

"Nope, stand on me, son" he grinned at Mansoor's surprised face. "It's amazing what people round here get up to and what you hear over the course of your time on the beat."

It didn't take them long to arrive at the charity shop where ignoring the curious glances of the customers, Alice McLean directed them through to the rear shop.

"Oh, Popeye," Mary Harris, wringing her hands nervously on her handkerchief, rose from the wooden chair to greet him, but he waved her back down and introducing his neighbour Fariq Mansoor, then removed his cap and said, "It's been a wee while since I saw you, Mary. How is Michael doing, hen?"

She could not know, but he had recognised how nervous she was and rather than delve right into the reason for her call, wanted her calmed first.

"Oh, Michael. Well," she grimly smiled, "we both know he's not going to get any better. I try to get across there at least four, sometimes five times a week, but it's so hard, seeing him like that."

"I can't imagine how you must be feeling," he drew up a second chair and placing it beside her, sat down and reached for her hand. "Right, now, why have you got me here and away from my roll and cuppa?" he joked.

She smiled and a little more relaxed, replied, "I heard about the murder up in Ruchill Park, Popeye. I was in there yesterday afternoon with my neighbours' two children. Giving her a wee break, you know? Anyway, when I was pushing the buggy up the hill towards the flagpole, I saw a young man walking up through the bushes in the same direction as me and I thought it was a wee bit suspicious?"

"What, because he was going the same way?"

"Aye…ah, no," she shook her head in confusion, then continued, "Well, what I mean is I had seen the same guy earlier in the morning, standing across the road on the corner of the Cross. Twice, actually I saw him and he was acting a wee bit suspicious."

"Define suspicious."

"Well," she slowly drawled as she collected her thoughts, "it looked to me like he was hiding, like he was not wanting to be seen, but his eyes were everywhere and I know I can't say for a fact, but to me he seemed to be watching something across the road. Do you know what I mean?"

"There's a word for that," he softly smiled, "it's called being furtive."

"Aye," she eagerly nodded, "that's what I mean. He was being *very* furtive."

His head jerked up for he suddenly recalled what was across the road from the corner that Mary described.

The bank.

And the bank and an ATM in the wall and that, he thought, might be interesting too.

He keenly stared at her and asked, "And what time was it that you were going up towards the flagpole?"

Her brow creased as she sought to recall, then replied, "I'm guessing here, mind, but I think it was just after four in the afternoon.

He didn't immediately reply, but recalled that morning reading the briefing paper that had been stapled to the Daily Briefing Register, asking that all officers with knowledge of any persons who frequented the Ruchill Park during midday and late evening provide the names to the murder inquiry team. If what Mary Harris had seen was correct, she might be a crucial witness and so he asked, "Who else have you discussed this with, Mary?"

"Nobody. I only found out from Alice about the murder and that's why I asked her to phone you. Why?"

"Well, what I'm going to ask of you is that you come with me to the office to speak with a detective and provide a statement. I'll call for a car to give you a lift to the office and I'll come with you. I would also ask that you don't speak to anyone else about what you saw."

"I told Alice…" her eyes widened as though in guilt.

He raised a hand and smiling, said, "I'll speak with Alice. So, you'll come with me to the office?"

A little flustered, she nodded as he turned to Mansoor who nodding in understanding, left the rear office to use his radio.

Carrying his holdall in his hand, Harry Henderson paid off the taxi outside the Millennium Hotel in George Square and stood on the pavement as it pulled away, his eyes darting back and forth, watching for any vehicle that he thought could be a police surveillance car that might have tailed him from the airport. Passers-by, had they paid attention, would hardly have noticed the average height, bespectacled and balding suntanned man wearing a creased white linen suit with a holdall held in one hand and a Panama hat in the other, for it was not unusual to see tourists stood outside the prestigious hotel.

Five minutes later and as satisfied as he could be that his taxi had not been followed, Harry walked the short distance round the corner into the side entrance to Queen Street railway station and jumped into a cab, politely instructing the driver to take him to the Hilton Hotel in William Street.

Just over five minutes later he was registering at the reception desk in his own name where, as Harry Cavanagh had promised, a package awaited Harry.

With a grateful smile he lifted the bulky package from the blushing young woman and thanking her, made his way to the elevator that took him to his room on the fifth floor.

Once the door had closed behind him, Harry breathed a sigh of relief and placing the holdall and his hat onto the king-size bed, hung his jacket on the back of the chair before wearily sitting at the desk with the package in front of him.

His hands on the package, his eyes narrowed when he thought of the pull at Glasgow Airport. The female detective called Mulgrew had struck him as being far smarter than her easy-going smile and demeanour indicated. It was the guy who accompanied her, however, that had piqued Harry's curiosity.

There was something vaguely familiar about him, but for the moment Harry couldn't quite recall whether it was the man himself or his name, Danny McBride.

He glanced at the package and smiled, guessing it must have been Harry Cavanagh himself who had wrapped it for there was enough sellotape holding it together to tow a car, but before opening it he glanced at the phone on the desk and realised he had a call to make. A couple of minutes later, the phone was answered and he said, "Hello, love. That's me here, safe and sound. The last place you stayed before you left."

He heard Donna gasp and reply in her sultry voice, "Hello there, lover. Any problems getting to where you are?"

He decided there was little point relating the pulls at the two airports and instead replied, "Nothing that caused me any difficulty."

However, Donna wasn't fooled, but knew there was a reason Harry didn't go into details and asked, "How is your aunt?"

"The latest word from our friend is that she's holding it together. I haven't had time yet to visit but hope to go over there soon."

"Good," she replied before adding, "You *will* give your aunt my love?"

"Of course," he smiled.

"And tell her she's always welcome here?"

"That too."

They spoke for another few minutes with Harry concluding that he would phone Donna with an update about Harriet and she warning him to take care.

Replacing the phone in the cradle, he smiled again and stared curiously at the package.

It took him a frustrating two minutes to unseal the package that he carefully emptied out onto the desktop.

The set of car keys had a large label attached that was printed with a registration number and informed him the hired red coloured Ford Focus was fuelled, parked in the underground car park of the hotel, that he was insured for a month's driving and there was a SatNav in the car.

According to the typed note in the packaging the mobile phone, an unlisted burner, was charged and had both Henry Cavanagh's office and personal mobile number already listed in the phones directory.

He flicked through the wad of crisp bank notes that fell from the package and pursed his lips. There was five thousand pounds in twenties, certainly enough to keep him in pocket money for the foreseeable future, though Cavanagh also had the foresight to include a Visa card in Harry's name with a PIN number and bank account details. The note informed him the Visa card was for a recently opened account with twenty grand available. However, the note continued, if for any reason Harry required more cash, funds would be transferred from Harry's own offshore bank account.

The last item was a little more of an eye opener for Harry.

He unwrapped the waxed paper to reveal a short recoil, semi-automatic Glock 17 pistol, a spare magazine and accompanying box of nine millimetre Parabellum ammunition.

Studying the handgun, Harry could see the weapon was not new for closely examining the scoring in the barrel and the scratches on the gunmetal, he opined the weapon had seen service and thought either with the military or perhaps a shooting club. He shook his head when he saw the serial number had been scored off and thought someone had wasted their time for he had learned from the Internet that recent techniques developed by the police Forensic departments throughout the United Kingdom had successfully identified the origin of many firearms used by criminals, even after their attempts to delete the serial numbers.

Stripping the weapon, Harry found it to be clean with a light smear of oil in the working Reassembling the weapon, he dry fired it twice and satisfied himself that it seemed to be in good working order.

Both magazines, he saw, were empty so loaded them each with ten bullets from the box, smiling as he thought that if he couldn't hit his target with twenty rounds, he would be as well to throw the bloody thing at whoever he was facing.

The last item was a right hand belt holster that would fit neatly beneath his suit jacket.

He read the unsigned note again and saw that his old friend had thoughtfully included the telephone number for Ward sixty-seven of the Neurological Unit at the Queen Elizabeth University Hospital in Govan as well as the post code, suggesting Harry use the SatNav to find his way there.

"Good man, Harry," he murmured his thanks to Cavanagh and reached for the phone on the desk.

Cap in hand, while he guided Mary Harris along the corridor towards the CID incident room, Popeye Doyle heard his name called out and turning, saw his sergeant, Anne Cassidy, one hand on her hip while she beckoned him to her with the other.

"Where the hell have you been, Constable Doyle," she hissed at him, her eyes darting behind him to stare curiously towards Mary.
"I was on a call, Sergeant. You sent me there or don't you remember?" he patiently reminded her. "Missus Harris here wished me to visit her and..."
"What, is she somebody from another wee doss place of yours, feeding you tea and cake while you should be out working?" she sneered at him.
Before he could reply and to both their surprise, Mary Harris took a couple of steps forward and voice quivering, said, "Excuse me, Constable Doyle. I'm very busy, you know. Now, you told me that I could be a vital witness in this murder your detectives are investigating. Can we get on with it, please?"
Neither officer could guess at the courage it took for the normally reserved woman to interrupt, but though her legs were shaking and she tightly grasped her handbag for support, neither would Mary tolerate this young, fair haired besom, polis woman or not, berating a fine man like Popeye Doyle, a man that the community liked and appreciated for his fairness and tolerance.
Cassidy's face turned pale and turning from staring at Mary to stare at Doyle, she said, "Witness? To the murder?"
"Aye, Sergeant," he took his cue and fought hard to refrain from grinning at Mary's cheek. "Missus Harris is a busy lady, so if you don't mind?"
She didn't respond, but turned sharply and returned to her office, slamming the door behind her.
Turning back to Mary, he winked and said, "Thanks, hen. Now, let me introduce you to DI McColl."

Turning restlessly in his bed, Kieran McMenamin shook his head as though trying to clear it of the nightmare he had endured.
No, not a nightmare, a mistake.
He'd made a stupid mistake that could get him banged up.
He had no regrets, no feelings of remorse about killing Lennie.
None.
The wee junkie shite deserved what he got for stealing from him, McMenamin decided.
Besides, he rationalised, the wee bastard was no use to anybody.

Lennie had been a hopeless addict who was on the way out anyway. It was only a matter of time before he'd turn his toes up and all McMenamin had done was hurry that day along, conveniently ignoring the fact that McMenamin himself was a user of both cannabis and occasionally cocaine, but convinced himself that unlike Lennie Robertson, McMenamin could quit any time he wished.
Or so he liked to believe.
Yes, he had done the wee junkie bastard a favour, putting him out of his misery like that.
Even if the polis ever found out it was him that had done it, they should thank him, not bang him up. He'd saved them a lot of work, for Lennie was forever getting lifted and jailed for his drug dealing. Aye, I've saved the cops a lot of work, he nodded to himself.
Now of course the only thing that was going to keep himself out of the jail and out of the polis hands was finding that wee junkie lassie who was trying to score off Lennie.
He had made his mind up.
He had to find her, the junkie that Lennie Robertson had called Maggie. Like it or not, she saw him attack Lennie and if the polis ever captured her for anything, anything at all, she'd give him up. His description and what she saw would be her get out of jail free card.
Teeth gritted, he beat rhythmically at the quilt cover with his fists, racking his brains as to how he might track her down.
But then he smiled.
If anyone knew the junkies in the Maryhill and Possil areas, it would be his old pal, Jackie Stone.
The problem is though, his brow furrowed, what story would he tell Jackie that would persuade him to give up the girl's address without alerting the dealer to why McMenamin wanted to find her.

The young woman called Maggie who was in Kieran McMenamin's thoughts was at that time squatting in the shadow of the building on the corner of Sauchiehall Street and Holland Street, a McDonalds paper cup between her feet, her knees drawn up and her arms wrapped tightly about her, for though it was a bright, warm morning and she was wearing her heavy black coat, Maggie Dalrymple was cold.

Her weary, wasted body, deprived for so long of nutritious food and sustenance, could no longer tolerate or fight off even the mildest of weather conditions, let alone the infection she incurred weeks before from the use of a shared needle.
In simple terms, she was dying though the date of her death was yet to be determined.
The pedestrians who hurried by the young woman either paid her no heed or were too embarrassed by her condition to acknowledge her and so her pitiful paper cup remained empty.
She had sat there for almost two hours, her fingers and toes numb and hovering between shivering consciousness and sleep as the chill from the shadowed building ate into her bones.
She didn't notice the elderly lady who walking by, slowed as she passed her then stopped. Leaning on her cane, she stared curiously at Dalrymple.
She paid no attention when the woman shuffled a few yards further on and then glancing about her, nervously tugged at her hijab and took a deep breath.
She was unaware of the woman slipping into a nearby takeaway shop and a few moments later, returning with a polystyrene cup of lentil soup.
She felt the gentle tap on her shoulder and eyes flickering as though uncomprehending, glanced upwards at the brown face of the woman who bent over, smiled and said, "As-salamu alaykum," and then in a heavily accented voice, add, "Please take," while offering the cup of soup towards the younger woman.
Startled, Dalrymple took the polystyrene cup and felt the heat of the soup flow through her fingers.
"Thank you," she mumbled, but the woman had straightened up and was already moving away.
She watched the woman walk off and carefully removing the lid from the cup, sipped at the scalding soup. As she stared into the cup, her eyes were moist at the simple act of charity and shoulders gently shuddering, she began to weep.
It took her almost five minutes to finish the soup, by then lukewarm and even though her stomach rebelled she managed to keep it down. With a satisfying sigh, she tipped the cup upwards to drain it of the final drops, then licked at the inside of the cup before using her fingers to scoop at remained of the vegetables at the bottom. Her

eyes narrowed at the state of her fingers, her once clipped and polished nails now dirt encrusted and chewed.

The soup, the first food she had consumed in almost thirty-six hours, had brought a fresh strength and revived her and using the wall, she pushed herself to her feet, ignoring the scornful glances of two young women who passing by, giggled at the state of her.

Embarrassed, she stooped to collect her paper cup then seeing it remained empty, threw it to one side.

Her watch had long ago been bartered for a hit, so she could only guess at the time and thought it to be midday.

Taking a deep breath, she decided there was no point in sitting about and she was too tired and too weak to attempt shoplifting in the stores further along towards the city centre.

Forcing one foot in front of the other, she began to make her way towards Charing Cross before the long walk back to the squat in the old tenement building in Napiershall Street.

It was as she was passing Charing Cross that she remembered.

One hand to her mouth, she stopped dead and gave a silent scream as she recalled the guy jumping from the bushes and attacking Lennie.

Seated at her desk, Myra McColl, now the Senior Investigating Officer in her first murder since being promoted to Detective Inspector, was irked that so far all they had achieved was identifying the victim as Leonard Robertson. No witnesses, no Forensic evidence of any use, though in fairness there might be something from under the victim's fingernails, she reminded herself, but not a bloody clue yet who had strangled the junkie.

Now, with DS Calum Fraser sat quietly in a chair in the corner to her left, she stared curiously at the nervous woman and the constable who sat before her and thought of all the people to turn up with what might prove to be something of crucial importance, it had to be Popeye Doyle.

She leaned forward onto her elbows, her hands clasped under her chin and with a reassuring smile, said, "Right, Missus Harris, or can I call you Mary?"

"Aye, of course, dear."

"Good. Well, I'm Myra and that makes it a bit easier all round, eh? Now, once again and let me see if I've got this right. From what you're telling me, you were looking after your neighbours two

young children…"
"Just to give her a wee break."
"Aye, good. So, you've one in the buggy, the wee girl and the wee boy is walking with you in Ruchill Park. You're pushing the buggy up the hill towards the area that's called the flagpole when you see a young man walking a short distance away in the bushes and who seems to be walking in the same direction. Correct?"
"Aye, that's correct," Mary nodded.
"You said you didn't think this young man had seen you or he didn't seem to be paying attention to you. Is that correct?"
"Aye, that's correct."
"The young man was then walking ahead of you and left the bushes to walk on the path in front of you, but still heading up towards the flagpole?"
Mary nodded.
"But you were wary because you believe you had seen the same young man earlier in the day, hanging about the corner opposite the charity shop where you volunteer part-time. Because of this you decided there was something not quite right about the young man so decided to turn back and didn't continue to the flagpole. Correct?"
Mary nodded, but her face was downcast for though at the time it has seemed so suspicious seeing the same young man three times in one day, the woman detective made it sound anything but and that it was simply a set of coincidences.
"Tell me again, please Mary, when you saw the young man twice on the corner, you were suspicious why?"
She shrugged and feeling a little foolish now, replied, "It was just the way he was acting," then glancing about, added, "Can I show you what I mean?"
McColl sat back in her seat and with a wave of her hand said, "By all means, yes please."
A little self-consciously, Mary got to her feet and with a quick glance at Doyle, said, "If you imagine this is the corner where the pub is at the Cross," she formed her hands into a right angle, "the young guy was doing this."
At that she craned her head forward as though peeking round a corner, then quickly withdrew it.
"As though he was hiding?" suggested McColl.

"Yes, exactly," Mary nodded, then continued, "And the second time I saw him, he had his hood up over his head and…" she stopped, her eyes fixed on a point above McColl's head and smiled.

"Mary?" McColl said.

"It was his hoodie," the older woman's eyes opened wide and she smiled with sudden realisation. "That's what was wrapped round his waist when I saw him again in the park. His hoodie," she beamed at McColl and turning, grinned at Doyle.

McColl turned and with a blank expression, glanced at Fraser before saying, "Mary, to reiterate, when you saw the young man at the corner…"

"Yes," Mary, seated again and now satisfied she wasn't being overly suspicious, interrupted, "when I saw him the first time he was acting strangely. When I saw him the second time, like I said he had his hood up and he ducked behind the corner when a police van was passing by. Now *that* made me really suspicious."

"And you are absolutely, one hundred per cent convinced it was the same young man you saw in the park later the same afternoon?"

"Yes, absolutely certain," Mary replied with a confident smile.

"But you didn't see anyone else? You didn't see this young man meet with someone?"

"No."

"Nor did you hear anyone else, no shouting or screaming, nothing like that?"

"No," Mary firmly replied.

McColl paused before opening her hands wide and said, "Mary, though of course I can't disclose details of our investigation, I can tell you that what you have told me and DS Fraser *is* very significant. All that remains now is that Calum here," she nodded to Fraser, "will take your formal statement and then we will arrange for you to view a number of photographs of young men of a similar age and description. While there is nothing to indicate this young man is responsible or the individual we are looking for, it is of course vital that we find him if for nothing else to eliminate him from our inquiry. I assume you will be able to identify this young man again?"

Mary paused before slowly nodding her head, but her hesitation was not lost on McColl who leaning forward, continued. "You have nothing to fear, Mary. For one, nobody other than my investigating team and Constable Doyle here knows that you are now a witness in this inquiry. If and I'm confident *when* we arrest the individual who murdered this young man Robertson, there likely will be a trial, but rest assured, your wellbeing and safety will be of paramount importance to us. You have my word on that and as I said, there is nothing to indicate the man you saw is the killer."

"Thank you, I understand," Mary quietly replied.

"Now," McColl turned again to Fraser, "please take Mary to an interview room and I presume we have photographic books available?"

Fraser grimaced when he replied, "We have, but how up to date they are, I'm not certain."

"No matter, I'm sure we'll turn something up," she cheerfully said, but more for Mary's benefit than confidence in the system.

"Popeye," she turned to him, "please wait for a moment."

Standing, she leaned across the desk to shake Mary's hand and waited till both she and Fraser had left the room before indicating Doyle close the door.

When they had resumed their seats, she said, "Well done. Any thoughts on who this guy might be?"

He slowly shook his head and replied, "Take your pick from a couple of hundred who live locally, Myra, and that's even assuming the guy *is* local. The description Mary gave me is a bit vague, but again, she's not a professional witness. What I am certain of is that Mary is a sharp woman and in the time I've known her, I believe she's not one to exaggerate. If she thinks the guy she saw was up to no good, then I believe her. Whether or not he's your killer," he shrugged and smiled, "when you find him, you can ask him."

His brow furrowed when he continued, "One thing that does niggle is that about the times that Mary saw the guy hanging about the Cross there were two muggings that occurred nearby. Now, from what Mary tells us, the guy she saw was standing directly across the road from the bank and that's where there's an ATM set in the wall."

"Ah," she remembered, but slightly annoyed with herself that she was so focused on the murder she hadn't given the street robberies any thought. "The old lady in Saracen Street and the man in Balmore Road? What, you think that our man might be involved in those?"

"Not beyond reasonable assumption," he shrugged again before adding, "It's very coincidental that he's hanging about there and then seen later at what proved to be the locus of a murder."

"The old lady…"
"Missus Henderson," he interjected.
"Yes. Have you followed up on that? I mean, has Calum Fraser spoken with you about your telephone call to Harry Cavanagh?"
"No," he replied, but was almost immediately wary.
"No matter," she indifferently smiled, then standing, added in dismissal, "Right then, again Popeye, thanks for bringing Missus Harris to us. If your sergeant wonders why you're off patrol, refer her to me."
"Oh, don't worry about that, Ma'am," he smiled in return, "I think that wee issue is already resolved.

He finally found an empty bay in the high rise car park and locking the Focus, followed the signs that directed him to Ward sixty-seven of the Neurological Unit.
The Staff Nurse who opened the security door for Harry Henderson stared at the suntanned man in the rumpled white linen suit, her face reflecting her curiosity as to who he had come to visit.
"Missus Harriet Henderson," he smiled disarmingly at her.
"Oh, right, come away in," she stood back to permit him to pass him by, then led him to a room further down the quiet corridor.
"It's not really visiting times," she explained, "but Harriet's notes said that her nephew would be arriving from abroad and to allow you to see her. That will be you then?"
"That'll be me," he confirmed with a nod and then to her unasked question, added, "Cuba."
"Oh my, you have travelled some distance," she smiled with surprise and opened a door into the room.
He felt his chest tighten when he saw his aunt lying unconscious on the bed, her white hair spread about the pillow and framing her pale face.
"Is there someone who can give me an update on her condition?" he asked.
"If you take a seat, eh, Mister…"
"Henderson. Harry Henderson."
He did as he was bid and reached out for his aunt's hand, surprised how cold and frail it seemed. He sat there for what seemed like five or more minutes with memories of the sharp tongued, but loving aunt who had raised him before the door opened to admit a pretty

young dark haired woman, a girl almost, who carried a brown cardboard file with her. Around her neck hung a stethoscope, worn as though it were some sort of declaration lest any unsuspecting member of the public not realise she was a doctor.

"Mister Henderson? My name's Jill McGhee. I'm the duty doctor for the minute," she smiled, displaying a brilliant white set of even teeth that seemed to Harry like an orthodontist's television advert.

"Now, let me see," she placed then opened the file on the foot of the bed. "Missus Henderson was admitted with what we initially diagnosed as a compressed fracture of the endocranium…" she paused then explained, "those are the bones that support the brain. Anyway, our information is that your aunt was attacked and it seems she fell heavily onto her head here," and with her left hand, indicated the back of her head. "The result of the blow when she landed on what seems to be something solid caused intracranial pressure and resulted in subdural haematoma or more commonly referred to as bleeding on the brain. Do you follow?"

"Yes," he slowly nodded, "but my immediate concern, Doctor, is what are her chances of making a full recovery?"

He didn't miss the hesitation before she replied, "You have to realise that Missus Henderson is not a young woman and, well, to be perfectly blunt, we really don't know."

"And what treatment are you providing?"

She didn't immediately respond, but then slowly replied, "The *consultant* has decided that for the minute we make Missus Henderson comfortable. He does not believe that she would survive intrusive surgery."

"But what do *you* believe?"

He watched her throat tighten and knew he was putting the young woman on the spot and guessed how uncomfortable she must be, however, her discomfort wasn't his problem, but his aunt Harriet's wellbeing was.

He closely stared at the young doctor and could only guess at the difficulty she was going through, but she surprised him when she quietly replied, "It's not really my place to make such a surgical decision, Mister Henderson," she glanced nervously behind her at the closed door before continuing in a soft voice, "but if I where the doctor in charge of your aunt, I believe I would consider surgery."

He glanced at his aunt, a frail woman in her early eighties and his eyes narrowed, for that's when it struck him. Though he would never admit to it, the likely real reason the consultant would not consider her surgery was the cost of such surgery against her possible survival.

He didn't immediately answer, then nodding, said, "Thank you for your honesty, Doctor. Who exactly is the consultant I should speak with?"

He saw her blanch and she was about to respond, but he held his hand up and with a grim smile, said, "Your candour won't be disclosed by me, doctor. Believe me, it's not just the medical profession that can keep a confidence."

The young woman visibly relaxed and replied, "Mister Jensen. He's not available right now because he's in surgery and likely won't be till sometime tomorrow. If you wish I can make an appointment for you?"

He glanced at his aunt and wondered if by tomorrow an appointment would be necessary, but nodded and said, "Please, yes."

"I'll get that arranged and see you're informed of the time before you leave, Mister Henderson and one other thing," she glanced at the file in her hand. "We have a Mister Cavanagh down as the point of contact for Missus Henderson. The thing is, if her condition should deteriorate I assume you would wish to be informed as soon as possible?"

He understood and fetching his mobile phone from his jacket pocket, provided McGhee with the number that she noted on the file.

McGhee was about to leave the room when she stopped and turning said, "Have you travelled far?"

His quizzical glance caused her to add, "You're very suntanned and, well, we don't see many white linen suits and Panama hats here in Glasgow, regardless of the time of the year."

He grinned and replied, "Cuba," but as the young woman left he glanced down at his suit jacket and thought it might be a good idea to get himself a change of clothes while he was here.

CHAPTER TWELVE

Shortly after his return to the Gartcosh Crime Campus, Danny McBride called three of his more competent staff to his office and asked the young analyst to close the door behind her before inviting them all to draw up chairs around his desk.

Glancing at them in turn, he stressed that what he was about to tell them would in the meantime remain between the four of them then proceeded to brief them on the Intelligence Report received from the Metropolitan Police Ports Control Unit at Gatwick Airport.

Recounting a summarised history of Harold Henderson, aka Headcase Henderson, aged fifty-seven years, a convicted murderer and primary suspect in the slaying of the McDonald brothers, William and Mickey, he continued and suggested that the three research the circumstances of the outstanding inquiry before commencing the tasks McBride had in store for them.

"Ma'am and I spoke with Henderson at Glasgow and put it to him that he was responsible for killing the McDonald brothers, but," he wryly shook his head, "while he said that neither of them was any loss to society, as you would suspect neither did he burst to killing them. Needless to say other than gossip and rumour, we have no evidence that he did murder the McDonald's. What he *did* tell us was that he had returned from Cuba because an elderly female relative had been admitted to hospital, but declined to provide any further information nor where he would be residing while he is here. Whether his story of a sick relative is true or not, right now we have no way of knowing."

He paused then continued, "Make no mistake, guys, Harry Henderson is a contract killer and the fact he's been out of the scene for a few years doesn't mean that he's not going to return to his old ways. He is one dangerous individual who is damned good at what he does and I say that without reservation because while through the years he is suspected for a number of murders, he's only been convicted for the one. So, if he *is* here for a hit, we stand a good chance of stopping and arresting him if we do our job properly."

"Okay, boss," said the male detective, "what do you need from us?"

"Malcom," he replied, "I spoke with the PCU at Glasgow Airport and they will trawl the CCTV footage of the passengers disembarking from Henderson's flight from Gatwick to see if they can obtain a good updated photograph of him." He smiled and added, "Henderson shouldn't be too hard to spot with his Panama hat and white suit. I want you to contact the PCU and provide your e-mail address for them to forward the photo. When that's done, print off a number of copies, say a dozen to begin with then contact the DCI in the Surveillance Unit and find out what resources she can call upon for an immediate job. Don't disclose what the job might be, just intimate that we might need a team at the rush. If there's any bitching and we both know what the bloody woman can be like," he grimaced, "don't take any crap from her. Simply refer her to Miss Mulgrew."

He turned to the younger of the two female analysts and said, "Alison. I know it's going to be a pain in the arse, but in the unlikely event Henderson *was* telling the truth, phone around the admission records of all the hospitals in the Greater Glasgow area and get a list of all elderly female patients who have been admitted within, say, the last five days. Obviously start with the name Henderson, but either way get a list that includes dates of birth, next of kin etcetera. If we don't have any luck, we'll cast our net wider. Yes," he grinned at her startled expression, "I know it will be painstaking and likely you'll have some of the records people complaining about Data Protection and all that crap, but it might be our only way to keep a track of Henderson while he's here."

Malcolm asked the question that was running through the minds of the three staff when he said, "We're guessing you and Ma'am believe he's spun you a yarn, that he's really here for some criminal purpose, boss?"

"Given his background, we can't afford to ignore the fact he is, Malcolm," nodded McBride who then turned to the second female analyst and said, "Jean. Trawl through Henderson's antecedent history and former list of associates. Somebody here must be expecting him to arrive. If he is here to do some damage, that person who has contracted him will be expecting him and if we can identify who it is then we might have an opportunity to identify Henderson's target. If he truthfully is here for an elderly relative, then again it's possible someone must have informed him of the woman's illness."

Jean raised her head from her notebook and asked, "What about the local cops in Cuba, Danny; the National Revolutionary Police Force. Is it worth contacting them to ask if they have any knowledge of Henderson over there? I mean, any recent visitors he might have had or somebody like that?"

He stared at her for a few seconds, surprised that she even knew anything about the Cuban police before replying, "Not such a bad idea, Jean, but if everything else fails we'll keep that on the back burner for now. But tell me, how the *hell* do you know what the polis out there are called?"

Jean blushed and replied, "I was over there on holiday a couple of years back with my partner. He's a big fan of Ernest Hemingway's books and dragged me round all the bars Hemingway frequented, most of which had cops patrolling outside because they're tourist traps and they're not averse to having a free drink with us travellers."

"Aye, well, if you can afford a holiday there I'll need to cut down your overtime hours," he quipped.

"Right then, any further suggestions? No?"

He waved at them, "Then get to it, people. Find out where Henderson is and why he's here."

He managed to find a parking bay in Howard Street and sipping a couple of pound coins into the machine, stuck the ticket on the inside of the windscreen before heading for the entrance to Slaters Menswear.

Stepping through the door, he smiled for it had been some time since he had worn anything other than shorts, brightly patterned shirts, open toed sandals and his trusty old Panama hat.

The young man who met him at the doorway on the first floor greeted him like an old friend and spent the next hour with Harry that resulted in his purchase of a half dozen dark blue coloured dress shirts, four ties, two each of navy or maroon colour, two off the peg navy coloured single breasted pinstriped suits that didn't require alteration, a selection of underwear, two pair of thick soled black brogues and finally,. A three-quarter length dark coloured rain coat. Recalling the hotel boasted a fitness room, he also purchased a pair of training shorts, a top and a pair of training shoes.

"Are you sure you don't want to look at something a little…brighter, sir? Say, something with a little colour?" the young assistant was clearly puzzled by Harry's almost funeral choice of outdoor clothing.

"No, I'm absolutely fine with these items," he smiled and as an added bonus for the assistant's solicitous attention, discreetly slipped the young man two crisp, folded twenty pound notes.

"Oh, thanks," the young man gushed and inquired if Harry needed any assistance with his purchases.

"Not at all," he replied. However, while living in Glasgow and before settling into his new life in Cuba, he had always dressed well and been almost fastidious about his appearance and so said, "but if you don't mind, I'll take a couple of minutes to change here and you can do me a favour by disposing of these clothes," he nodded to the linen suit, sandals, cotton shirt and almost with regret, the Panama hat.

"No problem, sir."

Fifteen minutes later, burdened with three black Slaters plastic bags and now wearing a dark blue shirt, maroon tie, one of the new suits and a pair of the brogue shoes, Harry returned to the parked car. However, had he been a little more observant, he might have seen the curiosity he evoked in the large man who seated in the driving seat of the Range Rover in the parking bay across the road, sat upright and keenly watched as Harry loaded the bags into the boot before driving off.

His eyes following the Focus as it turned into Stockwell Street, Sandy Craig lifted his mobile phone from the driver's door pocket and selecting a number from the directory, dialled.

When the call was answered, he smiled and said, "Hello there, Stevie boy. You remember Harry Headcase Henderson who skipped the country a few years back?"

He took a breath before adding, "Well guess what? It seems that Harry's back."

Waiting for the lift Kieran McMenamin tapped his fingers on the scratched and scored metal doors then impatiently kicked at them. At last the lift descended to the ground floor and without waiting for the elderly, well dressed woman to exit, pushed roughly past her and began to jab at the button for the ninth floor.

As the woman turned to remonstrate with him, he heard her say, "Dear me. Have you no patience, son?"

"Fuck off, ya old cow," he snarled at the stunned woman and as the doors hissed and closed, pretended to lunge at her, laughing when he heard her shriek and almost fall backwards as she tried to evade his grasp.

At last, the lift arrived at the ninth floor, but mindful of his last visit to Jackie Stone's flat he cautiously approached the door and placing his ear against it, listened to ensure there was no sounds of any beatings taking place within.

As satisfied as he could be he banged with his fist on the door, but prepared himself to run for the stairs if Stone was not alone or worse, if the cops were there.

"Who is it?" Stone's voice anxiously called out.

Almost with relief, McMenamin replied, "Jackie, it's me. Kieran. Open up, will you?

"Are you on your own?"

"Aye, for fucks sake," he slapped his palm against the chipped woodwork and hissed, "Open the door."

He listened to the rattle of a chain being loosened and then two keys turning in the Mortice locks before the door was cautiously opened by Stone who peering out at him, said in a low voice, "I'm rooked the now, wee man. I'm waiting on a delivery. If you come back in…"

However, McMenamin was in no mood to be stood at the door and pushed it against Stone who falling backwards, tried to cry out, but stopped when McMenamin raised a warning hand and said, "It's not smack I'm wanting, Jackie. It's something else."

Stone's eyes narrowed in suspicion and regaining his balance, slowly nodded as he turned towards the lounge door and said, "I don't have any dough, Kieran. I can't give you a bung, pal."

"It's not money I'm after," McMenamin patiently replied.

Walking through the hallway, he sniffed and smelled the distinctive odour of a smoked joint and realised what he hadn't noticed at the door; that Stone was high.

In the lounge, he saw the windows were wide open to freshen the room and inwardly smiled, thinking to himself, as if that would fool the polis if they kicked down the front door.

He sat down in the armchair while Stone, looking far older than his forty-two years and barefooted, was dressed in a stained Chelsea football top and blue tracksuit trousers.

Warily, he stared at McMenamin before slumping down onto the couch.

McMenamin could see Stone was just coming down from the high and felt that old familiar tingle in his veins as he wondered if he could persuade him to share some gear.

"So, what is it you want, Kieran?"

"My Nat King," he replied, grinned widely at Stone's surprised expression. "I've not had a shag for ages and I was wondering if you knew any local birds that might be looking for a hit for a wee deal of smack?"

Almost in disbelief, Stone stared at him and repeated, "Your hole? You mean you want me to set you up with a bird? For a deal?"

"Aye, do you know any birds?"

Befuddled, Stone nodded and replied, "Aye, I know a couple of birds that might do a turn for a deal of smack, but for fucks sake, Kieran. You could be talking about AIDS here, wee man. Are you off your head or what?"

McMenamin shrugged as though the risk of AIDS was not a problem and replied with a grin, "Look, I've shared needles before," he boasted, "and I'm always cautious, so trust me, Jackie my man. I'll not get AIDS. Now, do you know any birds that might be willing?"

"Do you not know any yourself?"

"Aye, but let's just say I'm looking for a change from the usual slags."

Stone slowly exhaled and then as if it just occurred to him, he said, "Did you hear about Lennie Robertson?"

McMenamin felt a cold chill creep up his spine and forcing himself to be calm, he tightly said, "No, what about him?"

"Got himself murdered up in Ruchill Park, I heard."

"Lennie Robertson? The junkie, you mean?"

"Aye, that's him," Stone slowly exhaled through pursed lips. "The word is that he'd owed somebody, but didn't pay. Anyway," he shrugged, "that's what people are saying."

"Aye, I think I've met him before or," McMenamin hastily added, "I might have heard his name mentioned. Have the polis been to speak to you about it?"

"Why would they speak to me," Stone was immediately alarmed. "I mean, I knew the guy, but for fuck's sake what would I know?"

"Just thought because Robertson was a junkie and you're on their radar, Jackie, they might have been up asking questions."

"Pish," he vigorously shook his head. "I've nothing to tell them."

They sat for a moment in uncomfortable silence, broken when Stone asked, "So, you're looking for a wee bird?"

"Can you help me out, pal?"

"Well," he drawled, "there's a young bird that does a turn for a hit, but I can't remember her name. About twenty or something. Black hair and always wears a long black coat. Speaks with a teuchter accent from up north or somewhere. Squats in a flat, one up in a funny kind of entrance to the close…" his eyes narrowed, "somewhere off Great Western Road I think it is. I dropped her in a hit at the squat once, a few months ago. She told me the place is a shitehole and fuck me, she wasn't kidding," he sniggered. "The flat's in an old Victorian tenement opposite a park," he narrowed his eyes, "and I think it's a doctor's surgery near to it too. Anyway, she's always fairly game for a hit, I mean, so I suppose she'll do you a turn."

He chortled with a schoolboy giggle and boastfully added, "I've shagged her a couple of times myself."

"How would I contact her if I was interested?"

"I don't know, unless you can find the squat and that's only if she's still staying there. Wait, no," his brow knitted as he recalled and raised a hand. "She sometimes hangs about Sauchiehall Street just along from Charing Cross. She's got a pitch there. Begging, I mean. At least, she did have, but I don't know if she's still hanging about there."

McMenamin refrained from the tingle of excitement, recalling the long black coat and certain in his bones that it was her, the lassie called Maggie.

"Ah, well, a bit too vague," he replied at last. "Do you not know anyone else?"

"There's always that Polish bird, her that hangs about the underground at St George's Cross," Stone sniggered.

"Aye, right, you're talking about Jolanta? No way, man," McMenamin forced a laugh and waved his hands across his body. "The last time I saw her she was on crutches because the veins in her legs had collapsed from too many injections."

"At least she wouldn't run off," Stone laughed uproariously.

"Anyone else?"

"Nah," Stone shook his head, "none that I can think of that don't have the AIDS or the Hep," he replied, referring to hepatitis.

"Well," McMenamin pushed himself to his feet, keen now to go on the hunt for Maggie, "I think I'll away and try to find my own bird, but before I go. Anything for me, Jackie? Anything at all?"

"Other than the stub of my last joint? I told you, Kieran. I'm waiting on a delivery, so if you come back, say, later tonight with some cash in hand?"

"Aye, well, we'll see," he replied and with a wave, left Stone sitting on the couch.

DI Myra McColl glanced up when her door was knocked, then pushed open by Detective Superintendent Cathy Mulgrew who said, "Not disturbing you, am I Myra?"

Getting to her feet, McColl replied, "Ma'am, not at all. Coffee?"

"That would be grand," Mulgrew smiled as she sat down in the chair in front of the desk.

Walking to the door, McColl beckoned forward a civilian analyst and said, "Any chance of two coffee's hen? Both with milk, please," before closing the door and returning to her seat.

"So, how is the inquiry progressing?" Mulgrew asked.

"Not as fast as I'd like," sighed McColl. "We had our first breakthrough his morning. One of the uniformed cops brought in a female witness who was walking in Ruchill Park about the time of the murder. Provided us with a description of a young man she saw walking through shrubbery towards the locus and recognised him as the same individual she had seen twice, earlier in the day, hanging about Saracen Cross about the same time that two assault and robberies were committed against a couple of pensioners."

"Is the woman a credible witness?"

"Seems to be," McColl pursed her lips. "The cop, Constable Doyle…"

"Is he the one they call Popeye?"

Surprised, McColl replied, "Do you know him, Ma'am?"

"Well, not really, but curiously I was in this office a couple of days ago passing on the Maryhill CID thanks to Chief Inspector Kane for some good Intel that Doyle had passed on. Anyway, sorry, I interrupted you."

"Oh, that's okay. Like I was saying, Doyle brought the lady to us and assures me that Missus Harris is a reputable and solid witness. However," her brow furrowed, "while I don't doubt she's telling us all she knows, her description could likely fit half the young men in the city, though she's confident she could identify him again."

"What about the two pensioners that were robbed. Can they provide a matching description that might tie it down to being the same suspect?"

"The old man who was robbed, he was dragged into the bushes and then thrown to the ground, searched and his wallet stolen after which he took a couple of kicks to the body."

She saw Mulgrew's lips tighten and added, "He's okay, Ma'am. Just a bit shaken after the attack. Unfortunately, he's half blind so other than telling us it was a young guy with a local accent wearing a hoodie who run off with some of his pension money and before you ask, he wouldn't be able to identify his attacker again."

"What about the second victim?"

The door knocked and was pushed open by a young woman who balanced two mugs of coffee on a plastic tray. Laying the tray down onto McColl's desk, she thanked the woman who smiled and left.

"The second victim, Ma'am," she handed Mulgrew a mug. "Regretfully, she was attacked in her close and suffered a head injury. I've allocated both inquiries to DS Calum Fraser and he's monitoring her condition. She remains unconscious for now and so we've been unable to obtain any kind of description of her assailant. Missus Henderson is an old lady in her eighties and…"

"Wait!" Mulgrew interrupted, more sharply than she intended. "Did you say her name is Henderson?"

"Aye, that's correct," McColl slowly replied.

"It's maybe just a coincidence, but do you have details of her next of kin?"

"Inquiry has so far failed to trace any relatives, Ma'am, but Popeye, I mean Constable Doyle spoke with a woman who cleans for Missus Henderson. She told Doyle that in any emergency, she was to contact an accountant called Harry Cavanagh who in turn would contact…"

"Her nephew, Harry Henderson," grinned Mulgrew.

McColl paused for a few seconds before eyes narrowing, she replied, "I think we're starting to read from the same page here, Ma'am. You know who Cavanagh and Henderson are?"

"Oh, aye, Myra. I know of Harry Cavanagh from old or rather I should say, of his reputation. And only this morning, I met with Mister Henderson who had just flown in from Cuba via Gatwick Airport. Now, if you don't mind, while I sit here enjoying my coffee,

I'd like you to phone Danny McBride at Gartcosh and you can tell him what you've just told me about Missus Henderson and if I'm not mistaken, I think Danny will be very pleased to hear from you."

Lying awake in her bed, Daisy Cooper yawned widely and wondered why it was that even though she had the best sleep of the nightshift, she still felt tired.
Forcing herself from the bed or rather, surrendering to the call of nature, she stumbled tiredly to the bathroom where after her ablutions she filled the bath with an aromatic bubble bath and lay soaking for almost thirty minutes.
Lying in the bath gave her time to ponder what she now knew and reflect on how she intended breaking the news.
Later in the bedroom, wrapped in her dressing gown and a towel about her wet hair, she glanced at the digital clock and saw that if as he'd promised Ian could persuade one of his assistants to lock-up, he'd be home in less than an hour.
Feeling revitalised after the bath, Daisy opened her wardrobe and selecting a half dozen outfits that she laid across the bed, finally chose a black, hip hugging dress that stopped a few inches above her knees.
Tonight, my girl, she thought with a smile, I'm going all out to dazzle my man, but then frowned as doubt took a hold of her.
Would it be enough?

He opened the boot of the Focus and retrieved the brightly coloured plastic bag, then turned and walked round the corner into Wellington Street.
He stopped and with an expectant smile glanced up at the ornate Victorian building before making his way towards the glass fronted entrance.
It had been some time since Harry had visited the building and he looked forward to renewing his friendship with his old pal, Harry Cavanagh.
Climbing the stairs to the second floor, he paused outside the door and after straightening his tie, pushed it open.
Seated at her desk, Cavanagh's secretary Helen, lifted her head as the door opened and her usual scowl was immediately replaced with a surprised grin as she leapt from behind her desk to throw herself at

Harry, squealing in delight as she wrapped her arms about his neck and smothered his cheeks with kisses.

"My favourite man!" she grinned at him, then her arms still wrapped about his neck, turned her head and with a foghorn voice, screamed, "Hoy! Harry! Get your arse out here to see who's arrived!" before turning her head back to him, then like a machinegun, rattled off, "Look at you, all suntanned and good-looking! How's Donna? Is she keeping well? Why did you not bring her with you? What did you bring me from Cuba?"

The door behind her opened to reveal the portly Cavanagh, spectacles sat atop his thinning hair, his garish tie undone and wide red braces holding up his suit trousers. Hands extended, he greeted Harry like the firm friend he was and said, "Good to see you, pal. Come away in."

Turning to Helen, he added, "Get the kettle on, hen."

Hands on short skirted hips, she scowled and replied, "Not before Harry tells me what he's brought me from Cuba."

"Ah," Harry smiled at her and from the plastic bag, fetched out a sky blue coloured, Cuban short sleeve Guayabera dress that he unfolded and held before her.

Her eyes widened and grabbing the dress from him, she murmured, "I love it!" before grabbing Harry's face in her hands and planting a noisy smacker on his lips.

"*Now* I'll get the kettle on," she grinned widely at him.

Leading Harry into his office, Cavanagh beckoned that he sit and his face widened with pleasure when Harry handed him a box of expensive Cuban cigars.

Opening the box, Cavanagh extracted then sniffed at a cigar and said, "Do you mind?"

"Go ahead," Harry waved at him and watched as he lit the cigar then deeply inhaled, but to Harry's quiet amusement almost immediately coughed his lungs out.

"God, it's been a while since I've smoked anything this good," Cavanagh spluttered and lifting a cup from a saucer, laid the cigar carefully down onto the saucer.

"Right then," he continued, "I take it you've been to visit Harriet?"

Harry nodded and recounted his discussion with the young Doctor McGhee.

Cavanagh slowly shook his head before replying, "I have to be honest, Harry. When I learned that Harriet had been injured I did consider getting her moved to one of the private hospitals for better care, but frankly," he sighed and again shook his head, "My research indicated the Neuro over at the new Queen Elizabeth is the centre for excellence and there isn't a private hospital that can match the treatment she will receive there."

"I've made an appointment for tomorrow to speak with her consultant, some guy called Jenson and I intend asking him why he won't operate."

"Have you considered that maybe the doctor you spoke with, this Doctor McGhee, has got it wrong? It seems to me that if Jensen is worried about Harriet's age, maybe he's right, maybe it *is* too risky for him to operate. I mean, we might be talking here about his experience over this lassie McGhee's inexperience."

"I thought about that and you're right," Harry nodded and let out a soft breath, "but I want him to tell me that. I don't want the information second hand."

"You mean what you really want is a second opinion," Cavanagh gently smiled.

Harry didn't get the opportunity to respond, for the door was opened by Helen who to their surprise, was wearing Harry's gift.

"What do you think?" she gushed as she laid the mugs down onto the desk and walking back and forth across the room, modelled the dress.

"Beautiful," Cavanagh smiled at her and glancing at the admiring man, it was then that Harry realised perhaps their relationship was what had been suspected by many over the years; a relationship that was more than employer and secretary.

When she'd left the room, Harry's expression became more serious when he asked, "Have you discovered anything at all about who did this to Harriet?"

Cavanagh slowly shook his head.

"We both know I've a web of people throughout the city and of course I put some feelers out, but all I learned was that there were two muggings within a short time in the Saracen area. An old man who got a kicking was robbed and Harriet. The Saracen polis don't have any suspects, but that might be because at the minute they're tied up with a murder inquiry. Some junkie strangled in Ruchill Park."

"The other mugging. Did the old man give a description?"

"That I don't know. My source," he smiled, knowing Harry Henderson could be utterly trusted, "she's a cleaner in the polis station. She's a smart cookie and always on the ball and passed me what she heard but to be honest, it's not that much. However, this guy that knows you, the cop Doyle. He might be the man to speak with. He's of the opinion that the guy who attacked Harriet was likely a junkie looking for cash."

"Doyle's been around for a long time now," Harry murmured, "so his opinion might be worth listening to. Is he the investigating officer? I thought it might be the CID who did the inquiry?"

"You're correct, of course. My cleaner tells me it's a Detective Sergeant Fraser who's dealing with Harriet's inquiry, but I haven't contacted him. I thought I'd wait and take direction from you before I phoned him."

"Leave that with me," Harry nodded.

His face twisted when he thought of his wee auntie Harriet being mugged and exhaling through pursed lips, spoke his thoughts aloud when he said, "Where there's a junkie, there's a local dealer and where there's a local dealer there's a local supplier. If I'm looking for the supplier," he turned to stare at Cavanagh, "where will I start?"

Cavanagh shrugged and replied, "We could be talking here about a guy called Nigel Faraday. Nobody had ever heard of Faraday when he muscled into the north side of the city. Came from nowhere with a pocketful of money and a head for finance. Doing very well so I hear and," he grimly smiled, "without *my* expertise which does rather surprise me. So," he leaned back in his chair and clasped his hands on his broad belly, "If you're looking for the local supplier for the north which of course will take in the Saracen area, Faraday's your man."

"How much do you know about him?"

"To my regret, very little. He runs a tight ship." His brow knitted when he continued, "There was talk of a few dissenters when he took over the running of the north side, but he always travels with a minder called Sandy Craig who…"

Harry held up a hand and interrupting, said, "Whoa! Sandy Craig who used to run with the Kinning Park team? Muscular guy with two little tear drops on the left side here," Harry used his fingers to indicate his own face, "just below the eye? Did some time for stabbing a copper? *That* Sandy Craig?"

"The very man," Cavanagh nodded. "As far as I'm away, Craig is much like your good self, Harry. Did time for the only one of the many crimes he committed and usually involving serious assault," he shook his head. "Anyway, as I was saying, Craig acts as Faraday's minder and driver." His eyes narrowed. "A white coloured Range Rover if memory serves me correctly. I find it rather odd Craig's working for Faraday because perhaps you won't recall, but another major player in the city these days is Stevie Watkins who I'm almost positive also run with the KP boys back then too."

His brow furrowed as from the recess of his mind he fought to recall the details, but then sighing, said, "Added to Craig's muscle, Faraday can call upon a number of thugs he hires who will at the drop of a hat make themselves available and not because they owe him any loyalty, but because he pays good cash in hand."

"And Faraday's address?"

"I'm told an executive flat somewhere on the Clydeside, but alas I do not have the exact details. You wish me to find out?"

"Wouldn't do any harm," Harry shrugged.

"Right," Cavanagh acknowledged and briskly rubbed his hands together. "Now, what's your plans while you're here? Your plans for this evening I mean?"

"I'm guessing you thought about taking me to dinner," Harry smiled, "but if it's all right with you, I'll head back over to the hospital and sit for a while with Harriet."

"That's to be expected, but here's what I'm thinking. The Hilton restaurant is open till late, so why don't I book a table for you and I for say, eight-thirty?"

"If you've no other plans?"

"Course I haven't," Cavanagh scoffed and then with a twinkle, added, "Would you mind if I brought Helen along? She'd only interrogate me tomorrow about everything anyway, so maybe better if she hears how you and Donna are doing, first hand."

"I'd be unhappy if you didn't bring her," Harry replied, once more endearing himself to his old friend.

"On that point," Cavanagh smiled at him. "Have you spoken with the lovely Donna since you arrived?"

Harry grimaced and shaking his head, replied, "I did intend giving her a call from a public phone at the airport, but thought it was too risky for both Gatwick and Glasgow are littered with CCTV cameras and I worried that I might be watched when I landed at both airports. If the cops saw me on a phone, they'd simply obtain a billing list from the phone and with the CCTV recording the time of the call, trace my home number in Cuba. It might have caused me all sort of complications. However, I gave her a quick call from the hotel just to let her know I'd arrived safely, but that's it so at least she knows I'm okay."

"Very wise of you. I'm sure she'll have been worried," Cavanagh nodded. "What about your arrival in the UK? Were there any other problems?"

"Maybe, but before I forget," he smiled. "Thank you for the contents of the package you had waiting for me at the hotel. As for other problems, I was hoping to keep a low profile, but I got a pull at Gatwick, probably because of my passport going through their machine and then again at Glasgow Airport from a female Detective Superintendent called Mulgrew and a DI Danny McBride. His name rang a bell, but I couldn't recall about what."

Cavanagh, his mind like a computer filing system, narrowed his eyes and replied, "Mulgrew? Good looking woman?"

"That'll be here," Harry smiled.

"I recall her name from one of the countless investigations the police have made into my affairs through the years, but McBride, yes; I know that name. He's the guy who was a witness when a cop and that bastard Brian Murphy fell from the top of a multi-storey building over in the south side of the city. McBride said his mate, the cop, was attacked by Murphy."

"Oh, yes," Harry slowly nodded, "I remember now."

He didn't think it necessary to tell Cavanagh that Wally McDonald had contracted Harry to kill Murphy and that Murphy's fortuitous demise with the unfortunate policeman saved him the job.

"What did this woman Mulgrew and McBride want?"

Harry smiled before replying, "Asked me if I bumped off the McDonald brothers."

"Ah," Cavanagh smiled too. "If they had any evidence you'd have been arrested so it sounds like you *might* be in the clear. What did you tell them about being here, back in Glasgow I mean?"

"Just admitted I was back to visit an elderly aunt, but not who or where she is or what happened."

"Perhaps just as well, though if the police put two and two together after that call I got from the guy Doyle, likely they will have worked it out by now."

"No matter," Harry shrugged. "I don't intend doing anything other than finding out who mugged Harriet."

"And when you do find them?"

"Better you don't know," he grimly smiled.

CHAPTER THIRTEEN

Ian MacLeod parked the car and sauntered wearily towards the front door. As much as he was looking forward to spending time with Daisy, the last thing he really wanted was to get dressed and go out, preferring instead to get something in and snuggling up with his fiancé on the couch in front of the television.

However, when he opened the door and saw her stood waiting for him in the hallway, his eyes opened and he changed his mind.

"Wow, you look stunning," he grinned at her.

"Good enough to show off in public?" she twirled and teased him.

"Oh, yeah," he nodded and moved forward to embrace her.

"Right, well, get yourself showered, Mister MacLeod, and I've laid out your clothes for you, so don't to be too long. I thought about ordering a taxi, but I decided I'll drive and you can have a couple of beers," she smiled.

"What? You're not drinking?"

"No," she sighed, disliking herself for the subterfuge. "I've just finished an exhausting nightshift and one glass will send me straight to bed and besides…" she narrowed her eyes, "I've other plans for when we get home, so I'll need to be wide awake."

He began to unbutton his shirt and with a grin, said, "Six o'clock, you say? Well, in that case I don't suppose there's time for…"

"No, there's not," she firmly replied, but with a smile and pushed him towards the bathroom.

He had walked up and down Napiershall Street twice and was fairly certain that the Victorian tenement opposite the parkland and adjacent to the medical centre was the building that Jackie Stone had spoken about. The problem was he didn't know which of the four close entrances led to the first floor flat for there were several entrances to shops and businesses that occupied the ground floors of the building. A further problem was that all the closes had secure entrances.

It occurred to Kieran McMenamin that he might hang about the bushes opposite the flats, but the building stretched around a corner towards Maryhill Road and he might easily miss the lassie Maggie if she passed by and besides, Stone had said he wasn't even certain if she still squatted there.

His eyes narrowed at a comment Stone had made, something about a funny kind of entrance to the close.

He glanced across the road towards a set of wide stairs that led from the pavement up towards what seemed to be the back court of the building.

He had made his decision.

Checking the roadway was clear, he pulled his hood up over his head and crossed over towards the stairs then made his way up to a metal gate that when he pushed at it, opened with a loud creaking noise.

He could see that to his left and his right were rear entrances to closes.

With growing confidence that he was in the right place, he moved left, but the close had a secure door that was locked and he reasoned that if Maggie *was* squatting, she probably didn't have a key to the close.

Mentally crossing his fingers, he moved to the close on the right where he saw the door was ajar and pushing it open made his way into the dark and foul smelling entrance.

Holding his breath against the fetid odour, he gingerly stepped among the refuse that was on the ground and came to a badly scarred, wooden door with nothing to indicate who lived there. Hesitantly, he pushed at the door and to his surprise, it swung slightly open.

Tempted as he was to call out, he held his tongue and breathing heavily, pushed the door further open, grimacing when it squeaked on rusting hinges as he quietly stepped through onto bare floorboards.

He guessed that the flats windows must have been covered over for the hallway was in darkness.

He held his nose between a forefinger and thumb against the smell of decay and rotten food, but particularly the stink coming from the room he suspected to be the bathroom. As he moved through the flat, peeking his head into room after room, he saw what seemed to be makeshift beds made up of old blankets and coats and realised that there was more than one person living there, though from the amount of rubbish in the rooms thought the occupants' tenancy was as squatters.

Checking the last of the rooms, he saw it to be unoccupied and breathed a sigh of relief.

As satisfied as he could be that he had discovered where the lassie Maggie was holed up, he decided that he wouldn't remaining in the stinking flat, but hang about outside for a couple of hours and wait to see if she returned there.

Sandy Craig reversed the Range Rover into a parking bay and thumbing through his phone directory, pressed the green button at Nigel Faraday's number.

"That's me downstairs when you're ready, boss," he told Faraday.

"Good, give me ten minutes," snapped Faraday and ended the call.

Craig sighed and returning the mobile phone to his pocket, thought about the man he had seen earlier in the day in Howard Street.

Harry Headcase Henderson, he smiled humourlessly.

Now, he idly wondered, what brought a bad bastard like him back to Glasgow?

The word was that Harry, never fond of his nickname he recalled, had got out of the city ahead of the polis posse just about the time that old Wally McDonald's sons Billy and Mickey had been done in. Fucked off and if further rumour was true, with old Wally's widow, Donna.

The rumour at the time was Harry was responsible for the murders, though as far as Craig knew, nobody had ever been convicted.

He startled when the rear door was pulled open and climbing in, Faraday said, "Good evening, Sandy. Take me to Ashton Lane."

"Boss," Craig replied and switching on the engine, but thought, whatever happened to 'please', you jumped up wee shite?

As he drove, he glanced in the rear-view mirror and seeing Faraday was cleanly shaved and wearing a suit, asked, "Big date tonight, boss?"

"An old acquaintance, Sandy. Somebody who owes me a favour." Several minutes passed before Faraday leaned forward and tapping Craig on the shoulder, said, "Tell me this. Have you happened to notice anyone or any vehicles paying particular attention to our coming and goings, Sandy?"

"What, you mean like the polis, boss? Like surveillance?"

"Yes, exactly."

"No," Craig shook his head. "Can't say that I have. Should I be keeping an eye open for them from now on?"

"I believe that it might be prudent to keep a weather eye open for our friends in blue," Faraday sat back into his seat. "I have the distinct feeling that they might have recently taken an interest in our activities. However, hopefully by tomorrow I will be in a better position to advise you."

Craig didn't respond, but his mind was working overtime and if he was correct, then Faraday was inferring he had someone in the polis who could provide him with information.

Now, he inwardly grinned, that would be someone worth knowing and decided when he'd dropped Faraday at Ashton Lane, he'd give Stevie Watkins another wee phone call.

He was handing in his Airwave radio and about to go off duty when Fariq Mansoor walked through the door, a piece of paper clutched in his hand.

"Popeye, that wee woman who we visited today in the charity shop," he handed Doyle the paper. "Is this related, do you think?"

He read the note and quietly asked, "When did this come in?"

"Couple of minutes ago. The bar officer knows we're going off duty and asked if we'd hand it on to the late shift to attend to it."

Doyle sighed and his shoulders visibly slumped. Reaching for a radio, he inserted a fresh battery and told Mansoor, "Before you go home, son, telephone the control room and inform them to mark me down for this call."

She was fortunate to find a parking bay relatively close to Ashton Lane where after parking her car then hand in hand, Daisy and Ian strolled slowly towards the restaurant entrance.
They were pleased the staff recognised them both and greeting them with smiles, showed them to a darkened booth at the rear of the room.
Their food order noted, they sat enjoying each other's company, Ian sipping at his beer while Daisy toyed with her freshly crushed orange and mutually agreeing to defer their discussion about the business till after their meal.
They were halfway through their main course when Daisy's attention was taken by a fair haired, handsome man who entered the restaurant alone and was shown to a table just out of sight of their booth.
For some unclear reason, he seemed familiar and while it puzzled her, she almost dismissed him until a few minutes later she saw a face that was familiar to her enter and almost immediately, was directed to a table in the same area as had been the man.
"Something wrong?"
She turned to Ian and smiled before replying, "No, love. Just someone who took my attention there. Nothing that will disturb us tonight.
"You're off duty, Sergeant Cooper," he gently chided her then pointing with his fork, added, "so concentrate on that excellent grub."
"Yes, sir," she pulled an obedient face, yet still couldn't get the couple out of her head.
It occurred to her that she could use the ladies' toilet, the door that was close by the table where the couple sat, but she thought that might be too obvious and dismissed the idea. No, she was out for a night with the man she loved and should concentrate on that, she decided and glancing at Ian, smiled happily.

He had been standing in the thick bushes in the park for what seemed like over an hour when he saw the figure shuffling up the road towards him, but it wasn't a woman, it was a young man who when he reached the stairs, glanced nervously about him before hurrying up and out of McMenamin's sight.

Junkie, he instantly dismissed the man and guessed he was one of the other occupants of the squat.
His brow furrowed in thought.
Should he go and question the junkie, find out if the lassie was still living there or hang on for another hour?
If he did return to the flat to ask the guy, it might show his hand and if the guy was her pal and tipped the lassie off that somebody was looking for her, she might not return there.
However, if he waited any longer in the bushes and she was no longer living there it was a complete waste of his time.
Impatient to get this over with, he made his decision and again pulling his hood up over his head, made his way across the road.

Identifying himself as Harriet's nephew, the smiling nurse pressed the button that permitted Harry entrance to the ward and confirming he knew where his aunt's room was, she left him to attend to another patient.
He was about to push open the door when through the window he saw a nurse and a tall, bearded man wearing a brown suit who Harry immediately and correctly guessed to be CID.
He hadn't been seen by either the nurse or the detective and for an instant was undecided whether or not to enter the room, for to do so would identify him to the detective to be Harry Henderson, convicted murderer and well known to the police.
As it was, the decision was taken from him for the detective turned and saw him.
Pushing open the door, Harry smiled and said, "Sorry, am I disturbing you?"
To his surprise, the detective extended his hand and said, "Mister Henderson? My name's DS Calum Fraser. I'm the officer assigned to your aunt's inquiry. I've just popped by to see if there is any change in her condition."
Shaking his hand, Harry replied, "Couldn't you have saved yourself a trip with a phone call, Mister Fraser?"
"Probably," Fraser smiled, "but I was over this way making a call about another inquiry anyway, so I didn't think it would do any harm to give the lady a visit, just on the off chance she might have been conscious. However," he sighed as he turned to glance down at the elderly lady, "it seems there is no change."

"If you gentlemen will excuse me," said the nurse, who slipped by Harry as she left the room.

"Are you any further forward in finding who did this?"

"I'm afraid not," Fraser shook his head, then staring keenly at Harry, added, "I understand that you might have some…" he hesitated before continuing, "connections in the Maryhill and Saracen areas, Mister Henderson. I'd be grateful if you hear anything and pass it to me."

Harry stared at him without responding, then slowly smiled.

"Let's not beat about the bush, DS Fraser. I'll presume you know of me and what my previous history was so let me be unequivocally clear," he quietly said. "I have returned to Glasgow because of my aunt's assault. You'll know that having been released on licence for a murder conviction, I'm restricted from associating with anyone in the criminal fraternity, therefore while I am here in Glasgow I have no intention of associating with *anyone* from my criminal past because frankly, I have no desire to return to prison. If the individual who did this is caught, then I will assume he will go to prison and I can get on with my life. If he is not caught and I do learn of his or her name…" he didn't complete the sentence.

However, as far as Fraser was concerned, the inferred threat was there and so he replied, "I have to inform you, Mister Henderson, that because of the circumstances of your relationship with the victim and your previous criminal history, if you in any way interfere with my investigation you could find yourself being the subject of police interest."

Harry softly smiled at the younger man and replied, "Listen, DS Fraser, because I don't think you're getting the message here. My wee aunt is a harmless wee woman who was widowed young, but raised me as her own and loved me as I love her and I have no intention of permitting the bastard that hurt her to get away with it. So, here's my thought. You guys catch him or her before I do and there will *be* no problem. Understood?"

Fraser was a younger man, but not easily impressed or intimidated by Harry's reputation and so replied, "It seems you and I have the same goal, Mister Henderson, but don't forget that if anybody turns up dead and we link that death to your aunt, you're the first suspect."

"Fair's fair," Harry opened his hands wide in acknowledgement and nodded.

Fraser turned towards the door and opening it, stopped to say, "For what it's worth, I hope she does recover, Mister Henderson. If there is anything that I can do that does *not* involve or assist you in committing a crime, you can contact me at Saracen office."
"Thanks for that," Harry nodded and watched as Fraser closed the door.
Placing a seat against the side of the bed, he sat down and taking his unconscious aunt's hand in his, softly said, "So, Aunt Harriet, I think that went well, don't you?"

Hesitating and preparing himself before knocking on the door, he decided to remove his cap.
He heard the footsteps approach and when it was opened, saw her smile in recognition, but his expression must have given him away for as she stared at him he saw the tears in her eyes forming as she reached a hand to her throat.
"I'm so sorry, Mary, so very, very sorry," said Popeye Doyle, then stepping forward he wrapped a supportive arm about her, using his other hand to push the door closed behind him as he led the weeping Mary to the kitchen.

Their sweet finished and a second bottle of beer ordered for Ian, Daisy's curiosity was getting the better of her and keen to see if the couple were still at their table, was about to excuse herself to visit the loo when the elderly owner of the restaurant in his crisp whites, attended at their table.
"My good friends," the elderly Abu Bakr greeted Daisy and Ian with a handshake and though his English was poor, he was accompanied by his niece who discreetly stood by his side and interpreted for him.
"Granddad asks if your meal was sufficient, but I think he means was it okay," she hid her smile.
"Tell him that if he's looking for a job," Ian grinned, "to come and see me at our café on Byres Road."
The offer caused the old man to break into a giggle and laughing, after a further handshake he waved goodbye and returned to the kitchen.
However his niece, a girl in her late teens with a broad Glasgow accent, stood shyly staring at Daisy before asking, "You're the

police lady, aren't you Miss?"
"Yes, I am," Daisy smiled.
"My cousin's always talking about you," she gushed a little more confidently. "He works in the same place you do and he's always telling us about you being a hero."
"Oh," her face reddened, "who's that then?"
"Furry. I mean, Fariq. We call him Furry because he's such a hairy bugger," then broke into her own fit of giggling.
"Oh, Fariq Mansoor. Yes, we're colleagues and he's a very good policeman and will do well in the service," she added, knowing it would please the girl who undoubtedly would relate the conversation to her family.
The girl excused herself and Daisy took the opportunity to leave the table on the pretence of attending the toilet, but when she approached the area of the table the couple had been sat at, she was a little disappointed to find it empty and presumed she had missed them leaving the restaurant.
Still, as she pushed through the door to the toilets, it troubled her that she had seen the dark haired man before and continued to wonder who he was.
It was later when driving home, she remembered.
Though his name didn't come to mind she was certain she had seen his photograph on an intelligence bulletin.

Harry arrived at the Hilton restaurant a little after eight-thirty and was directed to a table where he found Harry Cavanagh and Helen, still wearing her new dress, sipping cocktails.
"How's, Harriet?" Cavanagh asked.
"No change," Harry shook his head and smiled when Helen stood to come round to his side of the table to plant a kiss on his cheek.
Cavanagh waved over the young waiter and after ordering their meals, turned to Helen and said, "Undoubtedly pretty as you are, my dear, would consider taking a few moments to freshen your make-up?"
Wordlessly, Helen slid from her chair and walking from the table towards the foyer area, Harry noticed it wasn't just he and Cavanagh's eyes that followed the shapely young woman.
"I had a curious phone call from Stevie Watkins just before I left the office this afternoon," Cavanagh said. "Do you remember him?"

Harry shook his head and replied, "Should I?"

"Perhaps not," Cavanagh sighed and continued in a low voice, "He's the guy I mentioned who run with the Kinning Park team at the same time as Sandy Craig."

"Ah, I do recall you mentioning him."

"Anyway, when you left to join Donna, Watkins was an up and coming dealer just before you retired to the sun and now runs most of the east side of Glasgow and I hear has extended his network to parts of Lanarkshire too."

"What was the call about?"

"Well," Cavanagh drawled, "it seems that Watkins has learned you're back and wishes to meet with you. Told me he has a proposition for you."

Harry frowned and staring at Cavanagh, asked him, "If he wants to contact me how did he know to come to you?"

"It was no great secret, Harry, that after old Wally McDonald died and then when you…I mean, after his sons got knocked off, I helped Donna leave the country with what money I could raise from Wally's estate. You can also imagine that when Wally and his sons were dead, that left a vacuum in the north side of the city so," he grimaced, "given that I have a certain standing in the city for discretion and fairness, I was asked by a number of individuals to negotiate a settlement between those individuals who were keen to move in on Wally's area of operation." He stared keenly at Harry before adding, "Faraday and Watkins were two of those individuals. My part, for a fee of course, was simply to act as an arbitrator between these individuals to ensure that the transition of Wally's area of operation would occur without the necessity of gangland violence."

"And did it work?"

"Oh," he nodded with a smile, "I admit to being rather pleased with myself for though there was a modicum of bad feeling that resulted in the occasional shooting and slashing, it was nothing like what might have occurred if they had been left to deal with the situation themselves. Yes," he sighed, "I believe I did rather well, given the circumstances under which I was required to work."

"But that still doesn't explain how this guy Watkins knew to contact you about me."

"Ah, well, you of course recall that you didn't immediately leave the country after Donna, but spent some time settling your affairs, yes?" Harry slowly nodded.

"Well, during that time Watkins, who I have to say is a very devious individual and well worth the watching, approached me with an offer of employment for you, but," he held his hands up, "I took it upon myself on your behalf to refuse his offer simply because you had already intimated your intention to depart for Cuba. I hope I made the correct decision?"

"Yes, you did," Harry nodded then eyes narrowing, asked, "What did he want?"

"He's a very ambitious man is Stevie Watkins," he sighed, then continued, "As for Watkins contacting me today, I can only assume that having learned you were back he correctly assumed you would be in touch with me. How he discovered you were back," Cavanagh shrugged, "I've no idea."

Harry asked again, "Did Watkins say why he wished to contact me?"

"No, but it doesn't take a genius to work out what kind of work he might have for you.

Likely, he wants you to knock off some of his rival dealers."

"I'm not interested," Harry pursed his lips and added, "But if he phones again…"

He was interrupted by Cavanagh who passing him a slip of a paper, said, "Actually, he asked if you would give *him* a call. Stressed it would be worth your while."

An idea had been flitting through Harry's head and turning the slip of paper over in his hand, he said, "I assume I'm correct in thinking that Watkins will have knowledge of all the main dealers in Glasgow and that would include this guy Faraday who runs the Saracen area?"

"I suppose so," Cavanagh stared at him. "Why?"

"Just an idea," Harry softly smiled and courteously stood when Helen returned to the table.

It took them almost ten minutes to extricate themselves from the smiling staff of the Indian restaurant and stepping into Ashton Lane, Daisy turned towards Ian. Reaching up to kiss him, she stopped when she saw the CCTV camera that was angled to catch customers entering and exiting the door.

"What?" he stared suspiciously at her.

"Nothing," she grinned at him, an idea already forming in her head and taking his arm, they began to slowly make their way towards her parked car.

He listened before entering the smelly flat and heard a noise from a bedroom that faced the backcourts. A dim light could be seen from under the closed door and tiptoeing towards it, knocked on the door. "Who the fuck's that? Maggie? Piss off, I've no gear and no money, okay?"
Taking a deep breath that almost made him gag, McMenamin shoved open the door and raced in, catching the skinny, long-haired and bedraggled man by surprise as he pushed him against a wall, one hand at his throat and his fist raised as though to punch him.
"Who are you? What you want?" whined the man and even in the dim light McMenamin could see though he was older, perhaps in his thirties, he was frightened.
"I'm the DS! Where the fuck's the bird? Where's Maggie?" he snarled and with his open hand, slapped the man across the face.
The man's fear and confusion overtook his common sense for had he thought about it, the Drug Squad were unlikely to pay any attention to a lowlife junkie like him, but such was his terror that he thought only of his own safety and replied, "She's out. Begging. I saw her earlier in Sauchiehall Street, but she'll be back soon because she's no gear and she'll come looking to me for something! Honest, sir!"
"Where's your gear?"
"My gear?"
"Don't fuck with me! Where's your gear!"
"I've nothing, sir. Honest! I swear on my mother's grave!"
But McMenamin was having none of the man's lies and viciously slapped him again, this time drawing a sliver of blood from the man's mouth.
"There," he pointed with a shaky hand towards a small backpack, but then staring at McMenamin, his eyes narrowed and with sudden realisation, said, "You're not the polis! Who the fuck…"
But he got no further for McMenamin, his blood up, kneed him in the groin and taking a handful of his hair, battered the man's head off the wall then, for good measure, did it again until with a quiet sob, the man slid in a daze to the floor.

Shaking as the adrenalin raced through his body, he decided to teach the fallen man a lesson and savagely kicked at his body, time and time again until he was almost exhausted.

Then he heard a sob and turning, saw her stood in the doorway, her body framed in the dim light and her mouth open as shocked, she stared at him.

His face a sheen of sweat, he grinned at her and said, "Hello, Maggie. Nice to see you again."

CHAPTER FOURTEEN

Curiously, Mary Harris had a dreamless night or so she believed. When she awoke the sun was peeking through the crack in her bedroom curtain and lying there, it was almost a full minute before she remembered.

She clutched at the quilt with clenched hands.

Michael was dead; a heart attack the doctor had said.

She reached her hands towards her face and wearily rubbed at it as she recalled the events of the previous evening.

Popeye Doyle, bless him, coming to the door to break the news. Staying with her while she broke down in tears then as she sat nursing the tea he made her, fetching her phone book.

Hearing him phoning young Michael in Dorset in a firm, but quiet voice to break the sad news and then phoning New Zealand, but thoughtfully asking to first speak with Jenny's husband and telling him to break the news and thus lessen the shock of the phone call for his pregnant wife.

Then phoning Alice McLean, her fellow volunteer from the charity shop and asking her to come round and sit with Mary while he returned to the office to sign off duty. Returning later with his own car to drive her to the nursing home in Ibrox.

He brought her home and stayed with her until after midnight and refusing the services of her own doctor, she finally convinced him she would go to bed, that she would be okay on her own and admitting that she knew in her heart Michael's passing had just been a question of time.

Dear Popeye, she forced a smile; such a good man and such a good friend, not just to her and Michael, but to many people in the Saracen area.

He had left and promised that he would visit her in the morning and assist her with information about how to register Michael's death, to contact the undertaking service and the dozen other details she would need to deal with.

Still weary, she forced herself from the bed and after her morning toilet, went into the kitchen to boil the kettle.

She glanced at the clock, unable to believe it was almost nine o'clock then remembered the mug of hot, sweetened cocoa Popeye had persuaded her to drink before he left.

It was when she sipped at her tea that her inner reserve of strength took over and she determined then that she would not give in to her grief.

Not today anyway.

Finishing her tea, she made her way to the bathroom to get showered and prepare herself to face her first day as a widow.

DI Danny McBride gathered his three staff in his office and informing them that Harry Henderson's story about returning to Glasgow seemed to be true, nevertheless asked for the result of the inquiries he had tasked them.

"I have a dozen images from the Glasgow Airport CCTV, boss," replied Malcolm, "but to be frank, they're pretty poor. I also took the liberty of contacting the Gatwick Ports Coverage Unit and asked them for their CCTV images, but they were no better. If you want my opinion, Henderson was aware he might be photographed and kept that bloody hat on and tilted low in front of his face. As for a surveillance team, the DCI told me she can scramble one at an hour's notice if needed."

"Good work," McBride replied then said, "Alison. It seems your hard work was for nothing. We've learned from our colleagues at Saracen CID that Henderson's aunt was the victim of an assault and robbery and is currently detained at the city's new hospital in Govan."

"Thank God," she sighed. "Have you *any* idea how many pensioner patients were admitted to the Greater Glasgow hospitals over the last five days? It was like getting a list for God's waiting room."

Grinning, McBride turned to Jean and asked, "How did you get on?"

"Well, I hadn't heard of Mister Henderson before yesterday," she admitted, "but oh my, what a chequered history that man has. He's suspected for a number of unsolved murders throughout the Glasgow area over the last thirty years, though convicted for just the one, serving his twelve years in both HMP Peterhead and then latterly, HMP Barlinnie. However, he was released early due to his good behaviour and described by the Prison Authorities as a model prisoner. According to his antecedent history, he is acquainted with a number of criminal associates, but the only one he seemingly got on with was a drug kingpin called Walter McDonald who died a number of years ago and whose wife Donna apparently fled the country with McDonald's fortune. Coincidentally, it is McDonald's sons William and Michael, themselves violent offenders, that Henderson was last suspected of murdering."

"Anything in his antecedent history to indicate where he might be residing?"

"No, Danny, but if he's only here for a short time, is it possible he might be staying in a hotel?"

"Possibly," McBride mused then with a smile, added, "He arrived on his own passport so is likely using his own name. Trawl the Glasgow city centre hotels, Jean, and see if he's booked in with any of them." Tightly smiling, he continued, "Okay folks, thanks for that so let's get back to work."

Ian MacLeod was at the cooker making breakfast when Daisy, naked under her robe and barefooted, her hair in disarray and sniffing at the smell of toast and scrambled eggs, wandered into the kitchen.

"Thought I'd get you something to eat before I head out to work," he smiled at her.

Slipping behind him she wrapped her arms about his waist and nuzzling his back, replied, "Sure you're fit for work this morning? I mean, you had a bit of a busy night last night."

Laying the spatula down onto the worktop, he turned and grinning at her, said, "I'll manage," then his brow furrowed when he asked, "I know we settled the business of us getting an accountant, but wasn't there something else you said you wanted to tell me?"

She lifted her head and staring at him, smiled before replying, "Oh that? It'll keep till some other time, but right now," her fingers tiptoed down his shirt to his groin, "How much time do you have before you need to leave?"

Returning to his room after breakfast, Harry, dressed in a fresh shirt and navy blue tie, checked the room safe for the inch-long piece of hair he had placed in the door jamb then opened the safe to ensure the firearm had not been disturbed.

Relocking the safe, he returned the short hair to the door jamb then fetched the slip of paper Harry Cavanagh had given him before seating himself at the desk. He thoughtfully stared at the paper then with a sigh, dialled the number on his mobile phone.

His call was answered almost immediately.

"Hello."

"I'd like to speak with Mister Watkins, please."

"Who's this?"

"My name's Henderson?"

"Headcase Henderson?"

Harry flinched, for he had always hated the nickname, but taking a breath, replied, "Harry Henderson, yes."

"This is Stevie Watkins. Thanks for getting back to me, Harry. Can we meet?"

"I gather from what you told Harry Cavanagh this is about some business?"

"Aye, I'd like you to…"

"Please!" Harry hurriedly interrupted him. "I'd rather not discuss anything on the phone."

"Oh, aye, right. Good idea, Harry. Okay, do you know the red painted pub at the top of West Nile Street?"

Harry smiled at Watkins pitiful attempt to disguise the venue before replying, "Yes, I do."

"Say, eleven-thirty this morning?"

"How will I know you?"

"Don't worry about that, Harry," Watkins cheerfully replied. "I know you," then ended the call.

He slowly placed the mobile onto the desktop and staring at the wall, wondered at the call.

Could it be a set-up for some wrong he had caused Watkins in his past life or perhaps had hurt or killed someone known to Watkins?

His gaze turned to the safe located in the cabinet by the door. Should he take the firearm for his own safety?

But if it was a stet-up, why choose a public venue like a well-known Glasgow pub?

No, it was a meet, of that he was certain.

His instinct and the short call told him that Watkins, a man in his early fifties according to Harry Cavanagh, wasn't overly bright when he almost began to tell Harry why he wanted to hire him.

For heaven's sake, had the fool never heard of the police intercepting calls?

Undoubtedly he wanted to hire Harry to hurt or murder someone and likely it was a murder, for that was what Harry did best.

He glanced at his wristwatch.

He had an hour and a half before the meeting, time enough to walk to West Nile Street and be there well before Watkins turned up and if by chance he *did* suspect it to be a set-up.

Well, it also gave him time enough to walk away.

Lying in his bed, Kieran McMenamin was now convinced that he had tied up all the ends, that there was nobody to connect him to the murder of Lennie Robertson.

He listened for any sound, but hearing nothing and satisfied that both his father and sister had left for work, he decided to celebrate his relief. Rolling from the bed onto the floor, on his knees he reached and probed his fingers for the hole he had cut into the underside of the mattress from where he withdrew the small plastic bag.

Moments later he had rolled himself a joint and returning to his bed, lay there inhaling the cannabis cigarette while he idly stroked at his genitals and recalled with a smile how he had kicked the shite out of the junkie before dealing with the lassie called Maggie.

He was safe, of that he was certain and continued to hurriedly stroke at his genitals.

His eyes narrowed and his thoughts turned to the girl Maggie, remembering the fear in her eyes when she saw him.

Maggie.

His hand stopped and he became limp as doubt beset him.

Maybe he was being overly optimistic he wondered for after all, it was that prick Jackie Stone who had told him where to find her.

If the cops went to speak with Stone about Maggie, would he tell them that McMenamin had been asking about her?

Fucking right he would, he scowled and with a sigh realised that maybe all the ends weren't as tied up as he had thought.

Suddenly, the joint wasn't as enjoyable as he had thought and with a snarl, swung his legs from the bed and stamped his feet on the thin, stained carpet.

He had phoned in early and spoke with the duty sergeant, explaining that he needed the day off, that a friend had suffered a bereavement and he wanted to assist with the arrangements.
Aware that Popeye had just about a month left to serve, the obliging sergeant granted him time off against his forthcoming annual leave and now here he was, parking his car outside Mary Harris' close.
"Oh, Popeye," she seemed a little startled, "I didn't recognise you with your clothes on."
He resisted smiling at her unfortunate turn of phrase and though it was apparent she had been crying, asked, "How are you this morning, Mary?"
"Oh, where are my manners," she replied and standing to one side, said, "Come away in, Popeye. I've just put the kettle on again."
Closing the door behind him, she continued by answering his question, "I'm as well as can be expected, I suppose. I had a phone call this morning from my son Michael. He's travelling up from Dorset and should be here later this afternoon. My daughter Jenny called too from New Zealand, but she won't make the funeral. The doctor has told her that because she's eight months pregnant, there's a risk to the baby and under no circumstances should she travel. To be honest, I think that hurts even more than the death of her dad, knowing that she can't be here with me."
Ushering him into the kitchen, she stopped and staring at him, said, "It's awful kind of you to come by. Should you not be working?"
He sat down at one on the kitchen chairs and with a soft smile, replied, "I had some time lying, so I just took the day off."
Busying herself at the cooker, she turned and asked, "Have you had any breakfast?"
He raised a hand. "I'm fine. A cuppa will be grand, thanks," then added, "The reason I'm here, Mary, is that I thought I'd take you over to the nursing home again, when you're ready. There's things to do regarding the documentation. It isn't right that you should be catching buses at a time like this."
She couldn't reply, for his kindness choked her and taking a deep breath, could only nod.

He sat in silence while she poured the tea then when she sat in the chair opposite, said, "I phoned the DI this morning, Myra McColl, and told her about your bereavement. She won't be contacting you or anything, but asked me to convey her sympathy and when you're ready, to give her a phone call if there's anything else you can remember or if you happen to see the man you spoke about hanging about the Cross again."

"Popeye," she stared curiously at him the, her voice betraying her surprise, said, "I've known you all these years, but never thought to ask what your real name is?"

He smiled and replied with a grin, "My father was an Irish catholic and had a sense of humour, so he named me Cornelius after the Roman centurion who was baptized by Peter, but I'm happy with Popeye."

She returned his grin with a smile and wiping at her eyes with a handkerchief, she took another deep breath and in a practical, strong voice, said, "Okay, Cornelius, keep me right here. What forms do we need to collect and what certificates do I need to take with me?"

The bar officer saw him pass by while he was collecting his Airwave radio and called out, "Fariq, there's a phone call for you. You can take it through here at the bar if you want."

Lifting the radio then pushing his way through to the bar, he caught the eye of the bar officer who shrugged that she didn't get a name. Lifting the phone he formally said, "Constable Mansoor, can I help you?"

"Fariq, its Daisy Cooper. Do you have a minute?"

"Hi, Sarge," he replied, his face splitting into a wide grin, "what can I do for you?"

"I need a wee favour on the QT. Last night, my fiancé and I were at dinner in your grandfather's restaurant in Ashton Lane and I…"

"Was everything all right? I mean, did they treat you okay?"

"Oh, the food was delicious and you granddad's a sweet old man," she replied, "but that's not why I'm calling. The thing is I saw that outside the front door there is a CCTV camera and I was wondering if it is operational and does it record persons entering and leaving the restaurant and if so, if you know how long your grandfather keeps the recordings for?"

"Oh, yes, I know the camera. My grandfather had it installed about a year ago. There was a drunken bampot who gave the staff a hard time in the restaurant, making racial comments and just generally being a prat, so to protect his staff, my grandfather Abu Bakr had my cousin install it just in case the police ever needed evidence. As far as I remember it records real time onto a DVD player that's kept in the back of the restaurant. How long he keeps the DVDs, I'm not certain. Can I ask why you're interested, Sarge?"

"Well, I saw someone I thought I recognised and couldn't recall the name. The thing is though, Fariq, I'd like to view last night's DVD if that's possible, but I need to ask you to keep this strictly between us. Nobody else to know, understand?"

His eyes widened and believing that he was being asked to assist Sergeant Cooper in some sort of clandestine inquiry, without hesitation replied, "You're off duty today Sarge?"

"Yes, I am."

"Well, I finish at four, so what I'll do is phone my grandfather the now, have him keep the DVD from last night and if you give me your address, after I collect it from the restaurant I'll drop it off at your place."

"Are you sure that's not too much trouble, Fariq?"

"No bother, Sarge," he happily grinned.

In the spotlessly clean kitchen, dressed in a white shirt, red and blue striped tie and designer suit trousers, Nigel Faraday looked every inch the young business professional. Placing a cup beneath the spout of the expresso coffee maker he pressed the button and watched the brown liquid fill the cup. Adding milk, he lifted the cup and stepped from the kitchen through to the balcony to gaze across the River Clyde to the buildings being constructed on the opposite shore.

That's where the money is he mused as he sipped at the scalding liquid and again gave thought to investing his profits into the luxury property market, for he realised that sooner or later his rapidly expanding drug empire would come toppling down.

The trick was to get out before it all collapsed with him beneath it. He heard his mobile phone beep and fetching it from his trouser pocket, glanced at the text message.

They know about you but nothing to suggest they intend taking action at this time. No more. I've done enough

He reread the text and smiled.
His phone call and meeting had borne fruit and it was as he suspected.
Knowing and proving are two separate issues; however, the text made him even more determined to expedite his operations and clear his feet of any drug involvement before the cops came knocking at his door.
Setting the cup down onto the wooden railing he rapidly typed out a response.
I will decide when you have done enough. Remember…I know what you did
Then with a smug grin, he pressed the send button.

After a brisk walk, Harry arrived in West Nile Street a full thirty minutes before the arranged meet time and found a window seat in the small Italian café across the road that provided him, passing traffic aside, with a clear view of the pub's entrance door.
He opened that mornings edition of the 'Glasgow News', and read the front page headline that reported an investigation was being conducted by the CID in the Saracen area of the city after the body of a young man, said locally to be a drug abuser, had been discovered murdered in Ruchill Park. His attention deepened when he further read that the murder was being linked to the assault and robberies that had occurred against two elderly residents of the Saracen area, though it neither named the young man nor the other victims.
His brow furrowed for he thought it odd that the police would so openly link the three crimes and guessed that things hadn't changed that much, that there were still people employed by the polis who either couldn't keep their mouths shut or were accepting backhanders from the local journalists.
A taxi drew up outside the pub and his eyes narrowed, pretended to read his newspaper while drinking his latte and keeping his attention focused on the cab, but it was two women in their early thirties who exited to make their way in the general direction of the Sauchiehall Street precinct.
Just before eleven a gleaming black coloured Mercedes saloon stopped near to the door of the pub. As Harry watched, a young stocky built man got out of the front passenger seat while a heavyset

man got out the rear before the car drove off. While the rear passenger made his way into the pub, the younger man, his head shaved, wearing dark sunglasses and dressed in tightfitting jeans and a green bomber jacket, stood with his back to the wall of the pub at the door.

Clearly a minder, thought Harry and leaving a generous tip for the young waitress, left the café to cross the road towards the pub.

As he approached the door, he saw the man in the green bomber jacket, who wore sunglasses, seemed to be in his early twenties, about three or four inches taller than Harry with crude tattoos on his neck and hands that were crossed in front of him as he stood like a soldier on guard at the door.

Harry ignored the man as he entered the pub and his eyes adjusting to the dim light, saw the heavyset man seated at a table in the corner man. Grinning, the man rose to his feet and hand extended, greeted him with, "Harry Henderson. I'm pleased to meet you."

"Mister Watkins," Harry acknowledged the handshake and sat in the chair that permitted him a view of the door, but saw the minder had not entered the pub.

"Please, Stevie," Watkins jovially reached across to slap Harry good-naturedly on the shoulder, then continued, "I don't know what young Spud out there was expecting, but I think you just walked by him without a glance. Would that be right?"

"All I can say is that if he's a minder then you'd be better getting him better dressed and not so obvious. As you say, Stevie, perhaps he's looking for some sort of tall, well-built guy," he smiled, "but that's not me, is it?"

"So," Watkins glanced about him in an obvious show that he wanted Harry to know they weren't to be overheard, "Now that you're back, you'll likely be wanting to get some work, eh?"

"I'm only passing through for a short time, nothing more," Harry replied.

"Then why meet me here if you're not interested in work?" Watkins face expressed his curiosity.

Harry pursed his lips and shrugging, said, "I was hoping that as a courtesy you might be able to furnish me with some information."

Clearly puzzled, Watkins asked, "What kind of information?"

"I'm keen to know who's running the network in the Saracen area."

"Why would you want to know that?"

"Personal reasons, Stevie, but nothing that would harm you. You have my word on that."

"How do you know *I'm* not the guy running Saracen?"

Harry stared him in the eye before replying, "I'm told you have the east end of Glasgow tied up and are branching out into Lanarkshire. Or could it be that you might have an interest in the north side of the city too?"

Watkins didn't immediately respond, but stared at Harry before replying, "Would those personal reasons of yours involve doing some damage to the guy who is currently in charge of the north side?"

"Only he refused to tell me what I want to know," Harry chillingly replied.

"Surely Harry Cavanagh would be the man to know who's running the show in Saracen. I mean, its common knowledge that Cavanagh's got informants in every area in the city."

"He might know the name, yes, and perhaps where the guy lives," Harry agreed with a slow nod, "but you're the man that will know the nitty-gritty about the guy, the things that get told to you. Am I right?"

Flattered as Harry intended he should be, Watkins smiled as he nodded and replied, "Nigel Faraday. Hasn't been on the scene long. Didn't come up through the housing schemes like the rest of us because daddy's got money. No mug though and if there is any hint of a rammy he has a dozen names he can call on, hard men the lot of them," he shrugged. "Let's just say he won't get his own hands dirty with the seamier side of the game, but prefers to let the middle men handle the day to day running of the business."

He tapped at the side of his nose with a stubby finger and continued, "I've a source in his organisation who keeps me abreast of how he's doing, who he's meeting, when and where. Last night for example," he boasted, "I was told that Faraday met with an informant he has in the polis so the likelihood is that he's protected too, if you see what I mean."

Harry was about to respond, but the question remained unasked when his mobile phone rung.

Standing and stepping away from the table he said, "Hello?"

"Mister Henderson?"

"Who's calling?"

"Sorry, it's Staff Nurse Goodwin at Ward sixty-seven, I need to know I'm speaking with Mister Henderson. This is the number on the file I have."

He could feel his face pale and his stomach tighten before he replied, "Yes, Staff, I'm Mister Henderson. Is this about my aunt Harriet?"

There was a slight pause, almost he thought as if the nurse was gathering her breath to tell him. "Then I regret to inform you, Mister Henderson that your aunt, Harriet Henderson, has succumbed to her injury. If you should wish to visit, then Missus Henderson will remain with us for the next two hours or if you wish to…"

"No, that will be fine," he interrupted, rubbing with the heel of his hand at his forehead and far more curtly than he intended, before adding, "I'll be there within the hour. Thank you Staff."

He ended the call and turning to return to the table, Watkins eyes narrowed as he asked, "You look as if you've had bad news, Harry."

"Something like that. Now, Stevie, before I go what *exactly* is it that you want from me?"

The young woman, her fair hair bundled up on top of her head and wearing the skirted business suit clutched the folder to her chest as irritably she paced up and down outside the stairs and glanced again at her wristwatch.

The buggers were almost ten minutes overdue and…

A car pulled up sharply across the road and as she watched, a young couple in their late twenties exited the car, their apologies evident on both their faces.

"Sorry we're late," gasped the woman as they hurriedly crossed the road. "Bloody traffic was busier than we expected."

The estate agent flashed a tight, professional smile, conscious she had another viewing in Maryhill in just over fifteen minutes and replied, "That's okay, now, if you'd like to follow me," and turning began to step lively towards the stairs.

"You have to understand," she called over her shoulder, "the flat has been empty for almost a year and of course there is major décor and some repair work to be conducted. That," she turned and staring at the couple in turn as though imparting a confidence, "is of course reflected in the low price."

Leading the couple towards the close entrance, she continued her practised speech from the schedule she held informing them about

local transport, the proximity of the flat to the city centre and almost gushing added, "And of course there are some good local schools."
It was when they arrived at the open door of the flat the estate agent hesitated for she had never actually been inside the bloody dump, but putting on a brave face, continued, "Needless to say, because of the lack of recent occupants there is a lot of clearing out to do first, but again I'm certain the owner will take that into consideration regarding a discount in the schedule price."
However, she didn't mention the slimy sod had buggered off back to Southern Ireland to avoid charges of being a slum landlord just days before the council brought the case to court.
Tiptoeing across the debris in the dark hallway, the estate agent screwed her face up against the awful smell and was about to step over a bundle of clothes on the floor when glancing down, she saw the pale, dead face of Maggie Dalrymple whose mouth hung slackly open and whose open eyes stared back at her.

CHAPTER FIFTEEN

Strictly speaking though Napiershall Street wasn't part of her area of responsibility, DI Myra McColl responded to the telephone call from Phil Kennedy, the Maryhill CID Detective Inspector who was aware that McColl was already managing a murder inquiry where the victim was a drug abuser. Calling her from the locus of his double murder in the tenement squat, Kennedy had thought it prudent she met with him there.
Parking her car behind an ambulance, she stared curiously at the young woman who lay sobbing on the stretcher and was being attended to a by a paramedic while a couple in their twenties, the mans arm comfortingly over the woman's shoulder, anxiously stood nearby.
Identifying herself to a uniformed police officer, she asked, "Was somebody hurt?"
"No," the young officer repressed a grin. "Apparently the lassie in the ambulance is an estate agent and was showing them two," she nodded towards the couple, "the murder flat when she almost stood on a body. Took a hissy fit then collapsed in a faint. Been bawling her eyes out since me and my neighbour got here, Ma'am, so we thought it better to get her seen to. Care in the community and all

that shite," the young woman colloquially expressed her opinion of the police political correctness code.

She stared curiously at McColl and asked, "Are you the DI from Saracen that DI Kennedy's waiting on?"

"That's me, hen."

"Right, Ma'am, I'm to tell you to get yourself into a Forensic suit and go up to the locus. DI Kennedy is up there the now with the Scene of Crime people."

She was about to turn away when the young cop said, "Oh, and Ma'am. Do you have any perfume or hand cream in your handbag?"

McColl realised immediately why the question was asked and with a grim smile, replied, "Is it as bad as that?"

"Worse, Ma'am," the cop grimaced and held her nose between her thumb and forefinger.

Following the cop's instruction, McColl, now attired in a Forensic suit and with a liberal dab of fragrant hand cream rubbed under her nose, made her way to the dismal flat and remained on the cold landing while a Scene of Crime officer called the DI.

After introducing herself to Phil Kennedy, he said, "Glad you could make it, Myra. The reason I asked you to attend here is that the two victims are apparently known drug abusers and well…"

He didn't need to finish for they both knew that unlike the police, murder did not respect divisional borders and there was every likelihood the two crimes committed within a short space of time in a local area might very well be connected.

McColl handed Kennedy a printout of Lennie Robertson's antecedent history, saying, "When you identify your victims there's a list of names on here that might be useful in associating him with your two."

She nodded to the hallway and continued, "Now, how about a look at your victims?"

A moment later in the harsh light of a SOC halogen lamp, McColl stood over the body of Maggie Dalrymple as Kennedy said, "According to the casualty surgeon who attended, she's been strangled and as there is no apparent ligature marks, he reckons the bruising on her throat was likely caused by a pair of hands."

"Just like Robertson," she murmured and stepping warily over years of accumulated rubbish, followed Kennedy into the bedroom.

"However, it's a different story with this poor young fella," he shook his head. "The blood splatter and his wounds seems to indicate his head was bounced several times off the wall. There is also bruising to the torso as though he's taken a beating and likely at the same time he was murdered, though of course the PM will no doubt firm up on that."

Before she could respond, McColl's phone rung. The screen indicated the caller was DS Fraser so excusing herself, she left the flat and stepped out into the back court.

"Calum."

"Boss, I've just had word from the Neuro regarding Missus Henderson, the woman who was mugged," he reminded her.

McColl closed her eyes and already guessing the answer, asked, "And?"

"Unfortunately, she has succumbed to her injuries."

Murder's like bloody buses, McColl thought. You wait for ages, then when it arrives they all turn up together.

"Okay, Calum. I'll finish up here and head back to the office. What I need you to do is take a neighbour and head over to the hospital. Nobody touches the body till we get a PM performed. Right now Missus Henderson is ours and if anybody quibbles, remind them this is now a murder investigation and that's why we are seizing her body. When you are there get the staff to remove the body to the mortuary and see she's properly signed in and have your neighbour accompany the body from the ward to the fridge for evidential continuity purpose. I needn't remind you we'll need statements from the physicians and a list of the nurses who attended her, but don't bother with their statements for now. If we need them later, then we'll get them. Seize *all* documentation regarding her treatment. Again, any problems contact me. I'll get onto the Procurator Fiscal's Department and inform them of the death."

Her eyes narrowed as she added, "Robertson's PM is set for this afternoon. In the unlikely event there's an opening, try to persuade the mortuary staff to fit Missus Henderson's PM in about that time too and that could save us a double journey."

She screwed her face, trying to recall if she had forgotten anything and asked, "What am I missing?"

"You'll need to inform Ma'am," Fraser reminded her, then added, "and do you want me to set up a second inquiry team?"

"I'll phone Ma'am, but hold back re a second inquiry team. We just don't have the resources to investigate a separate murder," she bit at her lower lip before continuing. "I'll need to ask Ma'am if she can persuade the Murder Investigation Team to take on the second murder."

"Okay, boss, in that case shall I clear out the DS's room and make that available to them?"

"Good idea, Calum. One last thing."

"Boss?"

"Has Missus Henderson's nephew been informed?"

"According to the Staff Nurse I spoke with, she phoned him before she called us."

"Oh, joy," McColl absent-mindedly replied, her thoughts on the hurricane that was about to hit Saracen for she had little doubt that Harry Henderson would now be on the hunt for his auntie's killer.

The young cop Fariq Mansoor had gone just a few minutes when Daisy Cooper inserted the DVD into the machine and settled down on the couch to watch it.

Fast forwarding the time to when she thought the couple had left the restaurant, she intently watched and then unconsciously leaned forward as she saw the faces she thought she had recognised and pausing the recording, with a curious, deflated sensation, simply murmured, "Oh, my."

It was moments later when she remembered, when the name came to her and she frowned.

The man in McColl's thoughts had just arrived at the hospital and was met in the foyer by Harry Cavanagh.

"Bad business," the portly man shook his head and rubbed solicitously at Harry's arm.

"Thanks for coming," Harry nodded and together they walked towards the lifts, standing aside as the lift arrived and a porter pushed an empty trolley from it.

They entered the lift with no other passengers and while Harry pushed the button for the fifth floor, Cavanagh waited till the doors closed before asking, "How did your meeting with Stevie Watkins go?"

Harry slowly shook his head before replying, "Not the sharpest tool in the box, but okay I suppose."

Cavanagh turned to stare at him and replied, "So?"

Harry smiled and quietly replied, "He's keen to take over the drug business in the north side of the city and offered me thirty grand to knock off this guy Faraday. The only problem is that he believes Faraday is being protected by a cop who is providing him with inside information. How he learned this, he wouldn't say, but hinted he has his own source close to Faraday."

Cavanagh smiled before replying, "Oh, I believe we know who that will be," but got no further for the lift had arrived at the fifth floor.

They stepped out and made their way to Ward sixty-seven where Harry identified himself to the Staff Nurse who led them both to Harriet's room.

Cavanagh didn't miss the hesitance in Harry when they arrived at the door and with a supporting hand on his friend's back, they followed the young nurse into the room.

The dead woman lay on her back, the bandage still about her head and air tube remained attached to her mouth by tape.

Confused, Harry turned to the nurse and eyes flashing, angrily asked, "Why haven't you removed the bandage and that," he pointed to the tube.

Alarmed, the nurse took a step backwards, her hand groping for the door handle and replied, "I'm sorry, Mister Henderson. We've had instruction from the police, the CID I mean. They told us not to touch anything, that this is now a murder inquiry."

"Murder?" Harry's eyes narrowed then taking a deep breath, grimly stared at her and raising his hands as though in surrender, said, "I'm sorry, Staff. I didn't mean to scare you. Yes, you're correct of course. I realise that. It's just…" he felt his eyes water and his throat tighten as he stared at Harriet. He took a further deep breath, then turning to Cavanagh, said, "Let's get out of here. I don't want to see her like this."

Cavanagh nodded to the nurse and following Harry from the room, his legs worked overtime as he tried to keep pace with his enraged friend.

At the lift, he thought it better not to say anything, but when they were inside with the doors closed, softly said, "I'll take care of everything, Harry, stand on me about that."

Harry didn't respond, other than to nod as he stared at the aluminium walls of the lift.

At the ground floor, he took a few steps into the foyer then stopped and turning to Cavanagh, said, "Because I'm Harriet's only living relative, the cops will want to interview me. I'm heading over to Saracen office now and I'll give them a statement and that'll be done with it."

"What do you intend doing about this guy Faraday?"

"What I intend doing is finding the junkie who killed Harriet and to do that I'll need to follow the drugs," he stared grimly at Cavanagh. "First the supplier then the local dealer then the junkie, but don't worry, pal. I *will* get there in the end."

Watching Harry, his hands in pockets and head down as he walked off towards the car park, Cavanagh inwardly shuddered for he had little doubt that sometime today or maybe even tomorrow or whenever, somebody was going to suffer.

Detective Superintendent Cathy Mulgrew was at her desk when her secretary knocked on her door and said, "That's DI McBride here now to see you, Ma'am."

Immediately behind her, Danny McBride, in shirt sleeves and with his tie undone, thanked the secretary and entering the office closed the door behind him before taking the seat opposite Mulgrew.

"I heard the news about the woman who was mugged in Saracen dying in the hospital. If that doesn't set the proverbial cat among the pigeons," he sighed.

Mulgrew sat back in her seat and wearily rubbed at her temple with the heel of her hand.

"I'm not long off the phone with Myra McColl..." she stopped and stared with narrowed eyes at McBride. "Do you know her?"

"Met her a couple of times during inquiries. Recently promoted into the DI post at Saracen?"

"Yes, that's her. A good, hard working and experienced detective, but right now she's been thrown into the deep end, Danny. Bad enough she has to deal with the junkie who was strangled in Ruchill Park, but now this; Harry Henderson's auntie," she shook her head. "I can almost smell the blood in the water."

"Like you, Ma'am, I've only met him the once, but he doesn't strike me as the sort of man who will stand by and allow the police to catch

his auntie's killer. No," he shook his head, "I suspect Mister Henderson will go all out and that could mean bodies turning up."
"And that's why I asked you along here," she grinned at him.
"Suddenly I'm feeling that I'm not here to discuss our options," he warily replied.
She leaned forward onto her elbows and with a smile, said, "How would you feel about taking a break from behind your comfortable, coffee at your elbow, desk?"
His eyes opened wide with surprise. "What, you're getting rid of me?"
"No, you idiot, I'm asking you to take over the inquiry into Missus Henderson's murder and run it alongside Myra's Ruchill Park murder. You've been through the SIO/Murder Investigation course and before you came into the Intelligence field, you've worked on a number of murder inquiries as a DS, that and you have your knowledge of Harry Henderson, so maybe you can pre-empt any attempt he makes at railroading your investigation."
She raised her hand and continued, "I know it'll be tight working together in the same office because Saracen just doesn't have the available space for two major inquiries, but I want to leave the Maryhill office clear in case something else should develop."
She smiled and said, "Besides, Danny, it won't do your CV any harm having a murder inquiry under your belt and I'll be there to mentor you and available if you need any advice or whatever I can do to assist."
Still taken aback, he nodded and said, "Of course, Ma'am, I'll be glad to take it on," but privately worried that having been out of mainstream CID work for the preceding three years he was about to lead a team of detectives in a murder investigation, none of whom he knew.

Popeye Doyle parked the car outside the close and switched off the engine.
"Thank you, Popeye," Mary Harris said, "I don't think I could have got through today if you hadn't been there with me."
"It's just a shame that there's so many forms to be filled in," he sighed. "Unfortunately it seems that even in death there's a queue of people wanting this bit of paperwork or that bit of paperwork to be completed. Worse than the bloody polis," he growled, but then

slowly smiled and added, "Well, at least for another four weeks or so."

Clutching the paperwork in her hand, she said, "Will you come in for a cup of tea? I can put some dinner on too, if you're hungry?"

"A cuppa will be fine, hen, but I'm not ready to eat yet," he smiled.

Following her to the close entrance, she suddenly stopped and with a worried frown, turned to Doyle and quietly said, "I'm sure I left the front room curtains closed."

"Wait here," he ordered and quickly making his way into the close, stopped when he was confronted by a young man who opened Mary's door. He steeled himself to launch at the man, but was surprised when the man said, "Hello, Popeye, long time no see. Is that my mother you've brought home?"

Preparing dinner for their evening meal while she awaited Ian returning home, Daisy Cooper whipped off her apron before she answered the knock on the door.

Opening the door, she saw Fariq Mansoor wearing a tan leather jacket over his uniform shirt about to knock again then clearly embarrassed, he said, "Hi, Sarge. Sorry, but I got a flyer so I'm a wee bit early."

"Fariq, come in, come in," she smiled and stood to one side to permit him to pass.

"I got that DVD you asked about," he handed her the plastic DVD case, then his face showed his curiosity. "Is it really that important?"

"Important?" she distractedly repeated, glancing at the case while leading him along the hallway to the lounge.

"Well, you said not to tell anybody?"

Indicating he sit down, she offered him coffee or tea, but he declined and explained. "To be honest, my nose is bothering me. My grandfather Abu Bakr asked me why I wanted it too, but I just told him there was something happened in the Lane," he shrugged, "and that the CCTV above his restaurant door might have captured it."

"Well," she slowly drawled, "like I said on the phone, Fariq, I thought I saw someone in the restaurant that I recognised, but I'm not certain." She suddenly smiled and added, "If I'm wrong, it could prove to be very embarrassing for me, so I'd rather not involve you."

"But if you're correct?"

"If I'm correct," her brow furrowed, "it might prove more than embarrassing. It might prove to be…" her brow wrinkled as she sought the correct word, then said, "unprofessional."

The pretty young bar officer politely smiled at Harry while she phoned upstairs to report his arrival, then said, "DS Fraser will be with you in a moment, sir, if you'd like to take a seat," and pointed to the wooden bench behind him.

He nodded his thanks and sitting down onto the bench, inwardly smiled as he thought this was the first time he had ever actually entered Saracen police station through the front door, having on many occasions during his teenage years been pulled from the back of polis vans and dragged fighting to the charge bar.

He turned at the buzzing noise of the security door being opened and saw Fraser stood holding open the door.

"Mister Henderson, if you'd like to come through," Fraser formally invited him.

He had no sooner stepped through the door when Fraser stopped and turning, said, "First of all, I'd like to offer my condolence on the death of your aunt. To save you any further distress, I have to inform you that we're satisfied regarding your aunt's identification so there will be no need for you to attend any formal identification." He paused then continued, "On a personal note, I'm not a man who normally resorts to using bad language, but it's a fucking disgrace that an old lady of her years is attacked and murdered," he sadly shook his head.

Taken aback, Harry could only nod his surprise and gratitude for Fraser's comments before following the detective up a flight of stairs to an interview room.

"Can I get you something? Water, coffee, anything?" Fraser asked as he indicated Harry take a seat.

"No, I'm fine thanks."

"Right, give me a minute till I fetch a witness statement form," Fraser nodded and left the small room, closing the door behind him.

The few minutes alone gave Harry time to reflect on his aunt Harriet and he smiled.

His unmarried mother had left him with her sister-in-law Harriet when he was a toddler with the excuse she was off to London to find work, though neither Harriet nor any of his family who were alive at the time believed her or ever heard from her again.

Not that it mattered to a precocious two-year old Harry, for Harriet loved and cared for him like he was her own child; the child she and her husband Archie never had.

Growing up, he didn't remember his uncle Archie, his mother's older brother, other than through the photographs lovingly framed and perched on Harriet's front room sideboard. In the fullness of time he learned that Archie, less than three years after he and Harriet were married, had been conscripted as a National Serviceman into the army and killed during the Korean War conflict.

An upright and practising Christian woman, Harriet did her damned best to raise Harry as a good man, but more often than not was forced to belt him round the ears when he persistently got into bother. The punishment from the slightly built Harriet he could laugh off, but when she had cause to be really angry or upset with him it was the doleful look she could use that really hurt him more.

Seated there at the graffiti scarred desk, he realised that though she was his aunt and not his biological mother, Harriet had become his mum in all things but blood and it still irked him that tried as he had, she would not leave her friends, her church or her beloved Saracen to join him and Donna in the idyllic Caribbean island of Cuba.

And now some bastard has killed her.

Harry startled when the door suddenly opened to admit Fraser and a woman he judged to be in her late forties who Fraser introduced as Detective Inspector McColl.

"I'm very sorry for your loss, Mister Henderson," McColl said, but he noticed she did not extend her hand in greeting or sympathy.

He watched as she sat in the seat opposite and staring at him, said, "I was hoping we might have a wee word before Calum here takes your statement, Harry." She cocked her head to one side and pokerfaced, added, "Can I call you Harry?"

"I've a feeling I've no choice in the matter," he smiled humourlessly at her.

She returned his sombre smile and said, "In that case call me Myra. Well, Harry, I realise that this is obviously a painful time for you having suffered the loss of your aunt, but I want to stress that it's me and my colleagues who will track down the individual who did this."

She paused as though considering her next sentence, then said, "It would be naive to think that we don't know about you, Harry, the kind of man you are and what you're capable of, so here's a wee warning. If at *any* time I find out that you are in any way interfering with the investigation into the murder of Harriet Henderson, I will have you arrested for attempting to pervert the course of justice. Now," she stared fixedly at him, "you and me have been round the block a few times so we both know that perverting justice is a common law crime with no fixed penalty so believe me, Harry, when I tell you, being the convicted murderer that you are, that if I need to apply that charge against you I will request that any sentence awarded against you be the maximum…and I'm talking years here, do you understand?"

Harry softly smiled. He didn't for one second believe that McColl could influence a judge in any sentencing, but didn't think it was worth arguing with her either, so instead replied, "We seem to have got off to a bad start, Myra. I returned to Glasgow simply in response to my aunt having been admitted to hospital. Believe me when I tell you I am completely out of touch with what's going on in the city and I don't have the contacts I once had, so where would I start to find the guy who attacked her? No," he shrugged as he shook his head, "you'd be wasting your resources worrying about me. I'd rather you concentrate all your efforts on arresting the bastard who murdered Harriet."

Her eyes narrowed as she stared at him and didn't immediately respond, but then slowly smiled and replied, "Jesus, Harry, you almost had me going there."

Pushing herself away from the desk, she got to her feet and said to Fraser, "Take Mister Henderson's statement and then show him the door," then turning to Harry, added, "Don't forget our wee chat, Harry. And by the way," she surprised him with a broad smile, "tell Harry Cavanagh the flowers were beautiful."

At a corner table in the Weatherspoons lounge at Glasgow Airport, specifically chosen because the bar's CCTV camera did not cover the ten square yards where the table was located, Nigel Faraday sat opposite the swarthy man and watched as Miguel de Lugo sipped at his flavoured water.

Near the entrance and sat alone nursing a coffee, Sandy Craig, his head swivelling back and forth, kept a watchful eye open for anyone he suspected of being a surveillance officer.

"So, it's settled then," Faraday, immaculately dressed in a navy blue business suit and carrying an attaché case, quietly said. "The shipment will arrive in two days."

"Yes, my friend, it is settled," de Lugo, a strikingly handsome man in his late forties, replied in almost faultless English. "It only remains for me to request of you a delivery location and to provide you with the bank details for the transfer of the payment."

Lifting the case and setting it upon his knees, Faraday opened it and removed a sheet of paper that he handed to de Lugo who in turn offered a slip of paper with bank details printed on it.

Faraday began, "You will see that the paper contains details of the route from the M74 motorway to a lorry park called Oakbank Industrial Estate in Glasgow. The post code is also there, too. I've added the mobile number of a clean burn phone that has not yet been used to make or receive any calls. When your delivery driver crosses the border from England into Scotland, he is to phone that number and I will note the driver's mobile number when he calls. I will then send my people to await his arrival. During that time, they will confirm the area is cleared of any police. If the area is compromised that will give my people time to inform your driver of a new delivery location and post code."

de Lugo's eyes narrowed when he asked, "How can you be certain the Guardia…sorry, I mean the police will *not* be present at this location," he waved the sheet of paper.

Faraday smiled and leaning forward, replied, "Let us just say that I have eyes and ears that will inform me if there is any interest in that location."

"Ah," de Lugo smiled in understanding. "You have an informant in the police, yes?"

Faraday did not respond, but simply tapped the side of his nose with a manicured forefinger and smiled.

"Now," he continued to smile, "before you catch your return flight to Madrid, we have some time to discuss the payment and our future cooperation."

Smiling at de Lugo, Nigel Faraday might not have been so confident if he had known of the Spaniards thoughts, of his back-up plan if this new and rather naïve hombre should fail in this enterprise.

Kieran McMenamin was confident that there was nothing, absolutely nothing that could tie him to the three murders and with cocky swagger to his stride, walked along Saracen Street towards Ali's shop. He felt invulnerable, untouchable and watched with disdain the people who passed him by with almost a sneer on his face.
It still rankled that Ali had cheated him out of fifteen quid for exchanging the new notes for the used notes and now he was out to get even.
He slowed as he approached the shop and suddenly decided he would get a better view of who was inside from across the road. Skipping through the traffic and ignoring the angry car horn of a taxi driver, he safely reached the other side of the road. Now stood in the doorway of Saracen House, he leaned against the wall and for the next ten minutes watched the shop across the road.
It was common knowledge in the area that seven days a week, Ali was open from first light, serving his customers their morning newspapers, rolls and tobacco and usually closed up the shop about eleven at night. During opening hours, he removed the heavy metal grill from the front window and that, McMenamin sniggered, was what he intended punting in.
Should have brought a brick with me, he thought but decided that just before Ali closed up for the night, he would return and get his revenge.
With a cheery whistle, he stuck his hands in his pockets and decided to return home for his dinner.

CHAPTER SIXTEEN

The news of the two bodies discovered in a Napiershall Street squat broke to the media later that afternoon yet despite repeated attempts by the television news channels and the local newspapers, the police Media Department refused to impart any information other than the local Division were investigating two suspicious deaths.
However, the 'Glasgow News' editor, hoping to steal a march on his competitors, instructed his senior crime reporter to create a headlining story citing his fictitious police source that suggested a drugs war was the cause of the deaths.

Protest though he did at the lack of any substantive proof that this was the indeed the case, the reporter was reminded that his seniority in the cut-throat world of journalism depended on his editor and albeit with much reluctance, the story was submitted for editorial approval in that evenings edition of the newspaper.

Accompanied by her son Michael, Mary Harris thought it would do her no harm to get some shopping in and after visiting the Lidl store along the road, asked if Michael would accompany her to the charity shop where she wanted to thank her friend and fellow volunteer Alice McLean for her support and comfort after receiving news of her husband's death.
Walking in Balmore Road towards Saracen Cross and adjacent to Mary's tenement close, Michael stopped and said, "Wait here a minute. There's no need for us to carry the shopping when we're literally passing the house, mum."
She watched with quiet pride as he trotted across the road then returned a few minutes later when with a smile, he folded her arm into his and they continued towards the Cross.

Kieran McMenamin, still with his hands in his pockets, shouldered his way through the middle of two middle-aged women who shocked at his rudeness stopped and one of whom began to berate him with, "Hey, what the hell do you think you're doing, ya toe rag?"
He stopped and taking his hands from his pockets, clenched them into fists. Advancing towards the suddenly frightened woman, he snarled, "You speaking to me, ya fucking old slag!"
Both women flinched and stepped back, their eyes betraying their fear at McMenamin's aggressive behaviour.
Across the busy road the ruckus had attracted the attention of pedestrians who included Mary and her son Michael, but because of the noisy passing traffic on the busy road it was impossible to hear what was going on.
Staring across the road, they saw the women cling fearfully together as the young man hurriedly walked off past the pub on the corner and turn right into Bardowie Street.
Mary, her eyes wide with horror, clutched with both hands at Michael's arm and in a trembling voice, said, "It's him. That's the man I saw!"

Still dressed in his formal suit and wearing his black tie, Popeye Doyle decided before he returned home to call into Saracen office to collect his final salary documentation from his locker. Parking his car across the road, he locked it and made his way to the front entrance.

He was about to pull open the door when a slimly built suited man, his own height and wearing thin, steel framed spectacles, opened the door and extending his hand, smiled at Doyle.

For a brief second he was confused, then his eyes opened in recognition and instinctively taking the man's hand, he said, "Bloody hell, Harry Henderson!"

Harry continued to smile and said, "Hope you don't mind shaking the hand of a bad man, Popeye. I mean, if anyone sees you and me together, you won't get into bother because you know me, will you?"

With his own smile, Doyle shook his head and replied, "I'm too long in the tooth to worry about things like that, Harry." His smile turned to one of curiosity and eyes narrowing, he asked, "What are you doing in here, in enemy territory?"

Harry was about to laugh, but instead he shook his head and with a heavy sigh, said, "My aunt Harriet passed away earlier today. The CID are treating her death as murder and as her next of kin I was in giving a statement to a DS Fraser. On that point," he smiled sadly at Doyle, "I owe you, pal."

"Not at all, Harry, I'm sorry to hear about Harriet. I hadn't heard," and pointing to his own suit, added, "Coincidentally, I've been helping a friend. She's just lost her husband."

Doyle smiled sadly, then to his own surprise, asked, "Look, if you're not doing anything right now, fancy a coffee or a pint even?"

Harry took a deep breath and replied, "I'm not really into bevy these days and I'm driving too, but a coffee sounds fine. What do you have in mind?"

"Well, there's a Waterstones opposite the Hillhead Library in Byres Road that I occasionally use and it serves a decent coffee. If it's not too far out of your way?"

"I have a car over there," he nodded towards the Focus, "so see you there in what, twenty minutes?"

"I just have to collect something from my locker, so twenty minutes

then," Doyle acknowledged, then warned, "Watch where you park, the yellow peril are all over that area."
Waving cheerio for now, neither of them paid any attention to the young man, his head down, who guiltily walked past them on the opposite pavement as he hurried home.

Reacquainting himself with Myra McColl, Danny McBride and she quietly discussed their respective inquiries for a few minutes before being informed by the mortuary assistant that the pathologist was now ready to conduct the first post mortem on the body of Leonard Robertson.
"I've no objection is you being present if you wish," McColl said.
"It's a been a while since I've attended a PM," he replied, "so I might as well get started with your victim,"
In the bright light of the austerely furnished stainless steel dissection room, they respectfully stood with their fellow detectives who had been appointed to procure productions from the bodies while the Scene of Crime officer first took photographs then, as the mortuary assistant stripped the body of clothing, again photographed points of interest such as the bruising to the throat, needle marks and anything on the body that either the pathologist or more importantly McColl, considered might be of evidential value.
It was prior to the dissection procedure when the pathologist was finger-tip examining the body he frowned and called for his assistant to pass him a wooden fingernail scraper, no larger than a toothpick and a small brown paper bag. As they watched he gently scraped beneath the nails and as he did so, muttered, "Unless I'm very much mistaken, Miss McColl, I do believe there seems to be minute ectodermal tissue under the nail here that if we're lucky just *might* be sufficiently worth your Laboratory people to obtain some DNA sample."
McColl stiffened and wondered, was this the break she was looking for?
Handing the paper bag containing the scraper to the detective designated as the production officer, the pathologist continued, "I would suggest, young lady, you get that to your lab as soon as possible, eh?"
The detective turned questioningly towards McColl who nodded and

added, "Leave the collection of the rest of the productions with me. Ask the Lab to treat that as a priority."

Fifteen minutes later and the PM completed, the pathologist requested McColl, McBride and the remaining detectives return to the waiting room while the dissection room was prepared to receive the body of the next post mortem, Harriet Henderson.

Instructing Sandy Craig to accompany him to his top floor flat, Nigel Faraday made both he and the silent man a coffee before inviting Craig to join him on the balcony.

"I thought we would wait till we were settled here before I related how I got on with our Spanish friend," he began, sitting back in the reclining chair, his leg crossed across the other as he cradled his coffee in his hand.

Craig stared steadfastly at him, trying with difficulty to appear interested when what he really wanted to do was tear the arsehole a new one and throw him bodily over the veranda rails, then watch his body splatter on the pathway below.

Faraday smiled smugly, but wondered why he needed to explain the plan to the large muttonhead. In the same instance he decided what he was really doing was not just convincing himself the plan was fool proof, but with an inward smirk, congratulating himself on how smart he was.

In short, easy syllables, he recounted the deal made with Miguel de Lugo that the delivery of heroin would occur on Sunday, two days hence.

"The journey," he explained, "has commenced a week previously when an articulated lorry that had travelled from Turkey through Spain to the Port of Cadiz delivered a shipping container full of canned fruit to the ferry terminal. Thereafter the ferry will dock at Felixstowe where the container will be off-loaded onto a British registered articulated lorry and brought here to Glasgow."

He watched as Craig's eyes narrowed and then the big man asked, "Cadiz, boss? I would have thought that for Felixstowe, one of the French or Belgian or even a Dutch port would have been better."

He had never considered Craig to be anything but a musclebound idiot, a human torpedo who one simply pointed in the right direction and fired off to do his bidding and so was surprised by the big man's considered question.

"Yes, well," he smirked, "of course they are a lot closer, but think about it, Sandy. The Customs and Immigration people pay far more attention to these ports than they do Cadiz simply because geographically, those ports across the Channel present a threat not only for drug importation, but also by our brown and black friends who persistently attempt to slip unnoticed into the country. Every ship that docks at Felixstowe swarms with Customs and Immigration officers who keenly examine anything they don't like or suspect, eh? Now, by loading our container at Cadiz, we deflect a lot of interest from its contents, do you see?"

"What about when the container is loaded at Cadiz. Surely the Spanish cops or customs or whoever they are will give the container the once over?"

Faraday smiled like a man who had inside knowledge when he replied, "Our Senor de Lugo assures me that will not be a problem, that he has an inside man who will clear the container without any difficulty."

"And what about our side of the water. I mean, the cops are on the ball these days with their technical stuff and don't forget, there's always some junkie looking to make a deal for a get out of jail card."

"Don't worry about that, Sandy," he mysteriously replied. "I'm confident if Mister Plod takes any interest in us or what we're doing, I will get to know about it."

Craig didn't respond, but thought that more or less confirmed what he suspected; the prick had an inside man in the polis.

He paused as though digesting this information before asking, "How tight is this Spanish guy, this guy de Lugo? I mean, really; what do we know about him?"

"Trust me, Sandy," Faraday confidently replied as though speaking to a naive child, "I've done my homework. de Lugo had survived in this business for a long time. We can trust him."

"Aye, but sometimes people survive in this business," he slowly shook his head, "because they're too valuable for the cops to arrest."

"By that you mean?" Faraday's brow knitted at the comment.

"Well," Craig shrugged as he slowly replied, "it wouldn't be the first time the cops have ignored one drug dealers' business by balancing it against the arrest of a dozen more. Scales of justice if you like."

Faraday tightly smiled, but taken aback he wondered at these curious words of wisdom from Craig, a man who for the second time within as many minutes had surprised him.

"Here's what we'll do, Sandy," he finally replied as though bored with the conversation and in dismissal of Craig's opinion. "I'll leave you to organise the team to collect and distribute the shipment and you leave me to worry about the organisation of the deal. Agreed?"

Craig slowly nodded, inwardly aware that Faraday considered him to be a buffoon, but Stevie Watkins instructions to Craig had been explicit.

No move would be made against Faraday till we know where the delivery address will be, Watkins had warned him. Time, date and location first he had stressed.

Craig could feel his stomach tense and containing his excitement, tried to seem as casual as he could when he asked, "So, when and where does the container arrive here, boss?"

"Ah," raised a forefinger, "that my large friend will remain with me for now. As you quite correctly said earlier, there are always junkies or suchlike seeking to make a deal with our friends in blue so, need to know and all that, eh? Suffice to say it will be a night drop."

He sipped at his coffee and smiled benignly at Craig who mustering in his face what innocence he could, finally asked, "Just how much of the stuff do we expect to be delivered, boss?"

Faraday gently replaced his cup onto the saucer and sitting back in his chair, arched his fingers in front of his nose and with a wide smile, replied, "I calculate once the shipment has arrived and been distributed to our dealers, the purity assessed and adulterated for street sale, we're looking at a rough profit margin of between thirteen to fifteen million pounds."

Shocked, Craig's mouth fell open as he stared at him and for a heartbeat, just a sudden heartbeat, he *almost* made the decision to abandon Stevie Watkins employment for Faraday.

But then again, he inwardly thought as he returned Faraday's fixed smile and toasted him with his now cold coffee, it was worth more knowing the arrogant, poncey bastard wasn't going to survive to enjoy his millions.

Michael Harris had argued his mother's instruction that he take her to the police station and instead walked her home.

"I'll phone the police and they can come and visit you, okay?" he insisted, finally convincing her that was the simplest solution to her panicked recognition of the man they saw threatening the two women.

Just a little over ten minutes later while he was brewing his mother a calming cup of tea, the door knocked and opening it, DS Calum Fraser introduced himself and his colleague, DC Mhari Munroe.

Settled with Mary in her front room and accepting a cup of tea from Michael, Fraser asked, "And you are one hundred per cent certain it was the same man, Missus Harris?"

"Oh, aye, no doubt about it and you saw him too, didn't you Michael?"

Fraser half turned and smiling at Michael, replied, "While I accept that Michael saw the man earlier in Saracen Street, Missus Harris, he isn't to know if it's the same man *you* saw in Ruchill Park at the time of the murder."

"Maybe not and I agree," Michael interjected and a little bristly at Fraser's comment, "but what I *can* tell you, Mister Fraser, is that I believe my mother when she says it's the same man."

"Please," Fraser raised an apologetic hand and smiled, "I don't doubt your mother for one minute, Mister Harris, but you understand I have to be absolutely clear she's not mistaken."

Slightly mollified, Michael nodded, then eyes narrowing, added, "If indeed you do believe my mother saw the same man, then doesn't that make me a witness too? I saw the guy and I can identify him as the man my mother pointed to, the man she said she saw in Ruchill Park."

"A moot point, but yes, what it does is gives us the opportunity to take a statement and a description from you that with respect," he smiled and slightly bowing his head towards Mary, "will perhaps firm up on the description that Missus Harris has already provided."

"Is there anything in particular that stood out with this guy?" Munroe asked, turning her head from Mary to Michael.

Michael pursed his lips and first shaking his head, replied, "Just like any other of the deadbeats that hang around there at the Cross. You know the type, workshy and can't be arsed…" he took a deep breath and said, "sorry mum. I mean, the type who are quite content to get along on their dole money and won't bother looking for employment."

Mary sighed and then said, "There *was* one thing." She shrugged and added, "I don't really think it means anything, though."

"What was it, Missus Harris?" asked Munroe.

"Well, I know this sounds really silly, hen," her cheeks flushed and it was evident she was a little embarrassed, sitting on the edge of the armchair and wringing her hands together, "after he...I don't know, it was just a feeling I got. I mean when I saw him. Sorry. I mean when me and Michael saw him, we couldn't hear what was being said, could we, Michael? But we think he exchanged words with the two women and he certainly looked like he was frightening them, wasn't he Michael?"

She glanced at her son who nodded in agreement.

"Anyway," she continued, "he didn't hesitate. He just quickly started walking away and then he turned into Bardowie Street and put his hands in his pockets."

Confused, Munroe slowly repeated, "His hands in his pockets. Is that what you mean, Missus Harris?"

"No, hen, no," she vigorously shook her head. "What I mean is that he didn't look about him or anything. You know, like wondering, where am I? No, he knew exactly where he was going."

"I'm sorry, but..."

"What I *mean*," Mary persisted, "is that he walked away like he *knew* where he was going. Like he lives here. In this area. In Saracen."

****

Returned to Saracen office, Myra McColl introduced Danny McBride to her team and following him to his own incident room, McBride in turn introduced himself to the detectives seconded to him from the Murder Investigation Team.

Inwardly surprised at his nervousness, he was nevertheless relieved to see some familiar faces among the eight officers and three civilian analysts.

"I'll let you get on," McColl nodded and returning along the corridor to her own incident room to her surprise she found Detective Superintendent Cathy Mulgrew speaking with her team.

"Ma'am," she greeted Mulgrew, who nodded in acknowledgement and replied, "Thought I'd drop in, Myra and see how things are going. Calum here," she indicated Fraser, "was telling me you might have a wee update."

McColl turned questioningly towards the DS who recounted his visit to Mary Harris and her son.

"And she's certain it was the suspect from the park?"

"Yes, boss. I tried to sow a seed of doubt, but she's adamant it's the same man. What's of significance is that her son saw the man she pointed to and says he would recognise him again. Not that it's of particular evidential value," he hastened to add, "but he's given us a decent description, tying the suspect's age down as early to mid twenties. You'll recall in her first statement to us Missus Harris thought the guy might have been in his late teens."

"What about the two women this man they saw tried argued with? Is there any way we can trace them?"

"Unfortunately Missus Harris and her son were too busy trying to watch the man so they couldn't describe the women other than both approximately middle-aged."

"Nevertheless," McColl replied, "inform the uniform bar downstairs just in the off chance that the women come in to make a complaint about the man's behaviour."

Her eyes narrowed and she asked, "What's the odds of there being a CCTV camera in that area or along that stretch of the pavement?"

The detectives glanced at each other, but none had any information of cameras located in the street.

She addressed Fraser when she continued, "Maybe get onto the control room and see if any officer who works the beat there has knowledge of cameras in the street."

"Boss," Fraser nodded in acknowledgement.

"Now, let me get this clear in my head," McColl rubbed at her brow, "you also said that Missus Harris is of the opinion the suspect might live locally?"

"Just a feeling she has, boss," intervened Munroe who smiled and earned a grin from Mulgrew when she added, "but I never doubt the word of a wee Glasgow woman's intuition."

McColl smiled and with a sigh, replied, "If nothing else and if Missus Harris' intuition is correct, it might tie down the list of suspects to a couple of hundred rather than a couple of thousand. Right," she turned sharply and pointing to Munroe, continued, "Marilyn, as you're a fan of intuition, get onto the divisional intelligence collator with the son's description and see if she can come up with a name or names. Once you've done that, try your luck with the Force Intelligence at Gartcosh."

"Boss," Munroe nodded.

Turning to Mulgrew, she smiled and said, "I can treat you to a coffee, Ma'am, if you're interested?"

"Get the kettle on, Myra. I'm just going to pop into Danny McBride's incident room and I'll be back in ten minutes."

Harry parked the Focus in Observatory Road and walked round the corner to Waterstones in Byres Road.

He ordered the coffee at the counter, telling the young waitress to hold it till his friend arrived and turning, chose a table against the wall.

Sat down, he smiled and reflected on the chance meeting at the entrance to Saracen police station and like Doyle wondered at his agreeing to meet for coffee.

As the minutes passed by he thought of his choice of words to the waitress and pondered at what point he had decided that Popeye Doyle was now his friend.

The more he thought of it, the more he realised that he liked Popeye Doyle and that apart from Harry Cavanagh and, he smiled at the sudden memory, that old bugger Wally McDonald, Harry had never really counted any other man as a close friend. Holding that thought, he smiled for he hadn't considered the many pleasant and friendly local villagers where he and Donna now lived.

Yet, he exhaled, though he barely knew him some inner instinct told him that Popeye was a man he could trust, someone he could feel comfortable to be around without worrying what ulterior motive Popeye might have for his friendship.

Curious, he thought that of all the men who had passed through his life, the associates and acquaintances, one of the few with whom he felt most comfortable was a policeman.

He was startled from his thoughts when a voice said, "Penny for them," and turned to see Doyle grinning at him.

"I took the liberty of ordering you a cappuccino, Popeye," Harry smiled and as Doyle removed his coat and hung it over the back of the seat, he waved a hand to the waitress that they were now ready for their coffee.

"That's fine, Harry," Doyle stretched his back and wriggled comfortably, "and again, I'm sorry to hear about your auntie. I gather you were both close?"

"Close enough for me to hotfoot it over here from Cuba," Harry replied, then added, "Sorry, that sounded as though I'm performing a duty coming home. The truth is that Harriet raised me and was like a mother to me. The guy you phoned, Harry Cavanagh, was acting for me here in Glasgow. He saw to her needs and made sure she didn't go short on anything."

"That explains the new kitchen, the bathroom and the expensively furnished council flat," Doyle grinned.

"Aye, well, it's not as if I didn't want her with me," he grimly shook his head. "Believe me, Popeye, I tried to get her to come over to Cuba to live with me and my missus, but she just wouldn't give up her Thursday bingo, her pals in the Possilpark Parish Church and the tea dances she attended. That," he grinned and shook his head at the memory, "and her complaining the strong sun wasn't good for white people. You'll have guessed from that remark she wasn't what nowadays they call politically correct."

Doyle grinned again and staring curiously at Harry, asked, "You said your missus. Got yourself hitched?"

"Yes and no," he smiled. "Donna and I are, how can I put this? We went through a ceremony on the beach out there. The people in the local village are Catholic and a right good bunch too and though neither Donna nor I are particularly religious, I think the locals felt better when we went through what they call a blessing. The local priest is a decent man and kind of tipped us the wink that it would be acceptable to...well, you know," he unaccountably blushed, "unofficially tie the knot as it were. Anyway," he took a deep breath, "we invited the village, put on a bit of a feast, provided bevy and made a day of it."

"Donna. There was some talk when you disappeared. I take it Donna is the former Missus McDonald?"

"That's her," Harry confirmed.

"I never met the lady, but if you're happy, good for you."

"What about you, Popeye? Married or what?"

"Ah, no" he shook his head. "Never had the nerve to take the plunge."

"Seeing anyone?"

"Well, kind of," he screwed his face then almost conspiratorially added, "There's a lassie I was seeing for a while. An ambulance woman. Bobby, well, Roberta actually. Anyway," he exhaled, "I kind of messed up with her. It was her and her neighbour who attended the call when we found your aunt in the close and the last thing she said before she took your aunt away to the hospital was for me to keep in touch. I really don't know if she meant it, though."

"Well, you *won't* know unless you contact her and ask, will you, ya muppet," Harry grinned at him.

Doyle stared keenly at him. "You'll be heading straight back after the funeral?"

Harry stared down at his coffee cup and idly stirring the spoon in the cooling liquid, replied, "Probably."

"What does probably mean? Jesus, Harry," he hissed at him, "with your murder conviction and your reputation you do anything stupid and they'll be down on you like a ton of bricks. Remember your murder conviction. Life does mean life and you're out on license so if they catch you doing anything wrong, anything at all, you're banged up and the key thrown away."

"But what do you care, Popeye?" he slowly smiled at him. "You're out in four weeks or so, so you said."

"Aye, that maybe, but I still owe you a lot and besides," he grinned, "I always kind of liked you anyway."

"I've a question for you," Harry asked, sipping at his coffee.

"Shoot."

"DS Fraser told me that the Fiscal won't release Harriet's body till there's a defence PM. What does that mean?"

"Well, in the likelihood they arrest someone for her murder, the accused will undoubtedly engage or be appointed a defence lawyer who will arrange for a defence PM to be conducted."

"But Fraser told me there's to be a PM, that it is a statutory procedure in a murder inquiry, " Harry protested.

"Yes," Doyle defensively raised a hand, "but the defence will also have their own PM conducted usually by a different pathologist. The idea being that the defence PM might discover something that exonerates the accused, say for example your aunt didn't die because her head was bashed in…" he stopped and wide-eyed, cringed before adding, "Sorry, that was stupid of me, Harry."

"No, it's alright, Popeye. Go on."

"Well, like I said the defence PM is conducted to ensure that the Crown's cause of death, in this case your aunt being assaulted and suffering a head injury, was the actual cause of death and not, hypothetically speaking, that she died because of a stumble or poor hospital care or something like that."

"I see," Harry thoughtfully replied. "But what if they don't arrest anyone? How long will it be before Harriet is released for burial?"

"I can't say, Harry, but from what I know it might be weeks. However, it's not unknown when a body has lain for some weeks without a defence PM for the Fiscal to have an independent post mortem performed and the results retained to be handed to a defence team in the event of an arrest at some future date."

He stared keenly at Harry before continuing, "You're keen to get back to Cuba, aren't you?"

Harry smiled and nodded.

They sat in awkward silence for a moment, broken when Harry said, "When you telephoned Harry Cavanagh, he told me that you were of the opinion it was a junkie who attacked Harriet. Is that what you really think?"

"It seemed to be the rational explanation," he shrugged then his eyes narrowed. "Bloody hell, Harry, you don't think after all this time that somebody assaulted your aunt to get some sort of revenge against you, do you?"

"The thought *did* cross my mind," he admitted, "but no, you're right. I don't think it's anything to do with me."

It was as if he suddenly noticed, for his eyes narrowed and he said, "When I met you at your office, you were wearing a black tie, Popeye, and said you were at a bereavement. Had you been to a funeral this morning?"

"Ah, no. One of the locals, Mary Harris who lives in Balmore Road. Her husband was confined to a nursing home over in Govan and died yesterday. Dementia. He was a nice man and she's a lovely wee woman who works in the charity shop in Saracen Street. In fact," he half-smiled, "she's the CID's main witness in their other murder investigation. You might have read about it in the local papers. A young guy, a junkie, was strangled in Ruchill Park the other day. Mary's a good woman and was giving her upstairs neighbour a break and walking the lassie's weans in the park and saw what the CID now believe to be the main suspect for the murder. She came forward and gave a statement. A very brave and unassuming lady is

Mary," he sighed and reached for his coffee.

"You like her then," Harry grinned.

"Aye, but as a friend, nothing more."

"I did read about it in the 'Glasgow News', the junkie being strangled I mean," Harry nodded. "Any suspects?"

"Not that I'm aware of."

"And you helped the woman today, this Mary?"

He nodded. "Yes, well, her son came up from Dorset and he's staying with her till the funeral is by, but her daughter's been in New Zealand for almost seven years and pregnant with her third child, so she couldn't make it over. There's no way Mary can afford to travel over there and it's killing her, for the oldest boy was about three months old I think when they left Scotland and she has never even met the younger of the two grandchildren either," he shook his head.

"Decent of you to help her at this time," Harry sighed.

"Well," Doyle smirked, "I remember a young tearaway helping me in *my* time of need and it's something *I'll* never forget. Besides, it's no hardship helping a good woman like Mary. She's a cheery soul, never complains and just gets on with life."

"Can I ask you a question and there's no need to reply. I'm not looking to involve you in anything, Popeye."

"As long as it's a general question and you're not looking for information," he grinned in response.

"The DI at Saracen, the woman called McColl. What do you know about her?"

"To be honest, nothing. She's just been promoted into the post. Why?"

Harry smiled and replied, "While I was in giving the statement to the guy Fraser, she had a quiet word and more or less told me if I involved myself in the investigation into Harriet's murder, she'll twist my balls off."

"Ouch," Doyle grimaced, then recalling his conversation with McColl, continued, "She knows your pal Cavanagh or rather, she's had dealings with him in the past. When I suggested that I phone Cavanagh as it was me who attended the call to your aunt's close and me who found her…"

"How did you know to phone him, Harry Cavanagh I mean?"

"Your aunt has a cleaning lady called…" he tightly closed his eyes as he tried to recall the name then said, "Fleming, Agnes Fleming."

"She must be the woman he hired," Harry mused.
"Anyway, she gave me Cavanagh's phone number. So, when I suggested to McColl that I phone Cavanagh, her eyes lit up and she informed me that she knew Cavanagh and you as well. Course, I dizzied her and said I'd never heard of *you*, but I don't think she believed me."
"Funny," Harry's brow knitted, "I can't ever recall meeting her before."
"Likely your reputation precedes you," joked Doyle.
"So, digressing," Harry smiled at him, "what do you intend doing in four weeks when you retire?"
"Funny that," Doyle shook his head, "everybody keeps asking me the same question and to be honest, Harry, I don't have a damned clue! However," he deeply sighed then a little self-consciously added, "I'd like to be able to go on a high, you know? Have my colleagues say, 'Yeah, I remember Popeye Doyle. He was one of the good guys.' Something like that."
"Who knows, perhaps something will come along to make that happen," Harry smiled then continuing to smile, added with a twinkle in his eye, "Maybe you should give your ambulance woman a phone as well, eh?"

CHAPTER SEVENTEEN

Nigel Faraday dismissed Sandy Craig for the day with the instruction that if Faraday needed him, he was to be on the end of a phone call. It would have disturbed and shocked Faraday had he known that immediately after leaving the Clydeside flat, Craig had driven straight to the large Newton Mearns home of his real boss, Steven Watkins, where he now sat with Watkins in the drug dealer's opulent man-cave.
"I'd offer you a half, big man," said Watkins, waving to the well-stocked bar in the corner of the room, "but we can't be too careful with the old drink driving, not with the number of beasties patrolling these days in their unmarked cars."
"No, you're alright, Stevie," Craig waved away the offer. "Besides, that poncey bastard might be calling me later. He sometimes likes to go out and about at midnight, trawling the clubs in the city centre for a bird for the night."

"So," Watkins idly picked at his nose with his forefinger then inspected the mucus before flicking it away. "What's the ten four?"
"Well," Craig sat forward in his chair, "he met with the Spanish guy at the airport like I told you and then gave me a rundown on the delivery he's expecting. Says the gear is coming in through Felixstowe on Sunday then it's getting driven up here in an articulated lorry."
"Any idea what company?"
"Sorry, I never thought to ask, but apparently the lorry is supposed to be hauling tinned fruit, so I'm guessing the gear is in the tins."
"Just as well you didn't ask about what company though," sighed Watkins. "He might have got suspicious. Anyway, go on."
"When I asked him where the gear was being delivered to, he wouldn't say other than it will be a night delivery, but again he wouldn't burst to the time of the delivery."
Craig grinned as he continued, "He's told me to get a team together for the collection and distribution."
"Well," Watkins grinned too, "that makes things a lot simpler, eh? We'll use people we know, but not my boys just in case Faraday recognises any of them. How many were you thinking of getting together?"
Craig shrugged and said, "I'm thinking about seven or eight. I've a couple of shooters stowed away, so I'll give them out to people I can trust to act as the security and the rest can do the hauling."
Watkins eyes narrowed as he repeated, "Seven or eight bodies, Sandy? How much gear is coming in?"
Craig slowly smiled for this was the moment he intended savouring, the moment he would disclose what they were about to hijack.
"According to our man Faraday, after the gear is adulterated and washed clean by the dealers we sell to, we're looking at a profit margin of between thirteen and fifteen big ones."
Watkins face registered his confusion when he replied, "Seems a lot of bother for thirteen or fifteen hundred grand, Sandy."
Craig's face didn't alter, but inwardly took a deep breath and sometimes really wondered how Stevie Watkins managed to get where he was when he was so fucking thick.
After a short pause, he replied, "I'm talking thirteen or fifteen *million*, Stevie."

Watkins didn't move, simply stared at Craig as though he was joking, then bursting from his chair danced like a madman around the room before loudly shouting, "Ya dancer!" as he punched the air. "Thought you'd be pleased," Craig calmly said while he watched the hysterics with a wide grin.

Calmer now, Watkins loudly exhaled and reaching for a bottle of whisky from the bar, poured himself a larger that usual half and gulping it down, wiped his lips on the cuff of his shirt before saying, "You might be driving, pal, but I'm not. Bloody hell, Sandy, when we lift that amount of gear and get it dealt out the money will set us up for life."

"Or use the profit for a bigger importation, Stevie."

Sitting back down, Watkins stared curiously at him and asked, "What do you mean?"

"Well, once Faraday is out of the picture, the Spanish guy will need to deal with someone in Glasgow if he's to offload his gear, won't he? Why shouldn't that 'someone' be us?"

Watkins eyes narrowed. The big man made sense. This lift of Faradays heroin could lead to some serious money.

"We'd be stupid to do more than three, maybe four importations, though," Watkins said at last. "The other thing is, maybe it would make sense if we drip-feed this delivery of heroin out rather than punting it all at once. If we flood the market with the smack it will drive the price down."

"Good idea and I was thinking as well, Stevie, that we only do two more deliveries, three at a push," Craig replied. "You know what the cops are like these days, with their fancy technical stuff and worse than that; the bastards the polis run who'll sell their granny for a bung," he dry spit in disgust at the very thought of police informants. His eyes narrowed when he asked, "About Faraday, Stevie? Did your man Headcase take the job on?"

Watkins didn't immediately reply, his thoughts returning to the meeting with Harry Henderson in the West Nile Street pub, but then said, "Strange thing that. Headcase asked me what area Faraday covered with his network. I mean, it's no great secret," he shrugged, "so I told him the north of Glasgow. Maryhill, Wyndford, Summerston, Bishopbriggs, Milton, Balornock, Saracen, all round there, eh? Then he asked what I wanted done with Faraday and I just told him, make your own mind up, Headcase. I just don't want to hear anything about him ever surfacing from the River Clyde," he sniggered.

Craig smiled and asked, "Did you tell him when you want it done?"

"Well, obviously it needs to be after you find out where the delivery was coming in, so no, I've not given him a time or a date yet and as for how it's to be done; well, that's something I'll leave to Headcase, eh?"

Craig was thoughtful and brow furrowed, replied, "Headcase had the reputation of being an old fashioned gangster, always being tight and could *always* kept his mouth shut. If that's true, why don't we tell him to come along when Faraday gives us the delivery time and location and he can do the bastard right there and then?"

Watkins grinned evilly and staring almost knowingly at Craig, said, "You're wanting a poke at Faraday before Headcase kills him, don't you?"

Craig smiled humourlessly when he replied, "Nothing would give me greater pleasure than slashing that bastard wide open."

"Then why don't *you* do him? Would save us paying thirty grand to Headcase."

Craig's smile remained fixed, but inside his stomach was churning for he knew that if he murdered Faraday, the team who were going to be present would be witness to the murder and how could he ever be certain that none of the seven or eight of them would at some time in the future grass him in to the cops.

"No," he shook his head. "We stick to the plan, Stevie. Let Headcase do the bastard" he sneered, "I'll just be happy to watch."

Opening the front door, Ian MacLeod's nostrils were assailed by the aromatic smell of his favourite food; mince, tatties and mashed turnip.

"Smells delicious," he said when he entered the kitchen and wrapped his arms about Daisy Cooper's waist.

"Be ready in about fifteen minutes," she smiled at him then her face changed to reflect her dilemma when she added, "time for a cup of tea. I need to pick your brains."

He stared curiously at her before replying, "Let me get changed out of these work clothes and into my jeans and I'll be with you in a minute."

Less than five minutes later, their dinner simmering in the kitchen, Ian joined Daisy in the lounge where she had a cup of tea waiting for him and asked, "Is this about us moving home? Have you found somewhere?"

"No, not exactly," she absentmindedly replied.

Staring curiously at her, he eased himself into his favourite chair and taking the mug from her hand, watched as she activated the remote to switch on the television.

"I've a bit of a problem," she began as the pressed the green button for the DVD, "and I'm a little uncertain about how I should handle it."

He watched as the screen showed the doorway of the Ashton Lane restaurant and began to say, "Isn't that the…"

"Yes, from last night," she interrupted him before adding, "Just keep watching."

A moment later he turned towards her and said, "So, those two people are what I'm supposed to see?"

"Yes," her brow furrowed, visibly troubled.

"And their significance?"

"Well," she breathed deeply then slowly exhaled, "that's where my dilemma lies."

He scrolled down his mobile phone and smiled when he pressed the button for the selected number.

Seconds later, he heard the voice hiss in his ear, "I warned you, don't call me again!"

"Before you hang up," he quickly replied, "I need a little favour."

"No, no more favours, Nigel. I've done enough telling you that you're being watched! For fuck's sake! If I'm caught…"

"You won't be caught," he smoothly replied, then his voice hardened, "not as long as you and I stick to our arrangement."

"What arrangement? We don't have a bloody arrangement!"

"Oh, but we do. The arrangement is that you continue to provide me with some information when I require it and I do not inform your employers of our…how shall I describe it, past association?"

There was a pause and for a second he thought the line was disengaged, but then heard, "What is it that you need?"

"What I *need* is for you to never again to argue with me when

clearly, I quite literally have you over a fucking barrel!"
There was that pause again, he thought.
He listened and heard the sharp intake of breath before the response.
"Again, you *bastard*, what is it you need from me?"
He smiled and mentally likened himself to a fisherman having just landed a squirming and protesting trout.
"This coming Sunday evening," and without explaining why, he continued, "I want to know what resources your people intend deploying in a certain area of Glasgow."

Chewing softly at his inner cheek, a boyhood habit that seemed to resurrect when he found himself stressed, DI Danny McBride sat at the desk designated for that of the SIO and wondered what his next move would be. He was aware of the surreptitious glances his team cast towards him and taking a deep breath, stood and called for them to gather around him.
Walking to the front of the desk, he leaned back against it, his arms folded across his chest.
"Right folks, let's be honest here. Apart from a couple of faces, I neither know most of you and you don't know me, but here's the rub. We've got to work together and I'm confident that because I'm already aware from individually speaking with you all, this isn't your first murder inquiry, so working together we will get to the truth about who mugged and murdered this old woman. Now," he lifted a sheaf of papers from the desk behind him, "what we've got so far and remember, I've just been delegated the position as SIO so all my information is from statements and the briefing document; so feel free to correct me if I'm wrong."
He paused for breath, then continued, "Harriet Henderson was an eighty-six years old widowed woman who lived alone in a first floor flat in Saracen Street. Unless I'm way off the mark, I can't imagine that at her age she had any enemies who would want to kill her, so unless any of you have an alternative theory that I will absolutely listen to, I am going with the premise that because her purse was missing when she was discovered, her death is indeed the result of an assault and robbery gone wrong."
He paused and glanced about the team, but no one spoke.
"Right, I have one update for you that might or might not be relevant. The victim's purse was missing when she was found, but a

search of her home has disclosed she was a customer of the bank on Saracen Street and in the event that her attacker might consider using her bank card, I had the bank contacted to request that one, they be stopped and two, any misuse of the card be immediately reported to us. As a result of that inquiry, the bank has informed us that on the morning she was attacked, but prior to the time of the attack our victim withdrew eighty pounds from the ATM on the outside the bank. Regretfully and before you ask, there is no security camera linked to the ATM that the bank tell me is an old model. However, the bank assured us that the notes were all crisp and new and have provided us with the serial numbers so," he shrugged, "in the event you come across some sod with new notes, I don't need to tell you what action to take."

He glanced at the team and his eyes narrowed when he saw a young detective slowly raise a hand.

"Yes?"

"Sir, it was me who attended the initial call to the victims assault. I handed in a bank receipt that was discovered at the locus by Popeye…I mean, Constable Doyle, who was the first uniformed officer that attended the victims assault. It's definitely logged in the productions."

McBride turned towards Detective Sergeant Ian Prescott, the officer he had appointed as his office manager who immediately held up a both hands and said, "I'll check the ledger, boss. If it's there, it's a balls-up on my part."

McBride was inwardly angry, but to vent his wrath on Prescott in front of the team would only demoralise them further and so nodding, he crisply replied, "Do that Ian and as far as we're all concerned, ladies and gentlemen, let's get it right first time."

"Okay," he tightly smiled and held a hand up as he continued, "whether or not the culprit intended hurting our victim at the time of the assault and robbery is irrelevant; the woman's dead as a result and it's a murder we're investigating, so we won't lose sight of that. The official verdict of the pathologist that will be reflected in his report and what the evidence indicates from our colleagues in Scene of Crime is the victim struck her head when she fell back onto the stone stairs in the close where she lived. Pushed, shoved or her head deliberately banged off the step is for a jury to decide and not us. For the minute," he turned towards, "I'll be pleased if you get on with the Actions you have been designated and if there is any further information comes in, you will be informed at this evenings briefing before we knock off for the day."

He loudly clapped his hands together and asked, "Any questions?"

A hand was raised at the back of the room and a young woman said, "DC Copeland from the MIT, sir. What's the story we're being told about her nephew, this guy Harry Henderson? The word is he's a convicted murderer. Does he feature in the inquiry at all?"

McBride slowly shook his head and replied, "Harry Henderson, as you say, is known to us from some years ago. He was and remains the main suspect in the murder of two drug dealing brothers, but there was never enough evidence to charge let alone convict him of the murders. He left the UK shortly after the murders and tells us he has returned only because his aunt, our victim, was assaulted."

"Any likelihood his previous history and the attack on our victim are connected?" Copeland asked.

"We don't believe so, no," McBride replied then asked again, "Any other questions? No? Right then, folks. We'll speak later," he dismissed them with a tight smile.

Prescott approached McBride and with hands raised and a sigh, said, "The receipt is there, boss. My apologies."

"Okay, Ian, but let's have no more mistakes, eh?"

"Right boss. One other thing. I know there's a statement in the system from Henderson about his relationship with his aunt, but do you intend having another word with him? Maybe, reiterate Myra McColl's warning that he stand off from interfering in our investigation?"

"Not that the minute, Ian," McBride shook his head and smiled, but his smile hid a thought that had suddenly crossed his mind.

"Another thing, boss. The junkie that was murdered in Ruchill Park. It seems to me that the proximity of the killing to that of our two victims being mugged is very coincidental. Maybe I'm thinking out of the box here, but what's the likelihood of the culprit for the muggings and the junkie's murderer being the same guy?"

McBride's eyes narrowed as he contemplated Prescott's notion, then slowly replied, "It's not beyond reason, Ian, and certainly an option we'll need to look at. Our problem of course is that while Myra McColl's team have their witness, the woman who gave them a description of their suspect, we have nothing. Missus Henderson's dead and the old guy maintains he couldn't describe his attacker other than he thought the guy had a local accent and might have been in his late teens or early twenties. However," he scratched at an itch on his nose, "I agree that we could be looking for the same guy, so it won't do any harm for me to have another word with Myra about your suggestion. While you're at it, have someone trawl the crime reports for the last year from say, today's date; see if they can associate any previous reported muggings with these two latest ones."

As they parted, neither detective paid any attention to the elderly woman wearing the cleaners apron who was working her way around the room and emptying the bins beside the desks.

Harry Henderson said goodbye to Popeye Doyle outside the bookshop and through neither had made any fixed arrangement to meet again, Harry had taken what he thought was the unprecedented step of providing Doyle with his mobile phone number and the suggestion Doyle give him a call and they would do lunch or dinner. Shaking his head yet smiling at the thought, he inwardly admitted he enjoyed sharing time with Doyle and laughing as both recalled their early days in Saracen, the characters they both knew and the road their lives had taken since they last met.

He was walking round the corner towards his car when he heard his mobile phone ping with an incoming text message.

Moving to one side of the pavement, he stopped and opening the text, smiled.

As he had promised Harry Cavanagh, had sent Nigel Faraday's home address and post code.

Returning the phone to his pocket, Harry decided that he would return to the hotel and have a rest before his visit later that night to the flats where Faraday lived.

Hunched over the desk, she peered closely at the information on the screen, unconsciously mouthing the words of the report that she quickly read.

The door suddenly opened startling her and glancing up, she smiled nervously and said, "Good afternoon, Sarge."

Anne Cassidy's eyes narrowed and she stared suspiciously at the young blonde before replying, "What are you doing in here, in the sergeants room, DC Munroe, and why are you using Sergeant Cooper's computer?"

Munroe swallowed with difficulty and getting to her feet, she shrewdly hit the escape button on the keyboard before replying, "I was doing a check on a suspect, Sergeant. Daisy…I mean, Sergeant Cooper gave me her password for the Divisional Intelligence files and Briefings for current operations for the duration of the murder inquiry…for when she's off duty, I mean."

Cassidy placed her handbag onto her desk and staring steely-eyed at the young detective, snapped back, "What you *mean*, DC Munroe, is that by providing you with her password, you are suggesting that both Sergeant Cooper and you are in violation not only of Police Scotland protocol and code of practise regarding the misuse of our computer system, but also the Data Protection Act."

"I'm sorry, Sergeant," Munroe began, her cheeks flushed and yet angry at the manner in which she was being spoken to by Cassidy.

"I will speak with Sergeant Cooper, but in the meantime I suggest we keep this between us, DC Munroe," Cassidy turned away before adding, "You may return to your…inquiry."

When Munroe had left the room, Cassidy sat heavily down at her desk and pondered on what research the detective had been undertaking, but more importantly, wondered how she could use the information that Cooper had willingly disclosed her password, to her advantage.

Rising to her feet, her brow furrowed when she moved to stand over Daisy Cooper's desk.

The throaty roar of the diesel engine combined with the coarse language of the swarthy Turkish driver, his face beaded with sweat as he wrestled the large the articulated lorry round the Avenida del Peru and irritated at the public roadworks diverting him from his destination, the Liberian registered freighter that he knew was due to depart within the next four hours.

At last he pulled onto the access road, seeing the gates that led towards the container terminal a few hundred yards ahead.

Approaching the gates, he slowed in anticipation of the checkpoint and tried with difficulty to avoid looking at the two armed officers of the Guardia Civil, one who lazily cradled the automatic weapon in his arms and raised a hand to stop the approaching lorry.

The driver forced himself to be calm and reached for the paperwork in the file on the passenger seat, inwardly prayed that he would be recognised as the regular driver he was.
With a sigh of relief, he saw the familiar waddling figure of Carlos exit the brick built security gate and with a huge grin, reached down onto the floor of his cab to grab at the sleeve of strong and aromatic Turkish cigarettes favoured by the security team leader.
With an inward prayer to Allah, the driver prepared himself to be greeted and taking a deep breath, forced a fixed smile.

It had gone ten-o'clock when Harry parked the Focus among a row of private vehicles in bays below the three-storey building around the corner from where Harry Cavanagh's text said Nigel Faraday had his flat.
He wore his suit and a pair of the new shoes and a three-quarter length dark coat with the collar turned upwards.
He hadn't bothered with the belt holster, but in the right hand coat of the coat he carried the Glock.
Though he didn't anticipate having to use the handgun, he thought it prudent to bring it with him. But if the need to use it arose then he hoped more to frighten Faraday than kill him.
Though he had agreed terms with Stevie Watkins that he would murder Faraday, Harry fully intended reneging on their deal for he had no wish to involve himself in his previous life; other than perhaps if and when he caught up with the bastard who had murdered Harriet.
At the entrance to the flats he found the door was a security entry. Confirming Faraday's flat number from the text message, he ignored that button and pressed a ground flat button instead and when a woman's bored voice answered, he said, "Taxi for upstairs, but they're not answering the call."
"What? Oh, the lazy buggers!" the woman irately replied and pressed the entry button.
Pushing open the door, he quickly made his way to the flight of stairs just in case the woman decided to come out of her flat to confirm Harry was who he claimed to be.
Reaching the top floor, he saw that there was a spyhole set in the door to Faraday's flat, but realised if he placed his finger across the

small circle it would only make Faraday suspicious and with a sigh, knocked on the door.

He sensed rather than heard the presence on the other side of the door before a voice called out, "Who are you and what do you want?"

"Mister Faraday, my name's Harry Henderson. I apologise for calling so late in the evening, but I was hoping to have a word with you about the business in which you are engaged."

Harry was gambling that Faraday's curiosity might tempt him to open the door, but then heard him ask, "Are you alone? Are you the police?"

"I am alone and no, Mister Faraday, I'm not the police. My interests lie elsewhere. If you open the door I will stand well back and if you're not happy with what you see, you can quickly close the door again."

There was a moment's pause then Faraday called out, "Okay, do that."

Harry stepped back in the landing till his back was against the neighbouring door and stood with his hands unthreateningly crossed in front of him.

He heard the door being unlocked before it was then pulled open. The younger man who stood there was, Harry guessed, in his mid to late twenties with neatly trimmed fair hair, at least two inches taller than Harry, fit looking though not overly muscular and dressed in a light blue polo shirt and what Harry guessed were designer jeans. Faraday stared at him with curiosity.

Harry could see one hand raised as though ready to slam the door closed, but it was the hand Harry couldn't see that worried him for he suspected it held some sort of weapon.

"Okay, Mister Henderson, you've got my attention. What is it you want and what do you mean about my business?"

"I'm looking for someone who you may or may not know, but my information is that the individual I'm looking for is associated with you through your business, Mister Faraday. I would take it as a great favour if you would hear me out and even more so if you can help me."

Faraday's eyes narrowed as he slowly replied, "This individual. Why are you looking for this person?"

"Because they murdered someone who was very close to me, Mister Faraday."

Harry watched as Faraday turned pale and his eyes opened wide before he replied, "And do you believe I had something to do with this…this murder?"

"Not directly, no," Harry shook his head, "but like I said, you do have information that I need. Now, Mister Faraday, we can stand here and toss questions back and forth or you can invite me in where we can sit and I'll explain further."

"How do I know that you don't mean me some harm, Mister Henderson, that if I do invite you in you'll become," he paused then smiled, quickly assessing Harry to be an older and probably weaker man than he, before he added, "something of a problem for me to deal with?"

Harry opened his hands wide and replied, "If I meant you any harm, Mister Faraday, you wouldn't have seen it coming and I wouldn't be knocking on your door looking for information."

He watched as Faraday mulled this over before finally nodding and, his curiosity finally overtaking his good sense, opened the door a little wider and said, "Come in, then. Go straight through to the lounge."

Harry acknowledged with his own nod and as he passed Faraday in the doorway, saw that his guess had been correct for loosely in his hand, the taller man held a large bladed kitchen knife.

Smiling, Faraday said as he closed the door, "Just a precaution, Mister Henderson," and followed Harry through the hallway to the lounge beyond.

Inviting Harry to sit on the leather couch, Faraday sat opposite and laid the knife on the carpeted floor beside him before again asking, "What do you mean about my business?"

"I know you don't know me and likely have never heard of me, Mister Faraday, but I have some interesting contacts in the city who have told me about your drug dealing business and…"

"Now wait just one minute," Faraday angrily began to rise from his chair, but Harry held up his hand and continued, "I have no interest in what you get up to, none at all. What I am interested in is who your dealers in the north side of the city are. One of your dealers has supplied a junkie who is responsible for the murder of my aunt. A mugging, if you will that went badly wrong. My aunt died and that's why I want to find the individual responsible," he calmly added.

"How do I know you're not some undercover copper or a reporter?" Faraday stared suspiciously at him.

Harry reached into his inner jacket pocket and withdrew a business card that he reached across to lay on top of the coffee table between them.

"The card has the phone number of my accountant, Harry Cavanagh. I understand you have heard of him?"

Faraday slowly nodded.

"I know that Harry mediated for you and others in a recent territorial dispute and that you and the others trusted Harry at that time to make the correct decision regarding your individual businesses. If you contact him, he will vouch for me," he said, "and confirm what I have told you is the plain truth."

Faraday reached forward and lifting the card, peered at it before asking, "What if I were to supply you with names? What do you think will happen," he sneered at what he believed to be Harry's naivety, "that these people will suddenly just provide you with the tick lists of names of their punters?"

"They will if you instruct them too."

"And what if I refuse?"

Harry shrugged before calmly replying, "Then I will kill you and one by one, identify and kill your dealers till I find the individual I'm looking for."

Stunned, Faraday stared at Harry before responding, "Who the *fuck* are you that you think you can waltz in here and threaten me?"

"Well, firstly, I didn't *waltz* in. You invited me, Mister Faraday. Secondly," he slowly fetched the Glock from his coat pocket that he then menacingly laid on his lap, "I would suggest that tomorrow morning you telephone Harry Cavanagh and after he tells you *exactly* who I am, Mister Faraday, you will provide him with a list of your dealers and that way," he grimly smiled, "you get to stay alive." He stood up and returning the Glock to his pocket, quietly added, "I leave you to consider what I've said, but thank you for your time, Mister Faraday, and one more thing. Any information you provide to Harry Cavanagh will remain confidential. About that you have my word."

CHAPTER EIGHTEEN

The digital clock displayed almost six-thirty in the morning when Harry Henderson awoke and rising from the bed, fetched a nutritious energy bar from the shopping bag on the desk. While he munched at the bar, he opened one of the Slater's bags and dressed in the sports shorts and top then sitting on the edge of the bed, pulled on the training shoes.

Stamping down on the shoes to feel their comfort, he reached into the room's fridge and fetched out a bottle of chilled water that he drunk to wash down the bar. Ready now, he ensured the inch-long piece of thread at the safe remained in place and with a towel draped over his shoulder locked the room door behind him before heading for the lift that would take him down to the hotel's fitness room.

Dressed and ready to depart for her early shift, Daisy Cooper smiled at the sleeping Ian and blowing him a kiss, quietly closed the bedroom door.

She knew he would be annoyed that she didn't wake him before she left for work, but Saturday was a busy day for Ian and the staff in 'Daisy's Café' and so decided he needed the extra hour before he had to arise.

Moments later in her car, she smoothly drove away from the kerb and began to drive towards Saracen office, but her mind was a hive of activity.

Being Saturday, she knew that it was unlikely the Chief Inspector, Dougie Kane would be on duty at the office, though he might be working elsewhere in the city if there was a football game or a demonstration to be policed and only then if he was on the senior officer's duty list.

She did briefly consider calling him at home with what she had discovered and taking his advice on how she should proceed, but that would mean visiting him at home with the evidence of the DVD. However, she quickly discounted that idea for it was common knowledge in the office that Kane was a man who valued his off-duty privacy and while he was prepared to come out at any time for work related issues, he likely wouldn't appreciate a home visit about something that could wait till he resumed duty on Monday.

With a sigh and the decision made, Daisy concentrated on her driving as she sped through the quiet city.

Kieran McMenamin was hyped up, his body as tense as a tightly wound spring.
Lying in his bed, the joint smouldering between his fingers, he grinned at the memory of what he had done.
It was almost eleven o'clock and the darkness had set in.
He had watched the last customer, a tipsy old man stumble from the shop clutching a plastic bag to his chest as though afraid someone would snatch it from him.
By then he correctly guessed that Ali would be alone. His nerves tingling, he impatiently glanced up and down Saracen Street a dozen times, waiting for a break in the night-time traffic to make his move. With his hood up and the half brick in his hand, he had dashed across the road and with all his might, flung the brick through the window. Hearing with satisfaction Ali's cry of alarm that emboldened him, McMenamin raced off with a scream of joy through a nearby close and into the rear court.
Aye, he grinned to himself, that will teach the Paki bastard to mess me about and grinning widely at his self believed bravery, deeply inhaled on the remains of the joint.
As he exhaled, he could hear movement in the kitchen and figured his father must be doing a Saturday shift at his job while likely his sister Patricia was as usual staying over at her boyfriend's flat.
Good, he squirmed in the bed, that gave him the place to himself and decided that today, with the extra cash in his pocket, he'd pay a visit to Jackie Stone to find out if the delivery of gear Stone was awaiting had arrived.

Getting out of his car, Fariq Mansoor turned as a car drew up behind him and smiled when he saw the driver to be Daisy Cooper.
"Morning, Sarge," he greeted her with a smile and together they walked towards the entrance of the police station.
"Much on today, Fariq?" she asked as she passed through the entrance doors.
The young constable waved a greeting to the civilian bar officer then replied with a shake of his head, "Just the usual, showing Popeye the ropes and teaching him how to be a police officer."

"I heard that, you cheeky bugger," Doyle sneaked up behind Mansoor and playfully cuffing him on the back of the head, added, "Morning, Sarge."

"Popeye," she acknowledged him with a nod and then asked, "If you guys can square it with Sergeant Cassidy, I'm a bit short of patrol officers today so I'd be grateful for any help you can give me by attending calls. I'll phone her at her desk and confirm my request, but if you see her first…"

"I'll pass on your request, Sarge," Doyle nodded and with Mansoor, headed towards the Community Police office on the first floor.

Ten minutes later, the two officers were dressed and about to go downstairs to collect their radios when the door opened to admit a red-faced and flustered Anne Cassidy who was late, but to hide her annoyance at her tardiness, she barked, "What's keeping you two? I assumed you'd be out there already, attending any outstanding calls."

In an even and calm voice, Doyle related Daisy Cooper's request and added Cooper had already tried phoning her, but before he finished, Cassidy snappily interrupted, "If Sergeant Cooper wishes to utilise my officers she can come and ask me herself."

Doyle tightly smiled and replied, "I'll pass that on, Sergeant," and nodding that Mansoor
follow him, left the room.

Returning to his room, Harry Henderson first checked the piece of thread had not been disturbed before changing out of the sports clothes.

It had been a long time since he had the opportunity to enjoy a workout in a purpose built gymnasium, though had maintained his fitness at his home in Cuba by purchasing second-hand weights, making his own punch-bag and a strict regime of early morning swimming in the warm seas.

He was about to switch on the shower when he heard his mobile phone buzz with an incoming text message and opening the test, read that Harry Cavanagh wanted him to call by his office.

He returned to the en-suite and wondered; had Faraday taken his warning seriously or had he instead created a new enemy who might now be placing a contract out on him?

Sandy Craig, unshaven and not long out of his bed, paid off the taxi and first glancing curiously up at the building, then checked his wristwatch and slowly shook his head.

The text telling him to get his arse over to Faraday's flat had been out of the ordinary for the poncey git simply because it was normally his habit to lie late on a Saturday morning, yet here he was telling Craig that he needed him and now.

To his surprise, Faraday almost snatched the door off its hinges when he pulled it open and glaring at Craig, said, "Good, glad you're hear, Sandy. I've a job for you," before turning away in the expectation the big man would follow him.

Craig repressed a smile because it was obvious, not least because his posh accent seemed to have slipped away, that something had rattled Faraday.

In the kitchen, he nodded that Craig take a seat before offering him coffee, then continued, "I had a visitor late last night. A guy carrying a handgun. Bastard threatened me, too," he snarled.

Surprised, Craig refused the coffee then realising that Faraday was clearly rattled, asked, "Did you know him?"

"I didn't know him when like an *idiot* I let him into the flat, but he gave me this," he threw the business card onto the table, "with Harry Cavanagh's phone number on it and said *his* name was Harry Henderson. Does that name mean anything to you?"

Faraday didn't miss Craig's sharp intake of breath, but for the wrong reason for the large man did not expect Headcase to confront Faraday; no, after what he had agreed with Stevie Watkins, he expected Headcase to murder the bastard.

Faraday stared keenly at Craig before again asking, "So, you do recognise the name then?"

"Yes, boss, I do," Craig carefully replied. "Henderson's been out of the country for a while, but before he left he was the guy that you went to when you wanted someone to disappear. You know what I mean?"

Faraday paled and replied, "You mean, a killer?"

"A killer for hire, aye, and the very best at what he did."

His stomach clenched when he then asked, "What was he doing here?"

Faraday's brow furrowed and biting at a knuckle, he said, "Gave me a story that he's looking for someone who mugged his aunt; said he was close to her and that she apparently died because of the mugging. Load of crap if you ask me," he nervously paced back and forth across the kitchen floor.

Craig wasn't certain what he should tell Faraday, how much he should disclose about Headcase for Watkins instructions were quite explicit.

Nothing is to make Faraday suspicious, he had said; not until we learn the time and place where the delivery is being made. Then, when we have the information…

Now, thinking on his feet, he said, "Tell me *exactly* what Henderson wanted, boss?"

Faraday took a deep breath and replied, "He wants the names of our dealers in the north side of the city. Told me that he believes one of the dealers supplied the junkie who mugged his aunt, though how he knows that," Faraday shrugged, "he didn't say. It's the junkie that he's after. Told me that if I didn't come across he'd kill me, then find the dealers and kill them too."

Craig rubbed at his unshaven chin and looking up at Faraday, said, "You heard the news? The cops are looking for someone for murdering a junkie over in Ruchill Park. Why don't we tell Henderson that's the junkie who murdered his aunt? I mean, who's to say it wasn't, anyway?"

"Not a bad idea, Sandy," his voice dripped with sarcasm, "but that would infer we *already* knew who killed his aunt and the first thing the bastard would do is question how we came by that particular titbit, eh, and maybe then wonder if we were somehow involved."

"Aye, right enough," Craig conceded, then acutely conscious that Watkins wanted nothing to interfere with their plans, asked, "What do you intend doing, will you give him the names? I mean, he's a bad bastard to cross is Henderson and let's face it, he's not going to go to the cops and tell them the names of the dealers, is he?"

Faraday was aghast.

"What, you think I should give in to him, simply roll over and give him the names of our people?"

"From what you told me, boss, he's hunting just the one person, a junkie and don't forget, he came to you to ask. He could have just burst in here when you were on your own and well," he paused, letting the idea of what a madman like Headcase Henderson was capable of play with Faraday's imagination. "After all, what the fuck do we care what he does to a junkie and if it causes us the minimum of grief," he shrugged.

Faraday didn't immediately respond, recalling the visit and how calm and collected, sinister even, Henderson had been.

Finally, he said, "No. I told him I'd think about what he wanted from me, but I will not be intimidated by any bastard."

Craig didn't reply, but after a moment asked, "When I arrived, you said you'd a job for me? What job?"

Faraday stopped pacing and standing with his back to the worktop, his hand tightly grasping his mug, he replied, "Two things. First, I want you to get the team of muscle together for Sunday evening, say eight guys and make sure you get a Luton type van with a tail lift. I'll text you the location in the early evening after I speak again to my source and confirm the cops definitely won't be around. Secondly, I need you to find someone to deal with this guy Henderson before this gets out of hand."

"What, you mean…"

"Yes, Sandy, someone to…" he paused, the posh lilt to his voice returning as he smiled, "as you so succinctly put it earlier, make Mister Henderson disappear."

Daisy Cooper knocked on the door of the Community Police office and with a smile, leaned against the door post and said to Anne Cassidy, "Morning. I understand we had a bit of a mix-up this morning, Anne."

"Not really a mix-up, Sergeant Cooper," she turned in her chair and frostily replied, "more you commandeering my officers for patrol duties rather than those duties I intended for them."

Daisy didn't like Cassidy and thought her a bumptious, officious cow, but neither did she underestimate her and said, "For that I offer you my apologies; however, I'm certain you will appreciate that being under resourced as I am and with more calls to deal with than officers to attend them, your lads would be a great help. So, if you could lend them to me for the duration of the shift?"

"Oh, I think not, Sergeant Cooper, for had you the courtesy to first come to me rather than one of my subordinates…"

"Subordinates? Fuck me, Anne, Popeye Doyle is hardly a *subordinate*," she indignantly exclaimed. "The man has more service than you and me together and a damned sight more experience! I think you do him a great disservice by calling him a 'subordinate' and as for coming to you first," she narrowed her eyes and hissed, her dander now up, "perhaps if you improved your fucking timekeeping and were at your desk when I tried to get you on the phone *you* might have been in a position to give me a decision!" With that, she turned and stomped off, leaving Cassidy pale faced and shaking with anger.

Across the hallway in the Harriet Henderson murder incident room, the team had overheard Daisy's raised voice, her loud and angry exchange with Cassidy and burst into laughter that increased even more so when the irate Cassidy arose from her desk to noisily slam the office door shut.

DS Calum Fraser nodded to DC Munroe that he was ready to leave the stopped and said, "You seem a wee bit peaky today, Marilyn. Feeling okay?"

"Yes, of course," she vigorously nodded, but aware that she was blushing.

"If you're coming down with something, tell me. I'm not travelling in the same car if there's a risk of me catching some of your bugs," he joked.

"No, nothing like that," she shook her head then knowing he wouldn't let it go, added, "Just a personal thing, but nothing for you to worry about. Right, ready?" she forced herself to sound cheerful.

"Yes, ready," he agreed and accompanied her downstairs to their car.

Neither the Greek Captain of the aged and rusted Liberian registered freighter nor the majority of his Indian and Chinese crew were aware that the red and green painted container listed on the manifest contained anything other than tinned fruit.

However, the exception was the Turkish First Mate who while in his cabin and at the prearranged time used his global satellite phone to send a text message informing Miguel de Lugo that so far there had been no problems, that the ship was making good process and if the weather held, would dock on schedule at Felixstowe.

Mary Harris awoke suddenly, startled at the sound of someone in her kitchen but then smiled.

Michael had always been an early riser; a habit he had picked up from his father.

Rising from bed, she dressed in her robe and made her way to the kitchen where she saw her son, still in his pyjamas of shorts and T shirt, stood over the cooker.

The tantalising waft of bacon rose rose from the frying pan and turning, he smiled when he said, "Morning mum, couple of pieces and bacon and tea all right?"

"Lovely," she returned his smile, sitting down at the table and deciding not to admit that her usual breakfast was a cereal and glass of fresh orange juice.

"Sleep well?"

"Yes, I did," Mary replied. "And you?"

"Not bad at all," he tightly smiled, laying the plate and mug before her and it was then she realised there was something on his mind.

Watching as he sat down opposite, she asked, "Something up?"

"It's dad's funeral," he began, "well, not the funeral, but after the funeral I mean."

"And?"

He stopped chewing and took a slurp of tea before taking a deep breath and replying, "I'm worried about you, being here on your own I mean."

"But I'm not on my own, Michael. I have you and Jenny," she smiled.

"Jenny's in New Zealand mum and I'm…what I mean, is, I have my work down in Dorset and there's," he paused. "There's no real likelihood of me returning home. For good, I mean. We're making our life down there, you see."

"Oh, Michael," she smiled, her hand reaching across the table to hold his.

"It's not official or anything, but we're considering opening our own pharmacy," he continued at a rush. "The thing is, mum, we've both got good jobs down there and her family are all there and, well…"

Mary understood his concern and tightening her grip on his hand, said, "Listen to me, Michael Harris. I never considered that you might be worried about me and thinking you must move back here to be with me. Not for a second. You have your wife and your life in Dorset, a good job and now," she beamed, "I'm so pleased that you're thinking of going out on your own too. Your dad would have been so proud. As for me," she withdrew her hand and sat back, a cheeky smile on her face, "I have *my* job and my circle of friends and my life is here, so don't you be worrying about me."

He didn't immediately respond, but then asked, "Would you consider coming to live down south? In Dorset, I mean. I could find you your own place."

She slowly shook her head and with a smile to hide the ache in her heart, replied, "I told you, Michael I have my life here. Besides, if you and Janice have family, I'll be a regular visitor."

He nodded.

"So, with me having somewhere for me to visit on my holidays…right then, let's hear no more about you moving back here," she finished with a wave of her hand.

"Okay, mum," he replied, almost with relief. "Now eat your piece and drink your tea and we'll go and find me a suit for dad's funeral on Tuesday."

He drove some distance from Faraday's flat before pulling over into a supermarket car park and with a glance about him to ensure there was nobody parked nearby who would recognise him, fetched his mobile phone from his pocket.

Scrolling down the directory, he stopped at the entry called 'granddad' and pressed the green button.

"Sandy my man," Stevie Watkins voice echoed in his ear. "What's the latest then?"

"Bit of a hiccup, Stevie," Craig replied, his eyes darting back and forth as though he feared being overheard. "Couple of things to report starting with Headcase visited our man late last night."

"What! Did he do him in?"

"No," Craig unconsciously shook his head, "he was there for something else. Wanted to know the names of Faradays dealers. Told him he's looking for a junkie he thinks killed his auntie."

"You're shitting me!"

"Straight up. Said if Faraday didn't comes across he'd murder him then murder his dealers."

There was a pause and for a few seconds, Craig thought the connection had been lost before Watkins asked, "What did Faraday do?"

"Told Headcase he'd think about it but when I arrived this morning, ordered me to find someone to take care of Headcase."
He heard Watkins snigger before he replied, "Then why don't you do that, big man? Tell Faraday that you've found someone then all we have to do is tell Headcase when and where the delivery will be and watch while he does Faraday. Simple, eh? So, what's the other thing you want to tell me?"
Craig grinned and said, "It's definitely on for Sunday evening. He wants me to get a team of eight together and a Luton van with a tail lift, so I can only guess there's quite a lot of lifting to do."
"You still bringing the shooters?"
"Yeah, two of them. I'll handle one and give the other to…"
"To me," Watkins interrupted. "I'm too old to be humping gear about so you and me can do the security while the lifting is getting done."
"Fine by me. What about Headcase? He wanted the dealer's names sent to Harry Cavanagh by this morning. What if he visits Faraday again today because he didn't get the names and does him in? That puts paid to us getting the location of the delivery, doesn't it?"
"Good point, big man. Here's a thought. You know most of Faraday's dealers, don't you?"
"Yes," Craig slowly drawled.
"Then why don't *you* visit Cavanagh and tell him Faraday sent you with the names. That should satisfy Headcase for now and once he's killed Faraday, it's no longer our problem, is it?"
"No, it's not," Craig agreed with a grin and ended the call.

Fariq Mansoor replied to the radio message and said, "We've a call to Ali Rahmani's on Saracen Street, Popeye. Seems somebody punted his window in last night."
"Not before time," Doyle dryly remarked and with Mansoor by his side, plodded along towards the shop.

Harry Henderson parked the focus in a bay and after feeding the meter with a handful of coins, made his way to Harry Cavanagh's office.
He was surprised to find Helen dressed in a bright yellow tracksuit and seated at her desk who with a grunt, said, "He's in there

smoking those bloody cigars you brought him from Cuba. Place smells like a tobacco factory."

"Didn't think I'd find you here on a Saturday," he smiled at her as he dropped the paper bag of rolls and bacon on her desk.

"When's *he's* working," she nodded towards the closed door, "so am I."

Lifting the bag, she grinned and added, "Thanks, Harry, I'll get the kettle on."

He knocked politely on the door then opening it, waved away the fug of smoke that threatened to engulf him.

Cavanagh smiled at Harry's discomfort and rising from his desk, stubbed out the cigar in a tin ashtray before striding across the room to throw open the office windows.

"Sorry about that, Harry," he lifted a newspaper and began to waft it about his head. "I'd forgotten you're not keen on the smell of tobacco anymore."

"Not since I'd given them up, I'm not," he agreed and pulling a chair out from under the desk, sat opposite Cavanagh. "So, your text message. What's up?"

"I had an interesting phone call last night at home. You might recall me telling you that I had a woman who works in Saracen office?"

"Aye, a cleaner you said."

"That's her," Cavanagh nodded and leaned forward onto his elbows, his fingers interlaced as he stared at Harry. "Well, she called me last night to say that the overheard something that she thought we might be interested in."

Before he could continue, Helen stepped through the door carrying a tray upon which rested a plate with two rolls and two steaming mugs of tea and told Cavanagh, "Harry, that was a guy called Sandy Craig on the phone. Says he's acting for a Nigel Faraday and that he's coming to see you about a list."

Cavanagh nodded to Helen then turning to Harry, he asked, "A list?"

"I called on Faraday last night. Told him I needed a list of his dealers if I'm to track down the junkie who attacked Harriet." He smiled as he added, "I tried a little persuasion, but to be honest, I didn't think he'd come across." He pursed his lips before asking, "Is this the same Sandy Craig we discussed before?"

"It is, but before you left for the sunnier climate Craig was acting as muscle for Stevie Watkins. Remember I told you they run together in the old Kinning Park team? Well, that's the curious thing," Cavanagh shook his head. "As far as I'm aware and from what my various contacts have told me, Sandy Craig still *is* Stevie Watkins man, but he's now working as Faraday's right hand man."

"A plant and I'm guessing he's the man Watkins alluded to as his informant inside Faraday's network."

"Oh, I don't doubt it for a minute and you'll recall that Watkins boasted to you he is aware that Faraday has a police source? Well, that information can only have come from Craig and you'll recall," he winked at Harry "I already suspected I knew who Watkins source might be."

"Figures then that if you're correct and Craig *is* Watkins man then he'll already have informed Watkins who Faraday's dealers are. That places Watkins in pole position for if I was to do as he asks and bump Faraday off, Watkins would simply take over the running of an established network. Neat," he slowly nodded and pursed his lips. "Curious thing though. Why hasn't he already had Faraday dealt with?"

Cavanagh shrugged and shook his head before suggesting, "I assume you'll not want to be here when Craig arrives and you'll want me to take the list from Craig. Are there any questions I should ask?"

"Only which dealers Craig believes I should contact first. Now, what was it your source in the Saracen office found out?"

"Ah, it may be nothing, it may be something. It seems the CID have learned that shortly before your aunt was attacked she withdrew cash from a bank ATM at Saracen Cross. Eighty pounds in new notes. That and the man in charge of the inquiry, a DI McBride…"

"McBride," exclaimed Harry with a frown. "That's the name of the DI who was with the woman Mulgrew when they stopped me at Glasgow Airport. Coincidence, you think?"

"Who knows," Cavanagh shrugged. "Well, this man McBride seems to think that your aunt's attacker might be responsible for a similar attack on an old man shortly after Harriet was mugged. That and there might be a connection to the junkie who was murdered in Ruchill Park later the same day."

"Bloody hell," Harry's eyes widened. "If it is the same guy he's been busy, hasn't he?"

"Indeed," Cavanagh frowned, before adding, "Sandy Craig might be

on his way here now, Harry, so I suggest you make yourself scarce. I'll give you a phone later when he's gone and text you the list."
"I take it there won't be anything on paper?"
"Unlikely," Cavanagh shook his head. "I imagine everything he knows will be in his head."
Getting to his feet, Harry slurped the last of his tea and said, "I'll head off now and await your call."

CHAPTER NINETEEN

Stood behind his counter, Ali Rahmani glared at the two officers and said, "I'm telling you, I don't *know* who broke the window. Anyway, it's not *my* job to tell you guys, it's your job to find out who did it."
Mansoor turned towards Doyle and shaking his head, grinned and said, "Are we really in the middle of a city, Popeye? I'm just wondering because I'm sure I can smell bullshit."
"I'll report you," Rahmani poked a finger towards Mansoor. "You're being racist," he snarled at the young cop, "and not doing anything because I'm a Muslim."
"No," Mansoor angrily shook his head. "*I'm* a Muslim because I'm honest and law-abiding. You're just a thieving, lying…"
"Enough, Fariq," Doyle snapped at the younger man, then turning towards Rahmani, patiently said, "Look, Ali, we both know you're trying to give us the bums rush because you probably do know who punted your window in and let's face it; it's not the first time you and me have gone a few rounds because of your resetting stolen gear, eh?"
"Now wait a fucking minute…"
"No, Ali, no minute and don't be using bad language to me, okay?" Rahmani, his face flushed with anger, stared hatefully at Doyle then slowly nodded.
"The problem *you* have when you make your insurance claim," Doyle continued, "is you'll need the polis to confirm that it *was* a criminal act of vandalism and when we submit the crime report, don't forget your insurance company will likely pay for a copy. On the crime report we can either say you cooperated with our inquiry or that you refused to assist us. If the insurance company are not happy, that you refused to cooperate with us…well," he smiled, "the expense of replacing the plate glass window will be down to you,

won't it? Now, let me think," he stroked at his chin, "What's the going rate for a window that size?"

Rahmani turned pale and tight-lipped, said, "I don't know for certain who it was because I was cashing up at the time."

"But you have your suspicions, don't you?" Doyle coaxed him.

Rahmani took a deep breath and laying both hands flat on the counter, replied, "Look, I did a wee bit of business with a local guy. He wanted…" then stopped and shook his head.

"He wanted what?" Doyle pressed him.

"I'm not saying. I'm not grassing anyone up and besides, it might not have been him," Rahmani replied.

"It's like drawing blood," Mansoor sarcastically hissed, but quietened when Doyle gave him an icy glance.

"But this guy you're not grassing up," Doyle leaned companionably forward onto the counter. "He's the first guy that came to mind, isn't he? But don't worry about not giving us his name," Doyle stood upright and nodding to Mansoor that they leave, added, "Maybe he'll chip in and help pay for your new window, eh?"

Rahmani nervously licked at his lips, his glance darting from Doyle to Mansoor, then lowering his head, he said, "What if he finds out it was me that told you?"

"And who will tell him?" Doyle shrugged, "I mean, you didn't see anyone punting the brick through the window, did you?"

Rahmani shook his head before slowly replying, "No, I didn't see anyone."

"And we're unlikely to say, 'Hey Jimmy, Ali Rahmani gave us your name,' are we?"

He paused before continuing, "So, this guy. What was it that he wanted you to do for him that made him so upset with you?"

Rahmani didn't immediately respond, his Adams apple dancing a flamenco in his throat, but then said, "He wanted me to change some new notes for him. New for old and wasn't happy when I charged him a fee for doing it."

Doyle's face didn't change, but his stomach lurched when he remembered the ATM slip that he had discovered lying beside Harriet Henderson's unconscious body. Maybe it was just a coincidence, but his instinct told him no, he was on to something here.

"When you say new notes, Ali, how much are we talking about here and what kind of notes? What bank and the denomination of the notes I mean."

"Eh, four twenties I think. Aye," he nodded, "four new twenties and I think they were Royal Bank of Scotland."

"And where are the notes now?"

Rahmani's eyes creased when he replied, "Are they important? Is it something that…"

"Just answer the question."

"Gone," he shrugged. "Like I told you, I was cashing up when the brick came through the window. The takings for the day went into the cash bag and then I dropped them into the night safe in the wall of my own bank down in Charing Cross."

"And this guy's name?"

Rahmani, guessing that there was more to the story now that Doyle was interested in the new notes, replied, "I don't know his second name, but he's called Kieran."

"Kieran," Doyle slowly repeated then with a smile continued, "You'd better lock up the shop for now, Ali. You've a wee visit to make to the CID at the office."

Seated opposite Harry Cavanagh, Sandy Craig smiled and said, "Nice to meet with you again, Mister Cavanagh."

"Please," the rotund man smiled at him and reached for a pencil, "call me Harry. Now, this list you have, may we begin?"

"You do understand that my boss, Mister Faraday, is merely complying with Headcase's…I mean, Mister Henderson's request, as a courtesy? That Mister Faraday does not like to be threatened and if Mister Henderson was to even consider anything like that again there might be…" he hesitated before adding, "consequences."

"Indeed," Cavanagh continued to smile. "The list?"

"The list, yes," and proceeded to provide a number of names and addresses for Faraday's network of dealers in the north side of the city.

Once completed, Cavanagh laid down his pencil and arching his fingers in front of his nose, said, "Mister Henderson has a request of you, Mister Craig."

"Of me?"

"Aye, as you know from his conversation with Mister Faraday, he is hunting a particular individual, a junkie he suspects who is possibly responsible for his aunt's mugging and unfortunate demise. He asked that if you were him, who is the dealer you would suspect to be best placed to supply the product to that junkie in the Saracen area? Of course," Cavanagh held his hands wide apart, "he asks this as a favour and will be grateful for your advice."

Flattered, Craig took a deep breath and brow furrowed, considered for a moment before replying, "There are two I'd put at the top of my list; a guy who lives in the multi storey's up in Wyndford," then leaning forward, tapped the fourth name on the sheet of paper in front of Cavanagh.

"Jackie Stone. He's one of Mister Faraday's…." he grinned, "hardest workers."

He sat back down and continued, "But there's a name not on the list. A guy Mister Faraday has an interest in signing up. Collects his product from somebody over in the Govan area. A former boxer called Peter McGroarty," and gave the address in Ronaldsay Street.

As Cavanagh noted the name and address, Craig then said, "I hear Mister Henderson is back and looking for work. Is that correct, Harry?"

His face expressionless, he replied, "As far as I am aware he's only here in Glasgow in response to what happened to his aunt," but conscious of Craig being Stevie Watkins inside man, added, "though I did have cause to refer him to another client. But of course," he smiled, "I can't divulge any client names."

"No, of course not," Craig agreed, keen now to be away and report Cavanagh's admission back to Watkins.

He was gone just a few moments when Helen strode into his office and her eyes betraying her curiosity, said, "I don't like him, Harry. I watched him from the window when he walked out from the entrance downstairs onto Wellington Street. He was already on his mobile phone before he got out out of the main door. What did he want?"

"What he wanted, my dear, was to fire his boss's network in to our dear old pal, Harry Henderson and testing the waters to find out if Harry is back here for good or not. No doubt when you saw him on the phone he was calling his real boss, Stevie Watkins…"

"Another sour faced bastard," she interrupted.

"Aye, as you so succinctly put it and like Watkins, Sandy Craig is another man who can't be trusted and likely telling Watkins about his visit here."

"So, what's next?"

"What's next my love is that I will text Harry a couple of names and addresses from this list," he tapped with a stubby finger on the sheet of paper then grinning wickedly, added, "then perhaps you might wish to lock the outer office door and come I here and let me fiddle a bit with your undergarments."

Hands on her hips, she returned his grin with her own saucy smile before replying, "Oh, Harry Cavanagh, you *do* say the nicest things."

Michael Harris sighed for he had answered the door at least a half dozen times that morning, all to well-wishers either stopping by with a bereavement card to add to the dozen or so on the mantelpiece or handing in a plastic tub of food.

Now there was the bell again.

"I'll get it," he called out, but knew that no matter who it was his mother would extend an invitation to come in for a cup of tea and while most had gracefully declined, two spinster sisters stayed for over an hour, relating all the people they had known who had recently died.

And that's all my mum needs, he had thought as wearing a fixed smile he had kept them going with tea and biscuits.

Opening the door, he forced himself to again smile, but was genuinely pleased to see his mother's charity shop friend, Alice McLean, who stood uncertainly with her handbag clutched to her like a shield.

"Before you say no," he nodded to her, "come in Missus Mclean. I know she'll be pleased to see you."

"Sad times, son," she shook her head before giving him a brief hug. "How is she?"

"I'm fine, Alice," his mother said from behind him, patting her hair into some sort of shape after catching a quick fifteen minutes lie down in her bedroom. "Please, come through, Alice," then to Michael, "Can you pop the kettle on, son?"

"No bother," he headed into the kitchen.

In the front room, Mary bade her friend sit down on the couch while she occupied her favourite armchair.

"How are things at the shop?"
"Oh, we're getting by, hen, but don't you be bothering about that. You've enough going on without worrying yourself about the shop."
They chatted for a few moments, pausing when Michael brought through their tea and a plate of Abernethy's and continuing when he left them alone.
"I was in the bank this morning," Alice sipped at her tea, "and speaking with that young lassie; you know, the new teller? The girl with the right weird hairdo?"
"Aye," Mary nodded.
"You know the elderly lady that was mugged and then died? The lady on the television?"
"On the news, you mean?"
"Aye, the news. Anyway, it seems the police were down at the bank, she was telling me, because just before she was attacked the lady had used the ATM on the corner and withdrew money. According the lassie, the police think that the man that attacked her stole her money."
Mary's eyes narrowed, her mind in whirl. The young man she had seen standing on the corner, she had been almost certain he was watching something or perhaps someone across the road from the corner and she startled, spilling some of her tea onto the saucer.
"Mary? Are you okay, hen?"
"What? Oh, yes, Alice, I'm fine it's just that I *think* I've remembered something."

In his bedroom at the Hilton, Harry Henderson had just finished his phone call to Donna to assure her that yes, he was fine and no, he didn't want her making the trip back to attend Harriet's funeral. Besides, he had told her, there wasn't a date fixed for the ceremony because the police had not yet released her body.
"But you know I'll come if you need me," she had stressed.
He had smiled and assured her that he would be fine, causing her to laugh when he reminded her that he had Harry Cavanagh and the acerbic Helen to hold his hands if he was moved to tears.
He missed her laugh and his heart felt heavy when he had ended the call.
He turned when his mobile chirruped with an incoming text message.

Opening the text, he read that there were two addresses Harry Cavanagh suggested he begin with and rather than send them all, if the first two turned out to be bummers Cavanagh would send the remaining addresses two at a time thereafter.
He took a gulp of his bottled water and reading the first name and address muttered, "Jackie Stone."

Popeye Doyle introduced himself to Danny McBride who said, "You're the uniformed officer who discovered the victim?"
"Aye, sir, young Fariq Mansoor and me," he nodded.
"What can I do for you…" he smiled and asked, "Can I call you Popeye?"
"Everyone else does, so why not," Doyle grinned then continued, "When we found Harriet…I mean, Missus Henderson…"
"Did you know her?"
"Well, I knew her to see and say hello to, but it's her nephew who was known to me from a very long time ago," Doyle carefully replied.
"You mean Harry Henderson."
Surprised, Doyle nodded and replied, "Aye, that's him. Is he, I mean…"
"No," McBride shook his head. "he's not involved in the inquiry. If anything he's as a much a victim as his aunt, losing her like that. Now, I'm guessing you might have something for us?"
"Well, when we found Harriet, I also discovered a bank receipt from an ATM that indicated that earlier in the morning she had drawn…"
"Eighty pounds in twenties, yes, I'm aware of that," McBride interrupted with an unusual tension in his stomach.
"Right, well, young Fariq and I have just attended a vandalism that occurred last night in Saracen Street. A local shopkeeper come part time resetter of stolen property called Ali Rahmani. He, ah…" Doyle paused then said, "volunteered the name of a suspect for the vandalism, a guy who he had pissed off when he charged him extra for swapping eighty quid's worth of new RBS twenties for old notes."
McBride's eyes widened. Was this the break he needed?
"Where's this guy…eh?"
"Rahmani. I brought him in voluntarily, sir. He's with my neighbour in an interview room along the corridor."

"Did he cough the name of this guy with the new notes?"
"Told us he's called Kieran, but alleges he doesn't know his second name." Doyle shrugged and added, "Chances are he might be telling the truth about not knowing the surname, but the thing is I'm certain he definitely knows who this guy is and can identify him."
"What about you, Popeye. Do you know who he's talking about?"
"This is Saracen, sir. There's literally dozens of Kieran's, Patricks, Conor's, Sean's and every other Irish forename you can think of. And yes," he grinned. "After working the beat round here for nigh on thirty years, I don't think I'm boasting when I say I think I know most of them. At the minute though, I thought I'd report to you what we've discovered then I'm fetching some coffee for Mister Rahmani. He might not be the most honest of individuals, but I thought it better I keep him sweet till such times you or one of your team interview him."
McBride laughed and clapping Doyle on his arm, said, "Good work, Popeye," before turning and calling the office manager, Ian Prescott to him.

Just as Harry Henderson was about to depart the Hilton Hotel, Kieran McMenamin knocked softly on Jackie Stone's door, his breath held and prepared to run as he worried that Stone might have the polis or that guy Faraday and his bruiser in the flat with him. To his relief Stone nervously called through the door asking who was there and replying, he said, "It's me, Kieran."
The door opened and McMenamin's hopes were dashed for almost immediately upon seeing the bedraggled state of Stone he realised the delivery had not yet arrived for if it had, undoubtedly Stone would have been wasted.
"Come in, come in," Stone, dressed in a stained, once white tee shirt emblazoned with a scene for a Florida beach, black tracksuit bottoms and bare feet, waved him through the door before breathlessly asking, "Got any gear on you, Kieran?"
McMenamin closed the door behind him and following Stone into the front room, irritably replied, "No. That's why I'm here, Jackie. You told me you were expecting a delivery. Where the fuck is it then?"
Stone deeply sighed and coughing, flopped down into a stained and tattered armchair and said, "Monday at the latest, I'm told."

Standing over him, McMenamin idly kicked at Stone's bare feet and replied, "Monday? What the fuck use is Monday to me, Jackie. I've got dough in my pocket. If you can't provide me…"

"Wait a minute, Kieran," Stone almost pleaded, the pain in his eyes obvious as his body reacted to the withdrawal of his daily heroin fix. "I'm hurting here, man. Look," he squirmed in the armchair, his eyes reddened with lack of sleep, "If you've got cash, maybe I can sort out a wee deal with a guy I know and we can share a hit together, eh? What do you say, pal?"

McMenamin stared at him in disgust and sneeringly replied, "I came here to buy the gear to sell on, Jackie, not to become a fucking loser-user like you, ya junkie bastard," and again kicked at his feet, but more viciously this time. "I smoke the dope, aye, but I'm not going down the same road as you. What, you think I'm stupid or something?"

His frustration at not being able to procure the heroin from Stone enraged him and he felt an overwhelming urge to do the bastard, to kick the shite out of the helpless junkie just like he'd…

He stopped and staring down at the terrified Stone, evilly smiled. No, he forced himself to be calm, there was no point in hurting the smaller and weaker man because at some time in the future, he reasoned, he'd be back and buying the gear from him.

Shaking his head, he was about to leave the flat when Stone, hoping to reconcile himself with McMenamin, asked, "Did you find her, Kieran? The lassie I mean. Maggie?"

It was that simple question that sealed Stone's fate.

McMenamin stopped, his heart beating wildly in his chest and he took a deep breath.

Stone didn't know about Maggie being dead, he reasoned or he'd have had the sense not to mention her ever again.

In that heartbeat, he realised if the cops were ever to connect him to Maggie's death, to the murders of her and her junkie flatmate, it would be through Jackie Stone; the junkie who told him where to find her.

Turning, he swallowed deeply and quietly said, "Stand up, Jackie, I want to show you something."

"Show me what?"

"Just stand up, there's something in the veranda that I need you to see. Down in the car park. My new motor."

Puzzled, Stone pushed himself upright from the armchair and staring warily at McMenamin, replied, "You got yourself a motor, Kieran? What kind?"

"Just come and see," he replied, his voice as calm as he could be, but his hands were sweating and his mouth was dry.

Some inner sense told Stone that McMenamin was lying, that he meant him harm and he tried to bolt pass the younger, stronger man, but McMenamin was too fast for him and grabbing Stone by his long, greasy hair, pulled him towards the veranda door.

"No, Kieran, please," Stone begged, struggling futilely and his efforts to escape McMenamin's strong grip in vain.

Now McMenamin's arm was firmly around his neck while his free hand was clasped against Stone's mouth.

He tried to kick McMenamin, but the puny kick from his bare feet was ineffective, however, it caused McMenamin to unbalance and they fell struggling against the veranda door.

Releasing his grip on Stone's mouth, McMenamin pulled the door open as the older man tried to scream for help, but Stone's parched throat uttered no more than a croaked gasp.

McMenamin pulled him through the cracked, glass door into the cluttered veranda, knocking aside a large, plastic plant pot that spilled its contents of withered flowers and a handful of dried earth across the concreted veranda.

"No, please God, no," Stone's voice began to rise in panic.

Still holding him about the neck, McMenamin reached his free hand down and grabbing him by the seat of his trousers, he startled for he saw and felt the smaller man had wet himself and with fury and a sudden burst of adrenalin, heaved the weeping Stone over the metal railings.

Turning away, McMenamin resisted the urge to watch Stone fall to the ground nine floors below, but upon hearing his shrill scream, hastily made his way through the grubby flat towards the front door. Exiting the flat, he hurried towards the lift, completely unaware of the young Somalian mother at the door of her flat who hushed her child and held him close to her as she watched the tall, white man rush away from the door of the man who she had been warned was reputed to be a drug dealer.

CHAPTER TWENTY

"Boss?"

Myra McColl raised her head from reading the Action in front of her and stared with raised eyes at DS Calum Fraser.

"We've got a DNA hit on the skin sample that was under our victim's fingernails," he grimly stared at her.

She felt quick breath rise and asked, "Who?"

"Local ned, a Kieran McMenamin, aged twenty-three and a known associate of our victim, Lennie Robertson," Fraser replied.

"Do you know him?"

"No, not personally, but my neighbour Marilyn Munroe says he's a small time dealer, that he usually sticks to cannabis himself, but sells the hard stuff now and then when he's got cash in his pocket. Has a couple or three convictions, according to Marilyn."

"Do we have a current address for him?"

"Aye, we do. His antecedent history from his last arrest a three months months ago puts him living with his father and sister in Crowhill Street."

"Three months? No," she shook her head, "that's too long to take as a current address. He could have moved on from there in that time. I want you to call in the shift plainclothes. We have a wee job for them," then stopped and eyes narrowing in thought, said, "No, better than that. The cop, Popeye Doyle. It's more than likely he'll have better Intel about who's who and where people are biding from the time he's worked in this area. Get a hold of him and have him come and see me."

"Boss," he acknowledged with a nod.

"Right," she slammed both hands flat down onto her desk, "gather the team together for a quick briefing, but before we take any action against this guy McMenamin, I want a solid statement from the Lab boys that the DNA is a positive match for our suspect. Also," she rose to her feet and rubbed with the heel of her hand at her brow, "we'll need photographs of him to. As current as the Criminal Records at Gartcosh have got or," she stared at him, "check the divisional collators files too and see when the last photograph of McMenamin is dated."

She stared at Fraser and asked, "Have I missed anything?"

"You seem to have it covered," he smiled at her, then added, "I'll get onto the control room and have Popeye radioed to attend the office."

"Why are you looking for Doyle?" Danny McBride asked from behind him.

As McBride squeezed past him into McColl's office, Fraser stopped and turned towards McColl who replied, "I'm looking for Popeye to assist with some local intelligence regarding a suspect. We've had a break in the murder inquiry. It seems that the sample of epidermis taken from Lennie Robertson's fingernails at the post mortem has been identified as belonging to a local suspect, Kieran McMenamin and…"

McBride raised his hand to interrupt her and said, "Wait a minute. *Kieran* McMenamin?"

"Aye," McColl's face expressed her curiosity. "Do you know him?"

"No," he shook his head, "but call it coincidence or fate or whatever the hell you like, but you're aware that my victim Harriet Henderson had drawn eighty quid in new notes from the bank ATM just before she was assaulted?"

"Yes," McColl slowly nodded.

"Well," and he couldn't help but grin, "Popeye Doyle and his neighbour have just brought a shopkeeper to the office who Doyle tells me exchanged new notes for old for a man called Kieran on the evening the old lady was attacked."

McColl's glance darted from McBride to Fraser before she replied, "Don't do anything yet, Calum. Let's hear what DI McBride's new witness has to say before we go after this guy McMenamin."

Treading carefully along the busy upper floor corridor, Popeye Doyle was balancing three mugs of coffee on a plastic tray when the door to the Community Police office opened and he almost collided with Sergeant Anne Cassidy.

Glaring at him, she blocked his way and said, "Why aren't you on patrol, Constable Doyle."

"Assisting the CID with an inquiry, Sergeant," he cheerfully smiled, determined that the sour faced cow wouldn't provoke him into telling her what he really thought; not with so few days left to serve. No, he inwardly grinned. That could keep till he was retiring on his last day.

"Well," she huffily growled, "Once you've done with the CID, come and see me. I've some paperwork and a review I need to complete prior to your end of service."

With that she stomped off and taking a deep breath, Doyle continued to the interview room, but before he opened the door he heard the sound of scuffling.

Fuck, he thought and quickly laying the tray down onto the floor, pushed open the door to find the table pushed against a wall, a chair overturned and Fariq Mansoor's forearm holding Ali Rahmani by the throat against the far wall.

"Fariq!" he shouted and moving towards the younger officer, pulled his arm from Rahmani and watched as the heavyset man began to cough and slid down the wall to sit on the floor.

"What the *fuck* happened here?"

Panting, his eyes blazing with anger and a thin dribble of saliva sliding down his left cheek into his beard, the young officer replied, "When you left to get the coffee, he began to abuse me, called me a Malteser. I tried to ignore him, honest I did, Popeye, but when I told him to shut up he started slagging me off in Urdu…"

"A Malteser?" Doyle was confused and stared down at the breathless Rahmani who rubbed at his throat and whose eyes betrayed his hatred for Mansoor.

"Aye, you know; brown on the outside and white in the middle."

"Oh, you mean he was being racist?"

"Aye, then he spat on me."

Doyle's eyes flicked to the saliva on Mansoor's cheek and when the young officer raised a hand to wipe it off, he knocked Mansoor's arm away.

"Leave it!" he briskly ordered, then turning to the seated Rahmani, hissed, "Not only did you racially abuse a police officer, but you have also spit upon him and thereby exposed him to any infection you might have."

"I'm not infectious," Rahmani gasped, but Doyle turned away and with a swipe of his hand, activated the alarm bar on the wall.

Within seconds both unformed and plainclothes officers were crowding into the room.

Seeing Danny McBride among them, Doyle flatly said, "Sorry, sir, but your witness is now an accused," and before the stunned McBride could respond, reaching down he hauled Rahmani to his feet and formally arrested him.

To Mansoor, he loudly said, "Do not wipe that off, son," then turning towards a detective, added, "Please have someone take Fariq to the medical room to obtain a sample of the saliva on his cheek. Once that's done," he turned towards Mansoor, "Get someone to take you to the casualty at the Western Infirmary, Fariq. I want it logged that you have been exposed to a possible infection, okay?" Stunned, the younger officer could only nod as he was led away by the detective.

Taken aback at Doyle's assertiveness, the crowd of officer watched as with a firm grip on Rahmani's shoulder, he pulled the bulky figure along the corridor towards the stairs, but no one heard him tell the trembling man, "You, ya bastard! Spit on my young neighbour, would you? You're going nowhere except to the Sheriff Court tomorrow morning and when the CID come to see you, you tell them *every fucking thing* they want to know! Understood?"

Shaking, Rahmani could only nod and wondered how he had so suddenly and unexpectedly found himself in this situation.

Pulling the Focus into the street adjacent to the high-rise flats, Harry Henderson's eyes widened as he watched the large crowd to gather at the foot of the building.

Locking the car, he stepped over to the crowd and that's when he saw the two police cars and the ambulance parked in front of the building.

"What's going on, missus?" he asked an obese, middle-aged woman holding two plastic shopping bags, her shrunken face betraying her lack of teeth and her hair tightly bound in rollers and hidden beneath a colourful scarf.

"Another jumper," she shook her head. "Bloody shame. This used to be a great place to live before they moved the junkies and the immigrants in," she added with a sigh.

Harry glanced upwards at the high rise and involuntary shivered. He wasn't afraid of heights, but the thought of living in such a concrete edifice wasn't his idea of home and recalled an old fireman once telling him that no council with any regard to their tenants' safety should ever consider constructing a building that rose higher than a ladder could reach.

"Any idea who the jumper was?"

"No," she shook her head, then cackled, "but I'll bet you a pound to a penny some black bastard will be down at the social this afternoon claiming subsistence for funeral expenses."

"You're way out of order, missus," a young woman with cropped purple coloured hair turned on the middle-aged woman. "Some of these immigrants you're ranting about have been forced out of their own country and the last thing they need is to live next to an old racist windbag like you!"
"Who the fuck is you to call me old!" the woman retorted in fury, more concerned with the slight against her age than the fact she'd also been labelled racist.
Across the car park, Sergeant Daisy Cooper, alerted by the control room to attend the call, heard the raised voices and nodding to a constable to accompany her began to walk towards the shouting pair as the crowd parted into a circle whilst the two screaming women squared up to each other.
Seeing the two cops walking towards the crowd where he stood, Harry shrewdly decided to move on and walked a short distance away from from the pending breach of the peace.
"Listen to them two bampots," he heard a woman tell her friend. "Some poor sod has killed themselves and those two idiots are wanting to fight. As if we've not had enough entertainment today with the guy taking a header out of the flats."
Glasgow humour, he thought with an inward sigh, but then his ears pricked up when he heard an elderly man in the crowd say, "Aye, it was him right enough. That guy Stone. Willie Clarke was the man that found him. Said he was spread all over the car park like a jam sandwich."
Moving slowly through the crowd, he sidled up to the man and quietly asked, "Did I hear you say it was *Jackie* Stone?"
"Aye, Jackie Stone right enough, pal. Did you know him?" the elderly man turned to stare curiously at Harry.
He pursed his lisps and shook his head before replying, "Only by reputation. I live across there," he nodded in the direction of Maryhill Road, "but word gets about, you know? Heard Stone was a drug dealer."
The man's eyes narrowed in suspicion before he replied, "So they say, but I don't know anything about that. Excuse me," and pushed his way through the crowd away from Harry.
He realised that somehow he had caused the old man to be suspicious and decided there would be nothing to gain by hanging about.

As he made to leave he saw the crowd's attention had turned to the female sergeant and her male colleague, whose cap was bouncing along the road as the two officers struggled to separate the two protagonists.
He headed back towards the Focus, but not before he saw the cursing women being manhandled by the two cops towards a police van.
Sitting in the driver's seat, his instinct told him there was something wrong, that Stone's untimely death was no accident.
Could it be that someone did not want him to speak with Jackie Stone, but who and why not?
Fetching his mobile phone from his pocket, he scrolled down the text messages and with a sigh, murmured, "Well, if I can't speak to Mister Stone, let's hear what you have to say, Mister McGroarty."

Unaware of the police interest in him and contemplating his next move as he walked, it didn't faze Kieran McMenamin he had killed three people, but of course was unaware of the demise of Harriet Henderson.
With a cocky swing to his stride, he realised that if Jackie Stone didn't have access to the gear at the minute then it was unlikely there was any to be had locally.
No, he would just have to wait, but recalled Stone telling him it would be Monday at the latest before there was a delivery.
Teeth gritted, he realised that with Stone out of the picture he'd likely have no other option if he wanted to source gear he would need to return and get it from that bastard Peter McGroarty.
Still, if there is a shipment coming in, he thought, maybe it would be wise to have some real money in his pocket and avoid any more hassle from the former boxer.
He glanced at the time on his mobile phone and considered heading down toward Saracen Cross to keep an eye on the ATM at the bank. The old woman he mugged had drawn eighty quid and he wondered; with the number of pensioners using the busy machine he might get lucky again.
The decision made, he crossed the road and hurried along.

Danny McBride and Myra McColl caught up with Popeye Doyle just as he loudly slammed the cell door on a bewildered Ali Rahmani.

"Jesus, Popeye," McBride angrily began, "one minute you're telling me and DI McColl you've got a witness who might be able to identify the guy we're looking for regarding two murders and the next…"

He stopped when Doyle abruptly held up his hand and with a forefinger at his lips, nodded that they follow him along the cell corridor.

When out of earshot of Rahmani's cell, he said, "I've not charged him yet, sir. Let me explain. Ali Rahmani has been through the system before, but not for a racially aggravated assault that, if he *were* to be convicted, could get him some real time in the jail. Yes?"

McBride turned to glance at McColl before he nodded in agreement.

"Now," Doyle continued, "I know what he's like because he's right in the with the local neds in Saracen and believe me when I say I've often dealt with him before and he's a right cunning bastard. Getting your statement from him would be like getting blood from the proverbial and when it comes to an identification parade, as likely it will, I'll guarantee you that he will prevaricate and deliberately refuse to identify this guy Kieran as the man who gave him the new notes. However," he stared at them in turn, "*if* he believes there's a charge hanging over him, that he could go to jail and his business might suffer while he's banged up and by that I mean he gets hit in the pocket; well, he might be more than willing to work a deal with the CID."

McBride slowly smiled before replying, "And that deal would be we can get the charge dropped if he comes across with a statement and positively identifies our suspect Kieran?"

"That's what I'm thinking," Doyle shrugged.

"There's been a development since you spoke with DI McBride, Popeye," interjected McColl. "A skin sample from under Lennie Robertson's fingernails has been matched as belonging to a Kieran McMenamin and we're of the opinion that there is a likelihood McMenamin and the Kieran who exchanged the notes are one and the same man. Do you know McMenamin?"

Surprised, Doyle again stared from one to the other before replying, "Oh aye, Myra. I *do* know him. A bad young bastard. Lives with his…" his eyes narrowed as he tried to recall, "father and a sister I think it is, in Crowhill Street."

"Does he still live there?"

"Not certain," Doyle shook his head, "but I've certainly tested his address as there when I locked him up for drug dealing, but that several months ago. Heroin, I seem to recall, though I don't think he uses it himself."

"That confirms what DC Munroe told us," she nodded to McBride.

"I don't want you to think I'm being a smart arse," Doyle interrupted, "but you might want to get a move on interviewing Rahmani. If he gets time to think about it, he'll realise there are no witnesses to his assault on young Fariq and you'll have no leverage over him."

"He's right," McBride quickly agreed. "So, Myra, how do you propose we go about this?"

Opening the rear door of the police van, Daisy Cooper and two male colleagues had to physically manhandle both the enraged women out into the yard at Maryhill police office, who though they were handcuffed, continued to scream abuse, snarl and kick at each other as the three officers struggled to contain them.

It occurred to Daisy that a slap round the back of the head might be appropriate, but a quick glance at the CCTV cameras put paid to that idea, she grimly realised.

With some difficulty, the women were brought before the Duty Inspector at the charge bar where cautioned and charged with a breach of the peace, they suddenly seemed aware of their predicament and were led meekly to the female cells, the younger woman now sniffling and crying, "I'm sorry," while her co-accused muttered, "Fucking nonsense this. Getting locked up for nothing, so I am."

"Daisy," the Inspector called out to her, "when you're ready, there was a phone call for you from Saracen office. Sergeant Cassidy requests you call her back."

Acknowledging the information, Daisy made her way through to the writing room and dialled the number for the Community Police office.

"Sergeant Cassidy."

"It's Daisy Cooper," she tightly responded. "You're looking for me?"

"Yes, Sergeant Cooper. I was hoping to have a word with you about DC Munroe. I found her at your computer and when I asked what she was doing, she told me that you had provided your password to permit her access to the Divisional Intelligence network and Force Briefings regarding ongoing operations. Is that correct?"

"And you're telling me why?" replied Daisy, but her question was needless for she already knew why. Cassidy, tight-arsed and constantly practising her one-upmanship, was hoping to have some sort of leverage against Daisy.

"Well," Cassidy slowly drawled, "we both know it is a contravention of the Data Protection Act and the Police Scotland regulations to provide your password to an unauthorised individual who can then access sensitive intelligence issues."

It occurred to Daisy to tell Cassidy to shove the rules and regulations where the sun didn't shine, but instead, took a breath and replied, "Absolutely correct, Sergeant Cassidy, and that's why I cleared it with the Chief Inspector Kane before I gave DC Munroe the password. Now, I'm a bit busy arresting folk here, something I don't believe you have much experience with, so unless there's anything else?"

She could almost hear Cassidy's sharp intake of breath at the censure and smiled when Cassidy finally replied, "No, nothing else," before the phone went dead.

Daisy took a deep breath and slowly replaced the phone in the cradle.

All she had to hope now was that Cassidy was too embarrassed to actually speak with Dougie Kane for if she did, she'd find out Daisy had lied.

Harry Henderson drove into Ronaldsay Street and stopped near to the house whose number appeared on the text message.

Glancing at the house, he could see the front garden was untended and in disarray and thought if a bomb hit it, it might make some improvement. An old three seater settee was upended and lying against the wall at the side of the end-terraced house. Two council wheelie bins were on either side of the settee with their lids almost upright due to the number of the black bin bags stuffed in both.

He could see the curtains in the upstairs rooms were closed, but the curtains downstairs in what he guessed must the the sitting room, were open though there was no sign of anyone moving about.

A garish, shiny red coloured and new looking Mitsubishi Outlander was parked outside the house with the nearside wheels on the pavement and so close to the broken down fencing it made it difficult for anyone passing passing by on the footway.
As Harry watched, a young woman pushing a buggy was obliged to step out onto the roadway to get around the Outlander, her face angry and mouth chattering away as she cursed the inconsiderate owner.
"Fancy car, shitty house," he murmured to himself and got out of the Focus.
Locking it behind him, he made his way to the front door, but saw there was no nameplate.
He checked the text again and satisfied that this was indeed McGroarty's home, knocked on the door.
A minute passed and he was about to knock again when a young, dyed blonde haired woman wearing a gaudy orange coloured tracksuit with a fresh bruise under her left eye and sallow complexion, opened the door.
Staring at the suited Harry, Sharon Gale's eyes narrowed in hostility for her first thought was he was CID and sullenly said, "He's not in."
Harry, recognising the lie, replied, "Oh, you mean Mister Brown?"
Confused, she shook her head and said, "It's not Brown that lives here, mister, it's McGroarty. Peter McGroarty."
"Sharon, who the fuck's that at the door?" the male voice called from upstairs.
"So it's not Mister Brown's house," Harry smiled at her.
Turning her head back and forth as she sought to reply to McGroarty and deal with the stranger at the door, Gale became further confused and even more so when Harry, continuing to smile, gently took her by the wrist and to her surprise ushered her backwards into the hallway, then turned and closed the door behind him.
"Sharon! Are you deaf? Who the fuck is at the door?" McGroarty again called down.
Wide eyed and frightened, she stared at Harry who placed his forefinger against his lips to indicate she remain quiet, then called out, "You have a visitor, Mister McGroarty. I'll see you in your front room when you're ready."
Politely stepping to one side, he nodded that Gale lead the way into the front room and followed her in.

His first impression was that domesticity was not a strong point with either McGroarty or the young woman called Sharon, for the stained carpet, stained couch and armchairs, coffee table littered with empty beer cans, dirty dinner plates and overflowing ashtray were in complete contrast to the massive television that hung from the far wall. A sideboard against the adjoining wall was similarly littered with newspapers, magazines and all sorts of paper debris and the smell of fried food and old grease emanating through the open door that led into the compact kitchen nauseated him.
He turned when the door burst open to admit the shaven headed McGroarty, his bare chest and arms rippling with muscle and gaudy tattoo's.
Barefooted, he wore just a pair of grey coloured tracksuit bottoms.
"Who the *fuck* are you?" he snarled at Harry, flexing his muscular arms, his hands bunched into fists.
"Mister McGroarty, I apologise for disturbing you," he calmly replied with a slight smile and in doing so, almost absentmindedly prepared himself for violence by removing his spectacles that he placed in an inner pocket of his suit jacket. "I'm calling because I believe you might have some information that I require."
"Information? What information! I don't speak to you bastards!"
"By you bastards, I assume you think I'm a police officer?"
McGroarty's eyes narrowed. "You're not the CID?"
"No, Mister McGroarty, I'm most definitely *not* the CID," Harry replied with an amused smile.
McGroarty warily circled round the armchair that backed against the door so that there was just six feet between him and Harry, his fists still bunched but loosely held by his side.
"Before I knock the fuck out of you, I'll ask you one more time, pal; who are you and what do you want?"
Harry took a deep breath and slowly exhaled before replying, "I'm looking for a junkie, someone you might deal to. I've already spoken with your own supplier, Mister Faraday, who assures me of your cooperation. However, if you refuse to cooperate," Harry stared into McGroarty's eyes, "I will have no option but to hurt you until you provide me with the name I want."
McGroarty was confused. Who the fuck was Faraday, he was thinking, but his main concern for the moment was this weedy

looking bastard who had walked straight through his door and who was now threatening him.

Sharon Gale's head snapped from Harry to McGroarty who evilly smiled and replied, "You might have a couple of inches on me, old man, but I've got speed, fitness and a lot less fucking years than you have so what makes you think you can take me, eh?"

"Fair question," Harry smiled, "but first. Are you going to give me the answer I need?"

"Fuck off!"

"Wrong answer," Harry quietly replied then with a burst of speed that surprised McGroarty his right hand whipped round to the rear waistband of his trousers and when his hand returned, it held the Glock.

In one swift movement he fired and shot McGroarty in the left leg just above the knee.

Screaming, the former boxer fell back, clutching at the wound as blood spurted from the bullet hole.

Sharon Gale shrunk back into a corner of the room and her back against the wall, sunk to her haunches, her elbows tucked in and her hands clasped to her ears as in terror her mouth opened and she gave out a silent scream.

Holding the Glock out in front of him and pointed at McGroarty's other leg, Harry closed the gap between them and calmly said, "Now, I'll ask again, Mister McGroarty. Will you give me the answer to what I want to know?"

Biting back tears of pain as he clutched at the bleeding leg, McGroarty nodded.

Turning, Harry walked towards Gale and pulling her to her feet, politely said, "Please fetch a dishcloth or something similar from the kitchen. A clean one if you have such a thing," he added.

Staring fearfully at him, she nodded and made her way into the kitchen.

Crouching down in front of McGroarty, the Glock loosely held in one hand, he said, "Several days ago, my aunt was attacked by a junkie who stole her purse. She later died as a result of the injuries she received when she was mugged. My belief and information is that the junkie was probably supplied his drugs by one of Mister Faraday's local dealers who operate in the Saracen area, one of whom is you, Mister McGroarty."

"For fuck's sake, my leg," he sobbed. "I need a doctor and to get to a hospital."

"You'll need two doctors, one for each leg if you don't tell me what I need to know," Harry hissed at him. "Now, what do you know about a junkie mugging pensioners in the Saracen area?"

"Muggings? Fuck's sake, nothing! Jesus, it hurts!"

Harry placed the end of the barrel of the Glock again the kneecap of the uninjured leg and said, "Try to think harder, Mister McGroarty."

"You said her purse was taken?" said Gale from behind him.

Standing, Harry turned towards her as she stood visibly shaking in the doorway of the kitchen, a soiled dishcloth in her hands.

"That's right, her purse was stolen. Do you know something?"

She nervously passed him by and getting down onto her knees, pressed the dishcloth against McGroarty's wound.

"It's just…there was a guy…he said he found a purse," she got back up onto her feet and warily keeping her eyes on Harry, moved across the room and began to rummage through the papers and rubbish on top of the sideboard. "He said he found this in the purse."

"My leg, for fuck's sake I need a doctor!"

Ignoring McGroarty's plaintive cries, she handed Harry the black and white photograph and saw his face turn pale, unaware that he recognised the soldier in the photograph as his uncle Archie, Harriet's husband who was killed in Korea.

"Where did you get this?"

"He had it, the guy I'm talking about. Said it was his uncle or somebody. Said he got it from a purse he found."

"This guy, what's his name," he asked, his eyes boring into her.

She turned towards McGroarty, but Harry took her by the arm, his fingers digging painfully into the soft flesh and in a voice filled with venom, said, "Don't look at him! His name!"

Her voice almost a whisper, she replied, "Kieran McMenamin."

He released his grp on Gale and swallowed with difficulty then slipping the photograph into his jacket pocket, demanded McMenamin's address, but neither knew and seeing how frightened they were, he believed them to be telling the truth though both did describe McMenamin to be about six feet tall with dark brown hair and in his early twenties.

Drawing his face close to Gale, he said, "A minute after I'm gone, call an ambulance for him," he nodded to McGroarty.

Moving towards the injured man, he crouched and in a monotone voice, said, "When the police interview you, you do *not* name me. You do *not* describe me. You have *no* idea who I am. You will *not* give in to their pressure. You will deny giving me *any* information. You will simply tell them that a man not known to you entered your home and shot you in the leg. If you fail to follow my instructions, I *will* kill you before I am caught," then staring up at Gale, stone-faced added, "Both of you."
He paused and peering at her, said, "Do you believe I will kill you?" Gale vigorously nodded while McGroarty slowly did so too, his face wracked with pain.
"Then you can save your lives by doing as I tell you."
He stood upright and turning to Gale, nodded she follow him into the hallway where he said, "When this is settled, leave him. If you don't, then one day he *will* beat you to death."
At that he opened the door and fetching his glasses from his pocket, put them on as he walked out towards the Focus.

In the oily waters surrounding the Port of Felixstowe, the tug Captain first waved to the harbour pilot and then turning, beckoned to his crew to brace themselves as nudging and coaxing his smaller boat, the tug Captain manoeuvred the larger ship into the quayside where after gently bumping the buffers, the freighter's Captain ordered all engines stopped.
Within minutes, the Dockers had the ship securely berthed alongside the quay and in a well rehearsed and time conscious routine, the operators in their tall, blue painted cranes began the business of offloading the containers onto the dockside.
Once landed and their seals checked over by the Customs and Excise officers, the containers were discharged as legitimate cargo and conveyed by the laden container handling machines to their holding areas to await the transport that would deliver the containers to their final destinations.
On the deck of the freighter, the Turkish First Mate keenly watched the red and green coloured container and with relief, saw it chalk-marked by the uniformed Customs officer who moved onto the next container.

He waited till the officer was several containers away and ensuring he would not be overheard, from under his jacket brought out his global satellite phone and dialled the pre-set number.

CHAPTER TWENTY-ONE

With both teams crowded into Myra McColl's incident room, the two Detective Inspectors, acting in conjunction, informed the teams of the break in their inquiries; that Kieran McMenamin of Crowhill Street had been forensically identified by DNA as the chief suspect for the murder of Leonard Robertson and as a result of an interview with a local shopkeeper, McMenamin was also positively identified as the man who had exchanged four consecutively numbered twenty pound notes for old notes on the afternoon of Harriet Henderson's assault and robbery.

"At this time, albeit it's a Saturday," Danny McBride took up the briefing, "we have called out the manager and her assistant manager who work at Ali Rahmani's Charing Cross bank and the two of them are trying to trace the notes that Rahmani banked in the night safe there along with his takings for that day. If the staff *do* trace those notes and we keep our fingers crossed the notes are still in the bank," he exhaled, "then if the serial numbers match the serial numbers of the notes withdrawn from the ATM by our victim, we've got him for the two murders. And before you ask, we've two of the team down there waiting to collect the notes as evidence," he finished.

"Right now and as a result of this break in both cases," McColl, stepped forward, "DI McBride and I have agreed that we will run the two inquiries as one. Detective Superintendent Mulgrew has been informed of this latest development and of our decision to merge the inquiries and tells us she will be attending here shortly. Danny?" she turned to McBride.

"It's no secret," he smiled, "that not only are Myra and I new to being SIO's, but being new to this Division means that McMenamin isn't known to us. However, though he's not present, Constable Doyle or Popeye as most of you know him, has done a power of work in bringing us this result and also knows the suspect McMenamin. Right now, in plain clothes and accompanied by Marilyn Munroe who also has had previous dealings with McMenamin, the two of them have been sent in the old plain clothes van to watch McMenamin's address to try and establish if he's at home."

He held up his hand as he continued, "I realise that most of you probably want to go and kick in his door, but none of us," he stared around room at the two teams, "want this case against the suspect to fail because we didn't properly dot the I's and cross the T's, so Myra and I have agreed the arrest will be by Sheriff's Warrant. Based on the evidence we have so far collected, DS Calum Fraser is away knocking the duty Fiscal Deputes door to have a warrant written up and then he'll go hunting down a Sheriff for the signature."

He sighed and added, "We all know this might take a couple of hours, so in the meantime Popeye and Marilyn will monitor the comings and going at Crowhill Street and try to house our suspect. Myra?"

McColl stepped forward and holding up a sheet of A4 paper, said, "I have a list of names from the two teams, those of you who will act as the arrest team and those of you who, with Scene of Crime officers present, will act as the search team at the suspects house. Any questions?"

A number of officers shook their heads, but nobody spoke up and after instructing the two teams to remain in the office, she was about to dismiss them to coffee and tea when the door at the back opened to admit a uniformed officer who clearly anxious, made her way towards her.

"Ma'am, that's a call in to the uniform bar from the control room. Some guy from Ronaldsay Street has turned up at the casualty ward at the Western Infirmary with a gunshot wound to his leg. The Duty Inspector at Maryhill wants to know when the CID will attend."

"Shit," she grimaced and shook her head. "Just when I thought I was clearing my feet!"

Enjoying the cool of the evening on the balcony of his flat, Nigel Faraday ended the call and with a satisfied smile, decided a glass of his favourite Port might be appropriate.

The phone call from Miguel de Lugo confirming the shipment had been picked up at Felixstowe and was now being transported north to Glasgow was not just good news, but a tremendous relief. However, regardless of de Lugo's veiled threat that the payment should be released upon receipt of the shipment, Faraday had already made his mind up that once the delivery was made and dispersed to his dealers and they in turn were satisfied as to the purity of the heroin, only then would he instruct his off-shore bank to release the payment.

After all, he mused, it wouldn't do for a quantity of the shipment to be pure while the rest might turn out out be…well, *shite*, he smiled at his unaccustomed use of the vernacular.

Glancing at his watch, he wondered if this was the time to inform Sandy Craig of the delivery time and venue, reasoning it would do no harm to call him anyway and confirm that as instructed, Craig had recruited the men and obtained the van.

His call was answered almost immediately.

"Sandy. Mister de Lugo assures me that the operation is a go. How are things at your end?"

Fucking *operation*, Craig inwardly sighed; thinks he's some kind of military general, but replied, "All okay, boss. Are you calling with the time and location for the delivery?"

Faraday hesitated before replying, "Not quite yet, Sandy. I know that you trust the people you have hired, but they are not known to me, so let's keep it tight, for now, eh?"

Craig was about to remind Faraday that he was supposed to trust Craig, his right hand man, but conscious of Stevie Watkins warning not to antagonise Faraday so close to the delivery, he swallowed a bitter pill and replied, "Fair enough, boss, but I will need *some* warning to get my guys in positon just in case the polis decide to take a wee turn past the delivery location. Know what I mean?"

"You'll get an hour or two, Sandy," he said, amusing himself at what he believed to be Craig's nervousness.

"Anything else, boss?"

"The issue with our man Henderson. Have you contracted anyone yet?"

"That matter is being dealt with, boss," he glibly lied. "I wasn't certain if you wanted details."

"No, there's no need for that, Sandy. Just let me know when the job is completed," replied Faraday, for the last thing he wanted was to involve himself in a murder. No, he thought as he ended the call; that's why hired thugs like Sandy Craig.

"That's the close there where McMenamin lives with his father and sister," Popeye Doyle pointed out of the front windscreen of the rusting van towards the dilapidated two storey council property, fifty metres away and directly across the road from the grocery shop and Chinese takeaway.

Marilyn Munroe, like Doyle dressed in an old anorak and jeans, leaned forward in the driver seat and peering at the building, nodded. "I remember visiting the house," she said. "His father seemed a decent enough man and his sister was okay too, kept apologising for the trouble her brother was putting me to. If I recall correctly, she works in a hairdressing salon in Maryhill Road, I think it was."

"Aye, that seems to come to mind," Doyle agreed as he squirmed uncomfortably in the worn seat. "Right, I'll take first watch if you want to relax," he suggested.

They sat in comfortable silence for fifteen minutes before Munroe asked, "What plans have you got for your retirement?"

"Like I've told everyone else, the first thing I'm going to do is have a long lie-in," he grinned, "then I'll make it up as I go along."

"You're not married, are you?"

"Not so far. Why, are you offering yourself up as my new girlfriend?"

"Thanks," she blushed, "but I think I'll stick to someone my own age; however, if you're stuck for a date my granny's on her own these days."

"Ouch, that hurt," he smiled at her.

The hand held radio in his lap activated with the message that the warrant was typed up and DS Fraser was en route to have it signed by a Sheriff.

Acknowledging the information, Doyle informed the control room that so far there was no trace of the suspect.

DS Ian Prescott knocked on Myra McColl's door and entered to find her seated behind her desk with DI Danny McBride, suit jacket off and tie undone and Detective Superintendent Cathy Mulgrew, casually dressed in a black roll neck sweater, flared denim skirt and black knee high leather boots, seated in front of the desk.

"Sorry to intrude, Ma'am," he addressed McColl, "but that was DI Kennedy at Maryhill CID on the phone to the incident room looking for you. Asked if you could give him a call and said it is urgent."

"Thanks, Ian," she nodded to him before he left the room, then turning towards Mulgrew raised her eyebrows and said, "Ma'am?"
"Please, go ahead," Mulgrew nodded.
They sat in silence then heard McColl say, "Phil, it's Myra McColl, I believe you're looking for me."
As Mulgrew and McBride watched, they saw her eyebrows rise as she inhaled, then heard her say, "I have Ma'am and Danny McBride here with me. I'm about to put you on speaker, Phil."
Pressing the button McColl then said, "Go ahead, Phil, that's you on speaker."
"Ma'am, Danny," Kennedy's voice was loud and clear. "Like I told Myra, I've just had a phone call from the Forensic Laboratory at Gartcosh. In response to the hit Myra had with her junkie…her victim, I mean, in Ruchill Park, I asked the Lab to do a quick check regarding the trace evidence found under my female victim's fingernails. My inquiries to date have not discovered any apparent relationship with my victims to Myra's accused, this guy McMenamin, but the coincidence of Myra's victim being a druggie and my two victims also being druggie's was too coincidental so…"
"We're hanging here, Phil," Mulgrew tersely interrupted, "so what did the Lab say?"
"The DNA under Margaret Dalrymple fingernails is a match for Myra's suspect Kieran McMenamin, Ma'am. McMenamin is now my chief suspect for Dalrymple's murder and by association, the murder of her flatmate who we've positively identified as Francis O'Connor, aged thirty-two and recorded by us on several occasions as a drug abuser. O'Connor bled out quite substantially during his beating, so I've asked that when McMenamin is arrested all his clothing be examined for any trace evidence of O'Connor's blood type."
A stunned silence in McColl's office was broken when Mulgrew said, "Bloody hell! We've got a serial killer on our hands!"
She stared round at the two DI's and conscious that Kennedy was still on the line, quickly said, "In light of this new information, Phil, I think I'm going to have to combine all three incident rooms and as you have the larger one at Maryhill, we'll use that. I don't foresee any problems because with all the information already logged on the HOLMES system and due to the size of the major incident room you have there, all we have to do is transfer the personnel, move some of

the computers up to you and separate the inquiry teams with floor standing office screens."

She took a deep breath and slowly exhaling, added, "I know you guys might believe that I'm about to step on toes, but given the circumstances and enormity of what McMenamin is suspected of having done, I will assume the role of SIO for all three murder inquiries. However, I do *not* propose to be hands on, but will leave the running of your individual incident rooms to you three. I will act as the collator for all three inquiries and be available to assist or advise," she wryly grinned, "and of course take any flak that might come our way."

She glanced at both McBride and McColl and unconsciously leaned forward towards the speaker phone before asking, "Do any of you guys object or have an alternative idea?"

McBride and McColl both shook their heads while Kennedy replied, "No, Ma'am."

"What about the teams, Ma'am," McColl asked. "Should we inform them of this latest development?"

Mulgrew's brow creased and slowly shaking her head, she replied, "Not for now, Myra. While I'm sure you will trust them to be discreet, word might get out before we can make our accommodation arrangements at Maryhill and we'll have a hoard of media descending upon us, so let's leave it meantime. Once we're in situ and have McMenamin arrested, we can break the news then. Agreed?"

McBride nodded while both McColl and Kennedy said, "Agreed."

She got to her feet and waving McColl and McBride back down into their seats, said, "Right, I'll leave you guys to make the arrangements. I'll head back to Gartcosh and clear my desk before I head for Maryhill and besides," her brow wrinkled, "I'll need to phone the Chief Constable about McMenamin as well as our Media Department to give them the heads up that a shitload of reporters will soon be descending upon them."

Harry Henderson found himself a parking place in the Maryhill Shopping Centre and switching off the engine, sat for several minutes idly watching the shoppers while reflecting on his action in shooting Peter McGroarty.

He hadn't intended using the Glock, but if he was being honest with himself, the aggressive wee bugger would not have given anything up and more than likely it saved Harry from having to physically deal with him. Besides, he grinned, McGroarty was a former boxer and as he had said, a lot younger and probably fitter than the fifty-seven years old Harry.

Would McGroarty and his punch bag girlfriend keep their mouths shut?

He could only hope that their obvious drug dealing activities made them distrust the police and be unlikely to grass on Harry; that and his threat, he smiled, for neither McGroarty or the girl could know that he would never carry out such a threat.

Well, not to the girl anyway though he *would* consider doing McGroarty in.

Not that he pretended to be any kind of saint. It was just that the girl didn't deserve to be murdered if she did grass up Harry for after all, he *did* shoot her boyfriend in the leg but he had never broken his own rule of harming women, children or men of the cloth and wouldn't start now.

No, he would just have to trust that both would keep their mouths shut or at least till such time he left the country to return to Cuba.

Fetching his mobile phone from his jacket pocket, he dialled the only other number on his directory.

The call rung for less than twenty seconds before Popeye Doyle replied, "Hello, Annie. Give me a minute, hen," then Harry heard the sound of a car door opening and being closed.

"Sorry about that," Doyle said. "I'm out and about with a colleague. What can I do for you Harry?"

"I need an address, Popeye, and was kind of hoping that you might have it or be able to get it for me."

"An address? Who are you looking for?"

"A guy local to Saracen called Kieran McMenamin, about six feet tall, brown hair and in his early twenties."

He caught the sharp intake of breath before Doyle replied, "I'm sorry, Harry, no can do."

"You know him then?"

"Oh aye, Harry, I know him and so do your aunt's investigation team. They've already identified him as the chief suspect for her murder," said Doyle, choosing not to disclose McMenamin was also the suspect for the murder of the junkie in Ruchill Park.

"Is he in custody? You can tell me that, surely."

There was a pause before Doyle replied, "No, we're still looking for him, but believe me it's just a question of time."

In his car, Harry inwardly fumed at this setback, but realised it was nothing to do with Doyle and if nothing else, was grateful for the information.

"How close are the CID to arresting him?"

"Any time soon," Doyle said, not wishing to admit that with Munroe he was actively engaged in looking for McMenamin.

Harry smiled and replied, "You're not giving me anything else, are you Popeye?"

"That's not how it works, Harry, and besides, I happen to like you and don't want you to get banged up because of a shitbag like McMenamin. Believe me, when he's captured he'll be going away for a very long time and isn't it better he languishes in jail for the rest of his natural rather than getting a quick exit at your hands?"

"Maybe so, maybe so," Harry drawled, then asked, "You could do me one favour, Popeye."

"And that is?"

"Give me a call to let me know he's been arrested."

"That I *can* do, Harry, though likely you'll be hearing from the CID too. Keep in touch and we'll talk more over dinner some evening. My treat."

"I look forward to it," Harry smiled, yet deeply disappointed that McMenamin had been identified and was being hunted by the CID as well as him.

Ending the call, Doyle was climbing back into the passenger seat of the van and unaware that on the pavement some forty metres away behind him and albeit he was in plain clothes, Kieran McMenamin had recognised the well known local beat man as Popeye Doyle and glancing at the van, decided the copper and whoever was with him must be watching his close.

He froze in panic and legs trembling, turned about and hurriedly abandoned his idea of changing his clothes and going to Saracen Cross.

The Detective Sergeant and her Acting Detective Constable

allocated the inquiry into the apparent suicide of Jackie Stone who had jumped from the veranda of his ninth floor flat, followed the three white suited Scene of Crime Personnel into the flat.
Instructing the uniformed constable to remain on guard at the forced door, the DS, like her ADC wearing blue nitrile Forensic gloves, turned her nose up at the vile smell and smiled at the young ADC's comment, "My God, this place is a shithole. How can people live like this?"
"Did you know Stone?" he asked her.
"I had dealings with him, yes," she slowly admitted. "The guy was one of a number of local dealers and usually was wasted himself. Through the years the drugs had taken their toll on his body," she grimaced, idly picking up a broken ornament from a makeshift sideboard and peering at it, added, "and he looked like a walking skeleton."
She carefully replaced the ornament and with a shrug, continued, "I'm not surprised he committed sideways, the state he was in."
"Sideways?"
"Suicide, ya numpty," she grinned at the ADC.
"Sarge?"
She turned towards the white suited SOCO who stood at the open door of the veranda and saw him pull down the mask from his face.
"Your man that fell from the veranda here. We had a look at him and photographed him before he went into the shell," he said, referring to the casket used to collect dead bodies.
"And?" the DS moved to join the SOCO, her face expressing her curiosity.
"He wasn't wearing shoes or socks."
"And?" she impatiently repeated, her face indicating she expected more.
"Well," a little annoyed at her attitude, the SOCO shrugged before replying, "if he *wasn't* wearing shoes or socks and they're not lying here on the veranda, it seems a little odd that there are tread marks from what looks like a training shoe in the earth that's been spilled here," he pointed down at the overturned plant pot.
"Oh, shite," the DS's shoulders slumped as she and reached into her handbag for her mobile phone.

The owner and sole driver of the articulated lorry didn't know what

was in the container he had picked up from the Port of Felixstowe that he was hauling and didn't want to know either.
It was enough that he was being paid top price to deliver it to Glasgow.
Glancing through the windscreen at the dark clouds ahead, he was grateful for the upcoming rain for he knew that the Traffic cops on the motorways preferred to sit at service stations in their warm and cosy vehicles or instead be occupied attending to weather related crashes or drunk drivers and so, if the rain was heavy, less likely to pay attention to lorries travelling on a Saturday night.
His telephoned instructions had been quite explicit.
The container was to be delivered to an industrial estate in the north side of Glasgow and he had pre-set his SatNav with the address.
Once arrived there, he was to remain in his cab while the container was emptied and not to assist in the unload nor engage in any conversation with the men unloading the container.
Once unloaded, the empty container was to be returned to an address in Felixstowe that again had been entered into his SatNav.
He thought again of the dark-skinned, accented English speaking man who had recruited him, of the warning that if he at any time deviated from his instructions, his family would pay the price for his betrayal.
Now this, his third visit to Scotland in as many months that had earned him enough money to pay off not just the finance on his vehicle, but one more trip would see off his mortgage too.
Yes, he peered into the darkness as he drove and reluctantly admitted it; the price of silence was worth it.

CHAPTER TWENTY-TWO

Sitting hunched over on the unforgiving plastic chair in the casualty ward waiting room, a handkerchief clutched in one hand and a plastic beaker of sweet tea in the other, her knees tightly together but unable to keep her legs from shaking, Sharon Gale steadfastly refused to look at the detective seated opposite.
"Look, hen," DS Ian Prescott patiently tried again, "you can either speak to me here or we can go back to Saracen office and talk there, so once more; who was it that shot your boyfriend?"

"I don't know," Gale dully replied. "I've already told you, I was upstairs when he…I mean, they came in."

Prescott knew she was lying and the slip of the tongue confirmed his suspicions. It was one individual and likely a man right enough, not two masked men like that bastard McGroarty had told the ambulance crew.

"I don't want to talk to you anymore," Gale sniffed and nosily slurped at her tea, her outburst attracting the attention of the other walking wounded and their relatives who were seated near by and all pretending not to eavesdrop.

Turning to his colleague, Prescott told the DC, "Fetch the car to the front, Tommy. Miss Gale is coming with us," and made to stand, but her hand reached across the short space between them to stop him and he sat back down, his face registering his impatience.

"Look," she hissed with uncommon boldness, "you don't understand. I can't tell you anything because I don't *know* anything. I was upstairs when I heard the bang and when I came down, Peter was lying on the floor in the front room screaming and there was blood everywhere. I didn't know what to do, but I got a dishcloth and tried to stop the bleeding and I couldn't so I phoned the ambulance and…" she paused for breath. "I thought he was going to die," she began to softly weep, the plastic beaker tilting over, spilling the tea onto the floor and splashing Prescott's shoes.

Hastily drawing his feet away, he grabbed at the beaker to turn it upright and quietly said, "How did you know it was just one man, Sharon? Did you see him? Did he threaten you and that's why you won't tell us his name?"

"I don't know his name," she suddenly replied, then almost guiltily at the blatant lie, added, "and I didn't see him. Just Peter telling me a guy shot him."

"So," Prescott exhaled, "you're telling me an unknown man for some unknown reason came into your house and shot your boyfriend?"

Taking a deep breath, her mind recalling the piercing eyes and the gun in his hand, she nodded, her lips to tightly fixed they were almost as pale as her face.

Prescott rose to his feet and turning towards his neighbour, said, "Ask at the desk if they know when McGroarty will be out of surgery. We're getting nowhere here with her," he nodded down to Gale whose head bowed, ignored him.

She watched as Prescott moved towards the exit door to wait for his neighbour who joined him a few moments later.

She had not lied about knowing his name for he had not told them and with a secret smile, knew she had passed the first test, for the CID knew who Peter was and what he did and likely her brief experience with the police had taught her they would not waste much time trying to find out who shot him.

What the detective could not know and what she would never admit was that she was secretly pleased Peter had been shot for the thin, balding man with the gun had done what she never could or would dare to do; hurt the bullying bastard like he deserved.

She glanced at the door and recalling where McGroarty kept his stash and his wad of money, then remembered what the man had said about leaving the bastard and with a glance about her, got to her feet.

Fobbing off the questions and suspicions as to why they were being united into one office, DI Phil Kennedy was in the middle of making arrangements with his team to accept the Saracen inquiry teams into the Maryhill incident room when he was called to the phone.

"Boss?"

"Are you still at the suicide down at the Wyndford flats?" he asked his Detective Sergeant.

"Aye, and I'll be here for some time," the DS replied.

A chilling feeling run through Kennedy who rubbing his hand across his balding head, sat with his large backside on the edge of a desk and already guessing what was coming, said, "Tell me the bad news."

"We're looking at a possible murder. There's evidence that Jackie Stone might not have jumped, but been helped on his way by somebody else."

"And this evidence is?"

"At the minute, the SOCO people are looking at a footprint in dirt that was spilled from a potted plant on Stone's veranda."

"I'm presuming it's not his?"

"No, he went over the veranda barefooted."

"Shit!"

"But that's not all. I sent my Aide to knock on a couple of doors on the ninth floor and he's found a woman, an immigrant lady or more properly, an asylum seeker who's a possible witness. My lad managed to get some information out of her even though she's not a good English speaker. It seems about the material time Stone took his high dive, she saw a guy coming out of Stone's flat."

Kennedy perked up at this news and asked, "Can she describe him or identify him?"

"Well, there's the language problem of course, but she's given us a general description that fits half the junkies in Maryhill, but nodded that she can identify him again. Problem is the lassie's terrified he'll come back and get her and her wean and if you want an opinion, she's scared of the polis. Probably something to do with why she's fled Somalia. Can you send me down some troops and if you can dig up a family liaison officer from the Family Protection Unit, preferably somebody that speaks Somali or Arabic that I *think* are the languages the witness knows."

"I'll get onto the control rom and see who they can dig up," he replied, then added, "Stay where you are for now and I'll muster some people for you."

His brow creased and he asked, "The victim, Jackie Stone. The name's familiar. Isn't he…"

"He is or was," she corrected herself as she interrupted, "a local dealer in heroin."

"Right," he had a sudden inspirational thought, "once the SOCO team are done, turn the place over and try to find his tick book. There's bound to be one there. See if Kieran McMenamin's name features anywhere."

"Who? Oh, you mean the suspect for the two junkies murders? Do you think…"

"What I think is that McMenamin has been a very busy boy in the last few days. When your witness arrives here I'll arrange for his photograph to be shown to her and if I'm right," he paused and inhaled, "we might be looking at him regarding Stone's death as well."

Just been giving the all clear at the Western Infirmary, Fariq Mansoor charmed the receptionist into letting him use the phone to call the control room for a lift back to Saracen, but to his surprise was asked by the officer in the control room if he spoke Arabic.

"I'm a Muslim," he grinned and cheekily replied, "course I speak the language of Allah, ya heathen."

"Well, you impertinent bugger," the woman laughed, "in that case when the car arrives for you get yourself up to Maryhill office. As a matter of urgency, DI Kennedy needs someone for translation duties."

Still seated in Maryhill Shopping Centre car park, but now with a Greggs sandwich and bottle of water, Harry Henderson was at a loss. He now knew the name of the man he suspected mugged his aunt Harriet and who ultimately caused her dearth, but frustratingly so did the CID and now it was a race to find him.

However, with all the resources at their disposal, he had little doubt the CID would get to McMenamin first and that would scupper any chance he might have of exacting his revenge.

Perhaps Popeye was right, he mused. Maybe it would be better to let the judicial system have McMenamin, let him rot his days away in prison.

But that would depend on how many years he served, Harry's brow knitted.

Unaware that McMenamin was being hunted for multiple murders, Harry's thoughts began to torture him as he imagined how a trial would proceed.

He better than most knew that the system could be manipulated and once an experienced Queens Counsel persuaded a jury that Harriet was nearing the end of her life while McMenamin, likely a young man from a working class area and background, deprived of the benefits of a full education, was so desperate for money that his judgement was impaired and thus he resorted to stealing an elderly lady's purse.

There would be nothing said of the horror that Harriet, in the twilight of her life, experienced when she was grabbed and thrown down like a bag of rubbish to split her head and receive her mortal injury.

Nothing about the woman who had lived a good life, had raised her nephew when his own mother abandoned him, who had lost her husband in the service to his country and even after his death remained faithful to her love for him.

Nothing about the woman who every Sunday faithfully attended church and until her knees gave out, was a regular volunteer cleaner of the same church.

With no one to stand up for Harriet and her life, a sympathetic jury comprising mainly of working class peers and after McMenamin's Counsel had worked his magic, would see a groomed McMenamin in a nice suit with a sober countenance and recognise the hardships a young man from a council estate had endured and faced a life of no hope.

His defence would argue that he did not mean to hurt the old woman, that her injury was accidental and if the jury accepted that, then even before a guilty sentence was imposed the charge would likely be dropped from murder to Culpable Homicide.

Thereafter the sentence would probably be counted in single figures that could easily be dropped to five or six years if McMenamin toed the line and became a model prisoner.

Then what, he's out and about before he reaches his thirtieth birthday and enough time for him to have a full life with no regard for the hurt and pain he had caused Harriet Henderson.

Harry fumed and teeth gritted determined that no matter the cost, he would find McMenamin and Harriet's death would be avenged.

Reaching for the phone on the seat beside him, he dialled the first number in the directory and when the call was answered, said, "Helen, it's me. If he's not busy can you put me through to him, please?"

When Harry Cavanagh came onto the line, Harry said, "That source you have in the Saracen office. I need her to do something for me."

Myra McColl, like her opposite number at Maryhill office, was working with Danny McBride in ensuring the transfer of all data and equipment to Maryhill went without a hitch when DS Ian Prescott indicated he wanted a word with her in her office.

"The shooting," she rightly guessed as she settled behind her desk.

"Aye," wearily he slumped down opposite. "The victim is Peter McGroarty. A known drug dealer and all round bad guy. An ex-boxer who is still handy with his fists where the women are concerned," his lip curled and he spat out his dislike for the man, mentally recalling Sharon Gales bruised eye.

"He's not speaking, I assume?"

"We didn't get to speak with him, Myra, because he was undergoing surgery, but his live-in punch bag was there in the waiting room. A young lassie, a druggie I'm guessing, called Sharon Gale. Tried to get her to tell us who shot McGroarty and why, but she wouldn't talk to us and all she would say was it was one guy who came into the house, shot her man then left without her seeing him. McGroarty told the ambulance crew it was two masked men, but we believe that to be a load of shite."

"Any chance if you apply some pressure to this lassie Gale?"

He twisted his mouth and sighed before replying, "I'm not an expert on human behaviour, but if you were to ask me I'd say trying to pressure her would be a waste of time. Aye, she's undoubtedly a junkie, but there was something about her; something that made me think she wouldn't pee on me if I was on fire. I asked if she'd been threatened, but she countered by telling me she had not because she didn't see the guy."

"What's you next move?"

"I've left word with the hospital staff to contact me when McGroarty's out of surgery and can be interviewed. I've also asked that they keep the bullet for ballistic testing and I've arranged for a Scene of Crime team to call at the house in Ronaldsay Street and do what they can regarding anything of evidential value. However, I don't hold out any hope of McGroarty speaking to us so already I've him marked down as a waste of time."

He smiled when he added, "I've asked the Divisional drugs teams to accompany the SOCO people to give the house a wee turn and to try and find McGroarty's tick book. What is it they say?" he grinned. "It never rains but it pours?"

She returned his grin before asking, "What's your take on it, Ian? You've been in the Division a number of years now. Who shot McGroarty and why?"

"Could be a fall out among the local dealers," he shrugged, "which in turn might mean we could have a wee turf war on our hands or," he paused, "because he was shot in the leg and *not* an attempt to murder him, it might be someone giving him a warning. Who that might be," he shrugged again. "This is Glasgow, Myra, so have a look through the telephone book and take your pick."

In her office, Cathy Mulgrew first phoned her partner Jo to apologise and tell her that she was unlikely to be home for dinner, that she was heading back that evening to Maryhill office to take charge of a major inquiry.

"Are you okay? I mean, it's nothing risky?" Jo asked.

"No, nothing like that, sweetheart," Mulgrew replied with a smile, then added, "I'm sorry, but I need to run. I've the Chief to phone. Don't wait up, just get yourself off to bed and I'll join you when I get in."

"Yes, well, just be safe," Jo warned before she ended the call.

She was about to dial the Chief Constable's home phone number when her mobile chirruped and seeing the caller's name, answered with, "Hello Phil. What's up?"

"Hope I caught you before you phoned the Chief, Ma'am," replied Kennedy, then proceeded to inform her about the suspected suicide at Wyndford high rise flats that increasingly was now suspected to be a murder.

"And you think this suspect McMenamin might be involved?"

"I've no hard evidence yet, Ma'am, but I've a cop who speaks Arabic on his way here to Maryhill to interview a female asylum seeker I am told might have seen a suspect leaving the deceased's flat about the material time of his fall from the ninth floor. In the event it is connected to McMenamin, well…"

"No, Phil, you did the right thing giving me a heads up. I'll include your suspicions when I phone the Chief. Right," she glanced at her wristwatch, "I should be leaving here within the next half hour. How is the transfer of the two Saracen teams coming along?"

"So far, so good," he replied, then added, "Not to add to your concerns, Ma'am, but the hour is getting late and the three teams have been on all day and some of them are now on overtime. What do you propose when you get here?"

"I've thought about that, Phil. Once the teams are together, we'll give them a full briefing of what we know and then dismiss them for the night. As for overtime payment, I'll speak with the Chief about that and I'm sure he'll agree the extra funding from the major incident budget."

"Right, Ma'am, I'll see you when you get here and by that time I might have a better idea of what occurred down at the high rise flats."

Ending the call, Mulgrew drew a writing pad and pencil to her and tapping at her brilliantly white teeth with the thumbnail of her left hand, began to make a note of what she intended telling the Chief Constable.

Satisfied she had included all the details, she called his home phone number and when he answered, first apologised for disturbing him at home, but as she knew she would he dismissed her apology and reminded her that his instruction was that regardless of time or date, his senior staff must always apprise him of any ongoing or urgent inquiry.

In terse and concise detail, she summarised the circumstances surrounding the murders of four people and the likelihood that all four murders were committed by the same man who was now being hunted by her officers.

In addition, she continued, a fifth death now suspected to be murder was currently being investigated with the same suspect being considered as responsible.

"My God, Cathy," replied the Chief, the shock in his voice evident, "I don't care what it takes, but I want this man found!"

"We're doing all we can, sir," she assured him.

"Well, I agree with your assuming command as the SIO and moving your teams to the one incident room. Now, albeit I'm supposed to be off tomorrow, I'll be paying you an *unexpected* visit to bolster your team's morale. How does eleven in the morning sound?"

"That will be grand, sir," she replied.

"Well, when I turn up, try to look suitably surprised, eh?"

"Yes, sir," she smiled as he ended the call.

Night was falling as Kieran McMenamin, dressed in his dark, hooded top, jogging trousers and training shoes, trudged towards Glasgow's west end. The sight of Popeye Doyle and another cop in the van watching his close entrance had panicked him and for the hundredth time he wondered how they had got on to him.

More than that, he wondered for *what* they had got onto him.

His previous cockiness that he had got away with killing Lennie Robertson was gone and as for murdering the lassie Maggie and her

junkie flatmate, he was certain he hadn't left any trace of himself in the debris strewn squat.
Jackie Stone came to mind, but again he was certain no one had seen him leave Stone's flat.
His hood up and hands thrust into the pockets in the front, he wracked his brains to try and decide where he should go.
His stomach rumbled as he walked and decided his first stop would be a chippy.
That brought to mind how much money he had and he sickeningly realised that less than a hundred quid wouldn't get him very far if he had to get out of Glasgow.
Even though he hated the bastard, his first thought was to seek shelter at Peter McGroarty's place, but when he arrived at Ronaldsay Street he was shocked to see a CID car and a van parked outside with a woman wearing a white Forensic suit entering the house.
It occurred to him then that maybe McGroarty or that rat bag girlfriend of his had fired him into the polis, but then argued with himself that neither McGroarty or Sharon knew he had killed anyone.
In fact, he had told nobody, so what evidence did the cops have?
It occurred to him, albeit briefly, to go home and brazen it out, deny anything the cops might put to him, but he didn't trust the bastards and knew they weren't above fitting him up and planting their evidence on him.
No, that would be madness, he decided.
Right now, he turned to glance up at the skies that threatened to unleash their clouds of rain upon Glasgow below, he needed somewhere to hole up for the night and gather his thoughts. Make a plan to get himself out of Glasgow.
The old school he and his teenage mates used to screw for copper piping, he suddenly grinned and with a new spring in his step, hurriedly made his way towards Dowanhill Street.

Aware that Nigel Faraday wouldn't need him that evening, Sandy Craig drove his own, two-years old black coloured BMW from his tenement flat in Dennistoun's Thomson Street out towards Hamilton. Turning off the M74 onto the Raith Interchange he continued towards the town's council estate in Hillhouse and finally stopped outside a mid-terraced house in Fereneze Crescent.

Switching off the engine, he alighted from the car and glanced at a group of young teenagers who stood watching from a nearby corner, all dressed in the uniform common to that age of baggy sweat pants, hooded tops that covered their heads and training shoes. He watched one of the group pass a bottle of Buckfast to another as they silently stared at the big man.

He grinned for he knew his car was safe, but not because they recognised Craig.

The man he was visiting, like Craig a former door steward who now run his own drug network, ruled the area by fear and none dared interfere either with him or anyone visiting him.

Not if they wanted to continue walking on their own legs.

Striding along the neatly tended garden path, Craig noticed the CCTV cameras situated above the door and under the eaves of the roof.

The door opened before he reached it and a voice said, "Hello, stranger. Come for your toys?"

Jimmy Morrison, six feet four inches of solid muscle and bone, extended a hand towards Craig and with a cheeky grin, asked, "Did you bring me a present?"

Craig shook Morrison's tattooed hand and handed the powerfully built former amateur wrestler a boxed bottle of Aberlour double casked mature whisky.

Glancing at the gift, Morrison broke into a wide grin and slapping Craig heartedly on the back, invited him through to the plush front room where Craig saw Morrison's redheaded partner usher their two small children through to the kitchen before closing the door behind them.

He said, "I saw you've a couple of wee toys yourself, Jimmy, at the front door and in your eaves below the roofline. Expecting some kind of bother?"

"I've two cameras at the back as well and they're all tied in to the TV," Morrison proudly boasted and pointed to the massive state of the art set that was mounted on the wall. "That and the neighbours have been warned to let me know if they see anyone hanging about," he added.

Uncorking the Aberlour, Morrison offered Craig a dram that he politely declined.

Pouring himself three fingers, Morrison continued, "I've heard a whisper the local drug squad might be considering a visit so it's always best to be prepared," he grinned. "The front and back doors are reinforced with an inner steel casing and the windows are all bulletproof glass. Cost me a few bob," he shrugged, "but in our line, Sandy, it doesn't pay to take chances, eh?"

"Don't tell me you're keeping the gear in the house here?" Craig's face registered his surprise.

"No," he scoffed at the question, "but I'm not letting any bastard getting in here without me saying so, warrant or no warrant," Morrison shook his head. "It's a matter of principal. If the locals see me roll over for the cops, my hold on the area is weakened. Better to take a hit and keep my reputation, know what I mean," he winked.

The next couple of minutes were spent seated in deep conversation, discussing among other issues Morrison questioning why Craig still worked for Stevie Watkins and had not himself taken over Watkins network.

"I mean, Sandy, we both know it's just a question of time."

"Maybe so," Craig slowly nodded, "but right now isn't the time." Grinning widely, he added, "But keep me in mind, eh?"

Morrison gulped down his dram and licking at his lips, got his feet and said, "Now, about your toys. We'll take your car to collect them and you can drop me back off again, okay?"

Less than five minutes later Morrison was directing Craig to a local industrial estate off Pollock Avenue and had Craig drive around the estate for several minutes to satisfy Morrison that there were no police cars parked or prowling the area.

Directing Craig to stop at a metal fence, Morrison said, "Wait here." Watching, Craig saw him produce a set of keys from his pocket and unlocking the side gate in the fence, entered the yard behind and made his way to a building boasting several units where he disappeared through a door.

As he tensely waited he saw CCTV cameras mounted at each end of the metal fence and guessed those too would likely be networked into Morrison's television.

Some minutes later, Morrison reappeared carrying a bundled object under his arm and approaching the car he waved his hand upwards to indicate that Craig open the boot.

Pressing the button, Craig watched in the passenger's side mirror as Morrison bent over to lay the bundle in the boot and closing the lid, re-entered the BMW.

"Right then," he grinned at Craig, "you can drop me off. I've a date with a bottle of Aberlour."

Less than ten minutes later, Craig was passing Hamilton racecourse on his return to the Raith Interchange when he used the car's hands free to phone Stevie Watkins.

When the call was answered, he simply said, "That's me collected the toys, boss," then with a smile, ended the call.

After being dropped off at the front entrance to Maryhill police station, Fariq Mansoor cheerfully waved to the civilian bar officer who pressing the button to open the security door, said, "I've been told to tell you when you got here, Fariq, that you've to make your way up to the Family Liaison Unit suite on the first floor."

"Thanks," Mansoor acknowledged the instruction and headed for the stairs.

Deciding not to barge in, but to first knock on the door, he was surprised when it was opened by Daisy Cooper who stepped into the corridor and quietly closed it behind her.

"Sarge," he smiled at her.

"Glad you could make it," she returned his smile and asked, "What did the hospital say?"

"Oh," he shrugged, "they did an immediate saliva test for infection, but when I explained the bugger's spit didn't hit my mouth or anything," he involuntarily shuddered, "the doctor seemed to believe there is no risk so I'll get a written report in due course, but otherwise I'm good to go."

"Good," she smiled and brow furrowed, continued, "I've Missus Sureer Ahmed Kaar with her four years old daughter Yusar. Missus Kaar's English isn't great, but she's managed to tell me her name and that of her daughter and some other facts about herself. Mostly by sign language," she sighed. "I gather Missus Kaar is twenty-four and I've also managed to learn that she's been here now in the UK for nine months and is an asylum seeker. Her husband apparently was a teacher, but was murdered by a Jihadist faction a couple of years ago for teaching female children. She went into hiding with friends before fleeing the country on a plane to France, but for some unknown reason the French moved her on to here and she's wound up in Glasgow," then shrugging, added, "but why I don't know and neither does she, I think. Anyway, she seems to be an educated young woman and apart from Somali, she speaks French and Arabic and that's why you're here."

Mansoor slowly nodded and asked, "I know I've to take a statement from her, but what about?"

Daisy explained the suspicion of the CID that about the time of the death of a local drug dealer, Jackie Stone, Missus Kaar saw a man leaving Stone's ninth floor flat.

"The Detective Inspector is now treating Stone's death as murder and wants Missus Kaar to be shown a photograph of a suspect, Kieran McMenamin."

"McMenamin?"

"You know him?"

"Aye, well, not personally, but I know there's a lot of interest in him by the Saracen CID investigating the murders, Sarge."

"Oh, really," she hadn't known that, then asked, "Do you know how to operate the VIPER system?"

"Aye, we were shown in training. You want me to show her a selection of photographs on the computer and include McMenamin's photo?"

"Yes, well, take her statement first and if the description fits, we've a laptop for you to use with a number of photos already set to go and he's in there among them."

"You said her wee girl's four?"

"Yes," Daisy slowly nodded.

"Can you give me a minute?" he said, then sped away down the corridor.

Bemused, Daisy stared after him before returning to the room were the nervous woman sat with her child.

A few moments later the door knocked and was opened by Mansoor who stopped and stared wide-eyed at the young, slim and beautiful Somalian woman seated nervously on the edge of a comfortable armchair with her daughter stood by her side.

In front of them was a coffee table with a laptop lying open, but switched off.

Daisy inwardly smiled at the young man's confusion for even as a woman she recognised how attractive Missus Kaar was.

"Eh, ah, *As-salamu alaykum*," he finally stuttered, his free hand reaching to nervously stroke his beard.

Nodding her head slightly to one side, Sureer, aware of the young policeman's interest in her, shyly replied with a knowing smile, *"Wa-alaykum asalam."*

"May I?" he pointed to the little girl who open-mouthed, stared up at the tall, bearded Mansoor and in his other hand Daisy could see he had fetched a bar of chocolate and a can of Coca-Cola from the vending machine in the report writing room.

Good thinking, Fariq, she smiled at his thoughtfulness.

"Yes, of course," her mother replied as with a smile, he handed them to the child.

Drawing a chair towards him, he turned to Daisy and in English, said, "Any chance you might take the wee girl for a tour of the station, Sarge?"

"If it helps," she nodded and stone-faced, fought to refrain from smiling.

Turning to Sureer, he said, *"Sister, the police lady would like to show Yusar around the station if that's okay with you?"*

She didn't immediately respond, but then turning to the child, said, *"The nice lady would like to take you for a little walk while mummy speaks to the policeman. Will you do that for me, my love?"*

"Yes, mummy," Yusar nodded, her interest now mainly with the chocolate bar clutched in her hand.

They watched as Daisy gently took the Coco-cola from Yusar then holding the little girl's free hand, led her from the room.

He sat down opposite the young woman and fetching his notebook and pen from his pocket, was about to speak when she said, *"Your Arabic is very good, brother. Are you also an immigrant?"*

"Not me, sister," he cheerfully shook his head. *"I'm second generation Scottish, but I grew up speaking Urdu and Arabic at home as second languages and of course I attend the mosque. My grandfather arrived here from India before the country split in 1947 when Pakistan was created as an independent nation, but by that time he had made Scotland his home and was one of the first in this country to introduce curry restaurants into Glasgow. He still runs and cooks in his place in Ashton Lane,"* then realised Sureer was smiling at him, that his mouth was running away with him and he blushed.

"Right," he cleared his throat and hastily continued, *"let me explain why we need a statement from you."*

Fifteen minutes later, the statement noted, Mansoor turned the laptop towards him and signing onto the dedicated site, explained to Sureer what he was about to show her.

"This description you've given me," his eyes narrowed before he opened the site, *"It's very precise."*

It was her turn to blush as she explained, *"I was educated in a French convent school in my home city of Hargeisa which is the second largest city in Somalia. My father was very forward thinking and believed in female education. I studied art in my teenage years,"* she blushed again, *"and therefore have a good eye for detail."*

"So you're confident you will recognise this man again who you have described?"

"Yes, but…"

He saw her hesitation and gently asked, *"You are worried he might come for you?"*

"You have to understand where I come from, the police…" she sighed, her eyes widening at the memory of her home, *"the police do not protect people like me."*

"Well," he inhaled, *"you're here now and this policeman will protect you."*

"You are very gallant."

He swallowed with difficulty and wondered why the room was so warm before replying, *"It's not hard to be gallant with such a…"* then stopped, thinking maybe he was overstepping the mark, but then slowly said, *"With such a nice sister."*

She didn't reply, but demurely lowered her head and said, *"perhaps now I will look at the photographs, brother?"*

"Oh, yes, of course," he pressed the button that displayed a number of photographs, headshots of white males of a similar age and description provided by Sureer.

She didn't hesitate, but pointed directly at a photograph of Kieran McMenamin and said, *"Him."*

"You're certain?"

"Positive, brother."

He added her positive identification of McMenamin to her statement and taking a deep breath, said, *"Well, there's only one further thing to ask."*

"Yes?"
"How would you feel about you and Yusar having dinner with me at my grandfather's restaurant?"

The driver pulled into the overnight lorry park on the M6 motorway, strictly adhering to the instructions that he must arrive at the Glasgow location at the precise time typed on his work sheet; the document that should he be stopped by the coppers might save his arse.
Switching off the engine, he climbed from the cab and after locking it, made his way to the service station for his last meal of the day.

CHAPTER TWENTY-THREE

The sun shone through the broken window of the first floor classroom in the old Victorian school and created a light pattern on the opposite wall.
Now in a state of disrepair and disarray, the council had for several years debated whether to refurbish the building at an exorbitant cost or instead and against the wishes of the neighbourhood residents, sell the land and the building to a developer in an area that was already over populated and with it in the narrow roads about the building, the resultant parking problems.
His eyes were gritty and wearily forcing them open, he groped for his mobile phone to learn it was just gone seven in the morning, seeing too that the battery level was almost depleted.
Turning his aching body towards the wall, he growled at the memory of the circumstances that caused him to be here in this shithole.
He had slept badly, curled up on the wooden floor in an abandoned walk-in cupboard of the classroom, a collection of old sheets he had found in the cupboard cobbled together to make his bed with more sheets wrapped about him to act as his quilt.
His mouth was dry and he worked his jaw to ease the ache and savour again the salty taste of the fish and chips. He reached for the bottle of Irn-Bru to quench his thirst, annoyed that there was but a dribble left and angry that he had not had the foresight to buy more juice or something for his breakfast.

He shivered at the memory for unless Popeye Doyle and whoever was with the bastard were near to his close for some other purpose, he was being hunted by the cops.
Again and again he had wracked his brains, trying to figure out what they might know, what evidence they might have against him.
He hadn't left any trace of himself in the park, none at the squat and nothing at Jackie Stone's place, so what the *fuck* did they know?
No, he was sure he was clean, but the more he thought about it the more concerned he became.
He had watched the CSI programmes on the television, but who hadn't?
The way they can find even the tiniest clues was amazing, but it's not like that in real life; of that he was absolutely certain.
I mean, come on, he argued with himself; who finds wee clues hunting about the grass or in the squat, recalling the state that place was? That's just television make-believe, he sneered.
But the seed of doubt had been sown and lifting the sheets that covered him he glanced down at his clothing.
Was there something on his clothes he couldn't see?
The truth was, he just didn't know.
He expelled a burst of fetid air and used his hand to wave the smell away, conscious that he must soon release his bowels.
Staggering to his feet he stretched and realised he must leave the classroom to find a toilet, lifting the used chip shop paper as he made his way out of the room.
The darkened corridor was littered with debris, plaster fallen from the ceiling or refuse brought in by prowlers and thieves like himself.
Holes had been gouged in the walls by metal thieves after ripping out the copper piping. Broken desks and chairs lay simply abandoned when the building fell into disuse.
At last he found a girl's lavatory, but was annoyed to see that every porcelain item including the toilet bowls had been vandalised beyond repair.
Frustrated, he squatted in a corner of the room and made his toilet, using the chip shop paper to wipe himself clean.
Fastening himself, he glanced about the room and knew that he couldn't remain there, that he had to get away to somewhere safe and out of Glasgow.
But where?

Now stood in the corridor outside the toilet, he leaned his forehead against one of the unbroken windows, his breath creating a canvas of moisture on the glass and stared out into the early morning at the empty playground below.

A thought occurred to him, a thought so outlandish it caused him grin for tiredness, hunger, thirst and stress were now all combining to play havoc with his emotions.

What if he were to surrender to the cops? Go to Saracen station with his lawyer, that weasel Colin Drake, where he would then find out what they knew.

After all, they couldn't very well verbal or fit him up with Drake by his side, could they?

Tears of helpless frustration filled his eyes and not for the first time in his life he was frightened; no, not just frightened, but really shitting himself.

He slowly inhaled, then puffed his cheeks out as he blew through pursed lips.

That's what he would do, go to see the fat git at his office in Anderston and get Drake to accompany him to the cop shop.

The only problem was it was now Sunday and Drake's office would be closed.

He'd need to phone Drake's out of hours' number and persuade the slimeball to meet him.

Yes, he unconsciously nodded, that's what he would do.

If he told Drake the cops might suspect him of murder, the smarmy bugger would see an opportunity for getting his name in the papers and likely would hotfoot it to his office from whatever shithole he lived in.

He felt easier now that he had made his decision and rubbing at his eyes and nose with the sleeve of his hoody, fetched his mobile from his pocket, but then loudly cursed.

The battery was dead.

"Shit!" he screamed in frustration and had to refrain from angrily throwing the phone against the nearby wall.

There was nothing else for it.

He would need to leave the safety of the derelict school and find a phone, but then grimaced. All his numbers were in the mobile's directory, including Drake's out of hours' number.

Gritting his teeth against his bad luck, he realised he would have to get himself down to Anderston and Drake's office where the out of hours' phone number would be advertised on the window or above the door.

With a last cautious look about him, he started to make his way to the broken window on the ground floor where he had entered the building.

The meeting chaired by Cathy Mulgrew and attended by her three seated DI's; Myra McColl, Danny McBride and Phil Kennedy commenced that morning at five minutes after eight.

Stood propped with her back to the desk and her arms folded the first thing Mulgrew asked was if there had been any new information as to the whereabouts of their suspect, Kieran McMenamin.

While McColl and McBride both shook their head, Kennedy replied, "No, Ma'am. We've had officers stationed throughout the night outside his close and the warrant search of his house revealed nothing other than what seems to be a stash of personal drugs hidden in his mattress. Needless to say his father and sister were brought to the office, but neither knew of his actions nor where he might be. It seems that his father considers him to be shiftless and lazy while his sister, frankly, doesn't like him. However, there *is* a development."

Her interest piqued, Mulgrew asked, "That is?"

"You'll recall the apparent suicide of a local drug dealer, John Stone, known to us as Jackie Stone and our suspicions that he might have been helped on his way from his veranda?"

She nodded as Kennedy continued, "We have a witness who saw a man exiting Stone's ninth floor flat about the time he went over. The witness is an asylum seeker who resides on the same corridor with her child. Anyway, we used one of our own lads to interpret and note her statement and in short, using VIPER, she has positively identified that man as McMenamin."

"My God," Mulgrew exclaimed. "This bastard has been a busy boy hasn't he? How many is that we will now libel against him?"

"By my reckoning, Ma'am," interjected McColl, "Five murders."

Mulgrew rubbed wearily at her forehead and replied, "Last night I informed the Chief of my decision to assume the role of SIO and his response to my summary of the murders is no matter what it takes, we need to catch this man. Therefore, I have requested that every

CID office within the city will provide two additional detectives to the investigation."

"Maybe remind them to stick their two quid in the tea fund, ma'am," grumbled Kennedy.

"Aye, I will," she grinned. "Now, before we…"

The door knocked and was pushed open by DS Calum Fraser who said, "Sorry to interrupt, Ma'am, but I thought this was important enough," and handed her that mornings copy of the 'Glasgow News'.

The DI's saw her take a sharp intake of breath then turning the front page towards them, held it up for them to read the headline that exclaimed: SARACEN COPS HUNT SERIAL KILLER.

Glancing at the report, Mulgrew confirmed to the three others that the newspaper now had McMenamin's name.

"Well, that's the cat well and truly out of the bag now," sighed McBride.

"It was just a question of time," McColl thoughtfully added. "No matter how much we might trust our guys there's always one with a loud mouth who'll boast to a pal or a family member and let's face it; there's always money to be made for that kind of tipoff to the papers."

"Let's just be grateful they haven't included a photograph," Kennedy said. "Can you imagine the witch-hunt if that had happened?"

"We might still have to resort to that," Mulgrew shook her head. "We can't afford for this man McMenamin to kill someone else. Unless he's arrested by this evening, I'm afraid we might have no option but to issue his photograph and use the media to alert the public to the danger he poses," then turning to Fraser, dismissed him with a nod and a tight smile.

"Now," she stood upright, "I think it's about time that we get our heads together to brief the team on what we know."

As they discussed what the Detective Superintendent should tell the team, the three DI's individually gave some thought to who among their teams might have alerted the 'Glasgow News' to their hunt for McMenamin, but none of them considered a middle-aged cleaning woman who was well known and liked at Saracen office and who on occasion was employed by Harry Cavanagh.

Returning to his room after his workout in the hotel fitness room and before taking an invigorating cold shower, Harry Henderson first checked the safe was not been tampered with.

The hilarity and bedlam from the previous evening's wedding party had not died down till just after four that morning and try as he might, he couldn't sleep through the noise, listening as the hotel night staff continuously patrolled the corridor and urged the drunken guests to be quiet, all of which was ignored.

Glancing at the morning edition of the complimentary 'Glasgow News' delivered to his room, he smiled.

Harry Cavanagh's source in Saracen office had done her bit and now the CID's suspect Kieran McMenamin would be running scared and in Harry's experience, frightened people were more inclined to make mistakes.

Towelling himself dry, he dressed formally in a new shirt, suit and tie before heading downstairs for breakfast.

It was evident many of the guests had continued to drink throughout the night for a number of them, predominantly young men, were still dressed in their formal attire and continued to cause a ruckus in the dining room, their language loud and ripe.

Selecting a table as far from the large group as he could, he smiled at the flustered young waitress when ordering a pot of tea before attending to collect his buffet breakfast.

It was when he was at the hotplate filling his plate he saw one young man, he guessed in his mid-twenties, grab at the waitress's backside as she passed him by with a teapot held in one hand while her other hand supported the base of the teapot on a dishcloth.

Embarrassed, the young woman attempted to shrug the leering drunk off, but to Harry's surprise the drunk then leaned into towards her and bowed his head down onto her breasts while pretending to bite at them.

Shocked, the waitress shrieked and dropped the teapot onto the floor, causing the lid to fly off and some of the scalding liquid to splash onto the drunks' trousers.

"Ya stupid bitch!" he screamed at the waitress and shoving her with both hands, Harry watched as she fell heavily backwards onto the carpeted floor.

He did not intend intervening for in truth it was the staff's responsibility to deal with the drunk, but some ingrained chivalry caused him to lay his plate down onto an empty table and moving towards the waitress, Harry held out his hand and said, "Here, Miss, let me help you up."

As he grasped the waitress's hand, he felt himself being pushed from behind and heard the drunk say, "Who the *fuck* are you to get involved, ya baldy old bastard!"

Harry pulled the waitress to her feet then turning, grimly smiled at the drunk whose arm was extended and hand reaching out to push Harry again.

Feigning to his left, with lightning speed Harry took the drunks outstretched arm and with a sharp tug sent him flying directly into the stainless steel hotplate.

The drunk instinctively reached out both hands to prevent himself colliding with the hotplate, but to no avail for his momentum caused him to bodily collide with the steaming hotplate and both hands to sink into the large tub of extremely hot baked beans while his forehead crashed into the glass covered extractor unit above the hotplate.

With a scream, the drunk jerked back and fell whimpering onto the floor, his hands and the front of his suit now covered in the boiling bean sauce and blood oozing from the wound in his brow.

Without a backward look and ignoring the drunk's friends who hurried to his aid, Harry collected his plate and returned to his table. While the furore continued at the hotplate, he glanced up to see the hotel security escorting the burned and bleeding drunk and some of his noisier friends from the dining room.

Moments later the pale faced waitress arrived at his table with a fresh pot of tea that she laid down in front of him, then leaning forward, quietly said, "Thanks very much, sir. That bastard gave me one hell of a fright."

Harry grinned and nodded.

What he didn't see was his actions had provoked the curiosity of the hotel security manager, Peasy Byrne, a former Strathclyde Police detective who recognising the suited man quietly enjoying his breakfast, discreetly called the young waitress to him for a wee chat.

Dressed in casual trousers, shirt and tie and a sports jacket, Popeye Doyle was pleased that in the twilight of his career he was seconded to the major murder inquiry now being run from Maryhill office. Ignoring the ribald, but good-natured comments from his fellow

He didn't immediately respond and Mulgrew almost thought she was wasting her time, when to her surprise he sighed and said, "I knew Harry a long time ago. I didn't have any contact with him through the years he was making a name for himself nor when he was banged up, but I did see him the other day when he called at the Saracen office to provide a statement to DS Fraser. We exchanged a greeting and shared bit of craic," but decided not to mention their meeting at the Waterstones café in Byres Road.

"What's your thoughts on him?"

"Harry?" he smiled, a sidelong smile while his eyes wandered to the floor, then lifting his head, replied, "Curiously, he's a decent enough man and," he shrugged and continued, "I would trust him more than some of the cops I've had to work with through the years. As for trying to warn him off going after McMenamin; frankly Ma'am, I believe you would be wasting your time. But you can try and yes," he nodded, "I don't think it would do any harm having me along with you."

"Well then, we'll take my car and on the way I'll phone Peasy Byrne and find out if Henderson's still at the hotel."

He had returned to his room and removing his jacket and kicking off his shoes, lay on the bed with the mobile in his hand.

He pressed the button to call Harry Cavanagh and when the phone was answered by Helen, he smiled.

"Oh, it's yourself," she breathlessly replied in his ear. "Hang on, he's here."

He held the phone away from his ear when she bellowed, "Harry! Are you out of the shower yet? It's him, Harry Henderson!"

He could hear a shuffling then Cavanagh's voice saying, "Get us a coffee, eh sweetheart?"

Helen's outburst was lost as she left the room, then Cavanagh greeted him with, "Hello, Harry. Sorry about that. You caught me in the shower."

"In your bedroom?"

"Aye, I was just…oh," he laughed, "I see what you mean. Looks like I'm burst, eh?"

"I think that's been an open secret for some time," Harry smiled before adding, "I need a wee favour if at all possible."

"What kind of favour?"

"Have you seen this morning's 'Glasgow News'?"

"Oh, about your man? Yes, like you asked I got in touch with my friend at Saracen and looks like she did the business."

"Definitely and it means our man should be running scared by now. If I'm correct and the cops go all out to find him, they'll be turning over his address and every address known to them. A lowlife like him can't have too many places to run. Now, I've been thinking. Who do you suppose is the only person at this time that he might trust? The only person who might be in any kind of position to stand by him?"

There was a pause and he could almost imagine Cavanagh smiling before he replied, "His lawyer."

"Right. Now, I believe there's every reason to think that our man has already been through the system and unless the routine has drastically changed, every time he was arrested he'll have been asked the same question and that question and his answer will be logged on the police computer system."

"Do you want your lawyer contacted," answered Cavanagh.

"Correct," Harry couldn't help but smile. "Now, our problem is, who *is* his lawyer?"

There was that pause again before Cavanagh, his voice almost a whisper as it registered his shock, said, "Wait a minute, Harry, are you suggesting what I *think* you're suggesting?"

"And what is it that you *think* I'm suggesting?" Harry teased him.

"The cops computer, the system they use when an arrested person is charged. You think that somehow I can get into that? Find out who our man's lawyer is?"

"Can you? I mean, I don't profess to be an expert on computers, but it occurred to me that the computers at the charge bars must all operate from a common…what do they call it? The thing that connects all the computers in the different stations throughout the city so if somebody is arrested in one station it will indicate if he's later arrested in another part of the city."

"You're talking about a server, Harry; they call it a server."

"See," Harry grinned, "I knew you'd be right on the ball with this. So, with all your resources, do you have anybody in your…" he hesitated before continuing, "your employ who might be able to check that out for me?"

He listened to Cavanagh's breathing before the portly man replied, "There's a man who owes me a favour. Works out of Shettleston, but for Christ's sake, Harry, it's Sunday. He might not even be on duty."
"But you'll check for me?"
With a sigh, Cavanagh replied, "Of course I will. There *is* another possibility. I have someone who owes me and who works in the courts. If McMenamin has been through the system, he'll be recorded on their computers too and likely they'll have the details of whoever represented him at trial. Give me an hour…thanks, hen," Harry heard him say then the sound of Helen moving in the room. "I'll get back to you," Cavanagh finished before ending the call.
Laying the mobile on the bed beside him, he slowly exhaled and frustratingly knew there was nothing more he could do now other than wait.

With her son by her side, Mary Harris was about to leave after the Sunday service, but found herself cornered at the church steps by a succession of well-wishers, all who wanted to extend their sympathies for her loss.
A tap on her shoulder caused her to turn round where she saw her friend Alice stood there with her husband, his florid face and bulbous nose depicting his love of sweet sherry.
"Have you seen the paper this morning, Mary? The 'Glasgow News' I mean?" Alice asked.
"No."
"They're saying that they've identified the killer of the man in the park."
A cold hand clutched at Mary's chest. She felt her knees tremble and fearing she was about to collapse, reached out for her son who worriedly said, "Mum? Are you okay? What's wrong?"
A small crowd gathered around and it was suggested that feeling as faint as she was, Mary be taken to the vestry, but she raised a hand to decline, telling Michael, "I'm fine. Honestly. It's just…what Alice told me."
He glanced accusingly at Alice who wide-eyed, falteringly said, "I was just saying. The police, they know who killed the man in the park. It was in the paper."
"Aye, I know his father," someone in the crowd said. "A nice man, but that son of his…" and left the rest unsaid.

As quickly as it started, the word went round the assembled crowd about the police hunt for Kieran McMenamin and overshadowed any concern the crowd might have had for Mary.
Sensing his mother's discomfort, Michael took her by the arm and with Alice's husband solicitously supporting her other arm, led her away to begin the short walk towards her home.

In a cupboard at the uniform bar, Daisy Cooper was reaching for a fresh battery for her Airwave radio when she saw Fariq Mansoor passing along the corridor and with a smile, called out, "Hey, Furry, a word."
Surprised, Mansoor made his way towards her as she lowered her voice and said, "You never burst to *that* nickname, did you?"
"Would you, Sarge?" he replied, his cheeks blushing.
"Probably not," she grinned, then asked, "Was that Sergeant Cassidy I saw upstairs? I thought she didn't work Sunday's in her job."
"Usually she doesn't, but Popeye is away helping out with the murder investigation at Maryhill and left me to neighbour the Sarge," he moaned and rolled his eyes.
"Well, maybe today you can teach her something about beat duties, show her how to arrest someone," she slowly shook her head, the sarcasm oozing from her.
"Ouch," he pretended to shy away and joked, "Keep your claws in, Sarge."
"Did that come out like it sounded? My God, I'm getting bitter in my old age," though she thought Anne Cassidy had about as much interest in arresting neds as she had of catching her fingers in a door. Privately, Daisy believed that Cassidy avoided arrest situations for she did not wish to attend a court where her inexperience would show her up for the chancer she was.
"I'd better go in case she's wondering where I've got to," he pointed a finger upstairs, but as he walked away, Daisy recalled something and called after him, "Yesterday, Fariq, that witness you interpreted for. Well done."
"Oh, yeah, thanks Sarge," he gave her an embarrassed smile and headed for the stairs aware that if word got out he intended dating a witness in a murder investigation, well, he didn't like to think what the bosses would make of that.

Wearing a black coloured, silk dressing gown over his pyjamas, Nigel Faraday prepared himself a light breakfast and carried his cereal bowl and coffee onto the balcony where he sat facing the sunshine.

The noise of a small diesel engine cruiser making its way down the Clyde disturbed what was almost a perfect morning and he sighed. Much as he enjoyed living in the flat, his expected wealth from the sale of the shipment being delivered later this evening now meant he could afford something a little more upmarket and already his thoughts were turning to a secluded villa, but whether in Milngavie or Newton Mearns, he had not yet decided.

Sipping at his coffee, he smiled in anticipation of that evenings delivery, already having calculated the enormous profit he would make from the sale of the heroin.

His thoughts turned to Sandy Craig and smirked when he thought of the big oaf's eagerness to be told when and where the delivery would occur. The last text from Craig confirmed the van had been hired and the team were on standby and awaited his instructions.

On that point, he sighed and reached to the table for his mobile phone.

Scrolling down the directory, he chose the number he sought and began texting:

Any news re the placement of your people tonight. Any issues, I need to know immediately.

Pressing the send button, he replaced the phone onto the glass topped table and his eyes narrowed.

Once he had received confirmation the police had no interest in the venue, he would contact Sandy Craig with the time and details of the trucks arrival.

Satisfied he had done all that was needed, he slurped the last of the coffee and arose to head indoors for his shower.

DS Calum Fraser glanced irritably at his watch and telling the two detectives he'd meet them in the car, went looking for Marilyn Munroe.

Mounting the stairs to the first landing, he saw her standing with her back against a wall staring down at her mobile phone and more sharply than he intended, called out, "For heaven's sake, Marilyn,

what's keeping you."
Her head jerked up and he saw her face was pale when she stuttered, "Eh, it's my dad. My mum sent a text to tell me he's had a fall. Sorry," and began to make her way towards him.
"Look," he raised a hand to stop her. "If you need to go home, it's no big issue. I'll let the bosses know you need some personal time…"
She interrupted and shaking her head, replied, "Thanks, but it's fine, Calum. Honest. I was just taken aback, that's all. My sister will attend to it. It's no great deal. The silly bugger is always tripping over his feet. Right," she took a sharp intake of breath. "Let's go, shall we?"
When she stepped past her, he stared curiously at her as she began to make her way down the stairs.
It wasn't like Marilyn to ignore that kind of call for he knew she was devoted to her father, himself a former policeman who in his twilight years had been diagnosed with MS and was now profoundly suffering from the disease.
Well, he inwardly sighed, she knew best and followed her down the stairs.

He had found a small café in Argyle Street near to Berkley Street that was open for Sunday business and head down, ordered rolls and sausage and a polystyrene cup of coffee to take away.
The man serving him was too preoccupied by the two giggling young and scantily clad women who still dressed from their Saturday night out, were on a high, either with drink or drugs and didn't give Kieran McMenamin a second glance.
Which was just as well, for the glaring headline from the 'Glasgow News' newspapers stacked on the counter sent a chill through his body and resisting the urge to purchase a copy in case it drew the man's attention to him, paid for his rolls and coffee with his head down.
Leaving the shop, he made his way to a nearby close and pushing at the wooden door, was relieved when it opened and allowed him access to the rear yard where he squatted in the shade of the building to hungrily eat his rolls and drink his coffee.
His hunger and thirst abated, he licked at his fingers before rising to his feet and returning back through the close, checked the street to

make sure it was clear of any passing police vehicles before resuming his journey to Colin Drake's law offices.

Without any regard to the cones that prohibited cars from parking at the front of the Hilton Hotel, Cathy Mulgrew exited her Lexus and followed by Popeye Doyle, smiled at the doorman as she approached the entrance and and said, "CID. We're here to see Mister Byrne."
"Oh, aye, right Madam," the doorman nodded and courteously held open the door to permit them to pass through.
Expecting them, Peasy Byrne was stood to one side of the reception desk where the former cop greeted them both with a handshake and said, "Your man's still in his room. Do you want to go up or shall I have him informed you're here? I can make a room available if you wish to privately interview him."
Mulgrew pursed her lips and shaking her head, replied, "If the desk can inform him we're here in the foyer, I'm sure he'll be happy sitting with us in a public place. What do you think, Popeye?" she turned towards him.
"Suits us so I think it will suit him too, Ma'am."
In his room, Harry Henderson was surprised when the young woman called to inform him that a Miss Mulgrew and Mister Doyle were in the reception area and wished to see him, though not surprised they had finally tracked him down to his accommodation.
His first thought was that they had identified him as the shooter of Peter McGroarty, but then realised that couldn't be for if they had it was unlikely they would invite him to the reception area. No, if they had evidence and suspected him to be armed they would be more likely to batter down his door and follow that with a stun grenade; therefore, he guessed he was *not* being arrested.
With a half smile, he realised it was to do with the 'Glasgow News' having identified McMenamin as the killer of his aunt Harriet and *that* was why they wanted their little chat.
A few minutes later, he exited the lift and saw both officers seated in the comfortable chairs in the foyer, a table in front of them and courtesy of Byrne upon which a waiter was laying a pot of coffee, three cups, milk and sugar.
"Good morning, Miss Mulgrew," he greeted her and turning towards Doyle, nodded and said, "Popeye."

Seating himself down before Mulgrew with Doyle to his right, he asked, "To what do I owe the pleasure?"

"Shall I be mum," she leaned forward before either man replied and carefully poured coffee into the three cups.

"Just milk for me, please," Harry smiled at her.

"We heard you had a bit of a confrontation this morning. In the restaurant."

"Just a drunk hassling a wee lassie," he shrugged. "I only did what any man would have done. But that's not why you're here, is it?"

"No, it's not why we're here. You'll have seen this morning's newspaper…" she began.

"Couldn't miss it."

"…and *that's* why we're here. Can I call you Harry?"

He shrugged that it was fine by him.

"Is by any chance our suspect Kieran McMenamin known to you?"

"No," he shook his head, his lips bitterly tightening at the mention of the name.

She paused then said, "Do you have any idea where we might find him?"

"No."

"Have you been looking for him?"

"I only found out his name this morning," he lied and added, "from the newspaper."

She glanced at Doyle and continued, "Your reputation, Harry, precedes you and we are aware you maintain many contacts in Glasgow. The reason I'm here…"

"Is to warn me off," he interrupted with a scowl. "You think that if I go hunting this man McMenamin I'll kill him."

"Will you? Kill him I mean."

"I would need to find him first."

"How will you go about that?"

"Now you're assuming I intend hunting him."

"I think it's safe to say you didn't travel all this way from the Caribbean to see your aunt die then leave without exacting your revenge on the man that did it."

He lifted his cup and sipped at the steaming hot coffee before replying, "Have you people made any progress in finding the man who murdered Harriet?"

She shook her head and said, "I regret no, but we've teams out turning the homes of all his known associates."

"So you're satisfied that McMenamin is the man who killed my aunt?"

"The evidence seems to indicate that, yes."

He turned to stare at Doyle and said, "What about you, Popeye, you haven't said anything yet. You've worked that area all your service. What do you think?"

Doyle twisted his face and replied, "Miss Mulgrew is spot on, Harry. Kieran McMenamin is a bad wee shite. He comes from a decent enough family, but he's a lazy, shiftless bastard…pardon me, Ma'am," he nodded to her, "and I've no doubt that he's the man we're looking for and …"

He suddenly stopped and turned to glance almost guiltily at Mulgrew, a glance that wasn't missed by Harry whose eyes narrowed and said, "What? What are you not telling me?"

Mulgrew sighed and replied, "It'll come out in the wash anyway, Harry. The newspaper reported we're looking for a serial killer and they're not far off the truth. We suspect McMenamin for multiple murders and we're going all out to catch him. That's the real reason I'm here."

She raised her hand as though in warning and continued, "There is absolutely no need for you to risk getting yourself banged up for McMenamin. Remember, if you find him and harm him your previous murder conviction will mean you will *never* be released and," her eyes narrowed, "I understand you have a life in Cuba. Is it worth risking that life in the knowledge that McMenamin will go to prison for the rest of *his* life?"

"I'll take your warning on board, Miss Mulgrew, and I'm grateful for our little chat."

He rose to his feet and stared down at them in turn before adding, "Now that you know where I'm staying, can I assume that you will keep me updated of any development in your hunt for McMenamin? After all, I'm Harriet's next of kin so I believe I have a right to know."

She turned to Doyle and said, "Popeye, you and Harry go a long way back so I'll leave that to you, but," she turned to stare up at Harry, "the road goes both ways. If you have any information about McMenamin's whereabouts, I want to know. Understand?"

"Understood," he replied with a soft smile and turning away, made his way towards the lifts.

"Shit!" the driver of the articulated lorry kicked at the damaged tyre and glancing about him, wondered how long it would be before the recovery service arrived with a replacement.
He bit at his lip, a thin film of sweat beading on his brow and uncertain whether or not to make the call and inform the Spaniard that there might be a delay, knowing the bastard would be furious and worried that some blame might attach itself to him and his family.
He had no choice for already he was an hour behind schedule and fetching the mobile phone from his pocket, dialled the number.

CHAPTER TWENTY-FOUR

Sergeant Anne Cassidy was not a happy woman.
Not only was she working on a Sunday, but with all the vehicles tied up in the multiple murder investigation she was out on foot with the bloody probationer, Fariq Mansoor.
That and the fucking collar of her stab proof vest. No matter how much she bent it back for unaccustomed as she was to wearing it, it continuously chafed at her neck.
Now here they were, stood in Saracen Street and watching a half dozen bored uniformed officers and four mounted cops supervise an Orange Band belting out the Sash while their forty or so supporters traipsed along behind the band on either footway, wearing their ridiculous red, white and blue waistcoats, Rangers football tops and anything that symbolised their allegiance to the Crown. Behind the marching band a long line of impatient and angry motorists glumly gunned their engines in protest at the delay.
"They're not bad and can hold a tune, eh Sarge," Mansoor cheerfully remarked.
Cassidy turned and wordlessly stared at him, the look of disgust evident on her face.
Miserable cow, Mansoor thought and nodded greetings at the passing cops.
"Right, that's long enough for this nonsense. We'll return to the station," she began to walk off in the expectation he would follow

and added, "I've calls to make and paperwork to catch up on."
"But we've only been out for less than an hour, Sarge," he began to protest, but quickly shut his mouth when she darted a scowl towards him.
"Fine," he muttered and shaking his head at her back, caught up with her as she increased her stride.
"Here's an idea," he brightly began, "why don't I continue on the beat and if you need me, just give me a call on the radio, eh?"
"No way," she raised a hand and vigorously shook her head. "The regulations forbid you being unaccompanied with the level of service you have so far. I don't want to have to explain to the Chief Inspector why you were alone if you get into bother."
And that puts paid to that idea, he thought and wished his month's secondment was past and he was going back to *real* police work, not saddled with this lazy bugger.

To his impatient relief, the recovery mechanic finally replaced the damaged tyre and once the paperwork was sorted, he was on his way. He had travelled less than a mile when the text arrived. One eye on the road, he reached for his mobile and opened the text message.
Do not be late
was all it said and even though the cab was warm, he involuntarily shivered.

Rubbing himself down with the towel, Nigel Faraday heard the mobile phone whistle and wrapping the towel about him, made his way to the balcony to fetch the phone.
Opening the text, he read:
Nothing to suggest any police interest in you or what you're doing. Local CID tied up with murder investigations.
He smiled for he knew that the hold he had over his police informant was now firmly established, a source of information that would in the years to come benefit him enormously and a hold that he had no intention of relinquishing.
However, if the worst should *ever* come to the very worst, he had the name of a police informant that just might be useful as a bargaining chip.

Glancing at the time on his phone he decided he would wait a couple of hours then contact Sandy Craig with the details of the delivery.

The driver had made good time and glancing at the dashboard clock decided if he continued at his current speed he would arrive too soon which was almost as bad as arriving early.
The motorway road signs indicated one mile to the services at Gretna Green and his stomach told him it was time to eat.
That and now he had crossed the border he was instructed to phone a mobile number to inform the customer.
Besides, it would also give him the opportunity to clean himself, to check he hadn't developed a tail.

"My dear young Kieran, I almost expected to receive a call from the police, but not from yourself," Colin Drake's silky smooth voice almost whispered in his ear. "If I'm reading the newspaper correctly, what a devilish mess you seem to have landed yourself in, eh?"
"Cut the crap, Mister Drake, I need help and I need it now."
"I assume from your call that you are aware you are being sought for murder, young man?"
"Oh aye, I fucking know fine *why* they're looking for me, but I'm innocent and need your help."
"Of course you are," Drake's poofter voice felt almost like he was licking his ear through the phone and he shivered. How he hated they fucking queers, but taking a deep breath knew that needs must and for now he would ignore that the bastard was gay.
"Are you in a safe place at this time?"
"No, because there's nowhere fucking safe," he hissed. "My mobiles out of charge and I'm using a public phone in the Central Station and..."
"Kieran!" Drake interrupted. "Leave the Central Station immediately! The place is swamped with CCTV cameras and the police are currently using facial recognition software and we both know they already have your photo on file!"
"What...what should I do?" he glanced anxiously about him.
"Where will I go? I mean, how will I contact you without my mobile being charged?"
"Is it your intention to surrender to the police? Is that why you called me?"

"Yeah, I thought…"

"You thought you would give yourself up and you want me to accompany you to a police station to represent you lest our boys in blue should…how can I put this? Incriminate you with some of their more creative verbalisation?"

"Yes," he almost sighed with relief for queer or not, at least the slimy bastard was going to help him out of this fucking mess.

"Well, in the meantime you need to find somewhere safe until I get to you. I am at home and not yet dressed and that will take an hour or so. I will also have to contact the officer in charge of the investigation team…"

"You what! Why the *fuck* do you need to do that?"

"It's standard procedure in a case like this, Kieran, when you are being sought my dear boy. I need to let the officer in charge of the inquiry know that you are aware you are currently wanted for interview and that as an act of good faith you are willing to attend whatever office they choose for you to surrender yourself and the said interview. If indeed as is likely to happen you are arrested, there will be a court appearance and your cooperation by surrendering yourself will only stand you in good stead with the judge. Do you not see that?"

He didn't immediately respond, realising that it was naïve to believe Drake could get him out of this without him being arrested and slowly nodding, tightly replied, "Whatever you think best, Mister Drake."

"Now, the important thing is to get you somewhere safe while I negotiate with the police. Have you anywhere in mind?"

"Last night, I stayed in an old derelict school up in Dowanhill Street over in Partick."

"Wait till I take a note of this," Drake said, then continued, "If that's safe, then make your way back there till I come for you. Can you do that, Kieran?"

"Yeah, I can do that, but don't take all fucking day, Mister Drake. I don't like being out on a limb like this."

"I'll be as quick as I can, but like I told you. Get out of the Central Station as fast as you can and remember to keep your head down. Believe me, Kieran, it's far better you approach the police with me by your side than they arrest you without legal representation. So, make your way back to the school and watch for me arriving there sometime in the next couple of hours."

"Okay," McMenamin hurriedly replied and ended the call.

Laying down his mobile phone, Drake smiled.

If the 'Glasgow News' headline was correct, the publicity that would arise from representing a suspected serial killer, innocent or otherwise, would do no harm to his career as a defence lawyer and turning to his sleeping partner, gently kissed him on the cheek before getting out of bed and making his way into the en-suite.

The disturbed night by the noisy wedding party guests had tired Harry Henderson more than he realised and he had fell into a light sleep, but roused at the sound of a text message being received on his mobile phone lying beside him.

Yawning widely as he opened the message, he was suddenly awake and sitting up in the bed, smiled.

Harry Cavanagh had done well and reading the message, saw that not only had he discovered McMenamin's lawyer's name and added not just a phone number, but a home address too.

Sitting on the edge of the bed he slipped on his shoes and getting to his feet, opened the safe.

"Hello, boss," Sandy Craig greeted Nigel Faraday's call. "Got those details for me?"

"Sandy," he acknowledged him, having decided the time to inform Craig was now. "Are all the arrangements set for this evening?"

"They are, boss. The van's sitting at Fast Eddie's gaff and the rest of the team have been told to standby for my call."

"Do you have a pen and paper handy?"

"Right here, boss."

"Ten o'clock this evening, I want you and the team to be waiting in the Oakbank Industrial Estate off Garscube Road. There are two roads into the estate, but you and the team will enter the estate in the road that is just opposite Grovepark Street. Got that?"

"Grovepark Street, yes."

"Upon entering the estate, there is a right turn about fifty metres from the junction with Garscube Road that leads to a dead end. That section of the estate and the premises along the hundred yards of road to the dead end have no exterior CCTV cameras nor are there any buildings overlooking the area. Got that?"

"Yes," Craig replied, his teeth gritted and wondered if the poncey bastard thought him a complete fool.

"The driver of the delivery vehicle, an articulated lorry, will reverse into the dead end with his load; a red and green coloured container that will contain boxes of canned fruit. With the number of people you have at your disposal I believe the transfer should take no more than half an hour. Once the transfer is complete, the delivery is to be taken to a warehouse I have rented in Portman Street, over in Kinning Park. I'll text you the post code later."

"What about you, boss," Craig asked, his heart beating wildly in his chest. "Will you be there for the delivery tonight?"

"Hmmm," Faraday thought quickly. If he was there he could oversee the operation and ensure that none of the delivered heroin was squirrelled away by either Craig or any of the minions he had hired for the transfer, but on the other hand if he didn't attend the transfer and for any unknown reason, say a factor he had not considered and the police showed up, then he would avoid being arrested. None of the team hired by Crag were known to him nor he to them and other than Craig's word, nothing could link him to the delivery of the heroin. Therefore, as far as credibility went, his lawyer could easily defend him against any allegation made by a convicted criminal like Sandy Craig.

"Let me think on that, Sandy," he slowly replied.

"It's just that, well," Craig was now thinking on his feet, "You being the boss and that, the lads might feel more comfortable knowing you were there to take charge."

Faraday was no fool and realised he was being flattered, but why? Could it be that Craig was nervous of the responsibility?

Yes, his ego told him, that was it. For all the big man's bluster and street wisdom, when it came down to it, it was all about breeding and intellect and so persuaded himself that he must be there to take charge.

To Craig's relief, he replied, "Very well, I'll see you there at ten."

In the large and predominantly stainless steel kitchen, Stevie Watkins, wearing an apron and oven gloves, had just placed the Sunday roast into the lower oven when his wife came through from the lounge with his mobile in her hand and said, "That's a phone call for you, love," and mouthed, "Sandy Craig."

Shaking a glove off, he took his mobile from her and said, "Sandy, my man, how's it hanging?"

"We're a go for tonight, Stevie. Ten o'clock at an industrial estate off Garscube Road."

Closing the kitchen door as his wife returned to the lounge, he replied, "Will he be there?"

"Says he will, but took his time admitting to it so I'm not absolutely convinced he will turn up."

"Did he say what arrangement he has made for the gear after the delivery?"

"Told me he's rented a warehouse over in Kinning Park. Some place called Portman Street."

"Portman Street," Watkins repeated, then added, "Aye, I know it. Not far from Paisley Road Toll," he smirked, "but that's *not* where it will be going is it, big man?"

"No, Stevie, it won't," Craig grinned on his side of the call. "Will you be contacting Headcase?"

"Now that we know the delivery location, I'll give the mad fucker a phone and tell him to do it there," but his eyes narrowed as he thought, that's if Faraday turns up.

"Are all your boys informed yet?"

"No, I gave you the first phone call. The lads are on standby, so when we've finished talking…"

"Whose driving the van."

"Fast Eddie."

"I thought he was banged up, doing a four stretch?"

"Got out last month and keen to get back into earning good money."

"But the team you've recruited, they're all tight?"

"I got seven guys and they're all tight as a drum, Stevie, stand on me regarding that.

Besides," he smiled into the phone, "any fucker opens his mouth and he's a dead man."

"How are they getting to the location?"

"Two in the van with Eddie and the other four will travel in a car. I'll pick you up about nine if you want. Besides, I'll have the toys with me so it means we can be tooled up when we arrive at the location."

"Good. Right," he sighed, "I've a roast in the oven and Headcase to phone so I'll see you here at nine."
He ended the call and scrolled down the directory, stopping at Harry Henderson's number.

Parked in Fotheringay Avenue in Pollokshields, Harry said, "Hello, Stevie, I've been expecting your call."
"Where are you?"
He glanced up at the red Victorian sandstone tenement building and replied, "Just about to visit a new friend. Is this about that contract we discussed?"
"It is. The contract will be available to sign at ten o'clock this evening. I'll text you the location details. Are you still up for it?"
"For thirty grand, why not?" Harry grinned.
He could almost hear the relief in Watkins voice when the gangster replied, "And you'll be able to dispose of the contract too?"
However, Harry's suspicions were aroused so he replied, "Shouldn't be a problem, though I do have some questions, Stevie. I'm wondering what the contract will be doing this evening?"
Watkins could not help himself and trusting the convicted murderer as a confidante as well as excited by the thought of the money he was about to make, he boasted, "The bastard is taking delivery of a shipment of the hard stuff, Harry, but it's my guys who are doing the unloading. You do what you do best while he's there and…"
"Wait. You're telling me there will be *witnesses* when I do him?"
"Aye, but none that will open their mouths, Harry. Trust me, they're good men."
"How many *good men* are we talking about here, Stevie? Two, three?"
"Could be as many as seven or eight, Harry, but like I said…"
"They're all good men," Harry finished for him.
"I'll need that many to take delivery of the shipment, Harry," he explained, his mouth suddenly dry. "It's a big container."
"Well, maybe you trust them, but I don't have to trust them," Harry calmly replied, "so I might have to reconsider the contract here, Stevie."
"Now wait a minute, Harry. We have a deal here…"
"A deal that could land me back in the Big Hoose, Stevie boy!"
Watkins exhaled and to placate Harry, said, "Listen, I understand

you might feel a bit peeved that I didn't tell you about the team we've got handling the shipment, but these are all trusted men, Harry. Me and the big guy, Sandy I mean, we're going tooled up ourselves and we'll fucking plug any *one* of them that as much as looks at you sideways. You have my word on that."
There was no response from Harry, prompting Watkins to ask, "Harry? You still there?"
"Aye, I'm here, Stevie. I'm just thinking over what you told me. Right," he let his breath out, "Send me a text of the location and we'll get it done. But mind Stevie. One word or a suspicious glance from a cop and you're the man I'm looking at. Comprende?"
"Understood, Harry," Watkins replied with some relief.
Ending the call, Harry slipped the mobile into his jacket pocket and reaching into the glove box, fetched out the Glock.

Fetching a pot of tea from the kitchen, Michael Harris carefully carried it through to the front room and sat it upon the mat on the table beside his mother.
"Are you feeling any better, mum?"
"Aye, I'm fine," she smiled at him, then to assure him, added, "Really."
Kneeling beside her chair, he poured the tea into her favourite china cup and said, "You gave me a wee bit of a fright there, mum. What, with dad passing and now you to worry about."
She watched him take the chair opposite her and sighing, replied, "There's no need to worry about me, Michael. I'm fine, fit as a horse. I told you and you have to believe me. I just got a wee bit of a shock when I heard that they've identified him, the man I told the detectives about."
She reached for her cup, but hesitated when he said, "Are you worried that he might come after you, mum? Is that it? You're frightened?"
She paled and her lower lip trembled for that was exactly what she feared, that being alone, somehow the man would learn of her name and come looking for her to…she shivered, not daring to even think about it.
"I'm phoning Popeye Doyle,' he brusquely said and arose from his chair.
"No, Michael…"

But he wouldn't listen and lifting the phone, dialled the number for Saracen police office.

Daisy Cooper signed onto the Criminal Intelligence website and tapped in her password.
Moving the mouse to the query box, she typed the name in and hit the return key.
As she expected, there was just the one hit.
Unconsciously leaning towards the monitor, she scrolled down the page but to her surprise there were no recorded convictions and very little intelligence other than hearsay or uncorroborated allegations. Still, she thought, if the allegations were sufficient to create a unique file then someone somewhere and likely a detective in the Criminal Intelligence Department at Gartcosh must have an interest.
Scrolling to the next page, her eyes opened wide when she read the name of the supervisory officer who authorised the creation of the file.
Sitting back, she slowly smiled and muttered, "Well, well, well. What are the chances?"

Declining Popeye Doyle's offer to fetch her a coffee, he and Cathy Mulgrew made their way to the incident room where Mulgrew found DI's Myra McColl and Phil Kennedy deep in conversation.
"Anything yet?" she dumped her handbag onto a desk.
"No word yet," McColl sighed, "and as you can see," she waved a hand around the almost empty room, "the teams are out turning the houses of his known associates."
At the other end of the room, Popeye Doyle answered a ringing phone and a moment later approached the trio.
"Sorry to interrupt, Ma'am," he addressed Mulgrew then turned to McColl and said, "That was our witness Missus Harris' son Michael on the phone, boss. Says she's in a bit of a state since the paper broke the news that we've identified McMenamin. Says she's scared he'll come after her and asks if I could pop along to reassure her, if that's okay with you?"
"Aye, of course and…" McColl nodded, but stopped when Mulgrew interrupted, "Look, I'm excess baggage here at the minute with nothing to do and you guys have it covered. I'll accompany Popeye and speak with Missus Harris. That okay with you, Popeye?"

He was hardly going to say no, but smiling, replied, "I'm sure she would be reassured if the SIO tells her there's nothing to worry about, Ma'am."

"Right then, we'll take my car," Mulgrew breezily replied and with Popeye, headed for the door.

Both storm doors were open and hooked back flat against the porch wall of the first floor flat. He was about to knock on the frosted glass window of the stout wooden door when it was pulled open.

The tall, heavyset man in his mid fifties wearing a light blonde toupee, black corduroy trousers, open necked light grey coloured shirt and dark grey coloured sports jacket who carried a briefcase in his right hand was initially startled, but then stared curiously at Harry before asking, "May I help you?"

Harry, wearing one of the new navy suits, white shirt and crimson tie guessed that the man wasn't alarmed at the sight of a well dressed caller and replied, "Mister Drake?"

"Yes, that's me. How may I help you?"

His hands behind him, he stepped forward, forcing Drake to back off into the hallway who surprised, said, "Now look here, my good man! What the devil do you think…" but stopped, his eyes widening and his face paling when Harry brought his hands to his side and Drake saw that loosely held in the right hand was a handgun.

Drake swallowed with difficulty as with his left hand, his eyes boring into those of Drake's, Harry gently pushed the door behind him, hearing the Yale lock click as the door closed.

"Mister Drake," he calmly began, "we can make this easy or we can make this difficult. What would be your preference, sir?"

"Who…who are you?" Drake stuttered.

"My name is irrelevant. Again, easy or difficult?"

His eyes lowered to the gun held in Harry's hand that continued to point towards the floor. Forcing himself to appear calm, he replied with some effort, "Easy, if I must choose."

"A wise decision, Mister Drake. Now, I am going to ask you one very simple question. If you refuse to answer or lie and believe me, I *will* know if you *are* lying, then I will shoot you and shoot any other person I find in this flat. Man, woman or child, I'll kill you all. Do you believe me, Mister Drake?"

Terrified, Drake's mouth was as dry as week old toast and could only nod, his thoughts of his partner lying sleeping in their bed.
"Where is Kieran McMenamin?"
His eyes betrayed him and Harry realised that he was about to deny knowing McMenamin.
With blurred speed, he brought the barrel of the Glock upwards to point at Drake's forehead and again asked, "Where – is – McMenamin?"
Survival being his only thought, Drake replied, "He phoned me. From the Central Station. Said the police were after him. For a murder. His mobile…" he choked, his tongue protruding as he tried to work some saliva into his mouth, "He hasn't any charge in his mobile."
"That's *not* what I asked," Harry calmly said and with his thumb, worked the hammer back with an audible click that in the confined space of the hallway, sounded to Drake like a bell tolling.
"Jesus Christ, man, I can't just…"
"I *am* going to kill you now."
"Wait! Please!" Drake's terror and overwhelming desire to live overcame his legal obligations as hands raised to ward off the bullet, he dropped the briefcase and slowly sank to his knees, tears seeping from his eyes and his lips trembling.
"He's in a school. A derelict building, he said. Downhill Street over in Partick," he simpered, the tears now freely flowing down his cheeks. "I…I told him…" he quietly sobbed, "I would speak to the police about surrendering himself. That I would collect him from the…from the school. And take him…take him to the police. To represent him, I mean."
His head bowed, he was completely and utterly broken, ready to do anything that this man wanted rather than be shot.
"Who else have you told about his phone call?"
Sat back on his haunches and completely subdued, he stared up at Harry in surprise.
"What?"
"Who else knows McMenamin phoned you?"
"Why…nobody. I told no one else."
Continuing to point the gun at Drake's head, Harry stared back at him then in a low voice, said, "You will tell no one that McMenamin phoned you. You will tell no one that I visited you. If you do, I will

kill you and I will kill everyone dear to you. Do you understand?"
Numbly, Drake nodded.
"If the police come after me, I will arrange for you to be killed and everyone dear to you will be killed. Do you understand me?"
Again, Drake nodded, a glimmer of hope in his breast that this terrifying man might not after all shoot him and all it would cost was his silence.
"I know where you live, Mister Drake and there will *be* no hiding place. Do – you – understand?"
"I understand," he nodded again.
"I'm leaving now, Mister Drake, and I suggest that you completely forget this happened. You *will* stay silent, won't you, Mister Drake?"
"Yes, yes," he eagerly shook his head. "I will! I swear! I won't say anything!"
"Goodbye, Mister Drake," said Harry and within seconds, was gone.

In his car parked around the corner from Drake's building, Harry opened the glove box and before replacing the Glock, pulled out a Glasgow A to Z book of maps.
"Dowanhill Street," he muttered as his fingers traced down page eighty-two to the street then with a grim smile, threw the book on the passenger seat and switched on the engine.

CHAPTER TWENTY-FIVE

He had safely made it back to the old school, the only heart stopping moment when a panda car with three cops inside passed him by in Argyle Street, but they were too busy yapping to pay any attention to him and breathing a sigh of relief, he'd hurried on.
Now stood at a first floor window, he peeked out to the street below and wished he had both asked what kind of car Drake drove and worried that he had not told him exactly in the street where he was to collect him.
Without his phone, he had no idea of the time, but guessed it had been over an hour or more since he phoned the bastard.
"For fuck's sake," he irritably muttered, "how long does it take to phone the polis and come to an agreement?"

His stomach was beginning to rumble again and he wished now he'd had the sense to grab some grub on the way back. That and he needed a pee.
Unzipping his trousers, he stood to one side and urinating, boyishly giggled as he created a pattern against the wall.
Finished, he zipped up and glancing out of the window, saw that a new vehicle, a red coloured Ford car had stopped in a parking bay on the street outside.
His heart leapt.
Drake had arrived, but after a moment passed he wondered why the lawyer didn't get out of the car.
Was Drake thinking that he would join him in the car, he wondered? As he watched, the drivers door opened and a man got out, a man he didn't recognise; an old, baldy guy with glasses and wearing a suit who stood and looked up at the building.
Instinctively, he flinched back from the window, but then sneaked another glance.
He was certain the guy had not seen him for his head turned back and forth as he stared up at the building, but then to his surprise the guy held up his left hand, his fist closed and with the fingers of his right hand tapped several times at his wrist.
McMenamin's eyes narrowed as he wondered, what the *fuck* is he up to?
Then it clicked.
He's telling me time's wasting and to hurry up.
It made sense, he thought.
Drake's sent the guy to collect me while he deals with the cops. Elated that at last he had some help to get him out of this mess he was in, he waved from the window and with a grin, saw the guy waving back.
Scampering through the hallway, he hurried to the first floor window where he had entered and made his way round to Dowanhill Street and saw that the old guy was now sitting in the driver's seat waiting for him, the engine running.
Opening the passenger door, the guy asked him, "Mister McMenamin?"
"Aye," he clambered in and grabbed at the seatbelt, "that's me. Who the fuck are you, pal?"
"Oh, call me Harry," the man smiled.

"You have to understand, Missus Harris," Cathy Mulgrew sat facing her, "when we catch this man as undoubtedly we will, such is the severity of the crimes he is to be charged with that he will be remanded in prison until the time of the trial. I can assure you there is absolutely nothing for you to worry or concern yourself about. Kieran McMenamin will not contact or threaten or harm you. You have my word on that."

Mary took a soft breath and slowly exhaling, turned to stare at Doyle who sat on the couch with her son Michael and said, "Popeye?"

"Detective Superintendent Mulgrew is correct, Mary. You have nothing to fear but fear itself. It's a nonsense to suggest that this guy will even get to know your name. He's got a lot more to worry about than you," Doyle smiled encouragingly. "When we catch him he's going to the jail for a very long time."

"Aye, well, I suppose now that you've explained everything, I do feel a bit better and I feel such a fool," she smiled a little self-consciously.

"You're certainly not a fool, Missus Harris," Mulgrew returned her smile. "You're a very brave lady who came forward to aid us when we needed a witness to take our investigation forward and you're very important to us, isn't that right, Popeye?"

"Crucial to the case," he winked at Mary.

"So how close to catching him are you?" Michael asked.

Mary didn't miss their hesitation and continued, "You've no idea where he is, have you?"

"Not at the minute," Mulgrew admitted then added, "But I can share this with you. Kieran McMenamin is Police Scotland's number one priority at this time. We have more officers working on this investigation than ever did on the serial killer from the fifties, Peter Manuel or the Bible John inquiries. We'll catch him, have no worry about that. It's just a question of time."

"Is he local? To Saracen, I mean," Mary asked.

"Yes, he is local and while I'm not prepared to tell you where his family home is, suffice to say his father and sister with whom he resides are absolutely devastated that he's brought this shame to their family."

"Even though the boss can't tell you the address, Mary," Doyle leaned forward and conspiratorially grinned, "you know what the

jungle drums are like round here. His address and what school he went to, who his pals are and whether he takes brown or red sauce on his chips will be all over the place tomorrow."
"Aye, you're right enough," she smiled at him.
"So, Missus Harris," Mulgrew got to her feet and lifted her handbag, "if you believe we've satisfied your concerns we'll be off."
"You're sure you won't have a cup of something before you go?" Mary asked and also stood.
"No, you're fine but thanks for the offer. Popeye?"
"Right behind you, Ma'am," he winked at Mary before following Mulgrew to the front door.

DS Ian Prescott knocked on the DI's door and poking his head into the office, said to Phil Kennedy, "That's the Lab on the blower for you, boss. I'll transfer the call through."
Kennedy raised his eyebrows at McColl and when the call rang through, pressed the speaker button and muttered, "Let's hope it's good news."
"Aye, Phil? Gus Ferguson here at the Lab. The clothes and footwear your guys brought over for examination from the suspects house in Crowhill Street? A Kieran McMenamin?"
"Aye, what's the story, Gus?"
"Zilch on the footwear, however, we found minute traces of blood spotting on a pair of blue denims, but the remainder of the clothing was clear."
Kennedy glanced sharply at McColl and quickly asked, "These minute blood spots. Have you been able to identify whose blood it is?"
"Thought you'd never ask," they could almost hear Ferguson grin. "We've obtained DNA from the blood and matched it to…tell me," he teased, "have you had any good holidays recently, Phil?"
"Come on to fuck, Gus, and stop farting about! Whose DNA was on McMenamin's jeans?"
"Your male victim from the squat, Francis O'Connor."
"Yes!" Kennedy bellowed into the speaker, then continued, "Thanks, Gus."
Grinning, Kennedy gave McColl the thumbs-up and said to Ferguson, "That's a pint I owe you."
"And the rest," Ferguson grumbled before ending the call.

"So," McColl could not help but smile, "that's us got Forensic evidence for the lassie Dalrymple and now O'Connor. This bastard's arse is definitely hanging out of the window."
"Aye," Kennedy agreed, then with a sigh added, "all we have to do now is catch him."

Fed, watered and toilet completed, the driver yawned and climbed into his cab.
By his estimation, the remainder of the journey should take no more than two hours and he decided that if he was to arrive there on time, unload his container and be back on the road, he would return to London through the night. To do so, he would need to be rested and so decided to get his head down for the next few hours.
Setting the timer on his mobile phone, he pulled the window blinds and climbed into the bunk at the back of the cab.

"So, where are you taking me, pal?"
"Somewhere safe, Mister McMenamin," Harry replied, his eyes on the road as the Focus passed the sign for Milngavie.
"And you work for Colin Drake?"
"We've had some cooperation in the recent past, yes," Harry replied as he turned smoothly onto Auchenhowie Road.
"So, I take it he's dealing with the cops right now?"
"To be honest, Mister McMenamin, I'm not entirely certain what Mister Drake is doing right now," Harry said and slowed down to turn left into Dowan Road.
Passing the entrance to Langbank Farm, McMenamin turned to Harry and clearly confused, asked, "Where are you taking me again?"
Harry briefly glanced from the narrow road to smile at him and replied, "Where nobody will find you, Mister McMenamin."
He liked the old dude being so polite to him, calling him 'Mister McMenamin.' It made him feel he was somebody, that he was important.
They passed entrances to a kennel, a B&B guest house and a cattery and Harry could sense that McMenamin was getting suspicious, so said, "Nearly there, sir."
Slowing as they approached an opening on the left, he skilfully turned the Focus into the narrow lane and said, "Just up ahead, but

we'll need to walk to it now, if that's okay with you?" and gave him an encouraging smile.

Getting out of the car, McMenamin cried out, "Shit! I've stepped in something!" and with one hand on the roof of the Focus to balance himself, raised his foot to inspect the bottom of his left shoe.

"For fucks sake," he whined, "*where* are we going to?"

Stood beside him, Harry pointed along the lane and with a smile, said, "Only thirty yards ahead now, Mister McMenamin," and followed him as he stepped forward, muttering under his breath about how pissed off he was at having to walk in all this shite.

They had gone half the distance when McMenamin stopped and turning was about to complain when to his shock he saw Harry holding the Glock in his hand and that it was pointed at his face. Speechless, he could only stare at Harry who waved the barrel at him to indicate he keep walking.

Stumbling along in front, he thought about running off, but then gave up on that idea when Harry said, "If you try to run, Mister McMenamin, you're getting the first shot in the back of the knee. That, let me tell you, would be *extremely* painful."

At last the green foliage gave way to the edge of a small pool of water that glistened in the fading light.

"Where are we?" McMenamin, shaking and clearly frightened, turned to ask.

"This is known as the Ladies Pond," Harry replied. "When I was a wee lad growing up in Saracen…aye, that's right," he smiled and nodded at McMenamin's confusion, "I'm originally from Saracen. Anyway, when I was a lad growing up there, my auntie Harriet who I lived with, was a widowed lady and couldn't afford to take me on holidays. So what she did was make up picnics for the two of us and take me on bus trips to the countryside and the towns like Milngavie and Bearsden and swimming to Mugdock Reservoir, though it wasn't as fancy in them days as it is now. She also used to take me long walks and tell me about the importance of keeping fit and…"

"What the *fucks* this shite you're talking got to do with me!" McMenamin interrupted, his eyes fearfully watching Harry's tight hold on the Glock.

"Just a wee story to tell you why you're here, Mister McMenamin, that's all it is, so bear with me, please. Anyway, like I was saying," he waved the gun in the direction of the woods about them and continued, "These woods are known as the Beech Woods and over there," he nodded to his left, "are the Ladies Ride Woods and that's where the pond gets its name. See?"

"You're a fucking nutter, pal, that's what you are," McMenamin sneered, but his attempted bravado contradicted his chalk white face and his legs were shaking.

"Maybe not the right thing to tell a man who's pointing a nine millimetre Glock handgun at you, Mister McMenamin, is it?" Harry smirked.

"But *why* are you telling me this?" he demanded.

"Let me explain," Harry patiently continued. "My wee aunt Harriet sometimes brought me here too and I'd swim in the pond there. It's pretty deep so she'd always caution me to take care in case I got into difficulties. Now, why are you here, you asked?" and from a side pocket of his suit jacket he fetched out a photograph that he reached across to hand to McMenamin, all the while the Glock carefully pointed towards him.

Taking the photo, his eyes narrowed and staring at Harry, apprehensively asked, "Where did you get this?"

"Do you know who that soldier is?"

"Eh, aye," he began to bluff, "he was an uncle of mine that got killed in the war."

"Oh? What war was that?"

"The, ah, Second World War."

"And your uncles name was?"

"Billy. Billy McMenamin, but how the fuck did you get the photo?" he blustered.

Harry smiled and reaching out, took the photograph back from McMenamin's outstretched hand before replying, "You recall me mentioning my Aunt Harriet? Well, this is her husband Archie Henderson, killed in the Korean war, Mister McMenamin."

A cold chill swept through McMenamin.

The old lady in the close.

His instinct told him that he had been found out and that this situation he now found himself in was bad; very, very bad and sinking to his knees, his lips trembled and he began to softly cry and hands outstretched said, "I'm sorry, mister. I only stole the photo to impress my pals."

"No, Mister McMenamin, you stole the purse, but to get the purse you mugged the old lady who kept this photograph in her purse. Now, isn't *that* correct?"

"I'm sorry," all dignity and bluster now gone, he was openly weeping, his arms about him as he hugged himself and rocked back and forward on his knees.

If the man called Harry had screamed and shouted at him, cursed and abused him, somehow it might have been better, but this chillingly polite voice absolutely terrified him.

"I didn't mean to hurt her. She fell back onto the stairs. I swear on my mother's grave. I'm sorry!" he shouted, but his pleas fell on deaf ears, for Harry replied. "You didn't just mug her, Mister McMenamin. Harriet died because of the injury you caused her. An old harmless lady who spent her life raising and worrying about me. She was somebody I loved and *you* took her from me."

He took a deep breath, then softly added, "And now, Mister McMenamin, you have to pay for that."

"*Please!*" he begged, "Don't shoot me! I'll do anything! I'll confess to the cops, I'll…I'll…"

"What? You'll tell a court how sorry you are then get to spend the next few years getting three squares a day, television every night and have a *great* time boasting to your pals that you beat the system? Oh, no, Mister McMenamin," Harry shook his head. "That's *not* what's going to happen. Please get on your feet. Now!"

He lurched to his feet and urged by Harry, walked the remaining metres to the edge of the pond.

"Get in the water," Harry waved the gun at him.

"No, you don't understand," his head swivelled to stare at the blackness of the still waters behind him. "I can't swim!"

Surprised, Harry's first thought was that he needn't after all waste a bullet on the bugger before he said again, "Get in the water," then added, "or I shoot you where you stand!"

"Please," he sobbed, the tears rolling unchecked down his face.

Harry Henderson wasn't by nature a cruel man.

Yes, he was the first to admit that during his criminal life he had done some very, very bad things, but never tortured another human being the way he was now torturing this younger man.

But throughout his return to Scotland, he had felt a deep and unforgiving shame that he had not been there to protect Harriet, the woman who had nurtured and sheltered him during his formative years, the woman who had given him selfless love and though he had not turned out as she had wished, it was not her fault. No, he inwardly shivered, not her fault at all.

"Get in the water," he softly repeated.

McMenamin, with another glance behind him, backed into the cold water that now seeped through his training shoes, soaking his socks and the bottom of his jogging trousers and he involuntarily trembled.

"Please!" hands outstretched, he begged for his life.

"Keep going," Harry moved towards the water's edge, the Glock stiffly held in his outstretched hand and pointed at McMenamin's face.

Could he rush the old guy, he thought, his desperation to live urging him to go for the gun, but though Harry stood firmly holding the Glock a mere six feet away this wasn't television or a film; the distance between them was the difference between being shot in the face, the body or the head and he realised that cold and shaking, he had not the courage to spring forward and so did as he was told and backed towards the dark waters of the pond.

He could not know as Harry remembered that a few feet from the edge of the pool, the underwater shelf at the water's edge ended and gave way to a sharp six feet drop.

Hesitantly, he took another step back and placing his foot down, displaced the green scum at the edge of the pond then lowering his foot he failed to find solid ground. Losing his balance, he pitched backwards with a surprised shriek into the cold, murky water.

When his head hit the slimy pond and covered his face, the very act of crying out caused him to swallow a mouthful of water and he choked, inhaling not only the water, but the algae and bacterial slime that through the years had collected on the top of the pond. Gagging, he panicked and reached for the bank that now was more than six feet away for his floundering and falling backwards had caused him to be swept further towards the centre of the pond.

Again his head dipped into the darkness beneath the water and his arms flailed as they sought to catch some purchase, something to grab, but of course there was nothing.

Pokerfaced, Harry watched McMenamin slowly drown, the air from his lungs creating bubbles on the waters surface.

Twice, three times his head bobbed from the water, his mouth open as he tried to cry out.

Finally, with his arms held high and his hands reaching as though in supplication, there was a flurry of movement as the water thrashed wildly before he finally disappeared.
The Glock held loosely by his side, Harry slowly exhaled.
After a few minutes and satisfied McMenamin was indeed drowned, he turned away and made his way back along the narrow track towards the Focus, ignoring the wooden sign attached to the broken wooden post that lay in the overgrown grass and warned passers-by, 'Danger- No Swimming - Contaminated Water.'

CHAPTER TWENTY-SIX

Most of the four man teams had by now returned to Maryhill office, weary and dejected that their searches of the homes of anyone associated with Kieran McMenamin had both failed to locate him or find anyone who knew of his whereabouts.
Seated in the DI's room, Cathy Mulgrew was as dejected as her three Detective Inspectors and glumly said, "I don't see we have any option but to provide the media with his photograph, unless any of you guys have a better idea?"
"It's only been a few days, Ma'am," said McColl.
"Aye, maybe a few days, Myra, but it's ripping the arse out of the major investigation budget already and we *really* need a result on this, so, any ideas?"
In turn, they shook their heads with Danny McBride commenting, "About your comment to inform the the media. Failing to alert the public about McMenamin and the threat he poses will bite us in the arse, Ma'am, if we don't take some positive action to locate him and frankly, I can't think of anything other than using the full weight of both television, the newspapers and social media. At the minute we seem to have covered all angles. We've alerted the airports and port authorities who already have his photograph, we've turned the house of all known associates. What else *is* there for us to do?"
"Catch the bugger," she wryly replied, then with a shake of her grinned.
Glancing at the wall clock, she continued, "That's approaching seven o'clock now. What say we dismiss the teams and turn the incident room over to the nightshift, I treat you to fish suppers and while we're eating we go over everything we know so far?"

"Seems like a plan," McColl sighed and rising to her feet, opened the door to call a detective through to the office, then with a smile said, "Ma'am's got a wee job for you and don't forget to get me a couple of pickles as well."

In the privacy of his bedroom, Sandy Craig opened the parcel containing the two handguns and examined them in turn.
He favoured the Russian Nagant seven shot revolver, a souvenir brought home to the UK by a Scottish infantryman who had served in Bosnia and who was happy with the five ton that Craig paid for the weapon and the box of 7.62mm ammunition.
Holding the handgun, he stood in front of the mirror on the wardrobe door and pretended to fast draw it cowboy style from his trouser pocket, pointing at his reflection and snapping out, "Bang!"
Not that he expected to use the Nagant, but it wouldn't do any harm for the team to see him tooled up and besides, he was keen to flash the leather shoulder holster he had recently acquired.
With a grin, he placed the Nagant on the bedside cabinet and examined the old Enfield Mark II revolver, a swap two years previously with a stall holder at the Glasgow Barra's for a dozen deals of coke. The weapon was clearly very old, very worn and there were just five bullets for the cylinder chamber that normally would hold six. Aside from the five bullets that had come with the handgun, try as he had .38 ammunition wasn't that easy to come by these days. Examining the scarred and chipped wooden grip on the weapon, he held it up to point at his reflection and dry fired it. Grinning satisfactorily at the metallic click, he lifted the handgun to his nose and taking a deep sniff, inhaled the WD 40 he used to oil it.
The Enfield would do for Watkins, he sniggered, for he intended keeping the Nagant for himself.
After all, his brow creased as he recalled the conversation with Jimmy Morrison, he didn't expect to be Watkins right hand man all his days for Sandy Craig had his own ambitions.
He glanced at the digital clock on the bedside cabinet and decided there was time enough for him to make some dinner before he readied himself to collect Watkins at nine o'clock.

Dismissed for the night, the team collected their coats and crowded towards the door of the incident room to leave.

Among the throng, Popeye Doyle was chatting with a burly detective when his mobile phone chirruped to inform him he had received a text message.

Nodding goodnight to the officer, he stood to one side and his eyes widened when he recognised the new number that had sent the text.

Opening the message, he read: *phone me urgent*

Licking at his lips, he watched the last of the team disappear through the door and making his way to a window, called the number, then in a quiet voice, said, "Hello, Harry, what can I do for you?"

"We need to talk."

"When?"

"Now. I'm outside your office. Come out the main door and turn left. I'm parked fifty yards along the street. Bring your boss, Mulgrew."

"You mean the Saracen Office? Harry, I'm up in Maryhill office. Is it important?"

"Shit!" Harry snapped for he hadn't foreseen that. "You mentioned when we met for coffee that you'd like to retire on a high? Well, this *is* your high, Popeye. Get you and Mulgrew's arse down here right now and yes, it's *damned* important," and hung up.

Doyle stared at the phone and wondered, just what the hell was Harry up to?

He glanced at the closed door of the DI's office and thought, well, if Harry Henderson believes it's important, then so do I and quickly made his way to inform Cathy Mulgrew of the call.

"Do you have any idea what this is about, Popeye?"

"No, Ma'am," he ruefully shook his head, "but like I told you, if Harry Henderson thinks it's important, then it must be." He shrugged then added, "Maybe he's found out where McMenamin is and wants to turn him over to us."

"Do you really believe that?" she snatched a glance at him, ignoring the angry beep of the taxi horn she almost sideswiped as she continued to travel at speed towards Saracen Street.

Doyle, swallowing fearfully and bracing his feet against the foot well of her car, shook his head and though he would never realise it, prophetically replied, "No, I don't. I like Harry, but if *he's* found McMenamin, we never will."

Ten bone shattering minutes later, Mulgrew's Lexus skidded to a halt at the entrance of Saracen office and getting out of the car, she muttered, "This better not be a fucking waste of time. I'm starving and missing out on a sodding fish supper if it is!"

"There," Doyle nodded as he saw Harry emerging from the Focus further along the street.

They walked towards him, Mulgrew in the lead who irately greeted him with, "Mister Henderson. What the *hell* is this all about?"

Harry smiled at her ill-temper and nodding to Doyle, turned back to face her and said, "I expect to return to Cuba soon, but I want you to do something for me first and I'll give you something in return."

"What!" she stared at him as though he were mad and asked, "Give you what?"

"My aunt Harriet's body. I want to bury her before I go, not hang about till your PF decides her body can be released. I understand from someone I spoke with," he avoided looking at Doyle, "that her body can be held for some time for the purpose of a defence post mortem for McMenamin's counsel. Isn't that right, Miss Mulgrew?"

"Yes," she slowly drawled, "that *is* the current procedure. However, the PF can release the body of a victim if there are circumstances that dictate…"

She stopped and staring at Harry, asked, "What *exactly* are you offering for the release of your aunt's body, Mister Henderson?"

He slowly turned and smiling at Doyle, replied, "A retirement gift for an old friend."

Ian MacLeod had prepared dinner and set the table for Daisy's arrival home.

Hearing the front door open then close, he cheerfully called out, "Time for a pee and to wash your hands then I expect you to be at the table, Sergeant Cooper, and I'm keen to hear what happened at work about that thing, you know?"

He turned as she appeared at the kitchen door, her face pale and drawn.

Concerned, he said, "I'm a bit worried about you these days, Daisy. You're always so tired looking. Maybe we should consider seeing the doctor, get you a pick-me-up or something."

"Oh, it's nothing that won't be sorted in about thirty-four weeks," she smiled uncertainly at him.

"Thirty-four weeks? What the heck are you…" then the penny dropped, his eyes widening and his jaw dropping almost as far as his voice when he whispered, "You're pregnant?"

"Yes," she softly replied, unsure about his reaction. However, her fears were unfounded when moving towards her, he squeezed her with a bone crushing hug, but then stepped back and staring at her midriff, said, "Oh my God! Did I hurt…"

"No," she quickly replied, her voice tinged with laughter and a happy sob. "I'm fine," and reached to throw her arms about his neck as once more he embraced her, but more gently this time.

They stood for several minutes, enjoying the delight of their pregnancy until he led her to a chair and made her sit.

"I'm not an invalid," she joked, but kneeling beside her, his eyes filled with unshed tears, he could not speak such was his happiness. At last he took a deep breath and asked, "Have you told anyone at work yet?"

"No, not yet," her brow wrinkled as she added, "Once I declare I'm pregnant, I'll be transferred to an office job and put onto protected duties. Then there's the…"

She stopped and staring down at him, asked, "You're really happy, Ian, aren't you?"

"Happy? Dear God, how could I be but anything else, Daisy? The woman I love is pregnant with my child…" he grinned and continued, "You know what this means, though?"

"What?"

"You'll have no choice now. You'll need to marry me. You will, won't you? Marry me, I mean."

Now it was her turn to softly cry and not trusting herself to speak, bit at her lower lip and nodding, lowered her head onto his shoulder. They stayed uncomfortably like that for a moment, then Daisy raised her head and said, "What were you about to ask me? About work?"

"That? Oh, just if you had resolved the situation about the DVD."

"No," she sighed, "but when I go in tomorrow, I'll need to speak with the Chief Inspector about the pregnancy and that's when I'll inform him what I know. But right now," she grinned, "I'm eating for two, so is that dinner ready?"

The driver continued on the M74 and when approaching the junction

for Hamilton and Motherwell, realised he was a little ahead of schedule.
Time for a comfort break, he decided and turned into the service station a half mile beyond the junction.

At Cathy Mulgrew's instruction, Popeye Doyle hurried through to the Saracen office's uniform bar and seated himself at a computer. Now logged onto the system he hurriedly searched the Google maps for Oakbank Industrial Estate off Garscube Road and began printing off maps of the area.
In the DI's office upstairs, Mulgrew was on the phone to the Chief Constable seeking his permission to use his authority to scramble a firearms team.
"And you are certain, Cathy, this source's information is totally reliable?"
"I'm certain, sir. Without naming names, I believe his information to be one hundred per cent accurate, but the problem is that it's now time critical and regretfully there is no time to organise a Firearm Plan of Action. That's why I'm seeking your permission to call in the duty anti-terrorism armed patrols to back up the uniform arrest."
"So you *are* certain there might be gunplay?"
"The source is of the opinion that some of the players will be armed, at least two he says, though he has no information as to what type of weapons."
"How many opposition are there? Do you have that information?"
"I have the names of two of the main players, sir. Both actively engaged in drug importation in the Glasgow area. According to the sources information, the delivery is sizeable so it's fair to assume I believe there might anything between six to a dozen individuals employed to receive the delivery, sir."
There was a pause as the Chief Constable mulled over what he was being told before he said, "Is it an option if we were to deploy a couple of uniformed cars in the area to dissuade this delivery from taking place? I mean, rather than risk any of our officers or members of the public being harmed? Frankly, I don't like the idea of mounting an armed operation without there being a clear Plan of Action."
"That might defer the delivery sir, but we both know it won't cancel it and there is the real likelihood that the delivery might take place at

a future date when we do not have the heads up we now have. Also, as I said earlier, one of the main players is to be murdered at the location, or rather, that's what is being planned."

She heard him sigh and with a resigned voice, he replied, "Okay, Cathy. You have my permission and my authority to garner what resources you can in the time left to you. Good luck and keep me apprised of any developments."

"Sir," she acknowledged his decision with relief as she first ended the call then began dialling.

Sandy Craig passed through the electric wrought iron gates and into the driveway that led to Stevie Watkins palatial home in Newton Mearns to find Watkins, dressed in a black windcheater jacket, a black coloured polo neck sweater and black denims trousers, waiting at the door for him.

"Fuck me, Stevie," Craig grinned as he returned down the driveway towards the gates, "you look like the Cadbury's Milk Tray man."

"I like to look the part," Watkins said then added as he thumped at his chest, "and besides, this gear hides the fact I'm wearing a vest."

"A vest?"

"Aye, a bullet proof vest. Got it on e-bay," he smirked.

"What, you think somebody will be shooting at us tonight?"

"Doesn't do to take chances, Sandy my boy. That's why I'm top of the tree in this game, because I *don't* take chances."

Well, top of the tree at the minute, Craig thought, but time will tell, time will tell, then asked, "Did you get in touch with Headcase?"

"I did. Gave him the location for the night. Told him to get there about ten-thirty. By that time, you and the team should be finishing up and he can whack Faraday just before you leave. That way you'll not be working around a dead body, eh?" he started to laugh.

"What about you, Stevie? You can't be hanging about when Faraday arrives there. Where do you intend being?"

"Oh, don't worry about me," he indicated with his hands his black clothing. "I'm dressed for the part, aren't I? I'll find myself somewhere to hide from where I can watch you and when Headcase shows up, I'll pop out and enjoy the show as he does Faraday in. After all," he grinned evilly, "I need the bastard to know who it is that's responsible for him getting done and who's taking his shipment."

"Now," he turned towards Craig, "you brought the shooters?"
"Yours is in the glove box there," Craig nodded before adding, "It's a revolver with five rounds in the chamber. It's murder trying to get ammo for it, so if you need to use it, don't miss."
Opening the glove box, Watkins fetched the weapon out and holding it up to inspect it, Craig cried out in alarm, "For fuck's sake, Stevie! Bring it down! Somebody passing in a car seeing you flashing a shooter about is going to have the cops onto us!"
"Relax, big man," he grinned then boasted, "I know what I'm doing. It's not the first time I've held a gun, you know."
He turned to Craig and asked, "You've got a shooter as well, yeah?"
Craig patted at his left shoulder and replied, "Got myself a holster for mine. Any bastard shows his face that's not invited and he's getting it," he growled.
"Right then," Watkins nodded and grinned, "that's us ready."

Constable Fariq Mansoor was tired and hungry and making his way to the Community Police office to sign off, was surprised to see Sergeant Anne Cassidy hunched over her desk, a pen in her hand as she pored over a report.
"Hi, Sarge," he cheerfully greeted her. "Thought you had gone home."
"It's Sergeant, not *Sarge*" she irritably replied then added, "Is that you finished for today?"
"Aye, I got a wee bit held up with a breach of the peace, a fighting drunk from the parade earlier this morning."
"Well," she glanced at the clock, "you're only forty minutes late for getting off, so don't be thinking about claiming overtime."
"No, Sergeant," he sighed and was about to turn away, when she asked, "What's all the commotion downstairs?"
"Oh, the bar officer said that there's information come in about a drugs delivery tonight and the Detective Superintendent…Mulgrew is it?"
"Yes, Miss Mulgrew. Go on."
"Anyway, she's scrambling bodies from all over the Division to deal with it, but that's all I know."
"Well, I've paperwork to be getting on with so don't be letting anyone know I'm here," she instructed then lowering her head and waving her hand, indicated he could go.

With just one and half hours to make her preparations, Cathy Mulgrew, with Danny McBride hurriedly brought down from the Maryhill office and stood by her side, inwardly prayed that she had covered everything as best she could.

Now in the CID general office in Saracen police station, she addressed the six armed officers standing to one side of the room while Popeye Doyle handed each of the three two-man teams a copied map of the area upon which he had marked the position of the suspected delivery and where the unarmed officers were to be deployed.

"I can not stress enough that the information, though deemed to be A1, has come from a source with a criminal background and while I believe the information to be correct the source is unable to firm up what weapons might be carried by the opposition. Therefore," she stared at each of the teams in turn, "if you believe that you, a colleague or any innocent member of the public is in danger, you will follow your training and instructions in discharging your firearms. Are there any questions?"

"Prisoners, Ma'am," the only female armed officer asked. "Who will control them?"

"That will be down to DI McBride's team. Danny?" she turned to him.

"Once you are satisfied that the opposition do not present any armed threat, our colleagues and I," he nodded to the twelve uniformed and plain clothes officers designated as the arrest team, "will move in and use PlastiCuffs and deck them all until such times we sort out who's who."

"What about the delivery truck, Ma'am?" asked another officer.

Nodding to the Traffic sergeant and his constable, Mulgrew said, "Our Traffic colleagues will seize the driver and if he attempts to make off in the vehicle, we will have resources in place to act as cut-offs. Right, Sergeant?" she nodded to the Traffic supervisor.

"Right, Ma'am," he returned her nod.

"Another thing," she nodded to the two CID officers stood at the back, "DS Calum Fraser and his neighbour, DC Marilyn Munroe, will act as evidence gatherers so do not concern yourself about grabbing any items of evidential value, just concentrate on the role you've been assigned."

She took a deep breath and continued, "Look, folks, I know this is being done at a rush and for that I unreservedly apologise. This information came to us just a short time ago and while we have not had the time to prepare a proper Plan of Action …" she stopped and stared around the room. "What I'm trying to say is that no arrest or seizure of any shipment is worth any of you getting hurt. Under no circumstances are *any* of you to take *any* kind of risk. Is that clearly understood?"

There was a mumbled "Yes, Ma'am," from the officers present.
"Right then," she nodded as she inhaled, "kick-off is in about," she glanced at her wristwatch, "thirty minutes so get yourselves a last minute toilet break or cuppa and then we're a go. Thank you."

In the corridor outside the refreshment room, DS Calum Fraser turned back and said, "For heaven's sake, Marilyn, this is a hell of a time to be texting.
"Sorry, Calum, but it was my turn tonight to…oh, forget it," she angrily added and pressed the button to send the message as she swept past him.

Fast Eddie, a short, skinny man in his late fifties with more tattoos than teeth, kissed his wife goodnight before he left his flat in Hawthorn Street to join his two pals who waited for him beside the hired Luton van in the roadway outside.
"The other four are going there in Wullie's car," Eddie's pal told him as the three men climbed into the cab of the van.
"Any word from the big man?"
"No, nothing since the last text with the address of the location," Eddie replied and started the engine before adding with a grin, "So, it's a goer."

After showering, he dressed himself carefully, pleased that the black silk shirt and black tailored trousers matched and finally, slipped on the three-quarter length navy blue coat.
Turning back and forth, he critically examined himself in the full length mirror and smiling, liked what he saw.
Slipping the jacket back off for the meantime, he lifted his phone and pressed the button to call Sandy Craig.

In the BMW, Craig saw the incoming call to be from Nigel Faraday and placing a forefinger against his lips to warn Watkins to remain quiet, pressed the button for the hands free before greeting him with, "Hello, boss. That's me on my way to the location now. I take it I'll see you there?"

"Hmmm, it occurred to me we might travel together, Sandy. Save taking two cars."

Craig's head snapped around to stare at Watkins who drew a deep breath and grimaced.

"Maybe not a great idea, boss," Craig was thinking fast, "I'm almost there and I wanted to be first here to greet the team. Just in case they arrived and wondered why there was nobody here. If I turn back for you, it might make us late getting here."

There was a pause before Faraday, sounding slightly miffed, replied, "Fine, Sandy, we'll do it your way. I'll see you there."

He had just placed the phone down when it indicated receipt of an incoming text message and lifting it, his face paled when he read:
Not entirely definite but you might be compromised

"Shit!" he exclaimed and sat heavily down onto the bed.

What did *not entirely definite* mean?

It could only mean that his source wasn't certain of the facts, but only suspected the police might be aware of the delivery so there seemed little point at this late stage instructing the source to try and learn more.

What to do, what to do.

His face creased as he rubbed a worried hand across his jaw.

Was his source being over anxious?

If he attended the delivery and the police *did* arrive, he run the risk of being arrested.

However, if he did not attend and informed Sandy Craig and it proved to be a false alarm, he would miss the delivery.

His eyes creased.

The only thing connecting him to the delivery was Craig, a convicted criminal.

Should he warn Craig and text the delivery driver or should he instead stay clear of the location and hope for the best?

By not informing Craig and the driver he had everything to gain and nothing to lose for payment was to be made upon delivery and if there was no delivery…

He grimly smiled.
He had made his decision.
He would stay away, but let the delivery run its course and fervently hoped his source was simply being over cautious.

CHAPTER TWENTY-SEVEN

Harry Henderson glanced at the dashboard clock that indicated it was now fifteen minutes to ten.
Switching off the engine, he glanced up at the top corner flat in the red sandstone building in Lauderdale Gardens and with a smile thought Harry Cavanagh had done very well for himself.
Before getting out of the car, he unlocked the boot to satisfy himself the Glock remained hidden beneath the carpet.
Two minutes later he was knocking on Cavanagh's door and not surprised when it was the acerbic Helen, wearing a calf length black silk dressing gown, who opened the door.
"Harry!" she greeted him with a bone crushing hug, then stepping back with her hands on her hips, scowled and said, "What the hell possessed you to bring that git those foul smelling cigars!"
Behind her, Cavanagh, also wearing a calf length black silk robe though not as attractively as Helen, stepped out from the lounge door, a cognac glass in one hand and a thick Cuban cigar in the other, who grinned and called out, "Come in, old friend. You're just in time to join me for a brandy."
"He's driving, so he'll have coffee," Helen brusquely interrupted and stomped off towards the kitchen.
"I'm having coffee," Harry repeated with a grin and followed Cavanagh into the plush and expensively appointed lounge.
Indicating he sit, Cavanagh plumped down into a large leather chair and taking a deep breath, asked, "Am I to assume you have attended to the situation regarding Harriet?"
"It's attended to," Harry confirmed with a nod, for there was no need for Cavanagh to know details, but then thoughtfully added, "One thing. Before the Focus is returned to the hire company, you might consider having it deep cleaned, particularly the passenger seat. Also, the gift you left in the package? You'll find it under the mat in the boot. Might be an idea to have it disposed of."

"Will do," the heavyset man tightly smiled, the asked, "And as for your agreement with Stevie Watkins regarding Nigel Faraday? How is that to be resolved?"

That issue, Harry decided, was better explained and replied, "I made a deal with the cops. Watkins and his crew and Faraday's delivery of drugs in exchange for Harriet's body to be released for burial."

Cavanagh didn't immediately respond, but then narrow eyed, asked, "I take it that your deal will be tight?"

"Me, Detective Superintendent Mulgrew and Popeye Doyle."

"Ah, Constable Doyle. A man you trust?"

"Surprisingly, yes, I do trust him," Harry nodded.

"And Mulgrew?"

"Call it instinct, but I believe she'll keep her mouth shut too."

"Let's hope so," Cavanagh sighed as Helen, carrying a tray with a mug of steaming hot coffee and a plate of biscuits, entered the room and setting the tray down on a table next to Harry, said, "I'll leave you two old buggers to suffocate from that bloody smoke. I'm away to bed so, goodnight Harry."

Theatrically waving her hands in front of her face as she left the room, she closed the door behind her.

They both grinned before Harry, nodding to the departing young woman, asked, "It's official then? She's living here?"

"She still keeps her flat over in Shawlands and is always threatening to return there, but yes, she's living here now," Cavanagh happily replied and curiously, blushed.

"Well, I'm pleased for you both," Harry toasted his old friend with his mug.

"Any word when Harriet's body will be released?"

"No, but I'd like to contact a funeral home tomorrow morning and get things started."

"Leave that to me. I have some contacts in the profession," Cavanagh sipped at his glass. "I'll see that Harriet gets a good send off."

"I'm sure you will," smiled Harry.

The driver followed the SatNav instructions and slowed down as he approached the entrance to Oakbank Industrial Estate.

In the road seventy yards into the estate on the left, Fast Eddie and his six colleagues saw Sandy Craig's BMW approach them.

In the bushes that lay between the industrial estate and the canal that run behind, Stevie Watkins, the revolver clutched in his hand, quietly cursed as he stumbled through the undergrowth to obtain a position from where he could watch the shipment arrive.
He did not know that secreted in the bushes and lying flat on his stomach, not fifteen yards from where Watkins now crouched, was an unarmed plain clothes officer who quietly whispered into his Airwave radio, "One man into bushes near to me, carrying a firearm, a handgun I think, over."

Seated in a CID car two hundred metres into the estate, Cathy Mulgrew acknowledged the plain clothes mans message, then muttered, "Shit!"
She was about to tell the plainer to keep still, not to attract the attention of the gunman, but almost immediately following his first message, the plainer then excitedly whispered into the radio, "That's an artic lorry pulling into the road and following the BMW to the dead end. No, wait, the lorry's stopped and the reverse lights have come on. He's reversing back towards the entrance to the estate. Looks like he intends to…."
There was a brief pause then the plainer continued, "Yes." they could hear the excitement in the young officers voice. "He's done a three point turn and is now slowly reversing down the road, over."
In the driver's seat beside Mulgrew, Danny McBride sighed with relief. It had been a mad scramble getting the armed officers and the uniformed and plain clothes cops into positions where they could remain hidden, yet be at the handover location in less than a thirty seconds.
"That's worrying," Mulgrew muttered.
"Ma'am?"
"The man with the handgun. Where he is he's too far away from the armed cops to be able to react quickly. What is he, some sort of lookout doing his edgy for the polis?"
"Sounds like it," McBride agreed with a nod.
All the cops had their Airwave radio earpieces plugged in and heard Mulgrew say, "To all stations. We have an armed man in bushes at the entrance to the dead end road. No one and I repeat, no one is to approach this man. Alpha two," she addressed the plainer who was

closest to the unknown armed man, "at the shout, you *will* remain hidden. Do not attract his attention. Is that understood, over?"
"Roger," Alpha two acknowledged and thought, fucking right I'm not going anywhere near a guy with a gun.
"Alpha Six, permission," called the armed response officers supervisor.
"Alpha Six, go ahead," replied Mulgrew.
"Do you wish one of my teams to back up Alpha Two, over?"
She quickly thought and decided if the arrest went ahead and if the gunman made good his escape, then so be it. Better that than deploying a pair of much needed armed officers from the arrest location and so replied, "Negative, Alpha Six. All teams remain in situ until I shout go. Acknowledge," she ended.
In numerical order, the eight Alpha teams acknowledged her instruction, then Alpha Two interrupted and said, "That's the rear of the Luton van starting to load from the back of the lorry. Looks like the lorry driver is still in his cab, over."
"Good," Mulgrew grimly smiled, "we'll catch them while they've got their hands full."
She turned to McBride and asked, "Ready?"
He reached forward to hold the ignition key between his finger and thumb and nodding, replied, "Ready."
Mulgrew took a deep breath and pressing the button on her radio, said, "Go, go, go!"
McBride switched on the engine and with a screech of tyres, they headed for the lorry's location.

Wondering what the hell was keeping Faraday, Stevie Watkins attention was taken with the mumbled voices and mechanical noise as the Luton van's tailgate was lowered, but then to his surprise, heard the screech of tyres and saw a dark coloured saloon car with the headlights on full beam, skid by his position as it entered the roadway and drove towards the lorry.
It didn't take a genius to work out it was the polis and at the sound of raised voices shouting loudly, hurriedly got to his feet.
The young plainer, caught up in the excitement of what was about to happen, raised his head and stared at the brilliantly lit lorry cab caught in the CID car's full beam and the startled faces of the men at the back of the lorry.

Watkins, suddenly aware he might be surrounded by police, glanced about him and saw the raised head of the cop.
"Fuck!" he screamed and panicking, raised the Enfield revolver that he pointed towards the cop, but conscious that his hands were shaking and the barrel wavered in front of him.
He tried to call out, but his mouth was parched and unable to get any spit, he spluttered.
However, his choked cry it was enough to alert the young cop who turning his head, saw to his horror the man dressed in black who was now on his feet silhouetted against the roadway and pointing the gun towards him.

Sitting anxiously in his lounge, Nigel Faraday nervously tapped his fingers against the arm of the chair. He glanced at the clock and wondered why the *fuck* Sandy Craig had not yet called.

Sandy Craig turned at the shouts and his eyes widened at the sight of police officers scrambling from the bushes and over a wall as they rushed screaming towards his team.
Shouts of, "Don't move!" and "Lie down, lie down on your faces!" were interspersed with "Armed Police! Don't move!"
In the melee, three or four of his team tried to take off and and he saw them physically brought to the ground as they attempted to flee, though Fast Eddie began to fight with the officers while the remaining two and the lorry driver who exited his cab, threw themselves to the ground, their hands behind their heads as they surrendered.
It could only end one way.
Unseen, Craig sidled into the darkness of the building closest to the lorry and reached into his jacket for the Nagant.
Removing the weapon from the shoulder holster, he was about to creep away when a woman's gritty voice said, "Stand still and drop that fucking gun! If you as much as fart, I'll blow you're head off!"
Slowly turning his head, he saw the black clad figure wearing the Kevlar helmet standing a few feet away in the darkness and pointing her Heckler Koch assault rifle at his head.
A cold hand gripped his heart and as slowly as he dared, he stooped to place the Nagant onto the ground as the officer loudly called out, "Assistance here!"

Within seconds, two unarmed cops arrived to wrestle him to the ground and apply Flexicuffs to his wrists at the back.
Now firmly secured, the policewoman lowered her rifle and shaking her head, bent over to stare Craig in the eye and with a wide grin, snarled, "Boys and their toys, eh?"

The young plainer, now on his feet with his hands in the air and thoroughly frightened, stared at Watkins and stuttered, "I'm a police officer, pal. You shoot me and you're away for life."
Watkins glanced around him and realised that the noise, the screams and the shouts, were all coming from the area around the parked lorry, that there were no other cops nearby and with an evil grin realised none of the cops, nobody at all, knew he was there.
Nobody but this bastard he held the gun to.
Making his decision, he began to walk forward towards the unfortunate officer to close the gap between them and taking a tighter grip on the Enfield, squeezed the trigger.

In the middle of the confusion, Cathy Mulgrew and Danny McBride glanced around them at the arrested bodies lying flat on the ground and they both smiled.
"Good," she sighed through pursed lips. "No shots fired and nobody hurt," but then they heard the bang.

The Enfield was an old weapon, but still very reliable.
But that could not be said for the outdated ammunition.
When Watkins squeezed the trigger, the hammer with the fixed firing pin fell onto the base of the cartridge in the chamber.
Had the ammunition been new or as well cared for as the weapon, the explosion that occurred in the chamber when the firing pin struck the base of the cartridge would have sent the brass bullet through the 5.75inch barrel at a rate of 600 feet per second and at that short distance, undoubtedly struck the police officer.
However, because the ammunition was old it exploded in the chamber and blew back, breaking the thin pin that held the metal hammer in place and with the powder flash, sending the hammer backwards as a projectile towards Watkins face.

The flash as the cartridge exploded caused his skin to be burned and blistered, his eyebrows to be singed and eyes scorched, but it was the metal hammer that caused the real damage.
At an incredible speed, it seared through his right cheek, glanced off this jawbone and was ricocheted upwards into his brain before finally emerging from the top of his skull and lodging itself in a nearby tree.
Almost like a mannequin and still holding the useless firearm, he toppled backwards and fell to the ground stone dead.
Apprehensively, the young cop moved forward and hands still in the air, stared wide-eyed down at Watkins then said, "Holy Shit!" before violently vomiting on the ground beside the body.

CHAPTER TWENTY-EIGHT

Monday morning dawned with a frenzied media reporting on television, the radio and newspapers about the shootout at Oakbank Industrial Estate in the Maryhill area of Glasgow that resulted in the death of an armed criminal.
Never mind that there was no shootout, that the single death was actually the result of a misfire of a weapon used by the criminal involved, the media headlined the incident as coup for the police.
For the first time in days the hunt for the serial killer, Kieran McMenamin took second stage.
In his office at Tulliallan Police College, the Chief Constable poured coffee for a seated Cathy Mulgrew, who still dressed in the same clothes from the night before, looked tired and drawn.
As he listened to her account of the arrest of a number of criminals involved in the drug trade and the seizure of a substantial quantity of heroin, he asked, "And there's nothing that might in any way indicate we are responsible for the death of this man Watkins?"
"None at all, sir," she smiled gratefully as she accepted the cup and saucer.
Resuming his seat behind his desk, he used the silver spoon to idly stir at his cup and asked, "What about the man you believe to be behind the delivery, this guy Faraday?"
"Well, we have the source's information that the shipment was intended for Faraday. We have a statement from one of the accused, Sandy Craig, who is hoping to cut a deal with Crown Office to…"

"What kind of deal?" he snapped for cutting deals with criminals was a bone of contention between him and the Crown Office desk jockeys in Gartcosh.
"He's asked if the Crown drop the firearm charge against him and are lenient on the importation charge, he'll give us a statement against Faraday to confirm he was acting on his instruction."
"But you have *no* direct evidence against Faraday?"
"No sir," she sighed, "just the source's info and Craig's word."
"But you don't doubt Faraday is the man who is behind the importation?"
"I don't doubt it at all," she replied and curiously, though she could not admit to her Chief, trusted that Harry Henderson had told her the truth.
"The dead man, Watkins. At least he's a thorn out of our side," he sighed and sipped at his coffee.
"Perhaps so," she slowly said, "but now that Watkins and his henchman Craig are gone from the scene, that means his network is open for a takeover and Faraday is ideally positioned to move in there."
Her mobile phone chirruped and glancing at the screen, her eyes narrowed as she said, "Do you mind if I take this, sir?"
"Please, go ahead," he nodded.
She stood and moving to the window, took the call and moments later, a curious expression on her face, told him, "There's been a bit of a development, sir. I need to attend at Saracen office immediately. Can I get back to you, later?"
"I look forward to hearing from you, Cathy," he dismissed her with a nod.

Harry Henderson finished breakfast, aware that the young waitress he had rescued from the drunk was extra attentive and to his slight discomfort, stared doe-eyed at him all the while he was in the restaurant.
"Is there anything else I can get you, Mister Henderson," she hurried to him as he arose from the table, then in a lower voice added, "*Anything* at all?"
He refrained from smiling for Harry knew he was not the sort of man who usually attracted the attention of pretty women and replied,

"No, thank you. You've been more than helpful," and with a relieved sigh, made his way to the foyer.

He was intercepted before he got to the lift by a receptionist who said, "Mister Henderson. You had a call from a Miss Mulgrew. She asked if you could contact her at your convenience and left this number."

He took the slip of paper with a mobile number scribbled on it and thanking the receptionist, he made his way to his room where using his mobile, he called Cathy Mulgrew.

"Thanks for getting back to me, Harry," she said and from the background noise he realised she must be in a vehicle.

"You read the papers today?"

"Yes," he replied. "I saw you seem to have had a result last night. Who was the death that's being reported?"

"Steven Watkins. Tried to shoot one of my young officers, but the gun blew up in his face and killed him."

"Couldn't happen to a nicer guy," he sniffed.

"The reason I'm phoning is twofold; to thank you for what you did and to tell you I've made arrangements with the PF's office to have your aunt's body released. That should happen some time today if you wish to go ahead with making arrangements."

He didn't immediately respond and she asked, "Harry? You still there?"

"Yes...I'm here. Thank you."

"No, thank you, Harry. One other thing. Faraday didn't show at the location."

"He didn't?" Harry was surprised, then smiled. "Don't worry, Miss Mulgrew. I have no intention of hunting him down," then, he just couldn't help himself because he asked, "What about this man McMenamin? Has there been any sightings of him?"

"No, not yet," he heard her sigh before she added, "but don't worry, he'll turn up."

Yeah, he thought, when the gasses in his body expand and he rises to the top of the pond, but replied, "You *will* let me know, yes?"

"Yes," she confirmed and ended the call.

Placing the mobile on the bed beside him, he thought of Harriet and knew that while she would never condone him taking a life on her behalf, it satisfied his conscience that McMenamin, by all account a complete and utter wastrel, would never again harm a helpless old person.

Lifting the phone, he dialled Harry Cavanagh's number to inform him to go ahead and make the arrangements for Harriet's funeral.

Seated at her desk, but still feeling the effects of her late night participation in the arrest of the men and seizure of the drugs at the Oakbank Industrial Estate, DC Marilyn Munroe run a weary hand across her brow. The officers stood and seated elsewhere in the room, though most having had less than a few hours break after the incident, were buoyant and cheery while she felt like shit.

"Her Marilyn," one of her colleagues called over to her. "Some of us are going out this evening for a bit of a swally to celebrate the turn. Are you up for it?"

She managed a grin and shook her head.

After what had happened last night, she didn't feel like going anywhere.

She made her way to Chief Inspector Dougie Kane's office on the first floor and knocking on the door, pushed it open to find him behind his desk with Sergeant Daisy Cooper sat on one of the two chairs in front of him while Danny McBride stood in a corner.

A television on a trolley with a DVD player connected to it in the lower tray sat in a corner.

The two seated officers courteously stood when he entered, but Mulgrew waved them back into their seats and without preamble, said, "Tell me."

It was McBride who began by nodding towards Daisy and saying, "Sergeant Cooper here spoke to me this morning, Ma'am. She saw my name on an Intelligence report and sought my advice. When I heard what she had to say, I spoke with Dougie and well, here we are."

"And it's true, then?"

"It's better if you see the DVD, Ma'am," Kane replied and reaching for a control, switched on the TV then activated the DVD disc in the player.

As she watched the recording with the time and date prominently displayed in one corner, she saw a man and a woman exit a doorway and quite clearly, were together when they walked off.

"Play it again, Dougie, and this time Sergeant Cooper," she turned to her, "talk me through it."

"I was having dinner with my fiancé in the restaurant when I saw them come in. I didn't immediately realise they were together, but I recognised his photograph from Criminal Intelligence bulletins, Ma'am, though at the time I didn't recall his name. However, it piqued my curiosity and so I arranged for one of my cops to obtain the DVD."

Mulgrew didn't reply, but her lips tightened till they were white. She couldn't disclose to Daisy or Kane that as far as Harry Henderson knew and she had no reason to doubt him, Nigel Faraday, who should have been at the delivery last night but was conspicuous by his absence, had a police tout.

Now, unless two and two made five, it was clear why he didn't arrive.

He had been tipped off by his tout.

"Who else knows about this?"

"Nobody, Ma'am," Daisy replied, but then blushed and added, "except my fiancé Ian, but you have my word he won't have told anyone."

"What about the cop who obtained it for you?"

"He has no idea why I wanted it and to my knowledge, hasn't seen it. I trust him, Ma'am. He's a good young officer and if he knew I'm certain he would have mentioned it to me."

"Daisy, what you've discovered opens up a can or worms, but I'm glad you brought it to our attention. It also might explain a few unanswered questions. For the minute," she glanced at McBride and Daisy in turn, "can Dougie and I have the room?"

"Of course, Ma'am," he replied as Daisy rose to her feet, but before she left the room, Kane turned to Mulgrew and with a smile said, "Before she goes, that's not the only news Daisy brought to me this morning."

"Oh?"

Blushing, Daisy said, "I'm pregnant."

To her surprise Mulgrew, who like most of Police Scotland was aware of the younger officers heroism in the recent terrorist attack in Glasgow city centre, got to her feet and moved towards her. Enveloping her in her arms and with a huge grin, she said, "Congratulations to you both! Now, if there's *anything* I can do to help, either contact me through Dougie or call me direct and Daisy," she continued to grin, "That's an order, Sergeant."

When McBride and Daisy had left the room, Mulgrew, her face grim, said, "Well, no sense in hanging about, Dougie. Let's have her in."

While the police rejoiced at the successful operation of the previous evening, Mary Harris and her son Michael were joined by a number of family, friends and well-wishers at the Possilpark Church of Scotland in Saracen Street to celebrate the life of Mary's husband, Michael senior.

Among the many mourners who conveyed their sympathy and condolences was Popeye Doyle who Mary singled out to bestow her grateful thanks for all his kindness and compassion.

Following the ceremony, the small procession of cars proceeded to Lambhill Cemetery where Michael Harris was interred for, as Mary explained to her son, "It will give me somewhere to visit and besides," she smiled, "you know what your dad was like. He was never one for the heat."

DS Calum Fraser tapped DC Marilyn Munroe on the shoulder and expressionless, said, "Could you come with me, please? There's someone needs to speak with you."

He waited till she stood then accompanied her out of the incident room.

Chief Inspector Dougie Kane remained seated behind his desk while Cathy Mulgrew stood with her back against the wall by the side of the door.

When the younger woman entered, Kane said, "Please take a seat."

It was obvious from the outset that she was nervous and though she tried to appear outwardly calm, her legs were shaking and her hands clasped in her lap were held so tightly her knuckles showed white.

They had agreed that Kane would conduct the interview and so he began, "Before I caution you, I would like to give you the opportunity to explain this."

Pressing the button on the DVD player, she fought for breath while she watched the forty second recording of her exiting the restaurant door with Nigel Faraday.

Her face pale, she was close to tears when Mulgrew said, "May I examine your mobile phone, please?"
Numbly she handed the phone to Mulgrew who asked, "The password?"
"One-five-eight-nine," she replied, then muttered, "My birthday."
A minute passed while Mulgrew examined the text messages then with a subtle nod to Kane, said, "Tell me, Sergeant Cassidy. When did Faraday recruit you as his informant?"

The text message from Harry Cavanagh simply said: *All sorted. Harriet collected today and service tomorrow. 11 at her own church in saracen street. Burial or cremation?*
He paused before replying and involuntarily shuddered. There would be nobody left in Glasgow to visit her grave and besides, the thought of placing her in the cold ground rankled with him and so he replied: *cremation.*
Roger see you there was the response.
Standing in the entrance to the Hilton Hotel, he waited the five minutes for Cavanagh's man, a pimply faced youth with a sullen expression who didn't speak, to collect the car keys for the Focus and after handing them over, decided to take a walk to Sauchiehall Street and find somewhere for lunch.

DI Phil Kennedy nodded that Fraser could leave the room.
Kennedy had experienced a lot of bad things in his police career, but this was one of the worst things he had to do and sitting DC Munroe down in the chair opposite his desk, stood beside her and said in a soft voice, "I'm very sorry to break the bad news like this, Marilyn, but we've just had a phone call from your sister. I regret that your father died an hour ago."

Unwashed, unshaven and still wearing his dressing robe, he still couldn't believe it had happened.
With the mug of coffee growing cold by his elbow, he stared fixedly at the screen.
The BBC Scotland reporter, stood in front of the large tarpaulin that covered the entrance to the road into the estate, held the microphone in one hand as she brushed a strand of hair from her eyes and continued:

...and as you can see behind me, she turned and indicated the tarpaulin with her free hand, *the police have erected a barrier to prevent any view of the crime scene. However, sources close to this reporter have indicated that at least one of the nine or more violent criminals involved in this large importation of heroin has paid a heavy price for his participation in the drug trade,* and with a toothy smile, she ended with, *Over to you back in the studio.*
Shit! That could have been me, dead or arrested!
All through the exhausting, sleepless night he had worried that the police might show up at his door and time and time again, startled when he thought he heard movement on the landing outside.
His mobile phone rung and glancing again at it, refused to answer when he saw the Spanish number on the screen.
He reached for the control and switching the television off, sat back and sighed.
At least there was no evidence against him and the Spanish bastard could hardly blame *him* for what had turned out to be a right royal fuck-up!
Then the doorbell rang.

Through her tears and snivelling, she said, "I met him at university. I was sharing a flat with another girl called Lucy Barrowman. Lucy came from money people. Her family were landed gentry somewhere in Perthshire, I think it was. We started fooling around with cannabis," she turned a pleading eye towards Mulgrew and sobbed, "Christ! It was the life at Uni. We *all* did it!"
Not all of us, Mulgrew thought as Kane calmly said "Go on."
"Lucy, she was always into trying something new, something more daring and graduated to cocaine then heroin. Anyway," she sniffed, "I came in one day and found her with a needle in her arm and, well, she was dead. Overdosed. I didn't know *what* the fuck to do and called her father. The next thing I know is that there's a doctor there and she's being taken away in a private ambulance. They wouldn't even let me go to her funeral."
She paused, using the heel of her hand to wipe at her eyes and continued, "Nigel. He was one of the guys that supplied me and her. He told me that Lucy was quickly buried and the cause of her death was a heart attack, but I knew different. I didn't know *what* the fuck was going on, then five thousand pounds appeared in my bank

account and I received a phone call from a lawyer telling me that if I ever told anyone," her eyes tightened and her body was wracked with sobs, "I'd be taken to court and…and…"

"So, Sergeant Cassidy, you are a former drug abuser and not only colluded in covering up a drugs death, but accepted money to do so?" Kane asked.

"Yes," she loudly wept, her arms wrapped about her as head down, she rocked back and forth on her chair.

"And presumably, after learning you joined the police, Faraday used this information to force you to provide him with intelligence?"

Sobbing, she couldn't respond other than to nod.

Mulgrew stared at Kane and sighing, said, "I believe we've heard enough, Chief Inspector."

Staring down at the distraught Cassidy, she formally cautioned her then continued, "As of this moment, Sergeant Cassidy, you are suspended from duty pending further inquiries that I am certain will result in you facing a number of criminal charges. I am seizing your phone as evidence of your collusion with Nigel Faraday and expect in due course your legal representative will encourage you to provide a statement against Faraday, outlining everything you know of him. You will be escorted from this office and on no account are you to attend at any police office or contact any of your colleagues while you remain under suspension unless you are required to do so. Do you understand?"

She nodded twice.

Mulgrew opened the door and nodded to the two detective officers who in the corridor outside, stood waiting to escort Cassidy to the front door.

They watched as she quite literally stumbled through the door and out of the office.

Turning to Kane, Mulgrew said, "*Now* we've got Faraday."

He opened the door and to his surprise, saw a tall, stocky built black man stood there with shoulder length dreadlocks who wore a black tie, black coloured shirt, black suit under a three quarter length black coloured rain jacket, highly polished black shoes and a wide smile with teeth so brilliantly white they almost shone.

"Mister Faraday, Mister Nigel Faraday?" he politely asked, his hands behind his back and his London cockney accent so thick it could almost be cut with a knife.

"Yes," Faraday slowly drawled.

"Me Guvnor, Mister de Lugo, sends 'is regards and says to tell you that 'e's a very disappointed man that you let 'im down," and with that comment from behind his back the man drew a handgun fitted with a thick silencer and shot Faraday twice in the chest.

When he fell back twitching on the hallway carpet, the gunman shot him once more in the forehead.

Staring down at the body for a few seconds, the gunman was satisfied Faraday was dead and turning, made his way back down the stairs.

CHAPTER TWENTY-NINE

Harriet Henderson had been a member of the Possilpark congregation for over sixty years and it was no surprise to anyone when the church was not only filled to capacity, but overflowed to the pavement outside.

Seated in the front pew with Harry Cavanagh and the soberly dressed Helen, her nephew Harry had been taken aback by the numbers attending and even more so by those who recalled the lanky youth who had later become one of the City's most notorious criminal figures.

"I want to thank you for getting all this arranged so quickly," he whispered to Harry Cavanagh, who replied, "I didn't do it for you, ya scallywag; I did it for Harriet."

He smiled at Cavanagh's response and turned at the tap on the shoulder to find Popeye Doyle seated behind who quietly said, "My condolences, Harry. I liked your aunt. Never had a bad word to say about anyone" he paused and smiled before adding, "unless they deserved it, that is."

Harry returned Doyle's smile and replied, "Will I see you after? The Church has laid on a wee purvey in the hall."

"Aye, of course. I'll be there."

An hour and a half later, following the short service at the Glasgow Crematorium in Tresta Road, Harry travelled with Helen and Cavanagh back to the church hall.

Though he didn't intend remaining long, he found it difficult to ignore the number of predominantly elderly people who wanted to convey their regrets at Harriet's death or had a story to relate of her in life.

At last he found a quiet corner where Popeye Doyle joined him.

"Fair turn out, eh?"

"She never failed to surprise me," Harry smiled. "What about you, Popeye? Phoned that ambulance woman yet?"

"Bobby? Aye," his face reddened, "I gave her a call last night and we're going out for dinner on Friday. It's her first day off," he explained then keen to change the subject, said with a nod, "Come here a minute. There's somebody I'd like you to meet."

Harry followed him through the cacophony of noise in the hall where Doyle introduced him to Mary Harris.

"I'm so sorry about your aunt," she held tightly to his hand. "I knew Harriet. A good Christian woman and she'll be sadly missed, not least by the congregation here," she smiled before adding, "She was always popping into the charity shop where I volunteer, to donate some wee thing or other. A very kind lady too."

"Well, Mary," he fished in his trouser pocket, "I've no need for any of Harriet's things so you could do me a great service if you would take charge of clearing the house. Anything that the charity can use or sell, eh?"

"Oh, Mister Henderson…"

"Please," he smiled, "call me Harry."

"Mary was here at church yesterday, Harry," Doyle interrupted. "She laid her husband to rest."

A parishioner called to Doyle who excusing himself, stepped away to join a crowd of pensioners.

The light dawned on Harry and staring at Mary, he said, "I'm so sorry. I didn't realise who you were, Mary."

"Oh, that's all right," she blushed. "Michael was a good man, but the dementia took him after a stroke so in truth, I lost him some time ago."

"And if I recall," his eyes narrowed, "Popeye said you've family in New Zealand?"

"My pregnant daughter, her husband and my two grandchildren. They live in a place called Wadestown, outside Wellington. Not that I know anything about it," she blushed, "but the photographs Jenny sends me seem to indicate it's a nice place. She's always trying to get me to visit, but you know, the cost of getting over there," she shook her head. "I've a son in Dorset, but he had to return down there this morning to his job."

She leaned close and almost in confidence, said, "I had to persuade him to go for he's that worried about me. You see, I'm nervous about this man McMenamin they're looking for. I'm what the CID called a star witness, so, well," she blinked rapidly, her eyes filling with tears as she exhaled, "living on my own, you know?"

He stared at her, this anxious, good living woman and recognising the fear in her eyes, took a deep breath, then leaning in close, took her hands in his and said, "Tell me Mary, have you heard about me? What I used to do and please, I'm not proud of it, but I'm sure you *do* know that when I was younger I had a bit of a reputation?"

She stared nervously at him, unable to avert her eyes from his and the anxiety showing in hers when she slowly nodded.

He smiled tightly and continuing to tightly hold her hands, said in a low voice, "What if I were to tell you a secret? Can I trust you keep a secret, Mary?"

Again she nodded, not sure where this was going.

"Mary," he leaned in closer so that he was almost whispering in her ear, "nobody will *ever* have to worry about Kieran McMenamin again. Trust me on that."

"Never?" her voice faltered as she stared at him.

He stared meaningfully at her and slowly replied, "Never."

Dinner at the Hilton Hotel that night was an emotional time for Harry who made his lifelong friend promise that he and Helen, who dabbed at her eyes through most of the meal, would visit him and Donna soon.

The following morning, his bag packed, he caught the taxi to Glasgow Airport with a spring in his step.

He knew it was unlikely he would ever return to Glasgow and so he left with no regrets.

Passing through the security, he entered the departure lounge and lifted a complimentary copy of that morning's 'Glasgow News' to read that the incident at the Oakbank Industrial Estate was no longer headline news while the manhunt for Kieran McMenamin had been moved to page three.

He smiled at a quote from the officer leading the inquiry, Detective Superintendent Cathy Mulgrew, who reportedly said the police were optimistic about making an early arrest.

"Good luck with that," he muttered with a grin and made his way to the departure gate.

Popeye Doyle's leaving doo, held in a city pub, attracted a large number of serving and former colleagues representing all ranks who all had their own sometimes audacious, sometimes raucous stories to tell about the veteran cop.

To Doyle's delighted surprise, Chief Inspector Dougie Kane arrived with Cathy Mulgrew; Kane to provide the official farewell speech and Mulgrew to hand over the many gifts from Doyle's now former colleagues.

It was later than evening when a tipsy Doyle, ably supported by his new girlfriend Roberta 'Bobby' Dawson, who helped carry both him and his black bin bags of gifts home, that he opened a jiffy bag upon which was scrawled the one word; 'Popeye.'

Upending the bag, a note and an Emirates airline ticket fell from the bag.

Opening the note, he read: *Popeye, I know that you would never accept a gift from an old criminal like me, so I believe I've done the next best thing. Please ensure this ticket finds its way to the person who most needs it. Your old pal, Harry. PS Good luck with your ambulance woman.*

With glazed eyes, he lifted the open-ended First Class return ticket to Wellington International Airport in New Zealand and slowly smiled when he read the passengers name:

Mary Harris.

****

Needless to say, this story is a work of fiction and none of the characters represent any living individual. As readers of my previous books may already know, I am an amateur writer and therefore

accept that all grammar and punctuation errors are mine alone. I hope that any such errors do not detract from the story.
If you have enjoyed the story, you may wish to visit my website at:
www.glasgowcrimefiction.co.uk

I also welcome feedback and can be contacted at:
george.donald.books@hotmail.co.uk

Printed in Great Britain
by Amazon